At the breaking point, my body inhaled involuntarily. I closed my sightless eyes. Wrapped my arms around Lou, buried my nose in her neck. At least Morgane wouldn't have us. At least I wouldn't know life without her. Small victories. Important ones.

But the water never came. Instead, impossibly crisp air flooded my mouth, and with it, the sweetest relief. Though I still couldn't see—though the cold remained debilitating—I could *breathe*. I could *think*. Coherency returned in a disorienting wave. I took another deep breath. Then another, and another. This—this was impossible. I was *breathing underwater*. Like Jonah's fish. Like the melusines. Like—

Like magic.

Also by Shelby Mahurin

Serpent & Dove

Gods & Monsters

BLOOD
&
HONEY

SHELBY MAHURIN

HARPER TEEN
An Imprint of HarperCollinsPublishers

HarperTeen is an imprint of HarperCollins Publishers.

Blood & Honey

Copyright © 2020 by Shelby Mahurin

Map art © 2020 by Leo Hartas

All rights reserved. Printed in the United States of America. No part of this book may be used or reproduced in any manner whatsoever without written permission except in the case of brief quotations embodied in critical articles and reviews. For information address HarperCollins Children's Books, a division of HarperCollins Publishers, 195 Broadway, New York, NY 10007.

www.epicreads.com

Library of Congress Control Number: 2020938964

ISBN 978-0-06-287808-3

Typography by Sarah Nichole Kaufman

21 22 23 24 25   PC/LSCH   10 9 8 7 6 5 4 3 2 1

First paperback edition, 2021

For Beau, James, and Rose *who I love unconditionally*

PART I

Il n'y a pas plus sourd que celui qui ne veut pas entendre.
There are none so deaf as those that will not hear.

—French proverb

TOMORROW

Lou

Dark clouds gathered overhead.

Though I couldn't see the sky through the thick canopy of La Fôret des Yeux—or feel the bitter winds rising outside our camp—I knew a storm was brewing. The trees swayed in the gray twilight, and the animals had gone to ground. Several days ago, we'd burrowed into our own sort of hole: a peculiar basin in the forest floor, where the trees had grown roots like fingers, thrusting in and out of the cold earth. I affectionately called it the Hollow. Though snow dusted everything outside it, the flakes melted on contact with the protective magic Madame Labelle had cast.

Adjusting the baking stone over the fire, I poked hopefully at the misshapen lump atop it. It couldn't be called *bread*, exactly, as I'd cobbled the concoction together from nothing but ground bark and water, but I refused to eat another meal of pine nuts and milk thistle root. I simply refused. A girl needed *something* with *taste* now and again—and I didn't mean the wild onions Coco had found this morning. My breath still smelled like a dragon's.

"I'm not eating that," Beau said flatly, eyeing the pine bread as if it'd soon sprout legs and attack him. His black hair—usually styled with immaculate detail—stuck out in disheveled waves, and dirt streaked his tawny cheek. Though his velvet suit would've been the height of fashion in Cesarine, it too was now sullied with grime.

I grinned at him. "Fine. Starve."

"Is it . . ." Ansel edged closer, wrinkling his nose surreptitiously. Eyes bright from hunger and hair tangled from the wind, he hadn't fared in the wilderness much better than Beau. But Ansel—with his olive skin and willowy build, his curling lashes and his genuine smile—would always be beautiful. He couldn't help it. "Do you think it's—"

"Edible?" Beau supplied, arching a dark brow. "No."

"I wasn't going to say that!" Pink colored Ansel's cheeks, and he shot me an apologetic look. "I was going to say, er—good. Do you think it's good?"

"Also no." Beau turned away to rummage in his pack. Triumphant, he straightened a moment later with a handful of onions, popping one into his mouth. "*This* will be my dinner tonight, thank you."

When I opened my mouth with a scathing reply, Reid's arm came across my shoulders, heavy and warm and comforting. He brushed a kiss against my temple. "I'm sure the bread is delicious."

"That's right." I leaned into him, preening at the compliment.

"It *will* be delicious. And we won't smell like ass—er, *onion*—for the rest of the night." I smiled sweetly at Beau, who paused with his hand halfway to his mouth, scowling between me and his onion. "Those are going to seep out of your pores for the next day, at least."

Chuckling, Reid bent low to kiss my shoulder, and his voice—slow and deep—rumbled against my skin. "You know, there's a stream up the way."

Instinctively, I extended my neck, and he placed another kiss on my throat, right beneath my jaw. My pulse spiked against his mouth. Though Beau curled his lip in disgust at our public display, I ignored him, reveling in Reid's nearness. We hadn't been properly alone since I'd woken after Modraniht. "Maybe we should go there," I said a bit breathlessly. As usual, Reid pulled away too soon. "We could pack up our bread and ... picnic."

Madame Labelle's head jerked toward us from across camp, where she and Coco argued within the roots of an ancient fir. They clutched a piece of parchment between them, their shoulders tense and their faces drawn. Ink and blood dotted Coco's fingers. Already, she'd sent two notes to La Voisin at the blood camp, pleading for sanctuary. Her aunt hadn't responded to either. I doubted a third note would change that. "Absolutely not," Madame Labelle said. "You cannot leave camp. I've forbidden it. Besides, a storm is brewing."

Forbidden it. The words rankled. No one had *forbidden* me from doing anything since I was three.

"Might I remind you," she continued, her nose in the air and her tone insufferable, "that the forest is still crawling with huntsmen, and though we have not seen them, the witches cannot be far behind. That's not to mention the king's guard. Word has spread about Florin's death on Modraniht"—Reid and I stiffened in each other's arms—"and bounties have risen. Even peasants know your faces. You cannot leave this camp until we've formed some sort of offensive strategy."

I didn't miss the subtle emphasis she placed on *you*, or the way she glanced between Reid and me. *We* were the ones forbidden from leaving camp. *We* were the ones with our faces plastered all over Saint-Loire—and by now, probably every other village in the kingdom too. Coco and Ansel had pinched a couple of the wanted posters after their foray into Saint-Loire for supplies—one depicting Reid's handsome face, his hair colored red with common madder, and one depicting mine.

The artist had given me a wart on my chin.

Scowling at the memory, I flipped the loaf of pine bread, revealing a burnt, blackened crust on the underside. We all stared at it a moment.

"You're right, Reid. So delicious." Beau grinned wide. Behind him, Coco squeezed blood from her palm onto the note. The drops sizzled and smoked where they fell, burning the parchment away into nothing. Transporting it to wherever La Voisin and the Dames Rouges currently camped. Beau waved the rest of his onions directly beneath my nose, reclaiming my attention. "Are you sure you wouldn't like one?"

I knocked them out of his hand. "Piss off."

With a squeeze of my shoulders, Reid swept the burnt loaf from the stone and cut a slice with expert precision. "You don't have to eat it," I said sullenly.

His lips quirked in a grin. "*Bon appétit.*"

We watched, transfixed, as he stuffed the bread into his mouth—and choked.

Beau roared with laughter.

Eyes watering, Reid hastened to swallow as Ansel pounded on his back. "It's good," he assured me, still coughing and trying to chew. "Really. It tastes like—like—"

"Char?" Beau bent double at my expression, laughing riotously, and Reid glowered, still choking but lifting a foot to kick his ass. Literally. Losing his balance, Beau toppled forward into the moss and lichen of the forest floor, a boot print clearly visible against the seat of his velvet pants.

He spat mud from his mouth as Reid finally swallowed the bread. "Prick."

Before he could take another bite, I knocked the bread back into the fire. "Your chivalry is noted, husband mine, and shall be thusly rewarded."

He pulled me into a hug, his smile genuine now. And shamefully relieved. "I would've eaten it."

"I should've let you."

"And now all of you will go hungry," Beau said.

Ignoring my stomach's traitorous growl, I pulled out the bottle of wine I'd hidden amidst the contents of Reid's rucksack. I hadn't been able to pack for the journey myself, what with

Morgane snatching me from the steps of Cathédral Saint-Cécile d'Cesarine. Fortunately, I'd just *happened* to wander a bit too far from camp yesterday, securing a handful of useful items from a peddler on the road. The wine had been essential. As had new clothes. Though Coco and Reid had cobbled together an ensemble for me to wear instead of my bloody ceremonial dress, their clothing hung from my slim frame—a frame made slimmer, no, waiflike from my time at the Chateau. So far, I'd managed to keep the fruits of my little excursion hidden—both within Reid's rucksack and beneath Madame Labelle's borrowed cloak—but the bandage had to come off eventually.

There was no time like the present.

Reid's eyes sharpened on the bottle of wine, and his smile vanished. "What is that?"

"A gift, of course. Don't you know what day it is?" Determined to save the evening, I pressed the bottle into Ansel's unsuspecting hands. His fingers closed around its neck, and he smiled, blushing anew. My heart swelled. "*Bon anniversaire, mon petit chou!*"

"It isn't my birthday until next month," he said sheepishly, but he clutched the bottle to his chest anyway. The fire cast flickering light on his quiet joy. "No one's ever—" He cleared his throat and swallowed hard. "I've never received a present before."

The happiness in my chest punctured slightly.

As a child, my own birthdays had been revered as holy days. Witches from all over the kingdom had journeyed to Chateau le Blanc to celebrate, and together, we'd danced beneath the light of the moon until our feet had ached. Magic had coated the temple with its sharp scent, and my mother had showered me with extravagant gifts—a tiara of diamonds and pearls one year, a bouquet of eternal ghost orchids the next. She'd once parted the tides of L'Eau Mélancolique for me to walk the seafloor, and melusines had pressed their beautiful, eerie faces against the walls of water to watch us, tossing their luminous hair and flashing their silver tails.

Even then, I'd known my sisters celebrated less my life and more my death, but I'd later wondered—in my weaker moments—if the same had been true for my mother. "We are star-crossed, you and I," she'd murmured on my fifth birthday, pressing a kiss to my forehead. Though I couldn't remember the details clearly—only the shadows in my bedroom, the cold night air on my skin, the eucalyptus oil in my hair—I thought a tear had trickled down her cheek. In those weaker moments, I'd known Morgane hadn't celebrated my birthdays at all.

She'd mourned them.

"I believe the proper response is thank you." Coco sidled up to examine the bottle of wine, tossing her black curls over a shoulder. Ansel's color deepened. With a smirk, she trailed a suggestive finger down the curve of the glass, pressing her own curves into his lanky frame. "What vintage is it?"

Beau rolled his eyes at her obvious performance, stooping to retrieve his onions. She watched him from the corner of her dark eyes. The two hadn't spoken a civil word in days. It'd been entertaining at first, watching Coco chop at the prince's bloated head quip by quip, but she'd recently brought Ansel into the carnage. I'd have to talk to her about it soon. My eyes flicked to Ansel, who still smiled from ear to ear as he gazed at the wine.

Tomorrow. I'd talk to her tomorrow.

Placing her fingers over Ansel's, Coco lifted the bottle to study the crumbling label. The firelight illuminated the myriad scars on her brown skin. "*Boisaîné*," she read slowly, struggling to discern the letters. She rubbed a bit of dirt away with the hem of her cloak. "Elderwood." She glanced at me. "I've never heard of such a place. It looks *ancient*, though. Must've cost a fortune."

"Much less than you'd think, actually." Grinning again at Reid's suspicious expression, I swiped the bottle from her with a wink. A towering summer oak adorned its label, and beside it, a monstrous man with antlers and hooves wore a crown of branches. Luminescent yellow paint colored his eyes, which had pupils like a cat's.

"He looks scary," Ansel commented, leaning over my shoulder to peer closer at the label.

"He's the Woodwose." Nostalgia hit me in an unexpected wave. "The wild man of the forest, the king of all flora and fauna. Morgane used to tell me stories about him when I was little."

The effect of my mother's name was instantaneous. Beau stopped scowling abruptly. Ansel stopped blushing, and Coco stopped smirking. Reid scanned the shadows around us and slid a hand to the Balisarda in his bandolier. Even the flames of the fire guttered, as if Morgane herself had blown a cold breath through the trees to extinguish them.

I fixed my smile in place.

We hadn't heard a word from Morgane since Modraniht. Days had passed, but we hadn't seen a single witch. To be fair, we hadn't seen much of anything beyond this cage of roots. I couldn't truly complain about the Hollow, however. Indeed—despite the lack of privacy and Madame Labelle's autocratic rule—I'd been almost relieved when we hadn't heard back from La Voisin. We'd been granted a reprieve. And we had everything we needed here, anyway. Madame Labelle's magic kept the danger away—warming us, cloaking us from spying eyes—and Coco had found the mountain-fed stream nearby. Its current kept the water from freezing, and certainly Ansel would catch a fish one of these days.

In this moment, it felt as if we lived in a pocket of time and space separate from the rest of the world. Morgane and her Dames Blanches, Jean Luc and his Chasseurs, even King Auguste—they ceased to exist in this place. No one could touch us. It was . . . strangely peaceful.

Like the calm before a storm.

Madame Labelle echoed my unspoken fear. "You know we cannot hide forever," she said, repeating the same tired argument. Coco and I shared an aggrieved look as she joined us, confiscating the wine. If I had to hear *one more* dire warning, I would upend the bottle and drown her in it. "Your mother will find you. We alone cannot keep you from her. However, if we were to gather allies, rally others to our cause, perhaps we could—"

"The blood witches' silence couldn't be louder." I grabbed the bottle back from her, wrestling with the cork. "They won't risk Morgane's wrath by *rallying to our cause*. Whatever the hell our *cause* even is."

"Don't be obtuse. If Josephine refuses to help us, there are other powerful players we can—"

"I need more time," I interrupted loudly, hardly listening,

gesturing to my throat. Though Reid's magic had closed the wound, saving my life, a thick crust remained. It still hurt like a bitch. But that wasn't the reason I wanted to linger here. "You're barely healed yourself, Helene. We'll strategize tomorrow."

"Tomorrow." Her eyes narrowed at the empty promise. I'd said the same for days now. This time, however, even I could hear the words landed different—true. Madame Labelle would no longer accept otherwise. As if to affirm my thoughts, she said, "Tomorrow we *will* talk, whether or not La Voisin answers our call. Agreed?"

I plunged my knife into the bottle's cork, twisting sharply. Everyone flinched. Grinning anew, I dipped my chin in the briefest of nods. "Who's thirsty?" I flicked the cork at Reid's nose, and he swatted it away in exasperation. "Ansel?"

His eyes widened. "Oh, I don't—"

"Perhaps we should procure a nipple." Beau snatched the bottle from under Ansel's nose and took a hearty swig. "It might be more palatable to him that way."

I choked on a laugh. "Stop it, Beau—"

"You're right. He'd have no idea what to do with a breast."

"Have you ever had a drink before, Ansel?" Coco asked curiously.

Face darkening, Ansel jerked the wine from Beau and drank deeply. Instead of spluttering, he seemed to unhinge his jaw and inhale half the bottle. When he'd finished, he merely wiped his mouth with the back of his hand and shoved the bottle toward Coco. His cheeks were still pink. "It goes down smooth."

I didn't know which was funnier—Coco and Beau's gob-smacked expressions or Ansel's smug one. I clapped my hands together in delight. "Oh, well done, Ansel. When you told me you liked wine, I didn't realize you could drink like a fish."

He shrugged and looked away. "I lived in Saint-Cécile for years. I learned to like it." His eyes flicked back to the bottle in Coco's hand. "That one tastes a lot better than anything in the sanctuary, though. Where did you get it?"

"Yes," Reid said, his voice not nearly as amused as the situation warranted. "Where *did* you get it? Clearly Coco and Ansel didn't purchase it with our supplies."

They both had the decency to look apologetic.

"Ah." I batted my lashes as Beau offered the bottle to Madame Labelle, who shook her head curtly. She waited for my answer with pursed lips. "Ask me no questions, *mon amour*, and I shall tell you no lies."

When he clenched his jaw, clearly battling his temper, I braced myself for the inquisition. Though Reid no longer wore his blue uniform, he just couldn't seem to help himself. The law was the law. It didn't matter on which side of it he stood. Bless him. "Tell me you didn't steal it," he said. "Tell me you found it in a hole somewhere."

"All right. I didn't steal it. I found it in a hole somewhere."

He folded his arms across his chest, leveling me with a stern gaze. "Lou."

"What?" I asked innocently. In a helpful gesture, Coco offered me the bottle, and I took a long pull of my own, admiring his biceps—his square jaw, his full mouth, his copper hair—with unabashed appreciation. I reached up to pat his cheek. "You didn't ask for the truth."

He trapped my hand against his face. "I am now."

I stared at him, the impulse to lie rising like a tide in my throat. But—no. I frowned at myself, examining the base instinct with a pause. He mistook my silence for refusal, shifting closer to coax me into answering. "Did you steal it, Lou? The truth, please."

"Well, that was *dripping* with condescension. Shall we try again?"

With an exasperated sigh, he turned his head to kiss my fingers. "You're impossible."

"I'm impractical, improbable, but never impossible." I rose to my toes and pressed my lips to his. Shaking his head, chuckling despite himself, he bent low to fold me in his arms and deepen the kiss. Delicious heat washed through me, and it took considerable self-restraint not to tackle him to the ground and have my wicked way with him.

"My God," Beau said, voice thick with disgust. "It looks like he's eating her face."

But Madame Labelle wasn't listening. Her eyes—so familiar and blue—shone with anger. "Answer the question, Louise." I stiffened at her sharp tone. To my surprise, Reid did too. He turned to look at her slowly. "Did you leave camp?"

For Reid's sake, I kept my own voice pleasant.

"I didn't steal anything. At least"—I shrugged, forcing myself to maintain an easy smile—"I didn't steal the *wine*. I bought it from a peddler on the road this morning with a few of Reid's *couronnes*."

"You stole from my son?"

Reid held out a calming hand. "Easy. She didn't steal anything from—"

"He's my *husband*." My jaw ached from smiling so hard, and I lifted my left hand for emphasis. Her own mother-of-pearl stone still gleamed on my ring finger. "What's mine is his, and what's his is mine. Isn't that part of the vows we took?"

"Yes, it is." Reid nodded swiftly, shooting me a reassuring look, before glaring at Madame Labelle. "She's welcome to anything I own."

"Of course, son." She flashed her own tight-lipped smile. "Though I do feel obligated to point out the two of you were never legally wed. Louise used a false name on the marriage license, therefore nullifying the contract. Of course, if you still choose to share your possessions with her, you are free to do so, but do not feel obligated in any way. Especially if she insists on endangering your life—*all* our lives—with her impulsive, reckless behavior."

My smile finally slipped. "The hood of your cloak hid my face. The woman didn't recognize me."

"And if she did? If the Chasseurs or Dames Blanches ambush us tonight? What then?" When I made no move to answer her, she sighed and continued softly, "I understand your reluctance to confront this, Louise, but closing your eyes will not make it so the monsters can't see you. It will only make you blind." Then, softer still: "You've hidden long enough."

Suddenly unable to look at anyone, I dropped my arms from Reid's neck. They immediately missed his warmth. Though he stepped closer as if to draw me back to him, I took another drink of wine instead. "All right," I finally said, forcing myself to meet her flinty gaze, "I shouldn't have left camp, but I couldn't ask Ansel to buy his own birthday present. Birthdays are sacred. We'll strategize tomorrow."

"Really," Ansel said earnestly, "it isn't my birthday until next month. This isn't necessary."

"It *is* necessary. We might not be here—" I stopped short, biting my errant tongue, but it was too late. Though I hadn't spoken the words aloud, they reverberated through camp all the same. *We might not be here next month.* Shoving the wine back at him, I tried again. "Let us celebrate you, Ansel. It's not every day you turn seventeen."

His eyes cut to Madame Labelle's as if seeking permission. She nodded stiffly. "*Tomorrow*, Louise."

"Of course." I accepted Reid's hand, allowing him to pull me close as I feigned another horrible smile. "Tomorrow."

Reid kissed me again—harder, fiercer this time, like he had something to prove. Or something to lose. "Tonight, we celebrate."

The wind picked up as the sun dipped below the trees, and the clouds continued to thicken.

STOLEN MOMENTS

Reid

Lou slept like the dead. Cheek pressed to my chest and hair sprawled across my shoulder, she breathed deeply. Rhythmically. It was a peace she rarely achieved while awake. I stroked her spine. Savored her warmth. Willed my mind to remain blank, my eyes to remain open. I didn't even blink. Just stared, unending, as the trees swayed overhead. Seeing nothing. *Feeling* nothing. Numb.

Sleep had evaded me since Modraniht. When it didn't, I wished it had.

My dreams had twisted into dark and disturbing things.

A small shadow detached from the pines to sit beside me, tail flicking. Absalon, Lou had named him. I'd once thought him a simple black cat. She'd quickly corrected me. He wasn't a cat at all, but a matagot. A restless spirit, unable to pass on, that took the shape of an animal. "They're drawn to like creatures," Lou had informed me, frowning. "Troubled souls. Someone here must have attracted him."

Her pointed look had made it clear who she thought that *some-one* was.

"Go away." I nudged the unnatural creature with my elbow now. "Shoo."

He blinked baleful amber eyes at me. When I sighed, relenting, he curled into my side and slept.

Absalon. I stroked a finger down his back, disgruntled when he began to purr. *I am not troubled.*

I stared up at the trees once more, convincing no one.

Lost in the paralysis of my thoughts, I didn't notice when Lou began to stir several moments later. Her hair tickled my face as she rose up on an elbow, leaning over me. Her voice was low. Soft with sleep, sweet from wine. "You're awake."

"Yes."

Her eyes searched mine—hesitant, concerned—and my throat tightened inexplicably. When she opened her mouth to speak, to ask, I interrupted with the first words that popped into my head. "What happened to your mother?"

She blinked. "What do you mean?"

"Was she always so . . . ?"

With a sigh, she rested her chin on my chest. Twisted the mother-of-pearl ring around her finger. "No. I don't know. Can people be born evil?" I shook my head. "I don't think so either. I think she lost herself somewhere along the way. It's easy to do with magic." When I tensed, she turned to face me. "It's not like you think. Magic isn't . . . well, it's like anything else. Too much of a good thing is a bad thing. It can be addictive. My mother, she—she loved the power, I suppose." She chuckled once. It was bitter. "And when *everything* is a matter of life and death for us, the stakes are higher. The more we gain, the more we lose."

The more we gain, the more we lose.

"I see," I said, but I didn't. Nothing about this canon appealed to me. Why risk magic at all?

As if sensing my distaste, she rose again to better see me. "It's a gift, Reid. There's so much more to it than what you've seen. Magic is beautiful and wild and free. I understand your reluctance, but you can't hide from it forever. It's part of you."

I couldn't form a reply. The words caught in my throat.

"Are you ready to talk about what happened?" she asked softly.

I brushed my fingers through her hair, my lips against her forehead. "Not tonight."

"Reid . . ."

"Tomorrow."

She heaved another sigh, but thankfully didn't press the issue. After reaching over to scratch Absalon's head, she lay back down, and together, we stared up at the patches of sky through the trees. I drifted back into my mind, into its careful, empty silence. Whether moments or hours passed, I didn't know.

"Do you think . . ." Lou's soft voice startled me back to the present. "Do you think there'll be a funeral?"

"Yes."

I didn't ask whose she meant. I didn't need to.

"Even with everything at the end?"

A beautiful witch, cloaked in guise of damsel, soon lured the man down the path to Hell. My chest ached as I remembered Ye Olde Sisters' performance. The fair-haired narrator. Thirteen, fourteen at most—the devil herself, cloaked not as a damsel, but a maiden. She'd looked so innocent as she'd delivered our sentence. Almost angelic.

A visit soon came from the witch he reviled with the worst news of all . . . she'd borne his child.

"Yes."

"But . . . he was my father." Hearing her swallow, I turned, wrapped a hand around the nape of her neck. Held her close as emotion threatened to choke me. Desperately, I struggled to reclaim the fortress I'd constructed, to retreat back into its blissfully hollow depths. "He slept with La Dame des Sorcières. A witch. The king can't possibly honor him."

"No one will be able to prove anything. King Auguste won't condemn a dead man on the word of a witch."

The words slipped out before I could stop them. *A dead man.* My grip tightened on Lou, and she cupped my cheek—not to coerce me into facing her, but simply to touch me. To tether me. I leaned into her palm.

She stared at me for a long moment, her touch infinitely gentle. Infinitely patient. "Reid."

The word was heavy. Expectant.

I couldn't look at her. Couldn't face the devotion I'd see in those familiar eyes. *His* eyes. Even if she didn't yet realize—even if she didn't yet care—she would someday hate me for what I'd done. He was her father.

And I'd killed him.

"Look at me, Reid."

The memory flashed, unbidden. My knife embedding in his ribs. His blood streaming down my wrist. Warm and thick and wet. When I turned to face her, those blue-green eyes were steady. Determined.

"Please," I whispered. To my shame—my humiliation—my voice broke on the word. Heat flooded my face. Even I didn't know what I wanted from her. *Please don't ask me. Please don't make me say it.* And then, louder than the rest, a keening wail rising sharply through the pain—

Please make it go away.

A ripple of emotion flashed in her expression—almost too quick for me to see. Then she set her chin. A devious glint lit her eyes. In the next second, she whirled to straddle me, brushing a single finger across my mouth. Her own parted, and her tongue flicked out to wet her bottom lip. "*Mon petit oiseau*, you've seemed . . . frustrated these last few days." She leaned lower, brushing her nose against my ear. Distracting me. Answering my unspoken plea. "I could help with that, you know."

Absalon hissed indignantly and dematerialized.

When she began to touch me, to move against me—lightly, maddeningly—the blood in my face pitched lower, and I closed my eyes, clenching my jaw against the sensation. The heat. My fingers dug into her hips to hold her in place.

Behind us, someone sighed softly in their sleep.

"We can't do this here." My strained whisper echoed too loud in the silence. Despite my words, she grinned and pressed closer—*everywhere*—until my own hips rolled in response, grinding her against me. Once. Twice. Three times. Slowly at first, then faster. I dropped my head back to the cold ground, breathing ragged, eyes still clenched shut. A low groan built in my throat. "Someone might see."

She tugged at my belt in answer. My eyes flew open to watch, and I flexed into her touch, reveling in it. In *her.* "Let them," she said, each breath a pant. Another cough sounded. "I don't care."

"Lou—"

"Do you want me to stop?"

"No." My hands tightened on her hips, and I sat forward swiftly, crushing her lips against mine.

Another cough, louder this time. I didn't register it. With her hand slipping into my undone trousers—her tongue hot against mine—I couldn't have stopped if I tried. That is, until—

"*Stop.*" The word tore from my throat, and I lurched backward, wrenching her hips in the air, away from my own. I hadn't meant for it to go this far, this fast, with *this* many people around us. When I cursed, low and vicious, she blinked in confusion, hands shooting to my shoulders for balance. Her lips swollen. Her cheeks flushed. I clamped my eyes shut once more—clenching, clenching, *clenching*—thinking of anything and everything but Lou. Spoiled meat. Flesh-eating locusts. Wrinkled, saggy skin and the word *moist* or *curd* or *phlegm.* Dripping phlegm, or, or—

My mother.

The memory of our first night here flashed with crystalline focus.

"I'm serious," Madame Labelle warns, pulling us aside, "absolutely no sneaking away for any secret rendezvous. The forest is dangerous. The trees have eyes."

Lou's laughter rings out, clear and bright, while I splutter with mortification.

"I know the two of you are physically involved—don't try to deny it," Madame Labelle adds when my face flushes scarlet, "but no matter your bodily urges, the danger outside this camp is too great. I must ask you to restrain yourselves for the time being."

I stalk off without a word, Lou's laughter still ringing in my ears. Madame Labelle follows, undeterred. "It's perfectly natural to have such impulses." She hurries to keep up, skirting around Beau. He too shakes with laughter. "Really, Reid, this immaturity is most off-putting. You are being careful, aren't you? Perhaps we should have a frank discussion about contraceptives—"

Right. That did it.

The building pressure faded to a dull ache.

Exhaling hard, I slowly lowered Lou back to my lap. Another cough sounded from Beau's direction. Louder this time. Pointed. But Lou persevered. Her hand slid downward once more. "Something wrong, husband?"

I caught her hand at my navel and glared. Nose to nose. Lips to lips. "Minx."

"I'll *show* you minx—"

With an aggrieved sigh, Beau pitched upright and interrupted loudly, "Hello! Yes, pardon! As it seems to have escaped your notice, *there are other people here!*" In a low grumble, he added,

"Though clearly those other people will soon shrivel up and die from abstinence."

Lou's grin turned wicked. Her gaze flicked to the sky—now pitched the eerie gray before dawn—before she looped her arms around my neck. "It's almost sunrise," she whispered into my ear. The hair on my neck rose. "Shall we find the stream and . . . have a bath?"

Reluctantly, I glanced at Madame Labelle. She hadn't woken from our tryst, nor from Beau's outburst. Even in sleep, she exuded regal grace. A queen disguised as a madam, presiding over not a kingdom, but a brothel. Would her life have been different if she'd met my father before he'd married? Would *mine*? I looked away, disgusted with myself. "Madame Labelle forbade us from leaving camp."

Lou sucked softly on my earlobe, and I shuddered. "What Madame Labelle doesn't know won't hurt her. Besides . . ." She touched a finger to the dried blood behind my ear, on my wrist—the same as the marks on my elbows, my knees, my throat. The same marks we'd all worn since Modraniht. A precaution. "Coco's blood will hide us."

"The water will wash it away."

"I have magic too, you know—and so do you. We can protect ourselves if necessary."

And so do you.

Though I tried to repress my flinch, she still saw. Her eyes shuttered. "You'll have to learn to use it eventually. Promise me."

I forced a smile, squeezing her lightly. "It's not a problem."

Unconvinced, she slid from my lap and flung open her

bedroll. "Good. You heard your mother. Tomorrow, all of this ends."

An ominous wave swept through me at her words, at her expression. Though I knew we couldn't stay here indefinitely— knew we couldn't simply wait for Morgane or the Chasseurs to find us—we had no plan. No allies. And despite my mother's confidence, I couldn't imagine finding some. Why would anyone join us in a fight against Morgane? Her agenda was theirs—the death of all who had persecuted them.

Sighing heavily, Lou turned away and curled into a tight ball. Her hair fanned out in a trail of chestnut and gold behind her. I slid my fingers through it, attempting to soothe her. To release the sudden tension in her shoulders, the hopelessness in her voice. A hopeless Lou just didn't make sense—like a worldly Ansel or an ugly Cosette.

"I wish . . . ," she whispered. "I wish we could live here forever. But the longer we stay, the more it's like—like we're stealing moments of happiness. Like these moments aren't ours at all." Her hands clenched to fists at her sides. "She'll reclaim them eventually. Even if she has to cut them from our hearts."

My fingers stilled in her hair. Taking slow, measured breaths—swallowing the fury that erupted whenever I thought of Morgane—I wrapped a hand around Lou's chin, forcing her to meet my gaze. To *feel* my words. My promise. "You don't need to fear her. We won't let anything happen to you."

She scoffed in a self-deprecating way. "I don't fear her. I—" Abruptly, she twisted her chin from my grasp. "Never mind. It's pathetic."

"Lou." I kneaded her neck, willing her to relax. "You can tell me."

"Reid." She matched my soft tone, casting a sweet smile over her shoulder. I returned it, nodding in encouragement. Still smiling, she elbowed me sharply in the ribs. "Piss off."

My voice hardened. "Lou—"

"Just leave it alone," she snapped. "I don't want to talk about it." We glared at each other for a long moment—me rubbing my bruised rib mutinously—before she visibly deflated. "Look, forget I said anything. It's not important right now. The others will be up soon, and we can start planning. I'm fine. Really."

But she wasn't fine. And neither was I.

God. I just wanted to hold her.

I scrubbed an agitated hand down my face before glancing at Madame Labelle. She still slept. Even Beau had burrowed back into his bedroll, oblivious to the world once more. Right. Before I could change my mind, I hauled Lou into my arms. The stream wasn't far. We could be there and back before anyone realized we'd gone. "It's not tomorrow yet."

A WARNING BELL

Reid

Lou floated atop the water in lazy contentment. Her eyes shut. Her arms spread wide. Her hair thick and heavy around her. Snowflakes fell gently. They gathered in her eyelashes, on her cheeks. Though I'd never seen a melusine—only read of them in Saint-Cécile's ancient tombs—I imagined they looked like her in this moment. Beautiful. Ethereal.

Naked.

We'd shed our clothing at the icy banks of the pool. Absalon had materialized shortly after, burrowing into them. We didn't know where he went when he lost corporeal form. Lou cared more than I did.

"Magic has its advantages, doesn't it?" she murmured, trailing a finger through the water. Steam curled at the contact. "All of our fun bits should be frozen right now." She grinned and peeked an eye open. "Do you want me to show you?"

I arched a brow. "I have quite the view from here."

She smirked. "Pig. I meant magic." When I said nothing, she tipped forward, treading water. She couldn't touch the bottom of the pool, not as I could. The water lapped at my throat. "Do you want to learn how to heat water?" she asked.

This time, I was ready for it. I didn't flinch. I didn't hesitate. I did, however, swallow hard. "Sure."

She studied me through narrowed eyes. "You aren't exactly emanating enthusiasm over there, Chass."

"My mistake." I sank lower in the water, swimming toward her slowly. Wolfishly. "Please, O Radiant One, exhibit your great magical prowess. I cannot wait another moment to witness it, or I'll surely die. Will that suffice?"

"That's more like it," she sniffed, lifting her chin. "Now, what do you know about magic?"

"The same as I did last month." Had it only been a month since she'd last asked that question? It felt like a lifetime. Everything was different now. Part of me wished it wasn't. "Nothing."

"Rubbish." She opened her arms as I went to her, and I brought them around my neck. Her legs locked around my waist. The position should've been carnal, but it wasn't. It was just...intimate. This close, I could count every freckle on her nose. I could see the water droplets clinging to her lashes. It took all my resolve not to kiss her again. "You know more than you think. You've been around your mother, Coco, and me for the greater part of a fortnight, and on Modraniht, you—" She stopped abruptly, then faked an elaborate bout of coughing. My heart plummeted to my feet. *And on Modraniht, you killed the Archbishop with magic.* She cleared her throat. "I—I just know you've been paying attention. Your mind is a steel trap."

"A steel trap," I echoed, retreating into that fortress once more.

She didn't know how right she was.

It took several seconds to realize she was waiting for my response. I looked away, unable to face those eyes. They were blue now. Almost gray. So familiar. So . . . betrayed.

As if reading my thoughts, the trees rustled around us, and on the wind, I swore I heard his whispered voice—

You were like a son to me, Reid.

Gooseflesh erupted across my skin.

"Did you hear that?" I whipped my head around, clutching Lou closer. No gooseflesh marred her skin. "Did you hear him?"

She stopped talking mid-sentence. Her entire body tensed, and she looked around with wide eyes. "Who?"

"I—I thought I heard—" I shook my head. It couldn't have been. The Archbishop was dead. A figment of my imagination come to life to haunt me. Between one blink and the next, the trees fell resolutely still, and the breeze—if there'd been one at all—fell silent. "Nothing." I shook my head harder, repeating the word as if that would make it true. "It was nothing."

And yet . . . in the sharp pine-scented air . . . a presence lingered. A sentience. It watched us.

You're being ridiculous, I chided myself.

I didn't release my hold on Lou.

"The trees in this forest have eyes," she whispered, repeating Madame Labelle's earlier words. She still looked around warily. "They can . . . see things, inside your head, and twist them. Manifest fears into monsters." She shuddered. "When I fled the first time—the night of my sixteenth birthday—I thought I was going mad. The things I saw . . ."

She trailed off, her gaze turning inward.

I hardly dared breathe. She'd never told me this before. Never told me anything about her past outside Cesarine. Despite her bare skin against mine, she wore secrets like armor, and she shed them for no one. Not even me. *Especially* not me. The rest of the scene fell away—the pool, the trees, the wind—and there was only Lou's face, her voice, as she lost herself in the memory. "What did you see?" I asked softly.

She hesitated. "Your brothers and sisters."

A sharp intake of breath.

My own.

"It was horrible," she continued after a moment. "I was blind with panic, bleeding everywhere. My mother was stalking me. I could hear her voice through the trees—her spies, she'd once laughed—but I didn't know what was real and what wasn't. I just knew I had to get away. The screams started then. Bloodcurdling ones. A hand shot out of the ground and grabbed my ankle. I fell, and this—this corpse climbed out on top of me." A wave of nausea rolled through me at the imagery, but I didn't dare interrupt. "He had golden hair, and his throat—it looked like mine. He clawed at me, begged me to help him—except his voice wasn't right, of course, because of the"—she touched her hand to her scar—"the blood. I managed to get away from him, but there were others. So many others." Her hands fell from my neck to float between us. "I'll spare you the gory details. None of it was real, anyway."

I stared at her palms faceup in the water. "You said the trees are Morgane's spies."

"That's what she claimed." She lifted an absent hand. "Don't worry, though. Madame Labelle hides us inside camp, and Coco—"

"But they still saw us just now. The trees." I seized her wrist, examining the smear of blood. Already, the water had eroded it in places. I glanced at my own wrists. "We need to leave. Right away."

Lou stared at my clean skin in horror. "Shit. I *told* you to keep an eye on—"

"Believe it or not, I had other things on my mind," I snapped, hauling her toward the bank. Stupid. We'd been so *stupid*. Too distracted, too wrapped up in each other—in *today*—to realize the danger. She squirmed as she tried to free herself. "Stop it!" I tried to hold her flailing limbs. "Keep your wrists and throat above the water, or we're both—"

She stilled in my arms.

"*Thank* you—"

"Shut up," she hissed, staring intently over my shoulder. I'd barely turned—just glimpsing patches of blue coats through the trees—before she shoved my head underwater.

It was dark at the bottom of the pool. Too dark to see anything but Lou's face—muted and pale in the water. She held my shoulders in a bruising grip, cutting off the circulation. When I shrugged beneath her touch, uncomfortable, she clung tighter, shaking her head. She still stared over my shoulder, her eyes wide and—and empty. Combined with her pale skin and floating hair, the effect was . . . eerie.

I shook her slightly. Her eyes didn't focus.

I shook her again. She scowled, her hands biting deeper into my skin.

If I could've managed, I would've breathed a sigh of relief. But I couldn't.

My lungs were screaming.

I hadn't had time to draw breath before she'd pushed me under, hadn't been able to brace myself against the sudden, piercing cold. Icy fingers raked my skin, stunning my senses. *Stealing* my senses. Whatever magic Lou had cast to warm the water had vanished. Debilitating numbness crept up my fingers. My toes. Panic swiftly followed.

And then—just as suddenly—my eyesight blinked out.

The world went black.

I thrashed against Lou's hold, loosening the little breath I had left, but she clung to me, wrapping her limbs around my torso and squeezing, anchoring us to the bottom of the pool. Bubbles exploded around us as I fought. She held me with unnatural strength, rubbing her cheek against mine like she meant to—to calm me. To comfort me.

But she was drowning us both, and my chest was too tight, my throat closing. There was no calm. There was no comfort. My limbs grew heavier with each passing second. In a last, desperate attempt, I pushed upward from the ground with all my strength. At the jerk of Lou's body, the silt solidified around my feet. Trapping me.

Then she punched me in the mouth.

I rocked backward—bewildered, my thoughts fading to

black—and prepared for the water to rush in, to fill my lungs and end this agony. Perhaps it'd be peaceful, to drown. I'd never given it thought. When I'd imagined my own death, it'd been at the end of a sword. Perhaps twisted and broken by a witch's hand. Violent, painful endings. Drowning would be better. Easier.

At the breaking point, my body inhaled involuntarily. I closed my sightless eyes. Wrapped my arms around Lou, buried my nose in her neck. At least Morgane wouldn't have us. At least I wouldn't know life without her. Small victories. Important ones.

But the water never came. Instead, impossibly crisp air flooded my mouth, and with it, the sweetest relief. Though I still couldn't see—though the cold remained debilitating—I could *breathe*. I could *think*. Coherency returned in a disorienting wave. I took another deep breath. Then another, and another. This—this was impossible. I was *breathing underwater*. Like Jonah's fish. Like the melusines. Like—

Like magic.

A sliver of disappointment pierced my chest. Inexplicable and swift. Despite the water around me, I felt . . . dirty, somehow. Sordid. I'd loathed magic my entire life, and now—now it was the only thing saving me from those I'd once called brothers. How had it come to this?

Voices broke around us, interrupting my thoughts. Clear ones. Each rang out as if we stood beside its owner on the shore, not moored beneath feet of water. More magic.

"God, I need a piss."

"Not in the pool, you idiot! Go downstream!"

"Be quick about it." A third voice, this one impatient. "Captain Toussaint expects us in the village soon. One last search, and we leave at first light."

"Thank God he's eager to return to his girl." One of them rubbed his palms together against the cold. My brow furrowed. *His girl?* "Can't say I'm sorry to leave this wretched place. Days of patrols with nothing to show for them except frostbite and—"

A fourth voice. "Are those . . . clothes?"

Lou's fingernails drew blood now. I barely felt it. My heartbeat roared in my ears. If they examined the clothing, if they lifted my coat and shirt, they'd find my bandolier.

They'd find my Balisarda.

The voices grew louder as the men drew closer. "Two piles, it looks like."

A pause.

"Well, they can't be in there. The water is too cold."

"They'd freeze to death."

Behind sightless eyes, I imagined them inching closer to the water, searching its shallow blue depths for signs of life. But trees kept the pool shaded—even in the rising sun—and silt kept the water clouded. The snowfall would've covered our footsteps.

Finally, the first muttered, "No one can hold their breath this long."

"A witch could."

Another pause, this one longer than the last. More ominous. I held my breath, counted each rapid beat of my heart.

Tha-thump.

Tha-thump.

Tha-thump.

"But . . . these are men's clothes. Look. Trousers."

A haze of red cut through the unending blackness. If they found my Balisarda, I'd tear my feet from the silt by force. Even if it meant losing said feet.

Tha-thump.

Tha-thump.

I would not yield my Balisarda.

Tha-thump.

I'd incapacitate them all.

Tha-thump.

I would not lose it.

"Do you think they drowned?"

"Without their clothes?"

"You're right. The more logical explanation is that they're wandering around naked in the snow."

Tha-thump.

"Perhaps a witch pulled them under."

"By all means, go in and check."

An indignant snort. "It's freezing. And who knows what could be lurking in there? Anyway, if a witch *did* pull them under, they'll have drowned by now. No sense in adding my corpse to the pile."

"Some Chasseur you are."

"I don't see you volunteering."

Tha-thump.

A distant part of my brain realized my heartbeat was slowing. It recognized the creeping cold down my arms, up my legs. It pealed a warning bell. Lou's grip around my chest slowly loosened. I tightened my arms on her in response. Whatever she was doing to keep us breathing, to strengthen our hearing—it was draining her. Or perhaps it was the cold. Either way, I could feel her fading. I had to do something.

Instinctively, I sought the darkness I'd felt only once before. The chasm. The void. That place where I'd fallen as Lou lay dying, that place I'd carefully locked away and ignored. I fumbled to free it now, reaching blindly through my subconscious. But it wasn't there. I couldn't find it. Panic escalating, I tipped Lou's head back and brought my mouth to hers. Forced my breath into her lungs. Still I searched, but there were no golden cords here. There were no *patterns*. There was only freezing water and sightless eyes and Lou—Lou's head drooping against my arm, her grip slipping from my shoulders, her chest stilling against mine.

I shook her, my panic transforming to raw, debilitating fear, and wracked my brain for something—*anything*—I could do. Madame Labelle had mentioned balance. Perhaps—perhaps I could—

Pain knifed through my lungs before I could finish the thought, and I gasped. Water flooded my mouth. My vision returned abruptly, and the silt around my feet disbanded, which meant—

Lou had lost consciousness.

I didn't pause to think, to watch the gold flickering in my periphery take shape. Clutching her limp body, I launched to the surface.

PRETTY PORCELAIN

Lou

Heat radiated through my body. Slowly at first, then all at once. My limbs tingled almost painfully, nagging me back into consciousness. Cursing the pinpricks—and the snow, and the wind, and the coppery stench in the air—I groaned and opened my eyes. My throat felt raw, tight. Like someone had shoved a hot poker down it while I slept. "Reid?" The word came out a croak. I coughed—horrible, wet sounds that rattled my chest—and tried again. "Reid?"

Cursing when he didn't respond, I rolled over.

A strangled shriek tore from my throat, and I reeled backward.

A lifeless Chasseur stared back at me. His skin was bloodless against the icy shore of the pool, as most of said blood had melted the snow beneath him, seeping into the earth and water. His three companions hadn't fared much better. Their corpses littered the bank, surrounded by Reid's discarded knives.

Reid.

"Fuck!" I scrambled to my knees, hands fluttering over the

enormous, copper-haired figure on my other side. He lay face-down against the snow with his pants haphazardly laced, his arm and head shoved through his shirt as if he'd collapsed before he could finish dressing.

I rolled him over with another curse. His hair had frozen against his blood-spattered face, and his skin had turned an ashen blue-gray. Oh god.

Oh god oh god oh god

Pressing a frantic ear against his chest, I nearly wept with relief when I heard a heartbeat. It was weak, but it was there. My own heart pounded a traitorous beat in my ears—healthy and strong—and my own hair and skin were impossibly warm and dry. Realization swept through me in a wave of nausea. The idiot had almost killed himself trying to save me.

I flattened my palms against his chest, and gold exploded before me in a web of infinite possibilities. I skipped through them hastily—too panicked to delay, to think about the consequences—and stopped when a memory unfolded in my mind's eye: my mother brushing my hair the night before my sixteenth birthday, the tenderness in her gaze, the warmth of her smile.

Warmth.

Be safe, my darling, while we part. Be safe until we meet again.

Will you remember me, Maman?

I could never forget you, Louise. I love you.

Flinching at her words, I yanked at the golden cord, and it twisted beneath my touch. The memory changed within my mind. Her eyes hardened into chips of emerald ice, and she sneered at the hope in my expression, the desperation in my voice. My sixteen-year-old face fell. Tears welled.

Of course I do not love you, Louise. You are the daughter of my enemy. You were conceived for a higher purpose, and I will not poison that purpose with love.

Of course. Of course she hadn't loved me, even then. I shook my head, disoriented, and clenched my fist. The memory dissolved into golden dust, and its warmth flooded over and into Reid. His hair and clothing dried in a burst of heat. Color returned to his skin, and his breathing deepened. His eyes drifted open as I attempted to shove his other arm through his sleeve.

"Stop giving me your body heat," I snapped, tugging his shirt down his abdomen viciously. "You're killing yourself."

"I—" Dazed, he blinked several times, taking in the bloody scene around us. The color he'd regained in his skin vanished at the sight of his dead brethren.

I turned his face toward mine, cupping his cheeks and forcing him to hold my gaze. "Focus on me, Reid. Not them. You need to break the pattern."

His eyes widened as he stared at me. "I—I don't know how."

"Just relax," I coaxed, pushing his hair off his forehead. "Visualize the cord linking us in your mind, and let it go."

"Let it go." He laughed, but the sound was strangled. It held no mirth. "Right."

Shaking his head, he closed his eyes in concentration. After a long moment, the heat pulsing between us ceased, replaced by the bitter bite of cold, wintry air. "Good," I said, feeling that cold deep down in my bones. "Now tell me what happened."

His eyes snapped open, and in that brief second, I saw a flash of raw, unadulterated pain. It made my breath catch in my throat. "They wouldn't stop." He swallowed hard and averted his gaze. "You were dying. I had to get you to the surface. But they recognized us, and they wouldn't listen—" Just as quickly as it'd come, the pain in his eyes vanished, snuffed out as the flame of a candle. An unsettling emptiness replaced it. "I didn't have a choice," he finished in a voice as hollow as his eyes. "It was you or them."

Silence descended as realization clubbed me over the head.

This wasn't the first time he'd been forced to choose between me and another. This wasn't the first time he'd stained his hands with his family's blood to save mine. *Oh god.*

"Of course." I nodded too quickly, my voice horribly light. My smile horribly bright. "It's fine. This is fine." I pushed to my feet, offering him a hand. He eyed it for a second, hesitating, and my stomach dropped to somewhere around my ankles. I smiled harder. Of course he would hesitate to touch me. To touch anyone. He'd just undergone a traumatic experience. He'd cast his first magic since Modraniht, and he'd used it to harm his brethren. *Of course* he felt conflicted. *Of course* he didn't want me—

I flung the unbidden thought aside, cringing away as if it'd bitten me. But it was too late. The poison had already set in. Doubt oozed from the punctures of its fangs, and I watched—disconnected—as my hand fell back to my side. He caught it at the last second, gripping it firmly. "Don't," he said.

"Don't what?"

"Whatever you're thinking. Don't."

I gave a harsh laugh, casting about for a witty reply but finding none. I helped him to his feet instead. "Let's get back to camp. I'd hate to disappoint your mother. At this point, she's probably salivating to roast us both on a spit. I might welcome it, actually. It's freezing out here."

He nodded, still frighteningly impassive, and tugged on his boots in silence. We'd just started back for the Hollow when a small movement in my periphery made me pause.

His gaze cut around us. "What is it?"

"Nothing. Why don't you go on ahead?"

"You aren't serious."

Another movement, this one more pronounced. My smile— still too bright, too cheerful—vanished. "I need to take a piss," I said flatly. "Would you like to watch?"

Reid's cheeks flamed, and he coughed, ducking his head. "Er—no. I'll wait right—right over there." He fled behind the thick foliage of a fir tree without a backward glance. I watched him go, craning my neck to ensure he was out of sight, before turning to study the source of movement.

At the edge of the pool, not quite dead, the last of the Chasseurs watched me with pleading eyes. He still clutched his Balisarda. I knelt beside him, nausea churning as I pried it from his stiff, frozen fingers. Of course Reid hadn't taken it from him—from any of them. It would've been a violation. It didn't matter that witches would likely happen upon these bodies and steal the enchanted blades for themselves. To Reid, robbing his brethren of their identities in their final moments would've been an unthinkable betrayal, worse even than killing them.

The Chasseur's pale lips moved, but no sound came out. Gently, I rolled him onto his stomach. Morgane had once taught me how to kill a man instantly. "At the base of the head," she'd instructed, touching the tip of her knife to my own neck, "where the spine meets the skull. Sever the two, and there can be no resuscitation."

I mimicked Morgane's movement against the Chasseur's neck. His fingers twitched in agitation. In fear. But it was too late for him now, and even if it weren't, he'd seen our faces. Perhaps he'd seen Reid use magic as well. This was the only gift I could give either of them.

Taking a deep, steadying breath, I plunged the Balisarda into the base of the Chasseur's skull. His fingers stopped twitching abruptly. After a moment's hesitation, I rolled him back over, clasped his hands across his chest, and replaced his Balisarda between them.

As predicted, Madame Labelle waited for us on the edge of the Hollow, her cheeks flushed and her eyes bright with anger. Fire practically spewed from her nostrils. "*Where* have you—" She stopped short, eyes widening as she took in our rumpled hair and state of undress. Reid still hadn't laced his trousers. He hastened to do so now. "Imbeciles!" Madame Labelle cried, her voice so loud—so shrill and unpleasant—that a couple of turtle doves fled into the sky. "Cretins! Stupid, *asinine* children. Are you capable of thinking with the northernmost regions of your bodies, or are you ruled entirely by sex?"

"It's a toss-up on any given day." Marching to my bedroll, pulling Reid along in tow, I threw my blanket over his shoulders. His skin was still too ashen for my taste, his breathing too shallow. He pulled me under his shoulder, thanking me with a brush of his lips to my ear. "Though I am surprised to hear a madam being so prudish."

"Oh, I don't know." Sitting up in his bedroll, Beau dragged a hand through his rumpled hair. Sleep still clung to his face. "Just this once, I might call it prudence instead. And that's saying something from me." He arched a brow in my direction. "Was it good, at least? Wait—scratch that. If it was with anyone *other* than my brother, maybe—"

"Shut up, Beau, and stoke the fire while you're at it," Coco snapped, her eyes raking every inch of my skin. She frowned at whatever she saw there. "Is that blood? Are you hurt?"

Beau cocked his head to study me before nodding in agreement. He made no move to stoke the fire. "Not your best look, sister mine."

"She's not your sister," Reid snarled.

"And she looks better than you on her worst day," Coco added.

He chuckled and shook his head. "I suppose you're both entitled to your wrong opinions—"

"Enough!" Madame Labelle threw her hands in the air, wearisome in her exasperation, and glared between all of us. "What *happened*?"

With a glance up at Reid—he'd tensed as if Madame Labelle had stuck him with a fire poker—I quickly recounted the events at the pool. Though I skimmed the intimate parts, Beau groaned and fell backward anyway, pulling a blanket over his face. Madame Labelle's expression grew stonier with each word. "I was trying to maintain four patterns all at once," I said, prickling with defensiveness at her narrowed eyes, at the spots of color rising to her cheeks. "Two patterns to help us breathe and two patterns to help us hear. It was too much to control the temperature of the water too. I'd hoped I could last long enough for the Chasseurs to leave." I looked reluctantly at Reid, who stared determinedly at his feet. Though he'd returned his Balisarda to his bandolier, he still gripped its handle with his free hand. His knuckles were white around it. "I'm sorry I couldn't."

"It wasn't your fault," he mumbled.

Madame Labelle plowed onward, heedless of any and all emotional cues. "What happened to the Chasseurs?"

Again, I glanced at Reid, prepared to lie if necessary.

He answered for me, his voice hollow. "I killed them. They're dead."

Finally, *finally*, Madame Labelle's face softened.

"Then he gave me his body heat on the bank." I hurried to continue the story, suddenly anxious to end this conversation, to pull Reid aside and comfort him somehow. He looked so—so *wooden*. Like one of the trees growing around us, strange and unfamiliar and hard. I loathed it. "It was a clever bit of magic, but he almost died from the cold himself. I had to leech warmth from a memory to revive—"

"You *what*?" Madame Labelle drew herself up to her full height and stared down her nose at me, fists clenched in a gesture so familiar that I paused, staring. "You foolish girl—"

I lifted my chin defiantly. "Would you have preferred I let him die?"

"Of course not! Still, such *recklessness* must be checked, Louise. You know good and well how dangerous it is to tamper with memory—"

"I'm aware," I said through gritted teeth.

"Why is it dangerous?" Reid asked quietly.

I turned my head toward him, lowering my voice to match his. "Memories are sort of . . . sacred. Our experiences in life shape who we are—it's like nurture over nature—and if we change our memories of those experiences, well . . . we might change who we are too."

"There's no telling how that memory she altered has affected her values, her beliefs, her expectations." Madame Labelle sank in a huff onto her favorite tree stump. Breathing deeply, she straightened her spine and clasped her hands as if trying to focus on something else—anything else—than her anger. "Personality is nuanced. There are some who believe nature—our lineage, our inherited characteristics—influences who we are, regardless of the lives we lead. They believe we become who we are born to be. Many witches, Morgane included, use this philosophy to excuse their heinous behavior. It's nonsense, of course."

Every eye and ear in the Hollow fixed solely on her. Even

Beau poked his head out in interest.

Reid's brows furrowed. "So . . . you believe nurture holds greater sway than nature."

"Of course it does. The slightest changes in memory can have profound and unseen consequences." Her gaze flicked to me, and those familiar eyes tightened almost infinitesimally. "I've seen it happen."

Ansel gave a tentative smile—an instinctive reaction—in the awkward silence that followed. "I didn't know witchcraft could be so academic."

"What you know about witchcraft couldn't fill a walnut shell," Madame Labelle said irritably.

Coco snapped something in reply, to which Beau fired back. I didn't hear any of it, as Reid had lifted his hand to the small of my back. He leaned low to whisper, "You shouldn't have done that for me."

"I would do far worse for you."

He pulled back at my tone, his eyes searching mine. "What do you mean?"

"Nothing. Don't worry about it." I stroked his cheek, inordinately relieved when he didn't pull away. "What's done is done."

"Lou." He grabbed my fingers, squeezing gently before returning them to my side. My heart dropped at the rejection, however polite. "Tell me."

"No."

"Tell me."

"No."

He exhaled hard through his nose, jaw clenching. *"Please."*

I stared at him, deliberating, as Coco and Beau's bickering escalated. This was a bad idea. A very bad idea, indeed. "You already know some of it," I said at last. "To gain, you must give. I tampered with a memory to revive you on the shore. I exchanged our sight for enhanced hearing, and I—"

To be perfectly honest, I wanted to lie. Again. I wanted to grin and tell him everything would be all right, but there was little sense in hiding what I'd done. This was the nature of the beast. Magic required sacrifice. Nature demanded balance. Reid would need to learn this sooner rather than later if we were to survive.

"You?" he prompted impatiently.

I met his hard, unflinching gaze head-on. "I traded a few moments from my life for those moments underwater. It was the only way I could think to keep us breathing."

He recoiled from me then—physically recoiled—but Madame Labelle leapt to her feet, raising her voice to be heard over Coco and Beau. Ansel watched the chaos unfold with palpable anxiety. "I said that's enough!" The color in her cheeks had deepened, and she trembled visibly. Reid's temper had obviously been inherited. "By the Crone's missing eyetooth, you lot—*all* of you—need to stop behaving like children, or the Dames Blanches will dance atop your ashes." She cut a sharp look to Reid and me. "You're sure the Chasseurs are dead? All of them?"

Reid's silence should've been answer enough. When Madame Labelle still glared expectantly, however, waiting for confirmation, I scowled and said the words aloud. "Yes. They're gone."

"Good," she spat.

Reid still said nothing. He didn't react to her cruel sentiment at all. He was hiding, I realized. Hiding from them, hiding from himself . . . hiding from me. Madame Labelle tore three crumpled pieces of parchment from her bodice and thrust them toward us. I recognized Coco's handwriting on them, the pleas she'd penned to her aunt. Below the last, an unfamiliar hand had inked a brusque refusal—*Your huntsman is unwelcome here.* That was it. No other explanations or courtesies. No *ifs*, *ands*, or *buts*.

It seemed La Voisin had finally given her answer.

I crushed the last note in my fist before Reid could read it, blood roaring in my ears.

"Can we all agree it is now time to face the monsters," Madame Labelle said, "or shall we continue to close our eyes and hope for the best?"

My irritation with Madame Labelle veered dangerously close to distaste. I didn't care that she was Reid's mother. In that moment, I wished her not *death*, per se, but—an itch. Yes. An eternal itch in her nether regions that she could never quite scratch. A fitting punishment for one who kept ruining everything.

And yet, despite her cruel insensitivity, I knew deep down she was right. Our stolen moments had passed.

The time had come to move on.

"You said yesterday we need allies." I stuck my hand into Reid's, squeezing his fingers tight. It was the only comfort I could offer him here. When he didn't return the pressure, however, an old fissure opened in my heart. Bitter words spilled forth from it before I could stop them. "Who would we even ask? The blood witches clearly aren't with us. The people of Belterra certainly won't be rallying to our cause. We're witches. We're evil. We've strung up their sisters and brothers and mothers in the street."

"*Morgane* has done those things," Coco argued. "*We* have done nothing."

"That's the point, though, isn't it? We let it happen." I paused, exhaling hard. "*I* let it happen."

"Stop it," Coco said fiercely, shaking her head. "The only crime you committed was wanting to live."

"It matters not." Madame Labelle returned to her stump with a pensive expression. Though her cheeks were still pink, she'd mercifully lowered her voice. My ears rejoiced. "Where the king leads, the people will follow."

"You're mad if you think my father will align with you," Beau said from his bedroll. "He already has money on Lou's head."

Madame Labelle sniffed. "We have a common enemy in Morgane. Your father might be more amenable than you think."

Beau rolled his eyes. "Look, I know you think he still loves you or whatever, but he—"

"—is not the only ally we'll be pursuing," Madame Labelle said curtly. "Obviously, our chances of success are far greater if we persuade King Auguste to join us, as he will undoubtedly command the Chasseurs until the Church appoints new leadership, but there are other equally powerful players in this world. The loup garou, for example, and the melusines. Perhaps even Josephine would be amenable under the right circumstances."

Coco laughed. "If my aunt refused to *host* us with an ex-Chasseur involved, what makes you think she'll agree to *ally* with the real things? She isn't particularly fond of werewolves or mermaids, either."

Reid blinked, the only outward sign he'd gleaned the content of La Voisin's note.

"Nonsense." Madame Labelle shook her head. "We must simply show Josephine that she has more to gain from an alliance than from petty politics."

"Petty politics?" Coco's lip curled. "My aunt's *politics* are life and death for my people. When the Dames Blanches cast my ancestors from the Chateau, both the loup garou and melusines refused to offer aid. But you didn't know that, did you? Dames Blanches think only of themselves. Except for you, Lou," she added.

"No offense taken." I stalked to the nearest root, hauled myself atop it, and glared down at Madame Labelle. My feet dangled several inches above the ground, however, rather diminishing my menacing pose. "If we're living in fantasy land, why don't we add the Woodwose and Tarasque to the list? I'm sure a mythical goat man and dragon would add nice color to this great battle you're dreaming up."

"I'm not dreaming up anything, Louise. You know as well as I that your mother hasn't been idle in her silence. She is planning *something*, and we must be ready for whatever it is."

"It won't be a battle." I swung my feet in a show of nonchalance, despite the trepidation prickling beneath my skin. "Not in the traditional sense. That's not her style. My mother is an anarchist, not a soldier. She attacks from the shadows, hides within crowds. It's how she incites fear—in chaos. She won't risk uniting her enemies by presenting an outright attack."

"Even so," Madame Labelle said coolly, "we number six against scores of Dames Blanches. We *need* allies."

"For the sake of your argument, let's say all parties *do* form a miraculous alliance." I swung my feet harder, faster. "The king, Chasseurs, Dames Rouges, loup garou, and melusines all working together like one big happy family. What happens after we defeat Morgane? Do we resume killing each other over her corpse? We're *enemies*, Helene. Werewolves and mermaids aren't going to become bosom buddies on the battlefield. Huntsmen aren't going to forsake centuries of teaching to befriend witches. The hurt is too long and too great on all sides. You can't heal a disease with a bandage."

"So give them the cure," Ansel said quietly. He met my gaze with a steady fortitude beyond his years. "You're a witch. He's a huntsman."

Reid's reply was low, flat. "Not anymore."

"But you were," Ansel insisted. "When you fell in love, you were enemies."

"He didn't know I was his enemy—" I started.

"But you knew he was yours." Ansel's eyes, the color of whiskey, flicked from me to Reid. "Would it have mattered?"

It doesn't matter you're a witch, he'd told me after Modraniht. His hands had cupped mine, and tears had welled in his eyes. They'd been so expressive, brimming with emotion. With love. *The way you see the world . . . I want to see it that way too.*

Holding my breath, I waited for his validation, but it never came. Madame Labelle spoke instead. "I believe a similar approach will work on the others. Uniting them against a common enemy—forcing them to work together—might change each side's perceptions. It could be the push we all need."

"And you called me a fool." I kicked harder to emphasize my skepticism, and my boot—still unlaced in my haste to leave the pool—slipped from my foot. A scrap of paper fluttered from it. Frowning, I leapt to the ground to retrieve it. Unlike the cheap, blood-spattered parchment Coco had stolen from the village, *this* note had been written on crisp, clean linen that smelled like—like eucalyptus. My blood ran cold.

Pretty porcelain, pretty doll, with hair as black as night,
She cries alone within her pall, her tears so green and bright.

Coco strode to my side, leaning closer to read the words. "This isn't from my aunt."

The linen slipped through numb fingers.

Ansel stooped to pick it up, and he too skimmed the contents. "I didn't know you liked poetry." When his eyes met mine, his smile faltered. "It's beautiful. In a sad sort of way, I guess."

He tried to hand the linen back to me, but my fingers still refused to work. Reid took it instead. "You didn't write this, did you?" he asked, except it wasn't a question.

Mutely, I shook my head anyway.

He studied me for a moment before returning his attention to the note. "It was in your boot. Whoever wrote it must've been there at the pool." His frown deepened, and he passed it to Madame Labelle, who'd extended an impatient hand. "Do you think a Chasseur—?"

"No." The disbelief that'd held me frozen finally ruptured in a hot wave of panic. I snatched the note from Madame Labelle—heedless of her protest—and stuffed it back into my boot. "It was Morgane."

THE WISEST COURSE OF ACTION

Reid

An ominous silence settled over camp. Everyone stared at Lou as she took a deep breath to collect herself. Finally, she gave our silence a voice. "How did she find us?"

It was a good question. It wasn't the right one.

I stared at the crackling fire, envisioning Morgane's pale hand—her writing curved and elegant—as she spelled out destruction and doom.

I had a decision to make.

"You left camp, remember?" Madame Labelle snapped. "To take a *bath*, of all things."

"Chateau le Blanc is miles from here," Lou said. I could tell she was struggling to keep her voice reasonable. "Even if the water washed away Coco's protection, even if the trees whispered our whereabouts, she couldn't have gotten here so quickly. She can't *fly*."

"Of course she could. If properly motivated, you could too. It's simply a matter of finding the right pattern."

"Or maybe she was already here, watching us. Maybe she's

been watching us all this time."

"Impossible." I glanced up to see Madame Labelle's eyes darken. "I enchanted this hollow myself."

"Either way," Coco said, planting her hands on her hips, "why didn't she just snatch you from the pool?"

I returned my attention to the fire. That was a better question. Still not the right one.

Morgane's words floated back through my mind. *She cries alone within her pall, her tears so green and bright.* The answer was right in front of us. I swallowed hard around the word. *Pall.* Of course this was Morgane's plan. Grief thundered against the door of my fortress, but I kept it at bay, ignored the shard of longing that threatened to cut me open.

Slowly, methodically, I marshaled my thoughts—my emotions—back into order.

"I don't know." Lou answered Coco's question with a sound of frustration and started to pace. "This is so—so *her.* And until we know how she found me—or what she wants—we aren't safe here." She pivoted abruptly to face Madame Labelle. "You're right. We need to leave immediately. Today."

She wasn't wrong.

"But she knows we're here," Coco said. "Won't she just follow us?"

Lou resumed pacing, didn't look up from the path she wore in the ground. "She'll try to follow. Of course she will. But her game isn't ready yet, or she would've already taken me. We have until then to lose her."

"Marvelous." Beau rolled his eyes skyward, flopping grace-lessly to his bedroll. "We have an invisible axe hanging over our heads."

I took a deep breath.

"It's not invisible."

Every eye in the clearing turned to stare at me. I hesitated. I still hadn't decided what to do. If I was right—and I knew I was—many lives would be lost if we didn't act. And if we *did* act . . . well, we'd be walking into a trap. Which meant Lou . . .

I glanced at her, my heart twisting.

Lou would be in danger.

"Good God, man," Beau exclaimed, "now is not the time to play brooding hero. Out with it!"

"It was all in the note." Gesturing to the embers of the fire, I shrugged. The movement felt brittle. "Crying, tears, pall. It's a funeral." When I shot Lou a meaningful look, she gasped.

"The Archbishop's funeral."

I nodded. "She's baiting us."

Her brows dipped, and she tilted her head. "But—"

"That's only one line," Ansel finished. "What about the rest of it?"

I forced myself to remain calm. Collected. Empty of the emotion thrashing outside my mental fortress. "I don't know. But whatever she's planning, it's for his funeral. I'm sure of it."

If I was right, could I endanger Lou to save hundreds, perhaps thousands, of innocent people? Did risking her life to save the others make me any different than Morgane? One for the sake of many. It was a wise sentiment, but wrong, somehow. Even if it hadn't been Lou. The ends didn't justify the means.

And yet . . . I knew Morgane better than anyone here. Better than Madame Labelle. Better than even Lou. They knew La Dame des Sorcières as the woman. The mother. The friend. I knew her as the enemy. It had been my duty to study her strategy, to predict her attacks. I'd spent the last several years of my life growing intimately acquainted with her movements. Whatever she had planned for the Archbishop's funeral, it reeked of death.

But I couldn't risk Lou. I couldn't. If those few, terrible moments on Modraniht had taught me anything—when her throat had gaped open, when her blood had filled the basin—it was that I wasn't interested in a life without her. Not that it mattered. If she died, I would too. Literally. Along with dozens of others, like Beau and—and the rest of them.

My family.

The thought shook me to the core.

No longer faceless strangers, Morgane's targets were now the brothers and sisters I hadn't yet met. The brothers and sisters I hadn't yet allowed myself to dream about, to even think about. They were out there, somewhere. And they were in danger. I couldn't just abandon them. Morgane had as good as told us where she would be. If I could be there too—if I could somehow stop her, if I could cut off the viper's head to save my family, to save Lou, if I could prevent her from defiling my patriarch's last rites—

I was too distracted to notice the silence around me.

"You're reaching," Beau finally said, shaking his head. "You're drawing conclusions that aren't there. You want to attend the funeral. I understand. But that doesn't mean Morgane will be present too."

"What I *want* is to stop whatever she's planning."

"We don't *know* what she's planning."

I shook my head. "We *do*. She isn't going to spell it out for us, but the threat is clear—"

"Reid, darling," Madame Labelle interrupted gently, "I know you loved the Archbishop deeply, and perhaps you need closure, but now is not the time to charge heedlessly forth—"

"It wouldn't be heedlessly." My hands curled into fists of their own volition, and I struggled to control my breathing. My chest was tight. Too tight. Of course they didn't understand. This wasn't about me. This wasn't about—about *closure*. It was about justice. And if—if I could start to atone for what I'd done, if I could say goodbye . . .

The shard of longing burrowed deeper. Painful now.

I could still protect Lou. I could keep her from harm.

"You're the one who wanted to gather allies," I continued, voice stronger. "Tell us how to do that. Tell us how to—to persuade werewolves and mermaids to fight alongside each other. To fight alongside Chasseurs. This could work. Together, we'll be strong enough to confront her when she makes her move."

They all exchanged glances. Reluctant glances. Meaningful glances. Except for Lou. She watched me with an inscrutable expression. I didn't like it. I couldn't read it, and I could always read Lou. This look—it reminded me of a time when she kept secrets. But there were no more secrets between us. She'd promised.

"Do we . . ." Ansel rubbed the back of his neck, staring at his feet. "Do we even know if there'll be a funeral?"

"Or where it is?" said Beau.

"Or *when* it is?" said Coco.

"We'll find out," I insisted. "We'll be ready for her."

Beau sighed. "Reid, don't be stupid. If you're correct about this note—which I'm not convinced you are, by the way—we'd be playing right into her hands. This is what she *wants*—"

Absalon materialized at my feet just as I opened my mouth to argue—to explode—but Lou interrupted.

"It's true. This is what she wants." Her voice was quiet, contemplative, as she gestured between us. "It's exactly the sort of game she likes to play. Manipulative, cruel, divisive. She expects a response. She *craves* a response. The wisest course of action is to stay away."

The last she spoke directly to me.

"Thank the Maiden's flower." Madame Labelle heaved a sigh of relief, wiping a hand across her brow and gifting Lou a rare smile. "I knew you couldn't have survived this long without some common sense. *If* there is indeed a funeral and *if* Morgane indeed plans to sabotage it, we wouldn't have the necessary time to prepare. Travel along the road would be slow and dangerous with the entire kingdom searching for us. It would take nearly a fortnight to reach the Beast of Gévaudan's packland, and the melusines' home in L'Eau Mélancolique would be at least a week's journey in the opposite direction." She wiped her brow in agitation. "Beyond that, we'd need *weeks* at each place to foster the necessary relationships. I'm sorry, Reid. The logistics just don't work."

Lou watched me, waiting.

I didn't disappoint.

"Please, Lou," I whispered, stepping closer. "The wisest course of action isn't always the right one. This was my job. I've dealt with Morgane and the Dames Blanches all my life. I know how they operate. You were right before—Morgane incites chaos. Think about it. The day we met, she made an attempt on the king's life during his homecoming parade." I jerked my chin toward Beau at the memory. "She attacked the cathedral during the last of Saint Nicolas Day celebrations. Always, it's amidst a crowd. It's how she protects herself. It's how she slips away." I took her hand, surprised to feel her fingers trembling. "The Archbishop's funeral will have an assembly like the kingdom has never seen. People from all over the world will come to pay homage to him. The havoc she'll wreak will be devastating. But we have a real chance to stop her."

"And if no one joins us against her?"

"They will." Guilt ripped at my resolve, but I pushed it away. For now, I needed her to agree. I'd reveal this last bit of information when lives weren't at stake. "We don't need the blood witches or mermaids. The werewolves' land isn't far from Cesarine—a day or two's ride at most. We'll concentrate our efforts, focus on King Auguste and the Beast of—*Blaise*. We'll do whatever is necessary to persuade them. You said it yourself. Morgane isn't a soldier. She won't battle if we have equal footing." My thoughts raced faster, chasing different strategies. "She won't expect an alliance between the Chasseurs and werewolves. We'll ambush her . . . no. We'll create a diversion with the Chasseurs, drive her out of the city while the werewolves lie in wait. This could work," I repeated, louder now than before.

"Reid. You know this is a trap."

"I would never let anything happen to you."

"It's not me I'm worried about." With her free hand, she reached up to touch my cheek. "Did you know my mother threatened to feed me your heart if I escaped again?"

"That won't happen."

"No. It won't."

She dropped her hand, and everyone stilled, waiting. No one even breathed. In that moment, something shifted in our camp. Inadvertently, we'd looked to Lou for the final decision. Not Madame Labelle. Lou. I stared at her in dawning realization. She was the daughter of La Dame des Sorcières. I knew that. Of course I did. But I hadn't yet realized the implication. If all went according to plan . . . Lou would inherit the crown. The title. The power.

Lou would become a queen.

Lou would become the Maiden, the Mother, and the Crone.

She startled as if realizing this at the same moment I did. Her eyes widened, and her mouth twisted. It was an unpleasant realization, then. An unwelcome one. When she glanced at

Coco, looking deeply uncomfortable, Coco dipped her chin in a small nod.

"Right." Lou bent to crook a finger toward the cat at our feet. "Absalon, can you deliver a message to Josephine Monvoisin?" She shot an apologetic look at Coco. "This one should come from me."

"What are you doing?" Confusion laced my voice as I caught her hand, tugging her upright. "We should focus on Auguste and Blaise—"

"Listen, Chass." She patted my chest once before pulling away and crouching by Absalon once more. "If we're going to do this, we need all the help we can get. The mermaids *are* too far away, but the blood witches—maybe your mother is right. Maybe Josephine will be amenable under the right circumstances." To Coco, she added, "You said the blood camp is near?"

Coco nodded. "They usually camp in this area at this time of year."

Suspicion unfurled in my stomach as Lou nodded, whispering something to Absalon. "You said she wouldn't host an ex-Chasseur," I said.

Coco arched a brow pointedly. A smirk pulled at her lips. "She won't."

"Then what . . . ?"

Slowly, Lou rose to her feet, dusting mud from her knees as the cat vanished in a cloud of black smoke. "We're going to have to split up, Reid."

PAINTED HAIR

Lou

"White wine and honey, followed by a mixture of celandine roots, olive-madder, oil of cumin seed, box shavings, and a sprinkle of saffron." Madame Labelle carefully arranged the bottles on the rock we'd fashioned into a table. "If applied and left to alchemize for a full sun cycle, it will transform your locks to gold."

I stared at the many bottles, aghast. "We don't have a full sun cycle."

Her eyes cut to mine. "Yes, *obviously*, but with the raw ingredients, perhaps we could . . . speed the process." As one, we glanced across camp to Reid, who sulked by himself, sharpening his Balisarda and refusing to speak to anyone.

"No." I shook my head, pushing the bottles aside. The entire purpose of this futile exercise was to disguise myself *without* magic. After what had happened with Reid at the pool . . . well, we needn't poke the bear without reason. "Were there no wigs?"

Madame Labelle scoffed, reaching into her bag once more. "As inconceivable as it sounds, Louise, there were no costume shops in the small farming village of Saint-Loire." She slammed another jar on the rock. Inside it, *things* wriggled. "Might I interest you instead in a jar of pickled leeches? If allowed to bake into your hair on a sunny day, I'm told they yield a rich raven color."

Leeches? Coco and I exchanged horrified glances. "That is disgusting," she said flatly.

"Agreed."

"How about this as an alternative?" Madame Labelle fished two more bottles from her bag, throwing one to both Coco and me—or rather, *at* Coco and me. I managed to catch mine before it broke my nose. "The paste of lead oxide and slaked lime will dye your hair black as night. But be warned, the clerk informed me the side effects can be quite unpleasant."

They couldn't have been more unpleasant than her smile.

Beau paused in rummaging through Coco's rucksack. "Side effects?"

"Death, mostly. Nothing to fret about." Madame Labelle shrugged, unamused, and sarcasm dripped from her words. I didn't quite appreciate it. "Far safer than using *magic*, I'm sure."

Eyes narrowing, I knelt to inspect the contents of her rucksack myself. "It's just a precaution, all right? I'm *trying* to be nice. Reid and magic aren't exactly amicable at the moment."

"Have they ever been?" Ansel murmured.

Fair point.

"Can you blame him?" I pulled bottles out at random, examining their labels before tossing them aside. Madame Labelle must've bought the entire apothecary. "He's used magic twice, and both times, people have ended up dead. He just needs . . . time to reconcile everything. He'll make peace with himself."

"*Will* he?" Coco arched a dubious brow, casting him another long look. "I mean . . . the matagot showed for a reason."

The matagot in question lounged within the lower boughs of a fir, peering out at us with yellow eyes.

Madame Labelle snatched her rucksack from me. In a single, agitated motion, she swept the bottles inside. "We don't *know* the matagot is here because of Reid. My son is hardly the only troubled one in this camp." Her blue eyes flashed to mine, and she shoved a piece of ribbon in my hand. Thicker than what I'd once worn, but still . . . the black satin would barely cover my new scar. "Twice now your mother has attempted to murder you. For all we know, Absalon could be here because of *you*."

"Me?" I snorted in disbelief, lifting my hair for Coco to tie the ribbon around my throat. "Don't be stupid. I'm fine."

"You're mad if you think ribbon and hair dye will hide you from Morgane."

"Not from *Morgane*. She could already be here now, watching us." I flipped my middle finger over my head just in case. "But ribbon and hair dye might hide me from anyone who sees those wretched wanted posters—might even hide me from the Chasseurs."

Finished with the bow, Coco tapped my arm, and I let my hair fall, thick and heavy, down my back. I could hear the smirk in her voice. "Those posters *are* an uncanny likeness. The care with which the artist drew your scar—"

I snorted despite myself, turning to face her. "It looked like another appendage."

"A rather large one."

"A rather *phallic* one."

When we burst into a fit of cackles, Madame Labelle huffed impatiently. Muttering something about *children*, she stalked off to join Reid. Good riddance. Coco and I laughed anew. Though Ansel tried to play along with us, his smile seemed somewhat pained—a suspicion confirmed when he said, "Do you think we'll be safe in La Voisin's camp?"

Coco's response came instantly. "Yes."

"What about the others?"

Laughter fading, she glanced at Beau, who'd surreptitiously started digging through her pack once more. She knocked his hand away but said nothing.

"I don't like it," Ansel continued, bouncing his foot, growing more and more agitated. "If Madame Labelle's magic couldn't hide us here, it won't hide them on the road." He turned his pleading gaze to me. "You said Morgane threatened to cut out Reid's heart. After we separate, she could take him, force you back to the Chateau."

Reid had said as much an hour ago—or rather, shouted it.

As it turned out, he was much less keen on his *gather allies to confront Morgane at the Archbishop's funeral* plan when it meant we'd have to separate. But we needed the blood witches for this insane plan to work, and La Voisin had made it clear Reid wasn't welcome in her camp. Though small in number, their reputations were formidable. Fearsome enough that Morgane had denied their annual petitions to rejoin us in the Chateau.

I hoped it'd be enough for them to consider moving against her.

La Voisin was willing to listen, at least. Absalon had returned almost instantaneously with her consent. If we came without Reid, she'd allow us to enter her camp. It wasn't much, but it was a start. At midnight, Coco, Ansel, and I would meet her outside Saint-Loire, and she would escort us to the blood camp. In her presence, we'd be relatively safe, but the others—

"I don't know." When I shrugged helplessly, Coco's lips pressed tight. "We can only hope Helene's magic is enough. They'll have Coco's blood as well. And if worse comes to worst . . . Reid has his Balisarda. He can defend himself."

"It's not enough," Coco murmured.

"I know."

There was nothing else to say. If Reid, Madame Labelle, and Beau managed to survive the Chasseurs, Dames Blanches, cut-throats, and bandits of La Rivière des Dents—the only road through the forest, named as such for the teeth of the dead it collected—the danger would increase tenfold when they reached packland.

It was hard to say who the werewolves loathed more— huntsmen, witches, or princes.

Still, Reid knew those lands better than anyone in our company. He knew *Blaise* better than anyone in our company. I could only hope Madame Labelle's and Beau's diplomacy would serve them well. From what I'd heard of Blaise—which admittedly wasn't much—he ruled with a fair hand. Perhaps he'd surprise us all.

Either way, we didn't have time to visit both peoples together.

Tonight, we'd reconnoiter at a local pub to learn the exact date of the Archbishop's funeral. With luck, we'd be able to reunite in Cesarine before the services to approach King Auguste together. Madame Labelle maintained he could be swayed into a third alliance. We'd find out—for better or for worse—when we visited his castle.

Like Ansel, I didn't like it. I didn't like *any* of it. There was still too much to do, too much of the puzzle missing. Too little time. We'd piece together the rest at the pub tonight, but before we could do that . . .

"Aha!" Triumphant, Beau pulled two bottles from Coco's bag. She'd packed a motley assortment of ingredients to aid in her blood magic: some recognizable, such as herbs and spices, and some not, such as the gray powder and clear liquid Beau currently held aloft. "Wood ash and vinegar," he explained. When we stared at him blankly, he heaved an impatient sigh. "For your *hair*. You still want to dye it the old-fashioned way, correct?"

"Oh." Of their own volition, my hands shot up, covering my hair as if it protect it. "Yes—yes, of course."

Coco clutched my shoulder for moral support, shooting daggers at Beau with her eyes. "You're sure you know what you're doing?"

"I've helped many a paramour dye their hair, Cosette. Indeed,

before you, there was a buxom blonde by the name of Evonne."
He leaned closer, winking. "She wasn't naturally blond, of course,
but her other natural assets more than made up for it." When
Coco's gaze flattened—and her fingers tightened painfully on
my shoulder—Beau smirked. "Whatever is wrong, *ma chatte*? You
aren't . . . jealous?"

"You—"

I patted her hand, wincing. "I'll dismember him for you after
we've finished."

"Slowly?"

"Piece by piece."

With a satisfied nod, she strode after Madame Labelle, leaving
me alone with Ansel and Beau. Awkwardness loomed between
us, but I cut through it—literally—with an anxious swipe of my
hand. "You *do* actually know what you're doing, right?"

Beau ran his fingers through the length of my hair. Without
Coco to goad him, he seemed to wilt, eyeing the bottles of wood
ash and vinegar warily. "Never once did I claim to know what
I'm doing."

My stomach rose. "But you said—"

"What I *said* is that I helped a paramour dye her hair, but that
was only to piss off Cosette. What I actually *did* was *watch* a paramour dye her hair, while feeding her strawberries. Naked."

"If you fuck this up, I will skin you alive and wear your hide
as a cape."

He arched a brow, lifting the bottles to examine their labels.
"Noted."

Honestly, if a naked paramour didn't start feeding *me* strawberries soon, I'd burn the world down.

After pouring equal parts of ash and vinegar into Coco's mortar, he poked at it hopefully for several seconds, and an ominous gray sludge formed. Ansel eyed it in alarm. "How *would* you do it, though? If you magicked it a different color instead?"

Sweat broke out along my palms as Beau parted my hair into sections.

"That depends." I cast about for a pattern, and sure enough, several tendrils of gold rose to meet me. Touching one, I watched it curl up my arm like a snake. "I'd be changing something about myself on the outside. I could change something on the inside to match. Or—depending on the end color—I could take the hue, depth, or tone of my current shade and manipulate it somehow. Maybe transfer the brown to my eyes instead."

Ansel's gaze shifted to Reid. "Don't do that. I think Reid likes your eyes." As if afraid he'd offended me somehow, he hastily added, "And I do too. They're pretty."

I chuckled, and the tension knotting my stomach eased a bit. "Thanks, Ansel."

Beau leaned over my shoulder to look at me. "Are you ready?"

Nodding, I closed my eyes as he painted the first strand and kept my focus on Ansel. "Why are you so interested?"

"No reason," he said quickly.

"Ansel." I peeked an eye open to glare at him. "Out with it."

He wouldn't look at me, instead nudging a pine cone with

his toe. Several seconds passed. Then several seconds more. I'd just opened my mouth to prod him along when he said, "I don't remember much of my mother."

My mouth closed with a snap.

Behind me, Beau's hand stilled on my hair.

"She and my father died in a fire when I was three. Sometimes I think—" His eyes darted to Beau, who quickly resumed smearing the gray paste on my hair. Relieved, Ansel continued his dance with the pine cone. "Sometimes I think I can remember her laugh, or—or maybe his smile. I know it's stupid." He laughed in a self-deprecating way that I loathed. "I don't even know their names. I was too frightened of Father Thomas to ask. He did once tell me *Maman* was an obedient, God-fearing woman, but for all I know, she could've been a witch." He hesitated, swallowing hard, and finally met my eyes. "Just like—just like Reid's mother. Just like you."

My chest tightened at the hopefulness in his expression. Somehow, I knew what he was implying. I knew where this conversation was headed, and I knew what he wanted me to say— what he wanted, no, *needed*, to hear.

I hated disappointing him.

When I said nothing, his expression fell, but he continued determinedly. "If that's the case, maybe . . . maybe I have magic too. It's possible."

"Ansel . . ." I took his hand, deliberating. If he'd lived with his mother—*and* father—until he was three, it was highly unlikely the woman had been a Dame Blanche. True, she could've lived outside the Chateau—many Dames Blanches did—but even they rarely kept their sons, who were considered burdens, unable to inherit their mothers' magic or enhance their family's lineage.

Unbidden, my eyes cut to Reid. He whet his Balisarda on a stone with short, angry strokes.

How very wrong we'd been.

"It's possible," Ansel repeated, lifting his chin in an uncharacteristic display of stubbornness. "You said the blood witches keep their sons."

"The blood witches don't live in Cesarine. They live with their covens."

"Coco doesn't."

"Coco is an exception."

"Maybe I am too."

"Where is this coming from, Ansel?"

"I want to learn how to fight, Lou. I want to learn magic. You can teach me both."

"I'm hardly the person to—"

"We're headed into danger, aren't we?" He didn't pause for me to confirm the obvious answer. "You and Coco have lived on the streets. You're both survivors. You're both strong. Reid has his training and his Balisarda. Madame Labelle has her magic, and even Beau was quick-witted enough to distract the other witches on Modraniht."

The man in question scoffed. "Thanks."

Ansel ignored him, shoulders slumping. "But I was worthless in that fight, just like I'll be worthless in the blood camp."

I frowned at him. "Don't talk about yourself like that."

"Why not? It's true."

"No, it isn't." I squeezed his hand and leaned forward. "I understand that you might think you need to earn a place amongst us, but you don't. You already have one. If your mother was a witch, fine, but if she wasn't . . ." He slipped his hand from mine, and I sighed, longing to cut out my own tongue. Perhaps then I wouldn't need to eat my words so often. "You aren't worthless, Ansel. Never think you're worthless."

"I'm sick and tired of everyone needing to protect me. I'd like to protect myself for a change, or even—" When my frown deepened, he sighed and dropped his face into his hands, grinding his palms into his eyes. "I just want to contribute to the group. I don't want to be the bumbling idiot anymore. Is that so much to ask? I just . . . I don't want to be a liability."

"*Who* said you're a bumbling idiot—"

"Lou." He peered up at me, eyes lined with red. Pleading. "Help me. Please."

I stared at him.

The men in my life really needed to stop using that word on me. Disasters always followed. The thought of changing a single thing about Ansel—of hardening him, of teaching him to fight, to kill—made my heart twist, but if he felt uncomfortable in his skin, if I could help ease that discomfort in any way . . .

I could train him in physical combat. Surely no harm—and no bitter disappointment—would come from teaching him to defend himself with a blade. As for lessons in magic, we could simply . . . postpone them. Indefinitely. He'd never need to feel inferior in that regard.

"Of course I'll help you," I finally said. "If—if that's really what you want."

A smile broke across his face, and the sun dimmed in comparison. "It is. Thank you, Lou."

"This'll be good," Beau muttered.

I elbowed him, eager to change the subject. "How's it looking?"

He lifted a gummy strand and wrinkled his nose. "Hard to tell. I imagine the longer we let it sit, the stronger the color will be."

"How long did Evonne let it sit?"

"The hell if I know."

A half hour later—after Beau had finished coating each strand—Ansel left us to join Coco. With a dramatic sigh, Beau dropped to the ground across from me, heedless of his velvet pants, and watched him go. "I was perfectly content to loathe the little mouth breather—"

"He's not a mouth—"

"—but *of course* he's an orphan with no self-worth," Beau continued, unfettered. "Someone should burn that tower to the ground. Preferably with the huntsmen inside it."

A peculiar warmth started at my neck. "I don't know. At least the Chasseurs gave him some semblance of a family. A home. As someone who's lived without both, I can confidently say a kid like Ansel wouldn't have survived long without them."

"Are my ears deceiving me, or are you actually *commending* the Chasseurs?"

"Of course I'm not—" I stopped short, startled at the truth of his accusation, and shook my head incredulously. "Hag's teeth. I have to stop hanging out with Ansel. He's a terrible influence."

Beau snorted. "Hag's teeth?"

"You know." I shrugged, the uncomfortable warmth at my neck radiating across the rest of my scalp. Growing hotter by the second. "The hag's eyeteeth?" When he looked on, bemused, I explained, "A woman gains her wisdom when she loses her teeth."

He laughed out loud at that, but it didn't seem remotely funny to me now, not when my scalp was on fire. I tugged at a strand of hair, wincing at the sharp pain that followed. This wasn't normal, was it? Something had to be wrong. "Beau, get some water—" The word ended in a strangled cry as the strand of hair came away in my hand. "No." I stared at it, horrified. "No, no, *NO*."

Reid was at my side in an instant. "What is it? What's—?"

Shrieking, I hurled the gooey clump of hair at Beau's face. "You *idiot*! Look what you've—WHAT HAVE YOU *DONE*?"

He pawed the slime from his face, eyes wide and alarmed, and scrambled backward as I advanced. "I *told* you I didn't know what I was doing!"

Coco appeared between us with a flask of water. Without a word, she dumped it over my head, dousing me from head to toe, washing away the gray goop. I spluttered, cursing violently, and nearly drowned all over again when Ansel stepped forward to repeat the offense. "*Don't*," I snarled when Madame Labelle joined the group, her own flask poised for action. "Or I'll light you on fire."

She rolled her eyes and snapped her fingers, and with a puff of hot air, the water on my body evaporated. Reid flinched. "Such melodramatics," she said. "This is completely fixable—" But she stopped abruptly as I lifted a strand of too-brittle hair. We all stared at it together, realizing the worst in a heavy beat of silence.

My hair wasn't blond. It wasn't red or black or even the brassy color in between.

It was . . . white.

The strand broke off, crumbling in my fingers.

"We can fix this," Madame Labelle insisted, lifting a hand. "All will be as before."

"Don't." The tears in my eyes burned hotter than even my scalp. "No one else is going to lay a *fucking finger* on my hair." If I dyed it with another round of chemicals, the remaining strands would likely catch on fire, and if I used magic, I risked even graver consequences. The pattern required to change my hair from—from *this*—would be unpleasant. Not because of the color. Because of what the color represented. *Who* it represented. On anyone else, white, moonbeam hair could've been beautiful, but on *me* . . .

Chin quivering, nose in the air, I turned to Reid and slid a knife from his bandolier. I wanted to rage at him, to fling my damaged hair in his anxious face. But this wasn't his fault. Not truly. *I* was the one who'd trusted fucking *Beau* over magic, the one who'd thought to shield Reid from it. What a stupid notion. Reid was a witch. There would be no *shielding him* from magic— not now and certainly not ever again.

Though he watched me apprehensively, Reid didn't follow as I stalked across the Hollow. Hot tears—irrational tears, embarrassed tears—gathered in my eyes. I wiped them away angrily. Part of me knew I was overreacting, knew it was just *hair*.

That part could piss right off.

Snip.

Snip.

Snip.

My hair fluttered to the ground like strands of spider silk, pale and foreign. Delicate as gossamer. A strand floated to my boot as if teasing me, and I swore I heard my mother's laugh.

Jittery energy coursed through me as we waited for the sun to set.

We couldn't enter Saint-Loire for our reconnaissance until the sun went down. There was little reason to sneak into the pub if no villagers would be there. No villagers meant no gossip. No gossip meant no information.

And no information meant we still knew nothing about the world outside the Hollow.

I pushed abruptly to my feet, stalking toward Ansel. He'd said he wanted to train, and I still had Reid's knife from earlier. I flipped it from hand to hand. Anything to keep me from reaching up—*again*—to tug at my hair. The shorn ends just brushed the tops of my shoulders.

I'd thrown the rest of it into the fire.

Ansel sat with the others around the dying embers. Their conversation stalled as I neared them, and I had little trouble guessing what they'd been discussing. *Who* they'd been discussing. Fantastic. Reid, who'd been leaning against the nearest tree, approached cautiously. He'd been waiting for me, I realized. Waiting for permission to engage. I cracked a smile.

"How are you feeling?" He planted a kiss on top of my head, lingering on the white strands. For now, it seemed my tantrum trumped his own. "Better?"

"I think my scalp is still bleeding, but otherwise, yes."

"You're beautiful."

"You're a liar."

"I'm serious."

"I'm plotting to shave everyone's head tonight."

His lips twitched, and he looked suddenly sheepish. "I grew out my hair when I was fourteen. Alexandre has long hair, you know, in—"

"*La Vie Éphémère*," I finished, envisioning Reid with long, luscious locks that blew in the wind. I snorted despite myself. "Are you telling me you were a teenage heartthrob?"

One side of his mouth quirked up. "So what if I was?"

"*So* it's a pity we didn't meet as teenagers."

"You're still a teenager."

I lifted my knife. "And I'm still pissed." When he laughed in my face, I asked, "Why did you cut it?"

"Long hair is a liability in the training yard." He rubbed a rueful hand over his head. "Jean Luc got hold of it in a sparring session and nearly made *my* scalp bleed."

"He pulled your hair?" At my gasp, he nodded grimly, and I scowled. "That little *bitch*."

"I cut it afterward. I haven't worn it long since. Now"—his hands landed on his hips, his eyes glinting—"do I need to confiscate the knife?"

I tossed it in the air, catching it by the blade before sending it upward once more. "You can certainly try."

Quick as a flash—without breaking my gaze—he snatched the knife from above my head, holding it there out of reach. His eyes burned into mine, and a slow, arrogant grin touched his lips. "You were saying?"

Suppressing a delicious shiver—which he still felt, given his rumble of laughter—I spun and elbowed him in the gut. With an *oof*, he bent double, his chest falling hard against my back, and I pried the knife from his fingers. Craning my neck, I planted a kiss on his jaw. "That was cute."

His arms came around my chest, trapping me. Locking me in his embrace. "Cute," he repeated ominously. Still bowed, our bodies fit together like a glove. "*Cute.*"

Without warning, he lifted me into the air, and I shrieked, kicking my feet and gasping with laughter. He only released me after Beau sighed loudly, turned to Madame Labelle, and asked if we could depart ahead of schedule to spare his eardrums. "Will I need them in Les Dents, do you think? Or can I go without?"

Feet on the ground once more, I tried to ignore him—tried to keep playing, tried to poke Reid in the ribs—but his smile wasn't quite as wide now. The tension returned to his jaw. The moment had passed.

Someday, I wouldn't need to hoard Reid's smiles, and someday, he wouldn't need to ration them.

Today was not that day.

Straightening my shirt, I extended the knife to Ansel. "Shall we get started?"

His eyes widened. "What? *Now?*"

"Why not?" I shrugged, plucking another knife from Reid's bandolier. He remained wooden. "We have a few hours until sundown. You *do* still want to train, don't you?"

Ansel nearly tripped in his haste to stand. "*Yes*, I do, but—" Those brown eyes flicked first to Coco and Beau, then to Reid. Madame Labelle paused in dealing the former their cards. Instead of *couronnes*, they'd used rocks and sticks as bids. Pink colored Ansel's cheeks. "Should we—not do it here?"

Beau didn't look up from his cards. Indeed, he stared at them a bit too fixedly to be natural. "Don't presume we care what you're doing, Ansel."

Following Beau's lead, Coco offered Ansel a reassuring smile before she too returned to their game. Even Reid took the hint, squeezing my hand briefly before joining them without a word. No one turned in our direction again.

An hour later, however, they couldn't help but watch covertly.

"Stop, stop! You're flailing, and you're focusing too much on your upper body, anyway. You aren't Reid." I ducked beneath Ansel's outstretched arm, disarming him before he could sever a limb. Likely his own. "Your feet are for more than just footwork. Use them. Every strike should utilize both your upper- *and* lower-body strength."

His shoulders drooped in misery.

I lifted his chin with the tip of his sword. "None of that, *mon petit chou*. Again!"

Readjusting his form once more—twice more, a hundred times more—we parried through the greater part of the afternoon and into the evening. Though he showed little improvement, I didn't have the heart to end his lesson, even as the shadows around us deepened. When the sun touched the pines, he finally managed to knock my blade away out of sheer determination—and nick his own arm in the process. His blood flecked the snow.

"That was—you did—"

"Horrible," he finished bitterly, throwing his sword to the ground to examine his wound. Face still flushed—only partly from exertion—he shot a quick look in the others' direction. They all hastened to appear busy, gathering the makeshift plates they'd used for dinner. At Ansel's request, we'd trained right through it. My stomach grumbled irritably. "I was horrible."

Sighing, I sheathed my knife in my boot. "Let me see your arm."

He shook his sleeve down with a scowl. "It's fine."

"Ansel—"

"I said it's *fine*."

At his uncharacteristically sharp tone, I paused. "Do you not want to do this again?"

His face softened, and he dropped his head. "I'm sorry. I shouldn't have snapped at you. I just—I wanted this to go differently." The admission was quiet. This time, he looked to his own hands instead of the others. I gripped one of them firmly.

"This was your first attempt. You'll get better—"

"It wasn't." Reluctantly, he met my gaze. I hated that reluctance. That shame. I *hated* it. "I trained with the Chasseurs. They made sure I knew how terrible I was."

Anger washed through me, hot and consuming. As much as they'd given him, they'd taken even more. "The Chasseurs can eat a bag of dicks—"

"It's fine, Lou." He pulled his hand away to retrieve his fallen knife, but paused halfway down, gifting me a smile. Though weary, that smile was also hopeful—undeniably and unapologetically so. I stared at him, struck momentarily speechless. Though often naive and occasionally petulant, he'd remained so . . . pure. Some days I couldn't believe he was real. "Nothing worth having is easy, right?"

Nothing worth having is easy.

Right.

Heart lodged in my throat, I glanced instinctively at Reid's back across camp. As if sensing me, he stilled, and our eyes met over his shoulder. I looked away hastily, looping my arm through Ansel's and squeezing tight, ignoring the cold fist of dread in my chest. "Come on, Ansel. Let's end this wretched day with a drink."

CLAUD DEVERAUX

Reid

"I'm not drinking that."

I eyed the tumbler of liquid Lou offered me. The glass was dirty, the liquid brown. Murky. It suited the oily barkeep, the disheveled patrons who laughed, danced, and spilled beer down their shirts. A troupe had performed this evening as it passed through Saint-Loire, and the actors had congregated at the local tavern afterward. A crowd had soon followed.

"Oh, come on." She wafted the whiskey under my nose. It smelled foul. "You need to loosen up. We all do."

I pushed the whiskey away, still furious with myself. I'd been so hell-bent on convincing the others to gather allies, to confront Morgane—so blinded by my pathetic emotions—I hadn't considered the specifics.

"We aren't here to drink, *Lucida.*"

The thought of leaving her filled me with visceral panic.

"Excuse me, Raoul, but *you* are the one who insisted we reconnoiter at a *tavern*. Not that I'm complaining."

It was the kind of panic that consumed everything, required every bit of my focus to contain. I wanted to scream. I wanted to rage. But I couldn't breathe.

It felt a lot like drowning.

"It's the best place to gather information." With a twitch in my jaw, I glanced across the room to where Madame Labelle, Coco, and Beau sat amidst the raucous traveling troupe. Like Lou and me, Beau had hidden his face within the deep hood of his cloak. No one paid us any notice. Our ensembles were nothing compared to those of the performers. "We can't—" I shook my head, unable to collect my thoughts. The closer we drew to midnight, the wilder they ran. The more riotous. My eyes sought anything but Lou. When I looked at her, the panic sharpened, knifed through my chest and threatened to cut me in two. I tried again, mumbling to my fingertips. "We can't continue with Madame Labelle's plan until we assess the situation outside camp. Alcohol loosens lips."

"Does it, now?" She leaned forward as if to kiss me, and I recoiled, panic rising like bile. Thank God I couldn't see her face properly, or I might've done something stupid—like carry her into the back room, bar the door, and kiss her for so long she forgot her inane plan to leave me. As it was, I kept my muscles locked, clenched, to prevent me from doing it anyway. She slumped back in her seat with disappointment.

"Right. I forgot you're still being an ass."

Now I wanted to kiss her for a different reason.

Night had fully fallen outside. Only the fire in the grate

illuminated the grubby room. Though we sat as far away from it as possible, masked in the deepest shadows, its dim light hadn't hidden the wanted posters tacked to the door. Two of them. One with a sketch of my face, one with a sketch of Lou's. Duplicates of the ones littering the village streets.

Louise le Blanc, under suspicion of witchcraft, her sign had said. *Wanted dead or alive. Reward.*

Lou had laughed, but we'd all heard it for what it was. Forced. And under my picture—

Reid Diggory, under suspicion of murder and conspiracy. Wanted alive. Reward.

Wanted *alive*. It still didn't make sense in light of my crimes.

"See? All hope isn't lost." Lou had elbowed me halfheartedly upon seeing my indictment. In a moment of weakness, I'd suggested fleeing for the nearest seaport, leaving this all behind. She hadn't laughed then. "No. My magic lives here."

"You lived without magic for years."

"That wasn't living. That was surviving. Besides, without . . . all of this"—she gestured around us—"who am I?"

The urge to seize her had been overwhelming. Instead, I'd leaned low—until we were eye to eye and nose to nose—and said fiercely, "You are everything."

"Even if witches weren't watching the ports, even if we somehow managed to escape, who knows what Morgane would do to those left behind. We'd live, yes, but we couldn't leave everyone else to such a fate. Could we?"

Phrased like that, the answer had sunk like dead weight in

my stomach. Of course we couldn't leave them. But she'd still searched my eyes hopefully, as if awaiting a different answer. It'd made me pause, a hard knot twisting in my stomach. If I'd maintained we should leave, would she have agreed? Would she have subjected an entire kingdom to Morgane's wrath, just so we might live?

A small voice in my head had answered. An unwelcome one.

She's already done that.

I'd pushed it away viciously.

Now—with her body angling toward mine, her hood slipping—my hands trembled, and I resisted the urge to continue our argument. Too soon, she would leave for the blood camp. Though she wouldn't be alone, she *would* be without me. It was unacceptable. It couldn't happen. Not with both Morgane and Auguste after her head.

She can look after herself, the voice said.

Yes. But I can look after her too.

Sighing, she slumped back in her chair, and regret cleaved my panic. She thought I'd rejected her. I hadn't missed the way her eyes had tightened by the pool, then again in camp. But I wasn't rejecting her. I was protecting her.

I made stupid decisions when she touched me.

"How about you, Antoine?" Lou thrust the tumbler toward Ansel instead. "You wouldn't let a lady drink alone, would you?"

"Of course I wouldn't." He looked solemnly to the left and right. "But I don't see a lady here. Do you?"

Lou mustered a cackle and dumped the amber liquid over his head.

"Stop it," I growled, tugging her hood back in place. For just a moment, her hair had been visible to the pub. Though she'd sheared it, the color remained startlingly white. Distinct. It wasn't a common color, but it was a notorious one. An iconic one. None would recognize it on Lou, but they might mistake her for someone altogether worse. Even Lou had to see the similarities between her and her mother's features now.

Snatching my hand away before I could caress her cheek, I mopped up the whiskey with my cloak. "This is exactly why Madame Labelle didn't want you out in public. You draw too much attention."

"You've known your mother for approximately three and a half seconds, and already she's the authority. I can't tell you how exciting this is for me."

I rolled my eyes. Before I could correct her, a group of men seated themselves at the table next to us. Dirty. Disheveled. Desperate for a drink. "Fifi, love," the loudest and dirtiest of them called, "bring us a pint and keep 'em comin'. That's my girl."

The barmaid—equally filthy, missing her two front teeth—bustled off to comply.

Across the bar, Beau mouthed something to Lou, tapping his own teeth, and she snickered. Jealousy radiated through me. I moved closer instinctively, stopped, and scooted back once more. Forced myself to sweep the perimeter of the room instead.

"Migh' wan' a take it easy, Roy," one of his companions said. "Early morn tomorrow, and all."

Behind the disheveled group, three men in dark clothing played cards. Swords at their hips. Mead in their cups. Beyond them, a young couple chatted animatedly with Madame Labelle, Coco, and Beau. Fifi and a powerfully built barkeep tended the counter. Actors and actresses danced by the door. More villagers spilled in from outside, eyes bright with excitement and noses red with cold.

People everywhere, blissfully unaware of who hid in their midst.

"Bah." Roy spat on the floor. A bit of the spittle dripped down his chin. Lou—seated closest to him—scooted her chair away, nose wrinkling. "Horse broke 'er leg yesterday eve. We won' be goin' ta Cesarine after all."

At this, the three of us grew still. Unnaturally still. When I nudged Lou, she nodded and took a sip of her drink. Ansel followed suit, grimacing when the liquid hit his tongue. He tipped it toward me. I declined, quickly tallying the distance from Saint-Loire to Cesarine. If these men planned on leaving in the morning, the Archbishop's funeral was in a fortnight.

"Lucky, you are," another said as Fifi returned with their mead. They drank greedily. "Wife won' let me outta it. Says we have ta *pay our respects*. Bleedin' 'alfwit, she is. Old Florin never did me nothin' but peeve the wee ones durin' harvest."

The sound of his name hit me like a brick. These were farmers, then. Several weeks ago, we'd been dispatched to deal with another lutin infestation outside Cesarine. But we'd been *helping* the farmers, not hindering them.

As if reading my mind, one said, "His blue pigs did kill 'em, though, Gilles. That's somethin'."

Blue pigs. Fury coiled in my throat at the slur. These men didn't realize all the Chasseurs did to ensure their safety. The sacrifices they made. The integrity they held. I eyed the men's rumpled clothing in distaste. Perhaps they lived too far north to understand, or perhaps their farms sat too far removed from polite society. None but simpletons and criminals referred to my brotherhood—I winced internally, correcting myself—the *Chasseurs'* brotherhood as anything but virtuous, noble, and true.

"Not all o' them," Gilles replied gruffly. "We had a righ' proper riot after they lef'. The little devils dug up their friends' corpses and shredded my wheat in one nigh'. We leave out a weekly offerin' now. The blues would burn us if they knew, but wha' can we do? Cheaper than losin' another field to the creatures. We're caught between the rock and the hard place. Can hardly put food in our bellies as it is."

He turned to order another round from Fifi.

"Aye," his friend said, shaking his head. "Damned if we do, and damned if we don'." He returned his attention to Roy. "Migh' be for the best, though. My sister lives in Cesarine with 'er whelps, an' she said Auguste 'as set a curfew. People ain't allowed out after sundown, an' women ain't allowed out at all without gentlemanly chaperones. He's got his soldiers patrollin' the streets day an' nigh' lookin' for suspicious womenfolk after wha' happened to the Archbishop."

Chaperones? Patrols?

Lou and I exchanged looks, and she cursed softly. It'd be harder to navigate the city than we expected.

Gilles shuddered. "Can't say I rightly mind it. Wee folk are one thing. Witches are another. Evil, they is. Unnatural."

The other men mumbled their agreement while Roy ordered another round. When one of them diverted the conversation to his hernia, however, Lou shot me a quick glance. I didn't like the gleam in her eye. Didn't like the determined set in her jaw. "Don't," I warned, voice low, but she took a hearty swig and spoke over me.

"Oi, you 'ear what that lummox Toussaint was claimin'?"

Every eye at the neighboring table swiveled toward her. Disbelief kept me rooted to my chair, gaping along with the rest of them. Ansel let out a nervous chuckle. More squeak than anything. Lou kicked him under the table.

After another tense second, Roy belched and patted his stomach. "Who're you, then? Why're you hidin' yer face?"

"Bad 'air day, boy-o. Sheared the whole o' it off in a fit o' rage, and now I can' stand the sight of meself."

Ansel choked on his whiskey. Instinctively, I pounded him on the back. Neither of us tore our eyes from Lou. I couldn't see her grin, but I could sense it. She was enjoying herself.

I wanted to strangle her.

"Plus, there's the wart on me chin," she added conspiratorially, lifting a finger to tap her face. It disappeared within the shadows of her hood. "No amount o' powder can cover it up. It's the size o' Belterra, it is."

"Aye." The man who'd spoken before nodded sagely, deep in his cups, and peered at her through bleary eyes. "Me sister 'as a wart on 'er nose. I reckon yer all right."

Lou couldn't contain her snort. "These are me brothers"—she gestured to Ansel and me—"Antoine and Raoul."

"'Ello, friends." Grinning, Ansel raised his hand in a stupid little wave. "Pleased ter meet yeh."

I stared at him. Though sheepish, his smile didn't falter.

"Anyhoo," Lou said, tossing back the rest of her whiskey, "Antoine and Raoul 'ere can right empathize wit' yer lutin problems. Farmers, we are. Them blue pigs is ruinin' life fer us as well, and Toussaint is the worst o' them."

With a grunt, Roy shook his head. "He was just 'ere with 'is damn pigs this morn, and *they* said old Toussaint gutted Morgane on Christmas Eve."

"Shit o' the bull!" Lou slapped the table for emphasis. I pressed my foot over hers in warning, but she kicked my shin in response. Her shoulders shook with silent laughter.

"*But*—" Roy belched again before leaning in, gesturing for us to do the same. "—they said they 'ad ta leave for Cesarine right away because o' the tournament."

My stomach dropped. "The tournament?"

"That's right," Roy said, cheeks growing ruddier by the second. Voice growing louder. "They have ta refill their ranks. Apparently the witches took ou' a few of their own. People are callin' it Noël Rouge." He leered and wiped his mouth on his sleeve. "Because o' all the blood."

When Ansel passed me his drink this time, I accepted.

The whiskey burned all the way down.

The one with the warty sister nodded. "They're havin' it before the Archbishop's services. Tryin' to make a festival outta it, I think. Bit morbid."

Gilles downed his third pint. "Maybe I should enter."

The man laughed. "Maybe I should enter yer wife while yer gone."

"I'll swap 'er for yer sister!"

The conversation deteriorated from there. I tried and failed to extricate Lou from an argument about who was uglier—the man's sister or the witch in the wanted posters—when an unfamiliar voice interrupted. "Claptrap and balderdash, all of it. There is nothing so venerable as a wart on the visage."

We turned as one to look at the man who plunked into the empty seat at our table. Brown eyes twinkled above an unruly mustache and beard. The troupe's fiddler. He extended a weathered hand to me. Lifted his other in a cheery wave. "Salutations. Claud Deveraux, at your service."

Roy and his companions turned away in disgust, muttering about charlatans.

I stared at his hand while Lou readjusted her hood. Ansel's eyes darted to Madame Labelle, Coco, and Beau. Though they watched us surreptitiously, they continued chatting with the couple beside them. Madame Labelle dipped her chin in a subtle nod.

"Right, then." Claud Deveraux dropped his hand but not his smile. "You don't mind the company, do you? I must confess, I need a respite from all the revelry. Ah, you have libations." He waved a hand to his troupe before helping himself to the rest of Ansel's drink. "I am indebted to you, good sir. Truly, my deepest gratitude." Winking at me, he dabbed at his mouth with a plaid pocket square. "Where was I? Oh, yes. Claud Deveraux. That's me. I am, of course, musician and manager of Troupe de Fortune. Did you perchance attend our performance this evening?"

I kept my foot pressed on Lou's, beseeching her to keep quiet. Unlike Roy, this man had sought us out. I didn't like it. With a grudging sigh, she sat back and crossed her arms. "No," I said brusquely, rudely. "We didn't."

"It was a splendid affair." He continued his one-sided conversation with relish, beaming at each of us in turn. I inspected him closer. Pinstriped pants. Paisley coat. Checkered bow tie. He'd thrown his top hat—tattered and maroon—on the table in front of him. Even to me, his outfit seemed . . . bizarre. "I do love these quaint little villages along the road. One meets the most interesting people."

Clearly.

"It is unfortunate indeed we leave this very night, spurred southward by the siren call of crowds and *couronnes* at our Holy Father's committal." He waved an absent hand. Black polish gleamed on his fingernails. "Such a tragic affair. Such an ungodly sum."

My lip curled. I liked Claud Deveraux less and less.

"And what of you? Might I inquire as to your names?" Oblivious to the tense, awkward silence, he tapped his fingers against the table in a jaunty rhythm. "Though I do love a good intrigue. Perhaps I could instead hazard a guess?"

"That won't be necessary." My words fell leaden between us. Roy had given us all the information we needed. It was time to go. Standing, I caught Beau's eye across the room and nodded toward the exit. He nudged my mother and Coco. "My name is Raoul, and these are my friends Lucida and Antoine. We're leaving."

"Friends! Oh, how delightful!" He drummed his fingers louder in delight, completely ignoring my dismissal. "And such marvelous names they possess! Alas, I'm not *quite* as fond of the name Raoul, but do let me explain. I knew a man once, a big burly bear of a man—though perhaps he was a small surly man of a bear—and the poor dear caught a splinter in his foot—"

"Monsieur Deveraux," Lou said, sounding equal parts irritated and intrigued. Probably irritated *because* she was intrigued. His smile slipped when she spoke, and he blinked slowly. Just once. Then his smile returned—wider now, genuine—and he leaned forward to clutch her hand.

"Please, Lucida, you must call me Claud."

At the sudden warmth in his voice, at the way his eyes shone brighter than before, the muted panic in my chest roared back to life, hardened into suspicion. But he couldn't have recognized her. Her face remained hidden. This familiarity—perhaps it was another quirk of his personality. An inappropriate one.

Lou stiffened beneath his touch. "*Monsieur Deveraux.* While I usually welcome a complete stranger drinking my whiskey and fondling my hand, it's been a rough few days. If you could kindly *piss off*, I'd greatly appreciate it."

Roy—who'd never quite stopped eavesdropping—lifted his head and frowned. I winced.

Lou had dropped her accent.

Releasing her hand, Deveraux tipped his head back and laughed. Loudly. "Oh, Lucida, what a *delight* you are. I can't begin to convey how I've missed such black humor—the kind that bites your hand if you move too close—which, incidentally, I am appropriately and grievously contrite about—"

"Cut the shit." Lou shoved to her feet, unaccountably flustered. Her voice rang out sharp and loud. Too loud. "What do you *want*?"

But her hood slipped at the sudden movement, and whatever words Claud Deveraux had planned fell away with it. He gazed at her raptly. All pretense gone. "I simply wanted to meet you, dear girl, and to offer help should you ever have need." His eyes dropped to her throat. The new ribbon—slicker, larger than usual, harder to tie in a bow—had loosened from its knot, sliding down to reveal her grisly scar.

Fuck.

"What's happened ta you, then?" Roy asked loudly.

Beside him, Gilles narrowed his eyes to slits. He turned toward the wanted posters on the door. "That's a nasty scar you've got there."

Deveraux tugged her hood back in place, but it was too late.

The damage was done.

Roy heaved himself to his feet. He waved his glass tankard at Lou, swaying and trying to keep his balance. Mead spilled down his trousers. "You don't have no wart, *Lucida*. No accent neither. But you do look an awful lot like that girl everyone's lookin' for. That *witch*."

A hush fell over the tavern.

"I'm not—" Lou spluttered, looking around wildly. "That's ridiculous—"

Unsheathing my Balisarda, I rose with deadly purpose. Ansel followed with his own knife. The two of us towered behind her as the rest of Roy's companions lurched to their feet.

"Oh, it's 'er, all right." Gilles stumbled into the table, pointing at the poster. He grinned in triumph. "She cut 'er hair, dyed it, but she can't hide that scar. Saw it clear as day. That girl there is Louise le Blanc."

And in a clumsy, terrifying movement, Roy lifted his glass tankard and shattered it into a jagged blade.

MARIONETTE

Reid

Despite the nightmare our lives had become, I still hadn't fought alongside Lou in physical combat. At Modraniht, she'd been unconscious. At Ye Olde Sisters' performance, she'd been hiding her magic. And at the smithy, she'd killed the criminals before I could intervene. I hadn't been able to fathom how someone so small could kill two fully grown men with such efficiency. Such brutality.

Now I understood.

The woman was a menace.

She moved with unexpected speed, feinting and striking with both hands. When her knife missed its mark, her fingers flexed and her opponent toppled. Or stiffened. Or smashed into the bar, shattering tumblers and dousing the room with whiskey. Glass rained down on our heads, but she didn't slow. Again and again she struck.

Even so, Roy and his friends sobered quickly, and they outnumbered four to her one. Five when the barkeep joined the fray.

Coco ran to meet him, but I caught her, pushing her toward the door. "Take the others and go. They don't know your faces yet, but they will if you stay and fight."

"I'm not leaving L—"

"Yes"—I seized the back of her dress and hurled her out the door—"you are."

Eyes huge, Beau raced after her. Both Ansel and Madame Labelle looked likely to argue, but I cut them off, throwing a knife to pin Roy's sleeve to the wall. He'd swiped his tankard at Lou while her back was turned. "We'll meet you at camp. *Go.*"

They hastened after Coco and Beau.

Lou called something to me—parrying three men at once—but I couldn't hear her over the villagers' shrieks. They trampled each other in their haste to flee the witch with magic, but the men with makeshift swords proved equally frightening. Laughing, yelling, the three strode through the crowd toward the exit. One tore down Lou's wanted poster and pocketed it. He seized mine next. Grinning at me over his shoulder, he tapped his hair.

My hand shot to my fallen hood.

"Take your time." His voice reverberated through the panic, and he swiped a tankard from the nearest table, drinking deeply. His companions had successfully barricaded the door, trapping the remaining villagers. Trapping us. "We can wait."

Bounty hunters.

"Husband!" Lou thrust her palm out, and Gilles's and his friends' skulls cracked together. Moaning, they crumpled to the floor. "I *try* not to be needy, really, but a little help over here would be *grand*—"

Roy freed himself and tackled her. I sliced through the barkeep's leg, vaulting over him as he staggered, and sprinted toward them.

"Ugh, Roy, *mon ami*." Lou wrinkled her nose beneath him. "I hate to be indelicate, but when did you last bathe? You smell a bit ripe under here." With a retching sound, she bit the underside of his bicep. He reared backward, and I clubbed him in the head, hooking Lou's elbow and flipping her over my back before he could collapse on her. She kicked Gilles—who'd been trying to rise—neatly on her way down.

"You can't imagine how *toothsome* you look right now, Reid." Grinning wickedly, elbow still linked with mine, she spun into my arms and kissed me full on the mouth. I must've been insane because I kissed her back, until—

"Toothsome?" I pulled away, frowning. Adrenaline pounded in my chest. "Not sure I like that—"

"Why not? It means I want to eat you alive." She slashed at the last of Roy's friends as we dashed for the door. "Have you tried any patterns yet?"

The mountainous barkeep rose to block our path, roaring loudly enough to shake the rafters. Blood painted his leg crimson. "*Witch*," he seethed, swinging a club the size of Lou's body.

I blocked the blow with my Balisarda, gritting my teeth against the impact. "This is hardly the time—"

"But have you?"

"*No.*"

With an impatient sigh, Lou ducked beneath us to stab at Roy, who refused to stay down.

"I suspected as much." This time when Roy charged her, she rolled over his back and kicked him in the rear. He toppled over his friends' bodies, and Lou knocked away his sword. "Magic in combat can be tricky, but it doesn't have to end like this morning. The trick is to get creative—"

She broke off abruptly as Gilles seized her ankle. Winking at me, she stomped on his face. He crumpled against his friends and moved no more. Smashing my head into the barkeep's nose, I caught his club when he collapsed. The very foundation trembled on impact.

Breathing hard, I looked behind us. Five down. Three to go.

"Try to see beyond this disgusting little room to what lies beneath." Lou gestured wildly with her knife. Screaming anew, the trapped villagers scattered to hide behind overturned tables and chairs. "Go ahead. *Look*. Tell me what you see."

I returned my attention to the men at the door instead. True to their word, they'd waited. Pushing languidly from the wall, they drew their swords as we approached. "I suppose this means you aren't willing to simply step aside," Lou said with a sigh. "Are you sure that's wise? I am a witch, you know."

The one with the tankard finished his beer. "Did you know your head is worth one hundred thousand *couronnes*?"

She sniffed and came to a stop. "Frankly, I'm insulted. It's worth at least twice that. Have you spoken with La Dame des Sorcières? I'm sure she'd pay triple. For me, though. Not my head. I'd have to be *alive*, of course, which could present a problem for you—"

"Shut up." The man dropped the tankard, and it shattered at his feet. "Or I'll cut it off while you're still breathing."

"The king wants my *actual* head? How . . . barbaric. Are you sure you won't consider taking me to La Dame des Sorcières instead? I'm suddenly feeling quite sympathetic to her cause."

"If you surrender, we'll kill you quick," his companion promised. "Save the nasty business for after."

Lou grimaced. "How magnanimous of you." To me, she whispered, "They don't have Balisardas. Focus on the outcome, and the patterns will appear. Choose the one with the least collateral damage, but make sure you *choose*. Otherwise nature will choose for you. That's what happened this morning, isn't it?"

I gripped my own Balisarda tighter. "I won't need it."

"I'm trying to be patient, Chass, but we don't exactly have the luxury of time here—"

The first man's smile slipped, and he lifted his sword. "I said *shut up*. We have you outnumbered. Now, do you surrender or not?"

"Not." Lou lifted her own knife. It looked pathetically small in comparison. *She* looked pathetically small in comparison. Despite my deep, steadying breaths, the tension in my body built—built and built until I radiated with it, trembling with anticipation. "Wait, no, let me think." She tapped her chin. "*Definitely* not."

The man launched himself at her. I exploded, smashing my Balisarda into his gut, spinning as his companion attempted to maneuver past. My foot connected with his knee, and he buckled, driving his blade into my foot. Black spotted my vision as I wrenched the sword free.

With a feral cry, Lou darted toward the third, but he caught her wrist and twisted. Her knife clattered to the floor. She flicked a finger in response, and he crashed into the bar with enough force to splinter the wood. Coughing, she bent double. "Teachable moment," she choked. "I should've just killed the miserable bastard, but"—another cough—"I used the air around us to knock him backward instead, tried to—stick him on the wood. It knocked me pretty good in—in return. Make sense? I could've taken the air straight from my lungs instead, but he—he's too big. It would've taken too much air to move him. Probably would've killed me." She grinned to herself then, wider and wider until she was cackling. Blood trickled down her chin from her mouth. "And *then* how could I have claimed your father's hundred thousand *couronnes*—"

A knife flew at her from the wreckage of the bar.

She didn't have time to duck.

With a man on each arm, I watched in slow motion as she flinched, lifting a hand to stop the blade from piercing her heart. But the strength of the throw—the man's close proximity, his uncanny aim—was insurmountable. The blade would find its mark. There was nothing she could do to stop it. Nothing *I* could do.

Her fingers twitched.

And with that twitch, her eyes grew less focused, less—human. Between one blink and the next, the knife reversed direction and impaled its owner's throat.

Lou stared down at him, still smiling, her eyes shining with unfamiliar malice.

Except it wasn't unfamiliar. I'd seen it many times.

Just never on her.

"Lou?"

When I touched her, that terrible smile finally broke, and she gasped, clutching her chest. I pulled her behind me as the two men charged. She couldn't breathe, I realized in alarm. Despite her own warning, she'd given the air from her lungs to throw that knife—not as much as it would've taken to throw the man. Enough that red splotches had appeared in her eyes, enough that her chest worked furiously to replenish what it'd lost. "I'm fine," she said, struggling to rejoin me. Her voice was raw. Weak. I stepped in front of her. "I said I'm *fine.*"

Ignoring her, I swung my Balisarda wide—unnerved by her ragged breathing, the thick stench of magic in the air, the blood roaring in my ears—to drive the other two back, to shield her. But my foot throbbed, and I stumbled. "Let us leave," I said, voice low and desperate, terrified for them. No—not for them. For Lou. "Let us leave, and we'll let you live."

The first rose from beside his companion's corpse. His smile had vanished. Eyeing my injured foot, he pressed closer. "There are rumors, you know. In the city. They say you're the king's bastard son."

My thoughts scattered at this new information. How could they know? The only ones privy to that information were those in our own company: Lou, Ansel, Coco, Beau, and—

The last piece clicked into place.

Madame Labelle.

"We can help you," the second coaxed, shadowing the first's

steps. "We can free you from this witch's spell."

Every instinct screamed at me to engage. To fight, to *protect*. But those weren't the same things right now. I retreated faster, stumbling again. Lou steadied me.

"Please," she sneered. "He practically sleeps with his Balisarda, you idiots. I couldn't enchant him if I tried."

"Shut your mouth, *witch*."

"What of your dead friend?" she asked silkily. "Should he speak for me instead?"

I pushed her behind me again.

My eyes darted to the door, the windows. Too far. Though the rational part of my brain knew I maintained the advantage—knew my wanted poster said *alive*, knew they couldn't risk killing me—the same wasn't true for Lou. Her life was forfeit in this fight, which meant theirs were too. I'd have to kill them before they could touch her, before she could retaliate. Even outnumbered, I could dispatch them. Even injured. But if I engaged, Lou would too. She wouldn't let me fight alone.

Once more, she tried to move to my side, and once more, I moved her behind.

I couldn't allow her to fight. Not with magic. Not after what I'd just seen. She could damage herself irrevocably. Yet I couldn't leave her defenseless either. Clutching her hand, I backed her against the wall. Caged her with my body. "Reach inside my coat," I whispered as the men closed in. "Get a knife."

She knocked my Balisarda from my hand instead.

"What're you—?" I leapt after it, incredulous, but she beat me to it, sliding it under her foot as the men charged.

"Trust me!" she cried.

With no time to argue, I pulled two knives from my bandolier and met them strike for strike. My mind anticipated their every movement. My weapons became extensions of my arms. Even the sharp pain in my foot receded to a dull ache. Inexplicably agitated, I watched—disconnected—as my body feinted, dipped, and twisted with unnatural speed. Jabbing here. Kicking there. Soon the men slowed, bloody and winded. Hatred twisted their faces as they gazed at Lou. But she'd remained behind me, hadn't entered the fray—

I glanced back. My vision tunneled on her contorted fingers, and shock punched through me, stealing my breath. No. Not shock. Fury. Yes, I'd seen this before. I'd seen it many times.

She was using me like a fucking marionette.

At my expression, her fingers faltered, and my arms dropped to my sides, strings cut. Limp. "Reid," she whispered. "Don't—"

The men finally saw their opportunity.

The quickest of them spun around me, slashing my hands and knocking my knives to the ground. Before I could stop him, his companion had thrust his blade to my chin. The first quickly followed with a sword in my rib.

"Don't make this difficult, Diggory," one of them panted, punching me hard in the stomach when I struggled. "The king wants you alive, and we'd hate to disappoint him."

They jerked me around to face Lou, who'd swooped to retrieve my Balisarda.

"Easy, love." They pushed their blades deeper. Warning her. Warning me. A rivulet of blood ran down my throat. Slowly, Lou rose to her feet. Her expression was murderous. "That's right. No sudden movements. You can go ahead and slide that knife over here."

She kicked it toward the door instead, eyes flickering at something she saw there. I didn't dare look. Didn't dare draw attention.

She took a deep breath. Before our eyes, her expression transformed. Batting her lashes, she gave the men a saccharine smile. My stomach dropped. With her white hair—her eyes green tonight instead of blue—she looked like someone else entirely. "Did you know," she said, holding her hands erect, motionless, "that physical gesticulation is necessary to perform magic? We have to signal intent, otherwise we risk channeling patterns with errant thought. Gesticulation is manifestation." She recited the last as if from a textbook. Another smile. This one wider than the last. Sweeter. They stared at her in bewilderment. I stared at her with dread. "The smallest gesture will do. As you witnessed, I impaled your friend with a twitch of my finger. Took less than a second."

Their grip on me tightened.

"Lou." My voice was low, strained. "Don't do this. If manipulating mere memory is dangerous, you don't want the consequences of manipulating lives. Trust me." Her eyes flicked to the door and back. I swallowed hard, grimacing against the blade. She was stalling. That's all this was. But that smile—it unnerved me. I tried again. "There are two of them. Even if you kill one, the other—"

"—will slit his throat," the man on my left finished, pressing his knife deeper for emphasis. His hand was clammy. Cold. I could smell the perspiration through his clothes. She frightened them. Under pretense of struggling, I glanced behind us. My heart leapt to my throat. Ansel, Coco, Madame Labelle, and Beau were dragging Roy and his unconscious friends out the door. Why hadn't they listened to me? Why hadn't they *left*? Instead, they helped the last of the trapped villagers to safety. Claud Deveraux sifted frantically through the wreckage at the bar.

"I suppose you're right." Lou winked at me, and the facade cracked. Relief flooded my system. "But I certainly enjoy watching you squirm."

Losing his patience, the one on the right barreled toward her. "And *I'll* enjoy cutting off your mouthy—"

A crow of triumph sounded behind us, and the men finally turned.

Standing behind the bar—holding a lit match—Deveraux grinned. "Good evening, *messieurs*. I do hate to interrupt, but I believe it's in poor taste to discuss beheading a lady in front of her."

He flicked the match toward us, and the entire building exploded.

WHITE SHADOWS

Lou

Fire is such bullshit.

I'd already burned once—burned and burned on a metaphysical stake until I was nothing but a husk—but it seemed the flames hadn't gotten enough of me. They wanted another taste.

Well, too fucking bad.

I dove toward Reid as the pub detonated around us, flinging a hand toward the pattern that shimmered between us and the flames. The golden cord siphoned the icy fear from my chest—wrapping a protective barrier around us in cold, glittering crystals—before bursting into dust. We clung to each other, untouched, as the fire raged.

The bounty hunters weren't so lucky.

I tried not to enjoy watching them burn to a crisp. Really, I did. Without the fear I'd just sacrificed, however, there was only rage—a rage that burned hotter and brighter than even the flames around us. Blood from Reid's throat still trickled onto his collar, staining it. Even amidst our heinous trek through the wilderness—our week-long stay in the Hollow—he'd managed to keep his clothing immaculate. But not now. A couple of bounty hunters would've bested us if not for Claud Deveraux.

Speaking of which . . . where *was* Claud Deveraux?

Still fuming, I scanned the blazing pub for any sign of him, but he was gone.

Reid clutched me tighter as the bottles of whiskey behind the bar exploded. Glass pelted against our melting shield, and black, noxious smoke began to curl beneath it. I coughed, tugging his ear to my mouth. "We need to move! The shield won't hold much longer!"

Nodding swiftly, his eyes darted to the exit. "Will the shield move with us?"

"I don't know!"

He grabbed my hand, bolting through the flames toward the door. I hurtled after him—scooping up his Balisarda as I went—and forced myself to breathe. One thready gasp after another. My chest ached from earlier, and my head still pounded. My vision quickly blurred. Smoke burned my nose and throat, and I choked, the first tendril of heat licking up my spine. It razed my shoulders and neck, and my panic finally returned as the last of the shield melted.

Memory of another fire razed through me.

"Reid!" I shoved his back with all my might, and he tumbled out the door, sprawling in a heap on the ground outside. I collapsed beside him and buried myself in the frigid mud, heedless of decorum, rolling side to side like a pig wallowing in a sty. A sob tore from my throat.

"We have to move!" Reid's hands seized my own, and he

wrenched me to my feet. Already, more men had surrounded us, drawing makeshift weapons. Pitchforks. Hammers. The flames of the pub reflected in their hateful eyes as they loomed above me, and their shouts echoed through the fog steadily clouding my mind.

Witch!

Hold her!

Fetch the Chasseurs!

A heavy weight settled in my limbs. Groaning, I stumbled into Reid's side and stayed there, trusting him to support my weight. He didn't disappoint. My voice sounded muffled as I said, "My back hurts."

He didn't answer, instead prying his Balisarda from me and swinging it at the men, clearing a path. The world began to drift in a pleasant, distracting sort of way, like one's thoughts the moment before one falls asleep. Was that Claud watching us from the crowd? Somewhere in the back of my mind, I realized perhaps I'd caught on fire. But the realization was quiet and far away, and the only thing that mattered were Reid's arms around me, the weight of his body against mine . . .

"*Lou.*" His eyes appeared directly in front of me, wide and anxious and perfectly blue. Except—there shouldn't have been four of them, should there? I chuckled, though it came out a rasp, and reached up to smooth the furrow between his brows. He caught my hands. His voice drifted in and out of focus. "Stay awake . . . back to camp . . . the Chasseurs . . . coming."

Coming.

I'm coming for you, darling.

Panic punched through my stomach, and my laughter died abruptly. Shuddering against him, I tried to wrap my arms around his waist, but my limbs wouldn't cooperate. They dangled limply at my sides, heavy and useless, as I collapsed against him. "She's coming for me, Reid."

Vaguely aware of him hoisting me upward—of his mouth moving reassuringly against my ear—I struggled to collect my nonsensical thoughts, to banish the shadows in my vision.

But shadows weren't white—and this shadow was blinding, incandescent, as it tore through my throat and feasted on my blood—

"I won't let her hurt you again."

"I wish I was your wife."

He stiffened at the unexpected confession, but I'd already forgotten I'd spoken. With one last drowsy inhalation—of pine and smoke and *him*—I slipped into darkness.

CROSSES TO BEAR

Lou

I woke to voices arguing. Though the pain in my back had miraculously vanished, my chest still felt tight, heavy. Honey coated my tongue, so I almost missed the sharper, coppery taste hiding amidst its sweetness. I should've been apologetic, but exhaustion made it difficult to muster anything but apathy. As such, I didn't open my eyes right away, content to feign sleep and cherish the breath in my lungs.

They'd laid me on my stomach, and night air caressed the skin of my back. The *bare* skin of my back. I almost laughed and gave myself away.

The deviants had cut open my shirt.

"Why isn't it working?" Reid snapped. A hot presence beside me, he clenched my hand in his own. "Shouldn't she have woken up by now?"

"Use your eyes, Diggory." Coco's voice cut equally sharp. "Her burns have obviously healed. Give her internal injuries time to do the same."

"*Internal* injuries?"

I imagined his face turning puce.

Coco sighed impatiently. "It isn't humanly possible to move a knife—let alone throw one—with only the air in our lungs. She compensated by using the air from her blood, her tissues—"

"She did what?" His voice was dangerously soft now. Deceptively soft. It did little to hide his ire, however, as his grip nearly broke my fingers. "That could've killed her."

"There's always a cost."

Reid scoffed. It was an ugly, unfamiliar sound. "Except for you, it seems."

"Excuse me?"

I fought a groan, resisting the urge to insert myself between them. Reid was an idiot, but today, he would learn.

"You heard me," he said, undeterred by Coco's proximity to his arteries. "Lou is different when she uses magic. Her emotions, her judgment—she's been erratic since the pool yesterday. Tonight was worse. Yet you use magic without consequence."

All desire to shield him from Coco disappeared. *Erratic?* It took a great deal of effort to keep my breathing slow and steady. Indignation seared away the last of my fatigue, and my heart pounded at the small betrayal. Here I was—lying injured beside him—and he had the gall to insult me? All I'd done at the pool and pub was keep his ungrateful ass *alive*.

Eviscerate him, Coco.

"Give me specific examples."

I frowned into my bedroll. That wasn't quite the response

I'd expected. And was that—was that *concern* I detected? Surely Coco didn't *agree* with this nonsense.

"She dyed her hair with little to no forethought. She tried to strangle Beau when it went wrong." Reid sounded as if he were ticking items from a carefully constructed list. "She wept afterward—genuinely wept—"

"She dyed her hair like that for *you*." Coco's voice dripped with disdain and dislike, and I peeked an eye open, slightly mollified. She glared at him. "And she's allowed to cry. We don't all suffer from your emotional constipation."

He waved a curt hand. "It's more than that. At the pub, she snapped on Claud Deveraux. She laughed when she hurt the bounty hunter—even though she hurt herself in the process. You saw the bruise on her ribs. She was coughing up *blood*." He raked a hand through his hair in agitation, shaking his head. "And that was before she killed his friend and nearly herself in the process. I'm worried about her. After she killed him, there was a moment when she looked—she looked almost exactly like—"

"Don't you dare finish that sentence."

"I didn't mean—"

"*Stop.*" Blood still beaded Coco's hand, which clutched an empty vial of honey. Her fingers shook. "I don't have any comforting words for you. There is nothing comfortable about our situation. This sort of magic—the sort that balances life and death on a knife point—requires sacrifice. Nature *demands* balance."

"There's nothing natural about it." Reid's cheeks flushed as he spoke, and his voice grew harder and harder with each word. "It's aberrant. It's—it's like a sickness. A poison."

"It's our cross to bear. I would tell you there's more to magic than death, but you wouldn't hear it. You have your own poison running through your blood—which, incidentally, I'll boil if you ever speak like this in front of Lou. She has enough steaming shit to sort through without adding yours to the pile." Exhaling deeply, Coco's shoulders slumped. "But you're right. There's nothing natural about a mother killing her child. Lou is going to get worse before she gets better. Much, much worse."

Reid's fingers tightened around mine, and they both peered down at me. I slammed my eye shut. "I know," he said.

I took a deep breath to collect myself. Then another. But I couldn't ignore the sharp burst of anger their words had evoked, nor the hurt underlying it. This was not a flattering conversation. These were not the words one hoped to overhear from loved ones.

She's going to get worse before she gets better. Much, much worse.

My mother's face tugged at my memory. When I was fourteen, she'd procured a consort for me, insistent that I live a full life in only a handful of years. His name had been Alec, and his face had been so beautiful I'd wanted to weep. When I'd suspected Alec had favored another witch, I'd followed him to the banks of L'Eau Mélancolique one night . . . and watched as he'd laid with his lover. Afterward, my mother had cradled me to sleep, murmuring, "If you are unafraid to look, darling, you are unafraid to find."

Perhaps I wasn't as unafraid as I thought.

But they were wrong. I felt *fine*. My emotions weren't *erratic*. To prove it, I cleared my throat, opened my eyes, and—stared straight into the face of a cat. "*Ack*, Absalon—!" I lurched backward, startled and coughing anew at the sudden movement. My shirt—cut from my back in ribbons—fluttered at my sides.

"You're awake." Relief lit Reid's face as he sat forward, tentatively touching my face, sweeping a thumb across my cheek. "How do you feel?"

"Like garbage."

Coco knelt next to me as well. "I hope you nicked more clothing from that peddler. Your others quite literally melted into your back tonight. They were fun to remove."

"If by fun, you mean grotesque," Beau said, sidling up beside us. "I wouldn't look over there"—he waved a hand over his shoulder—"unless you'd like to see your love child of flesh and fabric. And Ansel's dinner. He parted with it shortly after seeing your injuries."

I glanced across the Hollow to where Ansel sat, looking miserable, while Madame Labelle fussed over him.

"You should change," Coco said. "It's near midnight. My aunt will be here soon."

Reid glared at her, shifting to block me from view. "I told you. Lou comes with me."

Coco fired up at once. "And I told *you*—"

"Shut up, both of you." The words leapt from me before I could stop them, and I cringed at their shocked expressions. They shared a quick glance, communicating without a word. But

I still heard it. *Erratic.* I forced a smile and stepped around Reid. "Sorry. I shouldn't have said that."

"Yes, you should've." Beau arched a brow, studying the three of us with unabashed interest. When he tilted his head, frowning as if he could *see* the tension in the air, I scowled. Maybe Reid had been right. Maybe I *wasn't* myself. Never before had I felt the need to apologize for telling him to shut the hell up. "They're incredibly annoying."

"Pot, meet kettle," Coco snapped.

"For the last time, I *go* wherever I want," I said. "Tonight was a disaster, but at least now we know the Archbishop's funeral is in a fortnight. It takes ten days of hard travel to reach Cesarine. That gives us only a couple of days with the blood witches and were-wolves." I skewered Reid with a glare when he tried to interrupt. "We have to proceed with the plan as discussed. We go to the blood camp. You go to Le Ventre. We'll meet back in Cesarine on the eve of the funeral. You'll send Absalon along with the time and place—"

"I don't trust the matagot," Reid said darkly.

Absalon flicked his tail at him in response.

"He certainly likes you." I bent down to scratch his ears. "And he saved us on Modraniht by delivering Madame Labelle's message to the Chasseurs. If I remember correctly, you didn't like that plan either."

Reid said nothing, jaw clenched.

"Le Ventre?" Beau asked, puzzled.

"It's packland," I said shortly. Of course he'd never journeyed into that murky corner of his kingdom. Most avoided it if possible. Including me. "La Rivière des Dents empties into a cold-water swamp in the southernmost part of Belterra. The loup garou have claimed it as their territory."

"And *why* is it called the stomach?"

"The teeth lead to the stomach—plus the loup garou eat anyone who trespasses."

"Not everyone," Reid muttered.

"This is a shit plan," Beau said. "We'll hardly reach Cesarine in time for the funeral, yet we're also expected to journey to Le Ventre? Not to mention the *insanity* that is approaching my father about an alliance. You *were* in the pub, weren't you? You saw the wanted posters? Those men were going to cut off your head—"

"*My* head. Not Reid's. For whatever reason, your father doesn't want him dead. Maybe he already knows about their connection, but if he doesn't, he'll soon find out. You're going to introduce them." I slipped back behind Reid to change into my new clothing. He was wide enough to block three of me from view. "Just so you know," I added to him, "the only reason I'm allowing this brute show of possessiveness is because your brother hasn't seen my tits yet, and I'm going to keep it that way."

"You break my heart, sister mine," Beau said.

"Shut up." Blood crept up Reid's neck. "Not another word."

Interesting. *He* didn't feel the need to apologize. A peculiar bitterness settled on my tongue, and I didn't particularly enjoy the taste—like regret and uncertainty and . . . something else. I couldn't name it.

"You should think about leaving soon," I told them. "After our rather spectacular excursion in Saint-Loire, the road will be crawling with bounty hunters. The Chasseurs might've turned around too. I know you're still uncomfortable with magic, Reid, but Madame Labelle will have to disguise you again. We can also ask to—"

I stopped short at Coco's laughter. She looked expectantly at Reid. "I can't wait to hear this."

Peeking at her from beneath Reid's arm, I asked, "Can't wait to hear what?"

She nodded to Reid. "Go on. Tell her."

He craned his neck to look down his shoulder at me as I slipped the scarlet shirt over my head and leather tights up my legs. I bent to lace my boots. Finally, he muttered, "I can't do it, Lou."

Frowning up at him, I straightened. "Can't do what?"

He shook his head slowly, the flush in his throat creeping up his cheeks. He clenched his jaw and lifted his chin. "I can't be around it. Magic. I won't."

I stared at him, and between one breath and another, the pieces clicked into place. His standoffishness, his disloyalty, his *concern*—it all made sense now.

Lou is different when she uses magic. Her emotions, her judgment— she's been erratic.

I'm worried about her.

There was a moment when she looked—she looked almost exactly like—

Like her mother. He hadn't needed to finish the sentence.

It's aberrant, he'd said.

Aberrant.

The bitterness coated my throat now, threatening to choke me, and I finally recognized it for what is was. Shame. "Well, isn't that convenient."

From beneath Reid's arm, I caught a glimpse of Coco hooking Beau's elbow and dragging him away. He didn't protest. When they'd disappeared from my view, Reid turned to face me, bending low to meet my eyes directly. "I know what you're thinking. It's not that."

"People don't really change, do they?"

"Lou—"

"Are you going to start calling me *it*? I wouldn't blame you." I bared my teeth at him, leaning close enough to bite. Never once in my eighteen years had I allowed anyone to make me feel the way I felt now. I resented the tears pooling in my eyes, the nausea rolling in my belly. "I'm aberrant, after all. *Erratic.*"

He cursed softly, his eyes fluttering closed. "You were listening."

"Of course I was listening. How *dare* you insult me to justify your own twisted narrative—"

"Stop. *Stop.*" His eyes snapped open as he reached for me, gripping my arms, but his hands were gentle. "I told you it doesn't matter that you're a witch. I meant it."

"Bullshit." I jerked away from him, watching in acute misery as his hands fell. The next second, I tackled him around the waist, burying my face in his chest. My voice was muffled, broken, as I squeezed him tight. "You didn't even give me a chance."

He held me tighter still, wrapping his body around mine like he could shield me from the world. "This is about magic, not you."

"Magic *is* me. And it's you too."

"No, it isn't. All those pieces you're giving up—I want them. I want *you*. Whole and unharmed." He pulled away to look at me, those blue eyes blazing with intensity. "I know I can't ask you to stop using magic, so I won't. But I can ask it of my mother. I can ask it of myself. And I can"—he brushed a strand of hair from my cheek—"I can ask you to be careful."

"You can't be serious." Finally, *finally*, I recoiled from his touch, my heart catching up with my head. "You're acting like I'm suddenly damaged goods, or—or a piece of glass about to shatter. News flash—I've practiced magic all my life. I know what I'm doing."

"Lou." He reached for me again, but I swatted his hand away. Those eyes burned brighter, hotter. "You haven't been yourself."

"You see what you want to see."

"Do you think I *want* to see you as—"

"As what? As *evil*?"

He gripped my shoulders hard. "You are *not* evil."

"Of course I'm not." I wiped a tear from my eye before it could fall, before he could see. Never before had I allowed myself to feel small, to feel *ashamed*, and I refused to start now. "You would willingly endanger your life—your mother's life, your *brother's* life—by refusing to use magic on the road?"

"I'm damned either way."

I stared at him for a long moment. The conviction in his eyes shone brutally clear, and it cut deeper than I'd anticipated. That wounded part of me wanted him to suffer for his foolishness. As they were, they'd all die on the road without magic, and if they didn't, they certainly would in Le Ventre. He was crippling them with prejudice, weakening them with fear. The weak didn't survive war.

Reid had to survive.

"No, you aren't." I stepped away from him, resigned, and squared my shoulders. His life was worth more than my wounded pride. Later—when all of this was over—I'd show him how wrong he was about magic. About me. "Before the pub exploded, Claud Deveraux offered help if I should ever need it. His traveling troupe leaves for Cesarine tonight. You'll join him."

TROUPE DE FORTUNE

Reid

The others protested little to Lou's *solution.*

I wished they would. Perhaps she'd listen to them. She certainly hadn't listened to me. When we'd packed our belongings—a whirlwind of mud, snow, and blood—I'd tried to reason with her to no avail.

This entire scheme, albeit clever, depended on one thing: Claud Deveraux.

We didn't know Claud Deveraux. More important, *he* knew *us*—or at least he seemed to know Lou. He'd been infatuated with her at the pub. He'd also seen her use magic. He knew she was a witch. Though I'd learned witches weren't inherently evil, the rest of the kingdom had not. If he helped us, what sort of person did that make him?

"Your salvation," Lou had said, stuffing my bedroll into my pack. "Look, he saved our asses tonight. He could've let us die, but he didn't. He obviously doesn't wish us harm, which is more than we can say about anyone else—and no one will think to look for you in a troupe of actors. You'll be hidden without magic."

She hurried down the hill toward Saint-Loire now. The others followed. I lingered behind, glancing back at the forest's edge. A single snowflake fell from the sky—still thick and heavy with clouds—and landed on my cheek. An eerie silence fell over the forest in its wake. Like the calm before the storm. As I turned away, two luminescent eyes reflected in my periphery. Large. Silver. I spun, the hair on my neck rising, but there was nothing except trees and shadows.

I strode after the others.

Actors bustled around the village square, hauling trunks, instruments, and props in preparation for departure. Claud Deveraux directed them. He flitted to and fro, clapping his hands in delight. As if there were nothing bizarre about packing in the dead of night, nor leaving before a storm.

Lou hesitated in the alley, watching. We all stopped with her.

"What is it?" I murmured, but she shushed me as Claud Deveraux spoke.

"Come, Zenna!" He bounded toward a plump woman with lavender hair. "We must depart before sunrise! Dame Fortune favors only those who begin their journeys under the new moon!"

I blinked more snowflakes from my eyes.

"Right," Zenna muttered, tossing an instrument into the smaller wagon. She wore a peculiar cloak. Deep purple. Perhaps blue. It glittered with what looked like stars. Constellations. "Except Dame Fortune abandoned Cesarine years ago."

"Ah, ah." Monsieur Deveraux waggled his finger at her reprovingly. "Never despair. Perhaps she will join us there."

"Or perhaps we'll be burned at the stake."

"*Absurdité!* The people of Cesarine need their spirits lifted. Who better to lift them than we? Soon, we shall whisk the patrons of La Mascarade des Crânes away to a world of frivolity and fantasy."

"Brilliant." Zenna pinched the bridge of her nose. Though her coloring resembled Coco's, her skin was scarless. She might've been attractive, but heavy cosmetics—kohl around her eyes, rouge on her lips—hid her true features.

"Seraphine and I deserve three percent of the cover to make this worth our while, Claud," she continued. "We're walking straight into Hell for this funeral, flames and all."

"Of course, of course." He waved his hand, already turning away to hurrah another actor. "But let's make it four."

Coco nudged Lou. This time, Lou didn't hesitate. "*Bonjour*, Monsieur Deveraux. You already know me from this evening, but my name isn't Lucida. It's Louise le Blanc, and these are my friends, Reid and Ansel Diggory, Cosette Monvoisin, Beauregard Lyon, and Helene Labelle."

Louise le Blanc. Not Louise Diggory. I kept my gaze forward. Impassive.

His brows lifted, and his eyes sparked with recognition. With surprise. They flitted over each of us before landing again on Lou. "Well, well, we meet again, little one! How delightfully unexpected."

The other actors paused in loading their luggage to watch us. Only two trunks remained on the ground, one too full to properly latch. Glittering fabric spilled out of it. Fuchsia feathers fluttered to the snow.

Lou flashed him a charming smile. "I'm here to accept your offer of help if it still stands."

"Oh?"

"Oh." She nodded and extended her arms to the wanted posters tacked around us. To the smoking remains of the pub. "You may not have noticed earlier, but my friends and I have made *quite* the impression on His Royal Majesty."

"Killing the Holy Father will do that," the young woman behind Deveraux said softly. She'd woven flowers through her curly hair and clutched a cross pendant at her throat. I averted my eyes, struggled against the rising emotion. It clawed through my chest, abrupt and untethered.

Lou's smile sharpened on the woman. "Do you know how many of my sisters your Holy Father killed?"

The woman shrank into herself. "I—I—"

Ansel touched Lou's arm, shaking his head. I stared at the feathers. Watched as the snow seeped into the delicate pink filaments. Just another moment. I just needed another moment to regain control, to master myself. Then my hand would replace Ansel's. I would help Lou remember. I would forget this withering, thrashing *creature* in my chest—

The curly-haired woman drew herself up to her full height. She was taller than Lou. Nearly as tall as Madame Labelle. "He still didn't deserve what happened to him."

You were like a son to me, Reid.

My breath caught, and the beast raged. I retreated further. As if sensing my distress, Lou stepped in front of me. "Oh? What *did* he deserve?"

"Lou," Ansel murmured. A part of me registered his glance in my direction. "Don't."

"Right. Of course, you're right." Shaking her head, Lou patted his hand and returned her attention to Deveraux. The curly-haired woman watched us with wide eyes. "We need transport into Cesarine, *monsieur.* Certain complications have arisen, and the road is no longer safe to travel alone. Do you have room in your wagons for a few more?"

"Why, of *course* we—"

"Only actors ride in the wagons." Zenna crossed her arms and skewered Claud with a glare. "That's the rule, isn't it? That you can't afford to feed and house us if we don't perform?" To Lou, she added, "Claud is a collector of sorts. He adds only the best and brightest talent to his troupe. The rare and unusual. The exceptional."

Fingerless gingham mittens covered Deveraux's hands, which he clasped with a smile. "Zenna, my sweet, the exceptional come in all shapes and sizes. Let us discount no one." He turned to Lou apologetically. "Unfortunately, however nettlesome, a rule is a rule, and a shoe is a shoe. Zenna is correct. I only allow actors to ride with the troupe." He swayed his head slightly, pursing his lips. "*If,* however, you and your *charming* companions take to the stage—in full costume, of course—you would become, in fact, actors—"

"Claud," Zenna hissed, "they're *fugitives*. The huntsmen will have our heads if we shelter them."

He patted her lavender hair airily. "Ah, poppet, aren't we all? Liars and cheats and poets and dreamers and schemers, every last one."

"But not murderers." A young man stepped forward, tilting his head at me curiously. Tall. Russet-skinned. Long black hair. Beside him stood a man with an uncannily similar face. No—identical. Twins. "Did you do it? Did you kill the Archbishop?"

My jaw locked. Lou answered for me, arching a brow. "Does it matter? He's gone either way."

He studied her for several seconds before murmuring, "Good riddance."

They hated him. Emotion thrashed, demanding admission, but I felt nothing. I felt nothing.

Deveraux, who watched the exchange—who watched *me*—with an inscrutable expression, smiled brightly once more. "So, what do you say? Are you, in fact, *actors*?"

Lou looked back at me. I nodded. A reflex.

"Excellent!" Claud parted his hands to the sky in celebration. The snow fell thicker now. Heavier. "And precisely what is your act, Monsieur Diggory? A handsome, gargantuan fellow like yourself is sure to please a crowd, especially"—he leapt to the smaller wagon, pulling forth a pair of leather pants—"in an ensemble such as this. With a fetching wig and top hat, perhaps a bit of kohl around the eyes, you are sure to enthrall the crowd no matter your performance."

I stared at him for a second too long. "Er—"

"He's a storyteller," Lou said quickly, loudly, stepping backward to clutch my hand. I recognized her shift in posture. The subtle lilt in her voice. She'd started her performance already. Distracting them from—from me. "He loves stories. And you're right. He'll look ravishing in those pants. Shirtless, of course."

She smirked and squeezed my fingers.

"Inspired!" Deveraux tapped his chin as he considered us. "Alas, I'm afraid we already have a storyteller in sweet, sweet Zenna." He nodded to the lavender-haired woman, who seized this fresh opportunity to protest. Sweetly.

"See? He's useless. If it were meant to be, Dame Fortune would've sent someone—"

"Can you use those knives?" Deveraux's kohl-rimmed eyes fell to my open coat, to the knives strapped beneath it. "We latterly lost our knife thrower to a troupe in Amandine, and"—he leaned closer, winking—"though I myself am disinclined to choose favorites, the audience is not."

"Oh, you *cannot* be serious, Claud." Eyes sparking, Zenna planted a hand on each of her hips. "Nadine's act was mediocre at best—*certainly* not better than mine—and even if it weren't, I'm not splitting tips with this lot. We don't even *know* them. They could murder us in our sleep. They could turn us into toads. They could—"

"Tell you that you have lipstick on your teeth," Lou finished.

Zenna glared at her.

"It's true," Beau said helpfully. "Right there at the side."

Scowling, Zenna turned to rub at her incisors.

Lou grinned and returned her attention to Deveraux. "Reid's knives are practically extensions of his limbs, *monsieur*. He'll hit any target you put in front of him."

"How marvelous!" With a last, lingering look at said knives, Deveraux turned to Madame Labelle. "And you, *chérie . . . ?*"

"I'm—"

"His assistant." Lou grinned wider. "Why don't we strap her to a board and give you a demonstration?"

Deveraux's brows climbed up his forehead. "I'm sure that's unnecessary, but I do appreciate your enthusiasm. Quite infectious, I tell you." He turned to Beau, sweeping into a ridiculous bow. His nose touched the tip of his boot. "If I might divulge, Your Highness, it is an exceptional and unparalleled delight to make your acquaintance. I'm positively *expiring* with suspense at the prospect of learning your myriad talents. Tell us one, if you please. How will you dazzle us on the stage?"

Beau didn't return his smile. His lip curled. "I won't be on the stage, and I certainly won't be wearing anything feathered nor fuchsia." At Deveraux's expectant look, he sighed. "I'll do your sums."

Deveraux clapped his mittened hands together. "Just so! For royalty, we shall make an exception!"

"And you?" Zenna asked, sneering at Lou. "Any special talents for the stage?"

"If you must know, I play the mandolin. Quite well, in fact, because—" She hesitated, dipping her chin in an uncharacteristic display of insecurity. Though small—nearly indiscernible—the movement unsettled me. Pierced the haze of my thoughts. "It doesn't matter."

"Tell us," I said softly.

"Well . . . my mother insisted I learn to play. The harp, the clavichord, the rebec—but the mandolin was her favorite."

I frowned. I hadn't known Lou could play a single instrument, let alone many. She'd once told me she couldn't sing, and I'd assumed . . . but no. Those calluses on her fingers weren't from swordplay. The *mandolin*. I wracked my brain, trying to picture the instrument, to remember the sound, but I couldn't. The only instrument I'd heard in childhood had been an organ. I hadn't cared to make time for others.

"Ha!" Zenna laughed in triumph. "We already have a musician. Claud is a virtuoso. The best in the kingdom."

"Bully for him," Lou muttered, stooping to save the fuchsia feathers from the snow. She didn't meet anyone's eyes. "I said it doesn't matter, anyway. I'm not joining the troupe."

"I do beg your pardon?" Claud accepted the feathers with a scandalized expression. The wind picked up around us. It nearly blew his hat to the rooftops. "I believe I misheard you in this gale."

"You didn't." Lou gestured to Ansel and Coco, raising her voice. Snow soaked her new cloak. She clutched it under her chin to keep herself concealed. "The three of us will be traveling in a different direction."

Deveraux flapped his hands, and the feathers scattered once

more. "Nonsense! Preposterous! As you have so succinctly sur-
mised, the road is not safe for you. You must come with us!" He
shook his head too vigorously, and the wind snatched his hat. It
spiraled upward and disappeared into the snow. "No. No, I fear
there is no question that our little rendezvous at the pub was
fated by none other than Dame Fortune herself. Furthermore, I
cannot abide you traveling the road alone. Nay, I refuse to have
that on my conscience."

"They will not be alone."

An unfamiliar voice. An inexplicable chill.

Lou and I stepped together, turning as one to the dark figure
beside us.

A woman.

I hadn't heard her approach, hadn't seen her draw near. Yet
she stood no more than a hand's breadth away, staring up at me
with eerie, colorless eyes. Uncommonly thin—almost skeletal—
with alabaster skin and black hair, she looked more wraith than
human. My hand shot to my Balisarda. She tilted her head in
response, the movement too quick, too bestial, to be natural.

Absalon wound between her emaciated ankles.

"Nicholina." Coco bared her teeth in a snarl. "Where's my
aunt?"

The woman's face split into a slow, cruel grin, revealing blood-
stained teeth. I pulled Lou backward, away from her. "Not here,"
she sang, her voice strange and high-pitched. Girlish. "Not here,
not here, but always near. We come to answer your call."

I felt her strange eyes on me as I heaved the last trunk into the wagon.

The others hastened to secure belongings, calm horses, check knots. Deveraux had pulled Lou aside, and they appeared to be arguing over the strange woman's arrival. I couldn't tell. Snow blew around us in a tempest now, eliminating visibility. Only two of the torches lining the street remained. The rest had succumbed to the storm.

Scowling, I finally turned to face her—*Nicholina*—but she was gone.

"Hello, huntsman."

I jumped at her voice directly behind me, startled by her close proximity. Heat flushed my throat, my face. "Who are you?" I asked. "How do you keep doing that?"

She lifted a skeletal finger to my cheek, tilting her head as if fascinated. The torchlight flickered over her scars. They disfigured her skin, twisted it into a macabre lattice of silver and blood. I refused to flinch away.

"I am Nicholina le Claire, La Voisin's personal attendant." Trailing a sharpened nail along my jaw, her lip curled. The girlish cadence of her voice vanished, deepening unexpectedly to a guttural snarl. "And I will not explain the secrecies of blood craft to a huntsman." Darkness stirred in those colorless eyes as she gazed past me to Lou. Her grip on my chin hardened, and her nails bit deep. Nearly drawing blood. "Or his little mouse."

Coco stepped between us. "Careful, Nicholina. Lou is under my aunt's protection. Reid is under mine."

"Mmm . . . *Reid.*" Nicholina licked her lips salaciously. "Your name on my tongue tastes like salt and copper and warm, wet things—"

"Stop it." I stepped away from her, alarmed, disgusted, and glanced at Lou. She watched us from beyond the wagons, eyes narrowed. Deveraux waved his hands at her emphatically. I strode toward them—determined to remove myself from this situation—but Nicholina shadowed my footsteps. Still too close. Much, *much* too close. The childlike lilt returned to her voice.

"My mice whisper such naughty things about you, Reid. Such wicked, *naughty* things. *Cosette, regret, and forget,* they cry. *Cosette, regret, and forget.* I can't attest, as I've never tasted huntsman—"

"And you won't start with this one." Coco hurried after us as Lou extricated herself from Deveraux. "He's married."

"Is he?"

"Yes." I lurched to a stop, whirling to glare at her. "So please maintain the appropriate distance, *mademoiselle.*"

She grinned wickedly, arching a thin brow. "Perhaps my mice were misinformed. They do love to whisper. *Whisper, whisper, whisper.* Always whispering." She leaned closer, and her lips tickled the shell of my ear. Again, I refused to react. Refused to give this insane woman the satisfaction. "They say you hate your wife. They say you hate yourself. They say you taste *delicious.*" Before I realized her intention, she'd dragged her tongue down my cheek in a long, wet movement.

Lou reached us at the same moment. Her eyes flashed with turquoise fire.

"What the hell are you doing?" With both hands, she moved to shove Nicholina away, but Nicholina had already floated backward. The way she moved . . . it was like she wasn't entirely corporeal. But her nails on my chin had been real enough, as was her saliva on my cheek. I jerked up my shirt collar, wiping at the moisture, heat razing my ears. Lou's fists clenched. She squared up to the taller woman. Vibrated with anger. "Keep your hands to yourself, Nicholina."

"*Keep them, keep them.*" Her eyes roved the exposed skin of my throat, dropped lower to my chest. Hungry. I tensed instinctively. Resisted the urge to clasp shut my coat. "He can keep them for me. Keep them and sweep them and slowly creep them—"

A low, menacing sound tore from Lou, and she stepped closer. Their toes nearly touched. "If you touch him again, *I'll* keep them for you. Each"—she took another step, closing the distance between them—"bloody"—she leaned closer still, body taut with anticipation—"stump."

Nicholina grinned down at her, unaffected, despite the way the wind rose and the temperature plummeted. Coco glanced around. Alarmed. "Silly mouse," Nicholina purred. "He hunts even now. Even now, he hunts. He knows his own mind, didn't tell me to stop."

"You lie." Even I heard the defensiveness in my voice. Lou stood rooted in front of me. She didn't turn around when I touched her shoulder. "Lou, she's a—"

"But *can* he stop?" Nicholina circled us now, like a predator scenting blood. "Hunt and stop? Or stop and hunt? Soon we'll taste the noises on his tongue, oh yes, each moan and sigh and grunt—"

"Nicholina," Coco said sharply, seizing Lou's arm when she lunged. "Enough."

"The snake and her bird, the bird and his snake, they take and they break and they ache, ache, *ache*—"

"I said that's enough." Something in Coco's voice changed, deepened, and Nicholina's smile vanished. She stopped circling. The two stared at each other for several seconds—something unspoken passing between them, something dark—before Nicholina bared her throat. Coco watched this bizarre display of submission for a moment longer. Impassive. Cold. Finally, she nodded in satisfaction. "Wait for us at the forest's edge. Go now."

"As you wish, *princesse.*" Nicholina lifted her head. Paused. Looked not to Lou, but to me. Her grin returned. This time, it was a promise. "Your little mouse will not always be here to protect you, huntsman. Take care."

The wind caught her words, blowing them around us with the snow. They bit at my cheeks, at Lou's cloak, Coco's hair. I took Lou's hand in silent reassurance—and startled. Her fingers were colder than expected. Unnaturally cold. Colder than the wind, the snow. Colder than Nicholina's smile.

Take care take care take care.

"Don't let her rile you," Coco murmured to Lou after she'd gone. "It's what she wants."

Nodding, Lou closed her eyes and took a deep breath. When she exhaled, the tension left her shoulders, and she glanced up at me. Smiled. I crushed her against me in relief.

"She seems like a real treat," Lou said, voice muffled by my coat.

"She is." Coco stared down the alley where Nicholina had disappeared. "The sort of treat that rots your soul instead of your teeth."

Deveraux approached through the snow. With a resigned sigh, he laid a hand on my arm. "The wagons are packed, *mon ami*. We must depart with the tempest, lest we miss our opportunity. Dame Fortune is a fickle mistress, indeed."

Though he waited expectantly, my arms refused to move. They held Lou in a vise, and I couldn't persuade them to let her go. I buried my nose in her shoulder instead, holding her tighter. Her cloak smelled unfamiliar. New. Like fur, damp earth, and the sweet, bitter scent of . . . something. Not magic. Perhaps wine. I frowned and pushed her hood aside, seeking her skin, the warmth I'd find there. But the unnatural cold in her hands had crept upward. It froze my lips as I brushed them against her throat. Alarmed, I met her eyes. Green now. So green.

"Be careful, Lou." I kept her cocooned within my arms, blocking the others from sight. Trying and failing to warm her. "Please. Promise me."

She kissed me instead. Gently disentangled herself. "I love you, Reid."

"It isn't supposed to be like this," I said helplessly, still reaching for her. "I should come with you—"

But she'd already stepped back, turned away. Clutched Coco's hand like she should've clutched mine. Her other reached for Ansel. "I'll see you soon," she promised, but it wasn't the one I wanted. The one I *needed*.

Without another word, she turned and vanished into the storm. I stared after her with a creeping sense of dread.

Absalon had followed.

THE MISSING PRINCE

Lou

The trees watched us, waiting, listening to our footsteps in the snow. They even seemed to breathe, inhaling and exhaling with each faint touch of wind in our hair. As sentient and curious as the shadows that crept ever closer.

"Can you feel them?" I whispered, cringing when my voice reverberated in the eerie quiet. The pines grew thicker in this part of the forest. Older. We could barely walk through their boughs, and with each step, they touched us, dusting our hair, our clothing, with glittering crystals of snow.

"Yes." Coco blew air into her hands, rubbing them together against the chill. "Don't worry. The trees here are loyal to my aunt."

I shivered in response. It had nothing to do with the cold. "Why?"

"Pretty lies or ugly truth?"

"The uglier, the better."

She didn't smile. "She feeds them her blood."

We smelled the camp before we saw it—hints of smoke and sage on the breeze hiding a sharper, acrid scent within them. At close range, however, one couldn't mistake the bite of blood magic. It overpowered my senses, burning my nose and throat, stinging my eyes. The tears froze in my lashes. Gritting my teeth against the bitter wind, I trudged onward, following Nicholina through snow drifts as high as my knees. "How much farther?" I called to her, but she ignored me. A blessing and a curse. She hadn't spoken a word since we'd left Troupe de Fortune in Saint-Loire. It seemed even she feared the forest after dark.

Coco inhaled the blood scent deeply, closing her eyes. She too had grown quieter over the past couple of hours—tenser, moodier—but when I'd questioned her, she'd insisted she was fine.

She was fine.

I was fine.

Reid was fine.

We were all *fine*.

A moment later, Nicholina halted outside a thick copse of pines and glanced back at us. Her eyes—so pale a blue they shone almost silver—lingered on my face before flicking to Coco. "Welcome home."

Coco rolled her eyes and moved to shove past her, but Nicholina had vanished. Literally.

"A real treat," I repeated, grinning despite myself at Coco's irritation. "Are all your sisters this charming?"

"She isn't my sister." Without looking back, Coco swept aside a branch and plunged into the trees, effectively ending the conversation. My grin slipped as I stared after her.

Ansel patted my arm as he passed, offering me a small smile. "Don't worry. She's just nervous."

It took every bit of my restraint not to snap at him. Since when did Ansel know more about Coco's feelings than I did? As if sensing my uncharitable thoughts, he sighed and hooked my elbow, dragging me after her. "Come on. You'll feel better after you've eaten."

My stomach growled in response.

The trees thinned abruptly, and we found ourselves on the edge of a rocky clearing. Campfires illuminated threadbare tents stitched together from bits of animal skin. Despite the inordinately early hour—and the cold and the darkness—a handful of witches huddled around the flames, clutching thick, matted furs for warmth. At the sound of our footsteps, they turned to watch us suspiciously. Though they ranged in age and ethnicity, all wore identical haunted expressions. Cheeks gaunt. Eyes hungry. One woman even gripped her auburn hair in her fists, weeping softly.

Ansel stumbled to a halt. "I didn't expect there to be so many males here." He stared at a young man roughly his age with undisguised yearning. "Are they . . . like Reid?"

His name cut through me like a knife, painful and sharp. I missed him. Without his steady presence, I felt . . . out of sorts. As if part of me was missing. In a way, I supposed that was true.

"Maybe. But if they are, I doubt they realize it. We've grown up believing only women possess magic. Our dear Chasseur . . . changes things."

Nodding, he tore his gaze away, cheeks pink. Coco didn't look at us as we approached, though she did murmur, "I should probably speak with my aunt alone."

I fought the urge to poke her in the cheek and *make* her look at me. When she'd spoken of her aunt's protection, of an alliance with her powerful kin, this was *not* what I'd envisioned. These witches looked as if they'd keel over from a strong wind, or perhaps even a sneeze. "Of course," I said instead. "We'll wait for you here."

"That won't be necessary." We all jumped as Nicholina materialized beside us once more. Her voice had lost its girlish pitch, and those silver eyes were flat, expressionless. Whatever show she'd performed for Reid's benefit, she didn't care to continue for us. "Josephine awaits the three of you in her tent."

"Can you stop doing that?" I demanded.

She twitched, every muscle in her face spasming, as if in physical protest to my question. Or perhaps to my mere voice. "Never address us, little mouse. Never, never, *ever*." Sudden life flared in her gaze, and she lunged, snapping her teeth viciously. Ansel reeled backward—pulling me with him—and nearly toppled us both. Though Coco stopped her with a quick, forceful hand, she'd still drawn near enough for me to feel the phantom brush of her teeth, to see the sharpened tips of her incisors. Waving skeletal fingers in my direction, she crooned as to a baby. "Or we will gobble you up whole. Yes, yes, we will—"

"*Enough*," Coco said impatiently, shoving her away. "Show us to our tents. It's late. We'll speak with my aunt after we've slept. That's an order, Nicholina."

"Tent."

"Pardon?"

"*Tent*," Nicholina repeated. She bobbed her head, resuming her maniacal performance. "Tent, tent, tent. A single tent is what I meant. One tent to share without dissent—"

"Share?" Ansel's eyes widened in alarm, darting to Coco. He released me to run a nervous hand through his hair, to tug at the hem of his coat. "We're sharing a tent? To—to sleep?"

"No, to fu—" I started cheerfully, but Coco interrupted.

"Why one tent?"

Shrugging, Nicholina wafted backward, away from us. We had no choice but to follow. The blood witches' gazes fell hard upon me as we passed, but all bared their throats to Coco in a gesture identical to Nicholina's earlier one. I'd seen this submission only once before tonight—when La Voisin had caught Coco and me playing together on the shore of L'Eau Mélancolique. She'd been furious, nearly dislocating Coco's shoulder in her haste to drag her away from me. Coco had showed her throat quicker than an omega showed its belly.

It'd unsettled me then, and it unsettled me now.

Echoing my thoughts, Ansel whispered, "Why do they do that?"

"It's a sign of respect and submission." We trailed several paces behind Coco and Nicholina. "Sort of like how you bow to royalty. When they bare their throats, they're offering Coco their blood."

"But . . . submission?"

After Coco had passed, the witches resumed glaring at our backs. I couldn't say I blamed them. I was a Dame Blanche, and Ansel had trained to be a Chasseur. Though La Voisin had allowed us to enter her camp, we were no more welcome than Reid had been.

"If Coco drank your blood right now," I explained, "she'd be able to control you. Temporarily, of course. But the Dames Rouges offer it to her and La Voisin freely. They're royalty here."

"Right." Ansel swallowed hard. "Royalty."

"*La princesse.*" Winking, I pinched his arm. "But still Coco."

He didn't look convinced.

"Why one tent, Nicholina?" Coco's hands curled into fists when Nicholina continued to hum under her breath. Apparently, her position as La Voisin's *personal attendant* afforded her more defiance. "*Tell me.*"

"You left us, *princesse.* Left us to rot. Now there's not enough food or blankets or cots. We die by the hour from cold or hunger. 'Tis a pity you couldn't have stayed away longer."

At Nicholina's chilling smile, Coco missed a step, but I steadied her with a hand on her back. When she pulled me to her side, lacing her fingers through mine, relief flooded through me. "Why does my aunt need to see us right now?" she asked, her frown deepening. "What can't wait?"

Nicholina cackled. "The son disappeared with the sun, went to rest below the rock. But he didn't come home, his body is gone, and vultures have started to flock."

"We don't speak wraith," I said flatly.

Coco—who possessed patience vastly superior to my own—didn't ask for clarification. Instead, her face twisted. "Who is it?"

"Who *was* it," Nicholina corrected her, her mouth still contorted in that disturbing smile. It was too large, too fixed, too—bloody. "*He's dead, he's dead*, my mice have said. Dead, dead, dead, dead, dead, dead, *dead*."

Well. I supposed that explained the weeping woman.

Nicholina drifted to a halt outside a small, threadbare tent at the edge of camp, separate from the rest. It overlooked the cliff's edge. In daylight, the sun's rays would warm this place, bathing the snow in a golden glow. With the uninhibited view of the mountains behind, the scene could've been beautiful, even in darkness.

Except for the vultures circling above.

We watched them dip lower and lower in ominous silence—until Coco tore her hand from mine and planted it on her hip. "You said he's missing," she said fiercely. "*Missing*, not dead. We'll speak with my aunt now. If she's organizing search parties, we'll join them. He might still be out there somewhere."

Nicholina nodded with glee. "Freezing to death slowly. Sloooowly."

"Right." Coco tossed her bag into our tent without looking inside. "Who is it, Nicholina? How long has he been missing?" Without warning, her bag came sailing back at her, knocking into the side of her head. She spun and swore violently. "What the—?"

From our tent stepped Babette Dubuisson.

Virtually unrecognizable without her thick makeup—and with her golden hair piled atop her head—she'd lost weight since we'd last seen her in Cesarine. Her scars shone silver against her ivory skin. Though fondness warmed her expression as she gazed at Coco, she did not smile. "We have known him as Etienne Gilly after his darling mother, Ismay Gilly."

Coco stepped forward, her relief palpable as they embraced. "Babette. You're here."

I frowned, feeling a bit as if I'd missed the bottom step on a staircase. Though Roy and his friends had confirmed our suspicions, muttering about *curfews* and *suspicious womenfolk* in Cesarine, I hadn't spared a thought for Babette or her safety. But Coco obviously had. My frown deepened. I considered Babette a friend—albeit in the loosest definition of the word—and I cared about what happened to her.

Didn't I?

"*Bonjour, mon amour.*" Babette kissed Coco's cheek before resting her forehead against hers. "I have missed you." When they parted, Babette eyed the fresh slash at my throat. I hadn't been able to salvage my ribbon. "And *bonjour* to you too, Louise. Your hair is *répugnant*, but I am happy to see you alive and well."

I offered her a wary smile, Reid's words returning with frightful clarity. *You haven't been yourself.* "Alive, indeed," I mused, smile fading. "But perhaps not well."

"Nonsense. In times such as these, if you are alive, you are well." Returning her attention to Coco, she sighed deeply. The sound lacked her signature melodrama. No, this sober, barefaced woman—with her tattered clothing and tangled hair—was not the Babette I'd always known. "But perhaps more than we can say of poor Etienne. You believe he still lives, *mon amour*, but I fear for his life—and *not* from the cold. Though we have known him by his mother, to the rest of the kingdom, Etienne Gilly would be known as Etienne Lyon. He is the king's bastard son, and he never returned from the morning hunt."

Larger than the others, La Voisin's tent had been pitched in the center of the clearing. Several wooden cages circled the ground around it, and glowing eyes reflected back at us. A fox lunged at the bars as we passed, snarling, and Ansel leapt into me with a squeak. When Babette snickered, Ansel blushed to the roots of his hair.

"Are these . . . pets?" he asked weakly.

"They're for blood," Coco said shortly. "And divination."

Nicholina glowered at Coco's explanation—probably a betrayal in her mind—before parting the bundles of dried sage hanging from the tent entrance. Babette pecked each of Coco's cheeks.

"I will find you after, *mon amour*. We have much to discuss."

Coco held her a second longer than necessary before they parted.

Inside, La Voisin stood behind a makeshift table, a smudge stick smoldering gently before her. Nicholina drifted to her side, picking up a rabbit's skin in one hand and a bloody knife in the other. The poor creature's various organs had been spread across most of the table. I tried to ignore her licking its blood from her fingers.

La Voisin looked up from the book she'd been studying and

fixed me with a cold stare. I blinked, startled at the smoothness of her face. She hadn't aged a day since I'd last seen her. Though she must've been thrice our age, no lines marred her brow or lips, and her hair—pinned back in a severe chignon—remained as black as the moonless night sky.

My scalp prickled as I remembered the wicked rumors about her at Chateau le Blanc: how she ate the hearts of babies to stay young, how she journeyed to L'Eau Mélancolique each year to drink the blood of a melusine—no, to *bathe* in it.

A long moment of silence passed as she studied Coco and me, her dark eyes glittering in the candlelight. Just as Nicholina's had done, her gaze lingered on me, tracing the contours of my face, the scar at my throat. I stared resolutely back at her.

She didn't acknowledge Ansel.

Coco finally cleared her throat. "*Bonjour, tante.*"

"Cosette." La Voisin closed the book with a snap. "You deign to visit at last. I see the circumstances finally suit you."

I watched in disbelief as Coco stared at her feet, immediately contrite. "*Je suis désolée.* I would've come sooner, but I . . . I couldn't leave my friends."

La Voisin strode around the table, parting the smudge smoke in waves. She halted in front of Coco, grasping her chin and tilting her face toward the candlelight. Coco met her gaze reluctantly, and La Voisin frowned at whatever she saw there. "Your kin have been dying while you cavorted with your *friends*."

"Babette told me of Etienne. We can—"

"I do not speak of Etienne."

"Then who . . . ?"

"Sickness took Delphine and Marie. Only last week, Denys passed from exposure. His mother left him to forage for food. He tried to follow." Her eyes hardened to glittering chips of obsidian. She dropped Coco's chin. "Do you remember him? He was not yet two years old."

Coco's breath hitched, and nausea churned in my own belly.

"I'm—" Coco stopped then, reconsidering. A wise decision. La Voisin didn't want her apology. She wanted her to suffer. To stew. Abruptly, Coco turned to me. "Lou, you—you remember my aunt, Josephine Monvoisin." She gestured between us helplessly. Taking pity on her, I nodded and forced a smile. It felt disrespectful after such a revelation.

"*Bonjour*, Madame Monvoisin." I didn't extend my throat. As children, Coco's first lesson to me had been simple: never offer my blood to a Dame Rouge. Especially her aunt, who loathed Morgane and the Dames Blanches perhaps even more than I did. "Thank you for granting us an audience."

She stared at me for another long moment. "You look like your mother."

Coco quickly charged onward. "And this—this is Ansel Diggory. He's—"

La Voisin still didn't acknowledge him. Her eyes never strayed from mine. "I know who he is."

"A *baby* huntsman." Licking her bottom lip, Nicholina edged closer, her eyes hungry and bright. "He is pretty, oh yes."

"He's not a huntsman." Coco's voice cut sharp enough to draw blood. "He never was."

"And that"—La Voisin's lip curled in unconcealed disdain—"is the only reason he remains alive."

At her aunt's black look, Coco cleared her throat hastily. "You . . . you said Etienne isn't dead. Does that mean you've found him?"

"We have not." If possible, La Voisin's expression further darkened, and the shadows in the tent seemed to press closer. The candles flickered. And her book—it *moved*. I stared at it with wide eyes. Though barely perceptible, the black cover had *definitely* twitched. La Voisin stroked its spine before reaching inside to remove a piece of parchment. On it, someone had drawn a crude map of La Fôret des Yeux. I leaned closer to examine it, despite my unease. Blood spatters dotted the trees of ink. "Our tracking spell revealed he is alive, but something—or someone—has cloaked his exact location." When her black eyes fixed on mine, my chest tightened inexplicably. "We searched the general area in shifts yesterday, but he was not there. We have expanded our search tonight."

I crossed my arms to keep from fidgeting. "Could he not have left on his own?"

"His mother and sister reside here. He would not have left without saying goodbye."

"We all know filial relationships can be fraught—"

"He disappeared just after I agreed to meet with you."

"A weird coincidence—"

"I don't believe in coincidences." She studied us impassively as we shuffled shoulder to shoulder in front of her—like naughty schoolchildren. A situation made worse by Coco and

Ansel towering over me on either side. I tried and failed to stand a little taller. "Your message said you seek an alliance with our coven," she continued. I nodded. "It said Reid Labelle journeys to Le Ventre as we speak, seeking a similar alliance with the loup garou. From there, you plan to approach the king in Cesarine."

A tendril of satisfaction curled through me. Reid Labelle. Not Reid Diggory or Reid Lyon. The name felt . . . right. Of course, if we adhered to the customs of our kin, he'd have the choice of becoming Reid le Blanc instead. If . . . if we handfasted properly, this time.

"That's correct."

"My answer is no."

I blinked, startled at her abrupt dismissal, but she'd already returned her attention to the map, tucking it back within her creepy little book. Nicholina giggled. In my periphery, she held the dead rabbit by its front paws, making its limp body dance. Heat washed through me, and my hands curled into fists. "I don't understand."

"It is simple." Her black eyes met mine with a calm that made me want to scream. "You will fail. I will not jeopardize my kin for your foolish quest."

"Aunt Josephine—" Coco started, pleading, but La Voisin waved a curt hand.

"I read the portents. I will not concede."

I struggled to keep my voice even. "Was it the rabbit's bladder that convinced you?"

"I do not expect you to understand the burden of ruling a

people. *Either* of you." She glanced at Coco, arching a brow, and Coco ducked her chin. I wanted to claw out La Voisin's eyes. "Every death in this camp is on my hands, and I cannot risk evoking Morgane's wrath. Not for you. Not even for my niece."

The heat in my belly built, growing hotter and hotter until I nearly burst. My voice, however, remained cold. "Why did you bring us here if you aren't even willing to listen?"

"I owe you nothing, Louise le Blanc. Do not mistake me. You stand here—*alive* and *well*—only by my benevolence. That benevolence is quickly waning. My people and I will not join you. Knowing this, you may now leave. Cosette, however, will stay."

And there it was. The real reason she'd brought us here—to forbid Coco from leaving.

Coco stiffened as if her aunt's black eyes had quite literally pinned her there. "Too long you have forsaken your duties, Cosette," La Voisin said. "Too long you have protected your *enemies* over your *people*." She spat the last, planting her palms against the table. Her nails bit into the wood. Beside her, the black book seemed to quiver in anticipation. "It ends now. You are the Princesse Rouge, and you will act as such from this moment onward. Begin by escorting Louise and her companion from our camp."

My jaw unlocked. "We're not leaving—"

"Until they find Etienne," Coco finished, straightening her shoulders. Her arm brushed mine in the barest of touches. *Trust me*, it seemed to say. I clamped my mouth shut again. "They want to help, *tante*. They'll leave only after they've found him—and if they do, you'll give them your alliance."

"*And* Coco will come with us," I added, unable to help myself. "If she so chooses."

La Voisin's eyes narrowed. "I have given my final word."

Coco wouldn't hear it, however. Though her fingers trembled slightly, she approached the table, lowering her voice. We could all still hear her. "Our magic cannot find him. Maybe hers can." Her voice pitched lower still, but gained strength. "Together, we can defeat Morgane, *tante*. We can return to the Chateau. All of this—the cold, the sickness, the death—it'll end."

"I will not ally with enemies," La Voisin insisted, but she cast a quick glance in my direction. Her brows furrowed. "I will not ally with *werewolves* and *huntsmen*."

"We share a common enemy. That makes us friends." To my surprise, Coco reached out and clutched La Voisin's hand. Now it was the latter's turn to stiffen. "Accept our help. Let us find Etienne. Please."

La Voisin studied us for a moment that felt like eternity. At long last, she pulled her hand from Coco's grasp. "*If* you find Etienne," she said, lips pursing, "I will consider your proposition." At Ansel's and my sighs of relief, she added sharply, "You have until sunrise. If you have not found him by then, you will leave this camp without argument. Agreed?"

Indignant, I opened my mouth to argue such a ridiculous timeframe—less than a handful of hours—but something brushed my ankle. I glanced down in surprise. "Absalon? What are you . . . ?" Hardly daring to hope, I whirled toward the tent entrance, but there was no towering, copper-haired man standing there, no half smiles or clenched jaws or flushed cheeks. I frowned.

He wasn't here.

Disappointment bit deep. Then confusion. Matagots generally stayed with those who'd attracted them. Unless . . .

"Do you have a message for me?" I asked, frown deepening. A tendril of panic bloomed. Had something already gone wrong on the road? Had he been recognized, captured, discovered as a witch? A million possibilities sparked in my mind, spreading like wildfire. "What is it, Absalon? *Tell* me."

He merely meowed and wove between my ankles, human intelligence gleaming in his feline eyes. As I stared at him, bewildered, the last of my anger sizzled away. He hadn't stayed with Reid. He hadn't come to deliver a message. Instead, he'd simply . . . come. Here. He'd come *here.* And that meant—

"You named the matagot?" La Voisin blinked once, the only outward sign of her surprise.

"Everyone deserves a name," I said faintly. *They're drawn to like creatures. Troubled souls. Someone here must have attracted him.* Absalon stood on his hind paws, kneading the thick leather of my pants with his front. Instinctively, I knelt to scratch behind his ear. A low purr built in his throat. "He didn't tell me his, so I improvised."

Coco's brows knitted together as she glanced between me and Ansel—clearly trying to decide who the matagot had followed here—but La Voisin only smiled, small and suggestive. "You are not what I expected, Louise le Blanc."

I didn't like that smile. Straightening hastily, I nudged Absalon away with my foot. He didn't move. "Shoo," I hissed, but he merely gazed balefully back at me. Shit.

The auburn-haired woman from before interrupted us, peeking inside the tent. She held the hand of a child, a miniature version of herself. "The midnight search party has returned, my lady." Sniffing, she wiped away a fresh tear. "No sign of him. The next party has assembled."

"Do not fear, Ismay. We will find him." La Voisin clasped her hands, and her voice softened. "You must rest. Take Gabrielle back to your tent. We will wake you with developments."

"No, I—I must rejoin the party. Please do not ask me to sit idly while—while my son—" She broke off, overcome, before gritting her teeth. "I will not rest until he is found."

La Voisin sighed. "Very well." When Ismay nodded in thanks, guiding her daughter out of the tent, La Voisin inclined her head to me. "If you agree to my terms, you will join the next party in their search. They leave immediately. Nicholina will accompany you, as will Ismay and Gabrielle. You may also take your familiar and companion." She paused. "Cosette, you will attend me."

"*Tante*—" Coco started.

"He's *not* my familiar—" I snapped.

But La Voisin spoke over us, her eyes flashing. "You try my patience, child. If I am to consider this alliance, you will find Etienne before the first light of day. Do we have a deal?"

ONE STEP FORWARD

Reid

The weight of the knife was heavy in my palm. Solid. The blade balanced and sharp. I'd purchased it from one of the finest smiths in Cesarine—a smith who had later consorted to kill my wife with a couple of criminals. *Blue pig,* he'd spat after I'd given him to the authorities. In all our years of business, I hadn't known he despised me. Just like the farmers in Saint-Loire. All because of my uniform.

No. That wasn't true.

All because of *me.* My beliefs.

Golden stars took up most of the spinning board. Leather cuffs hung from four strategic points on the circular wood—two for an assistant's hands, and two for their feet. The top of the board had been stained with something that looked suspiciously like blood.

With a halfhearted flick of my wrist, I threw my knife. It lodged dead center.

Deveraux erupted into applause. "Well, that was quite—quite *extraordinary*, Monsieur Diggory! Really, Louise wasn't fibbing when she spoke of your bladed prowess!" He fanned himself for a moment. "Ah, the crowd will positively *exalt* your performance. The Dagger of Danger, we shall call you. No, no—Knife Strife."

I stared at him, alarmed. "I don't think—"

"Argh, you're right, you're *right*, of course. We have not yet found the perfect appellation. Never fear! Together, we shall—" His hands shot skyward abruptly, fingers splayed as if framing a portrait. "Three-Fingered Red? It takes three fingers to perform, yes?"

"Any more, and it would just be uncomfortable." Lounging behind us on a spangled blanket, Beau laughed. The remains of his lunch littered the ground beside him. "Might I suggest *Le Petit Jésus* as an alternative?"

"Stop." I took a deep breath through my nose. Heat worked up my throat, and even to me, the word sounded tired. I'd thought to use the break in travel to practice. An egregious lapse in judgment. "I don't need a stage name."

"My dear, dear boy!" Deveraux clutched his chest as if I'd insulted his mother. "Whatever else shall we call you? We cannot simply announce you as Reid Diggory." He flapped a hand, swatting away my protests. "The *couronnes*, dear boy, just think of the *couronnes*! You need a name, an *identity*, to whisk the audience into their fantas—" His hand stilled mid-swipe, and his eyes lit with excitement. "*The Red Death*," he said with relish. My heartbeat faltered. "That's it. The clear winner. The obvious selection. Come one, come all, to witness the horrible, the hellacious, the *handsome* Red Death!"

Beau doubled over with laughter. I nearly threw another knife at him.

"I prefer Raoul."

"Nonsense. I have *clearly* articulated my feelings on the name Raoul." Deveraux dropped his hands. The feather on his hat bobbed in agitation. "Never fear, I have every confidence the honorific shall grow on you. But perhaps a respite is in order in the meantime? We might instead outfit you both for your grand debut!"

Beau rose hastily to his elbows. "I told you I won't be onstage."

"Everyone in the company must model the appropriate attire, Your Highness. Even those collecting tickets and tips from the audience. You understand, I'm sure."

Beau fell backward with a groan.

"That's the spirit!" From his sleeve, Deveraux pulled a measuring tape. "Now, I'll just need a few measurements—a negligible amount, really—and all will be set. May I?" He gestured to my arm. When I nodded, he stepped into my space, engulfing me in the scent of wine.

That explained a lot.

"For the remainder of our journey," he prattled, unfurling his tape, "might I suggest you bunk with the twins in the amber wagon? Your mother may join you. Your brother, however, may better suit the scarlet wagon with Zenna and Seraphine. Though I sleep little, I will accompany him there." He chortled at an unspoken joke. "I've been told Zenna and Seraphine are the fiercest of snorers."

"I *would* be better suited to Zenna and Seraphine's wagon." I could hear the smirk in Beau's voice. "How perceptive you are, Claud."

He barked a laugh. "Oh no, dear boy, I fear if romance is what you seek, you shall be markedly disappointed. Zenna's and Seraphine's very souls are intertwined. *Cosmic*, I tell you."

Beau's expression flattened, and he looked away, muttering about piss poor luck.

"Why the sleeping arrangements?" I asked suspiciously. After bidding Lou goodbye, I'd spent the remainder of the night riding up front with Claud. He'd tried to pass the time with conversation. When I hadn't kept up my end, he'd started to sing, and I'd regretted my grave error. For *hours*.

"You're quite contrary, aren't you, Monsieur Diggory? Quite prickly." He peered up at me with a curious expression before dropping to measure my inseam. "'Tis nothing nefarious, I assure you. I simply think it wise for you to consider pursuing a friendship with our dear Toulouse and Thierry."

"Again, *why?*"

"You might have more in common with them than you think."

I glanced over my shoulder at Beau. He frowned at Deveraux. "That's not cryptic at all."

Deveraux sighed and stood once more, patting the mud from his corduroy trousers. *Violet* corduroy trousers. "If I might be frank, *messieurs*." He turned to me. "You have recently suffered a rather traumatic event and are in desperate need of platonic companionship. Your forefather is gone. Your brotherhood has abandoned you. Your self-loathing has cleaved a physical and emotional cleft between you and your wife. More important, it has cleaved a cleft within *yourself*."

Sharp, hot anger spiked through me at the unexpected reprimand. "You don't even know me."

"Perhaps not. But I do know you don't know yourself. I know you cannot know another until you do." He snapped his fingers in front of my nose. "I know you need to wake up, young man, lest you leave this world without finding that which you truly seek."

I glared at him, the beginning of shame flushing my neck. My ears. "And what's that?"

"Connection," he said simply, spinning his tape into a tidy roll. "We all seek it. Accept yourself, accept *others*, and you just might find it. Now"—he turned on his booted heel, smiling cheerily over his shoulder—"I suggest you partake in your midday meal. We soon continue to Domaine-les-Roses, where you shall woo the crowd with your knife-wielding prowess. Ta-ta!"

He strode off whistling a merry tune.

Beau snorted in the ensuing silence. "I like him."

"He's *mad*."

"All the best ones are."

His words sparked others—sharper ones now. Words that bit and snapped within my mind, seeking blood. *Claud is a collector of sorts*, Zenna had said. *He adds only the best and brightest talent to his troupe. The rare and unusual. The exceptional.*

My suspicion deepened. His curious look, his meaningful smile . . . was it possible he knew my secret? Did he know what I'd done on Modraniht? It wasn't likely. And yet—Morgane knew. I wasn't fool enough to believe she'd keep that knowledge to herself. When it best suited her purposes, she'd reveal it, and I would burn. And perhaps I deserved to burn. I'd taken life. I'd played God—

No. I retreated from my spiraling thoughts, breathing deeply. Marshaling my mind into order. Into silence. It lasted only seconds before another unwelcome question crept in.

If Deveraux *did* know, did that mean—were the twins also witches?

You might have more in common with them than you think.

Scoffing, I unsheathed another knife. In all my years around magic, in all *Lou's* years around it, we'd never heard of another male witch. To stumble upon two others this quickly after Modraniht was the least likely possibility of all. No. Less than unlikely. Absurd.

Claud is a collector of sorts.

Closing my eyes, I focused on emptying my mind of thought. Such speculation did little good. I had one purpose now—to protect Lou, to protect my unknown brothers and sisters. I couldn't know them if they were dead. I breathed in through my nose. Out through my mouth. Retreated to my fortress. Relished the darkness of my lids.

It didn't matter if the twins were witches.

It didn't matter if Deveraux knew I was one.

Because I wasn't a witch if I didn't practice.

I wasn't a witch.

Heedless of my conviction, gold flickered to life in the darkness, and there—soft at first, so soft I nearly missed them—voices began to hum.

Seek us, seek us, seek us.

My eyes snapped open.

When Beau cleared his throat behind me, I jumped, nearly dropping my knife. "You aren't seriously planning on strapping your mother to that board, are you?" he asked. "You could decapitate her."

In response, I hurled the knife—end over end—toward the center of the board. It sank deep beside the first one.

"Now you're just posturing." He rose from his blanket, stepped to my side for a better view. To my surprise, he tugged another knife from my bandolier, studying it in his hand. Then he threw it.

It thudded against the board like a dead fish before falling to the ground.

A beat of silence passed.

"It would seem"—Beau straightened his coat with as much dignity as he could muster—"I'm shit at this."

I snorted despite myself. The knot in my chest loosened. "Was there ever any doubt?"

A self-deprecating grin broke over his face, and he pushed my shoulder halfheartedly. Though tall, he stood a couple of inches shorter than me.

"When's your birthday?" I blurted.

He arched a black brow. So different from my own. "The ninth of August. I'm twenty-one years old. Why?"

"No reason."

"I'm older than you, if that's what you're wondering."

"I wasn't, and you're not."

"Come now, little brother, I told you my birthdate. It's only fair you reciprocate." When I didn't answer, his grin spread. "Your silence is damning. You really *are* younger, aren't you?"

Pushing his hand from my shoulder, I stalked toward the amber wagon. My neck burned.

Cots lined the walls inside, built above and below storage shelves like pieces of a puzzle. Pillows overflowed. Though threadbare, silk and velvet and satin covered each of them. Trunks had been shoved in the corners, along with a battered rack of costumes and a half-dressed mannequin. My chest twisted.

It reminded me of Soleil et Lune's attic.

Except for the incense. Frankincense and myrrh burned within a small porcelain pot. The smoke funneled out through a hole in the roof.

I hurled the entire pot outside into the snow.

"Easy there." Beau dodged the projectile, following me into the wagon. "Have the resins personally offended you?"

Again, I didn't answer. He didn't need to know it reminded me of the cathedral. Of . . . him.

I collapsed onto the nearest cot, tossing my bag to my feet. Rummaging for a dry shirt. When my hand caught instead on my journal, I pulled it out. Trailed my fingers across the worn cover. Flipped through the crinkled pages. Though perhaps I'd been foolish to pack such a sentimental token, I hadn't been able to leave it behind. Absently, I paused at my last entry—the evening I'd visited the king after burning Estelle.

My father.

I traced the words on the page, not truly seeing them. I'd done my best not to think of him, but now, his face crept back into my thoughts. Golden hair. Strong jaw. Piercing eyes. And a smile—a smile that disarmed all who looked upon it. He wielded it like a blade. No—a deadlier weapon still. A blade could not disarm his enemies, but his smile could.

As a Chasseur, I'd seen it from afar my entire life. Only when he'd invited me to dine with him had I witnessed it personally. He'd smiled at me the entire night, and despite Lou writhing alone in my bed—burning alive for her sister's sin—I'd felt . . . seen. Appreciated. *Special.*

Beau had inherited that smile. I had not.

Before I could lose my nerve, I asked, "What do our sisters look like? Violette and Victoire?"

Beau paused in examining the contents of the nearest trunk. I couldn't see his face. If my abrupt question surprised him, he didn't say. "They look like me, I suppose. Like our mother. She hails from an island across the sea. It's a beautiful kingdom. Tropical. Much warmer than this nonsense." He waved a hand toward the snow outside before plucking a crystal orb from the nearest trunk. "They're twins, you know. Prettier than my mother and me. Long black hair and blacker eyes, not a blemish on either of their faces. Like paintings—and my father treats them as such.

That's why you've never seen them. They're rarely allowed outside the castle walls."

"How old are they?"

"Thirteen."

"What do they"—I leaned forward eagerly—"what do they like? Do they read? Ride horses? Play with swords?"

He turned and smiled that smile, then. But it looked different on him. Genuine. "If by play, you mean bash their big brother over the head, then . . . yes. They like to *play* with swords." He eyed the journal in my hand. "And Violette likes to write and read. Victoire not so much. She prefers to chase cats and terrorize the staff."

A warmth I'd never known spread through me at the picture he painted. A warmth I hardly recognized. It wasn't anger or humiliation or—or shame. It was something else. Something . . . happy.

It hurt.

"And our father?" I asked quietly. "What's he like?"

Beau's smile faded then, and he dropped the lute he'd been plucking back into the trunk. His eyes narrowed as he faced me fully. "You know what he's like. Don't paint us like a fairy tale, Reid. We aren't one."

Closing my journal with more force than necessary, I pushed to my feet. "I know that. I just—I've—" I exhaled hard and threw caution to the winds. "I've never had a family."

"And you still don't." He shook his head in exasperation, eyeing me as if I were a stupid child in need of admonishment. "I should've known you'd do this. I should've known you'd want to *bond*." Stepping closer, he stuck a finger in my chest. "Listen carefully, *little brother*. This isn't a family. It's a noose. And if this brilliant plan of yours goes awry, we'll all swing from it—you, me, Violette, Victoire, and every other poor bastard our father has fucked into existence." He paused, and his expression softened infinitesimally before hardening once more. He kicked open the wagon door. "Make peace with it now, or we'll break your heart."

He left without another word.

The sway of wheels woke me. Groggy, disoriented, I jolted from my cot. My head pounded—doubly so when I cracked it against the shelf overhead—and my neck ached. I rubbed it with a muttered curse.

"Sleep well?" Madame Labelle regarded me over the brim of her teacup. Jade with gold filigree. The scent of spiced pears pervaded the wagon. Mulled perry, then. Not tea. It rippled with each roll of the wheels. Late afternoon sunlight filtered in through the window, as did Deveraux's cheery whistle.

"What time is it?" I asked.

"Around four o'clock. You've been asleep for hours. I didn't want to wake you." She offered me a second cup, along with a small smile. "Would you like some? I'm quite partial to perry after a long nap. Perhaps you are too?"

A hopeful question. A transparent one.

When I didn't answer, she prattled on, spinning her own cup

in her hands. Around and around. A restless gesture. "My mother brewed it for me when I was a girl. A grove of pear trees grew in the valley near the Chateau, and it was our secret place. We'd harvest the fruit at the end of summertime and hide them all over the Chateau, waiting for them to ripen." Her grin broadened as she looked up at me. "And we'd weave the blossoms into crowns, necklaces, rings. Once I even made Morgane a cape of them. It was glorious. Her mother—Louise's grandmother—organized a dance that May Day just so she could wear it."

"I'm allergic to pears."

I wasn't, but I'd heard enough. Her smile fell.

"Of course. Forgive me. Perhaps some tea instead?"

"I don't like tea."

Her eyes narrowed. "Coffee?"

"No."

"Wine? Mead? Beer?"

"I don't drink alcohol."

She set her cup down with an angry *clink*. "As you're sitting healthy and whole before me, I presume you drink *something*. Pray tell me what it is, so I might indulge you."

"Water."

She downright scowled then, abandoning her saccharine act. With a wave of her hand over the pot of perry, the spiced scent in the air vanished. The sharp bite of magic replaced it. Mouth pursed, she poured crystal-clear water into my cup. Pushed it roughly toward me.

My gut twisted, and I crushed my palms against my eyes. "I

told you. I don't want to be around—"

"Yes, yes," she snapped. "You've developed a renewed aversion to magic. I understand. One step forward, two steps back, and all that rubbish. I'm here to give you a gentle push back in the right direction—or a not so gentle one, if necessary."

I fell back to my pillow, turning away from her. "I'm not interested."

The next second, water doused the side of my face, my hair, my shoulder.

"And I am not finished," she said calmly.

Spluttering, pushing aside my sopping hair, I lurched upright once more to seize control of the conversation. "The men in the tavern knew I'm the king's bastard. How?"

She shrugged delicately. "I have contacts in the city. I requested they spread the word far and wide."

"*Why?*"

"To save your life." She arched a brow. "The more people who knew, the more likely it was to reach Auguste—and it did. You're wanted *alive*, not dead. Once he discovered the connection, I knew he'd want to see you again, to . . . study you. Your father is nothing if not vain, and children make impeccable mirrors."

"You're *insane*."

"That is not a polite word." She sniffed and smoothed her skirts, folded her hands in her lap. "Especially in light of Louise's new situation. Do you call *her* insane?"

"No." I forced my clenched teeth apart. "And you don't either."

She waved her hand. "Enough. You've made it perfectly clear

you don't desire a friendship with me—which is fortunate, indeed, as you're in desperate need of not a friend, but a parent. It is to that end I now speak: we will not defeat Morgane without magic. I understand you've had two less than ideal experiences with it, but the whole is greater than the sum of its parts. You must put aside your fear, or you will kill us all. Do you understand?"

At her tone—imperious, *sanctimonious*—anger tore through me, sharp and jagged as shattered glass. How dare she speak to me like a petulant child? How dare she presume to *parent* me?

"Magic is death and madness." I wrung out my shirt, stalking to join her at the table, tripping over my bag in the process. Swearing viciously at the tight quarters. "I want no part of it."

"There is more in this earth than in all your Heaven and Hell, yet you remain blind. I have said it before, and I will say it again. *Open your eyes*, Reid. Magic is not your enemy. Indeed, if we are to persuade Toulouse and Thierry into an alliance, I dare say you'll need to be rather less critical."

I paused with a fresh cup of water to my lips. "What?"

She regarded me shrewdly over her own cup. "The entire purpose of this endeavor is to procure allies, and two powerful ones have just landed in our lap. Morgane will not expect them. What Morgane does not expect, Morgane cannot manipulate."

"We don't know they're witches," I muttered.

"Use that thick head of yours, son, before it falls from your shoulders."

"*Don't* call me son—"

"I've heard of Claud Deveraux in my travels. What lovely Zenna professed is true—he surrounds himself with the exceptional, the talented, the *powerful*. I met a woman in Amandine years ago who'd performed with Troupe de Fortune. Rumor had it she could—"

"Is there a point to this?"

"The *point* is that Toulouse and Thierry St. Martin—probably even Zenna and Seraphine—are not what they appear. No one batted an eye when Lou revealed herself as a witch. They were far more concerned with *you* as a Chasseur, which means someone in this troupe practices magic. Claud wants you to befriend Toulouse and Thierry, yes?"

You might have more in common with them than you think.

I forced a nod.

"Excellent. Do it."

Shaking my head, I downed the rest of the water. As if it were that simple. As if I could disguise my disdain for magic and—and *charm* them into a false friendship. Lou could've done it. The thought curdled in my gut. But I could neither forget that look in her eye at the pub, nor the way she'd removed my Balisarda to control me. I couldn't forget the feel of the Archbishop's blood on my hand. My ex-brethrens' blood. My chest tightened.

Magic.

"I don't care if the St. Martins are witches." My lip curled, and I pushed away from the table. We'd stop for dinner soon. I'd suffer even Deveraux's singing to escape this conversation. "I have no intention of bonding with any of you."

"Oh?" Her eyes flashed. She too sprang to her feet. "You seemed intent on bonding with Beauregard. You seemed to care a great deal about Violette and Victoire. How do I earn such coveted treatment?"

I cursed my own carelessness. She'd been listening. Of course she'd been listening—filthy eavesdropper—and I'd shown her my soft underbelly. "You don't. You abandoned me."

In her eyes, our last moment on Modraniht unfolded. Those thousand moments. I shoved them all aside. "I thought we'd moved past this," she said softly.

I stared at her in disgust. Yes, I'd given her peace with her last breath, but that gift—it'd been for me too. She'd been dying. I couldn't spend the rest of my life haunting a ghost, so I'd let her go. I'd let it *all* go. The pain. The bitterness. The regret. Except she hadn't died, she hadn't *left*, and now she haunted me instead.

And some hurt couldn't stay buried.

"How does one move past being left to die in a garbage bin?"

"How many times must I tell you? *I* didn't—" She shook her head, color heightened and eyes overbright. Tearful. Whether angry or sad, I didn't know. Her voice was small, however, as she continued. "I am sorry, Reid. You've led a tumultuous life, and the blame in part is mine. I know this. I understand my role in your suffering." Catching my hand, she rose to her feet. I told myself to pull away. I didn't. "Now *you* must understand that, if given the choice, I never would've left you. I would've forsaken everything—my home, my sisters, my *life*—to keep you, but I cannot change the past. I cannot protect you from its pain. I *can* protect you here and now, however, if you let me."

If you let me.

The words were living things in my ears. Though I tried to bury them, they took root, suffocating my anger. Swathing my sorrow. Enveloping it. Enveloping *me*. I felt—warm, unsteady. Like lashing out and railing against her. Like falling down and clutching her skirt. How many times had I wished for a parent to protect me? To love me? Though I'd never admitted it—never *would* admit it—the Archbishop, he hadn't been—

No. It was too much.

I pulled away from her, sinking onto my cot. Staring at nothing. A moment of silence passed. It might've been uncomfortable. It might've been tense. I didn't notice. "I love pears," I finally mumbled, near incoherent. She still heard. The next second, she'd pressed a hot cup of perry into my hands.

Then she went for the kill.

"If you wish to defeat Morgane, Reid—if you wish to protect Louise—you must do what is necessary. I am not asking you to practice magic. I am asking you to tolerate it. Toulouse and Thierry will never join us if you scorn their very existence. Just—get to know them." After a second of hesitation, she added, "For Louise."

For yourself, she'd wanted to say.

I stared into the perry, feeling sick, before lifting it to my lips. The steaming liquid burned all the way down.

THE WHITE PATTERN

Lou

After two hours of trudging through the shadows of La Fôret des Yeux—pretending not to jump at small noises—a sudden realization clubbed me in the head.

Gabrielle Gilly was Reid's half sister.

I studied the little girl's back through the pines. With her auburn hair and brown eyes, she clearly favored her mother, but when she glanced at me over her shoulder—for the hundredth time, no less—there was something in her smile, the slight dimple in her cheek, that reminded me of Reid.

"She keeps looking at you." Ansel tripped over a stray limb, nearly landing face-first in the snow. Absalon leapt sleekly from his path.

"Of course she does. I'm objectively beautiful. A masterpiece made flesh."

Ansel snorted.

"Excuse me?" Offended, I kicked snow in his direction, and he nearly tumbled again. "I don't think I heard you correctly. The *proper* response was, 'Goddess Divine, of course thy beauty is a sacred gift from Heaven, and we mortals are blessed to even gaze upon thy face.'"

"Goddess Divine." He laughed harder now, brushing the snow from his coat. "Right."

Pushing him away with a snort of my own, I bounded atop a fallen log to walk beside him. "You can laugh, but if this plan of ours doesn't go tits up, that'll be my title someday."

Pink crept into his cheeks at my vulgarity. "What do you mean?"

"You know—" When the log ended, I hopped down, shooing Absalon away again. "—if we kill Morgane, I'll inherit the Triple Goddess's powers in her stead."

Ansel stopped walking abruptly, like I'd clubbed him in the back of the head. "You'll become the Maiden, Mother, and Crone."

"Goddess Divine." I smirked, stooping to pick up a handful of snow, but he didn't share my humor any longer. A furrow appeared between his brows. "What's with the face?" I asked, packing the snow between my palms. "That's how it works. La Dame des Sorcières possesses divine power as a blessing from the Triple Goddess."

"Do you *want* to become La Dame des Sorcières?"

I hurled the snowball at a tree, watching as it exploded on the limbs. What an unexpected question. Certainly no one had ever asked it before. "I . . . I don't know. I never thought I'd live past my sixteenth birthday, let alone plot a revolt against my mother.

Inheriting her divine power seemed far-fetched, even as a child."

He resumed walking, albeit slower than before. I fell into step beside him. But after several instances of him glancing at me, looking away, opening his mouth, and shutting it again, I'd had enough. I made another snowball and chucked it at his head. "Out with it."

With a disgruntled look, he knocked the snow from his curls. "Do you think you'll be able to kill your own mother?"

My stomach twisted unpleasantly. As if answering some unspoken call, Absalon dropped from a pine overhead to saunter along behind me. I didn't look at him—didn't look at anyone or anything but my own boots in the snow. My toes had gone numb. "She hasn't given me a choice."

It wasn't an answer, and Ansel knew it. We lapsed into silence.

The moon peeked out overhead as we continued our search, dappling the forest floor in light. The wind gradually ceased. If not for Nicholina floating along like a specter beside Ismay and Gabrielle, it would've been peaceful. As it was, however, a bone-deep chill settled within me.

There'd been no sign of Etienne.

If I am to consider this alliance, you will find Etienne before the first light of day. Do we have a deal?

As if I'd had a choice.

When I'd called for a pattern to find Etienne—standing at the edge of camp with everyone's eyes on my back—the golden threads had tangled, coiling and shifting like snakes in a nest. I hadn't been able to follow them. At La Voisin's expectant look, however, I'd lied my ass off—which was why I now wandered through a random copse of spruces, trying and failing not to watch the sky. Sunrise couldn't be too far away.

I took a deep breath and examined the patterns again. They remained hopelessly knotted, spiraling out of control in every direction. There was no give. No take. Just . . . confusion. It was like my third eye—that sixth sense enabling me to see and manipulate the threads of the universe—had . . . blurred, somehow. I'd never known such a thing was possible.

La Voisin had said someone was shielding Etienne's location from us. Someone powerful. I had a sick suspicion who that might be.

After another quarter hour, Ansel sighed. "Should we maybe . . . call out for him?"

"You *should*." Nicholina cackled in front of us. "Call him, call him, let the trees *maul* him, boil and butter and split and saw him—"

"Nicholina," I said brusquely, still keeping one eye on the patterns. "I think I speak for everyone here when I say to *shut up*."

But she only drifted backward, clutching the inky hair on either side of her face. "No, no, no. We're going to be the best of friends, the three of us. The very best of friends." When I arched an incredulous brow at Ansel, she cackled louder. "Not him, silly mouse. Not him."

A branch snapped ahead, and if possible, she laughed all the louder. "The trees in this forest have eyes, little mouse. She spies, she spies, she spies, little mouse—"

"*Or* it could be a wounded Etienne." I unsheathed my knife

in a single, fluid movement—unnerved despite myself—and whirled toward the noise. "You should go investigate."

Still leering, Nicholina vanished between one blink and the next. Ismay stared ahead, visibly torn between investigating the source of the noise and protecting her daughter. She clutched Gabrielle's hand tightly.

"Go." I approached them with caution, but I didn't sheathe my weapon. The hair on my neck still prickled with unease. *She spies, she spies, she spies, little mouse.* "We'll take care of your daughter."

Though Ismay pressed her lips together, she nodded once and slipped into the trees. Gabrielle waited until she'd gone before sticking her hand out to me, wriggling with excitement.

Then she opened her mouth.

"My name is Gabrielle Gilly, and *you* are even shorter than they said. Practically elfin! Tell me, how do you kiss my brother? I heard he's as tall as this evergreen!" I tried to answer—or perhaps laugh—but she continued without breath. "I suppose I should call him my half brother, though, shouldn't I? *Maman* doesn't like you being here. She doesn't like me knowing about him, but she's gone for the moment and I don't really care what she thinks, anyway. What's he like? Does he have red hair? Nicholina told me he has red hair, but I *don't* like Nicholina very much. She thinks she's so clever, but really, she's just weird. Too many hearts, you know—"

"Hearts?" Ansel shot me a bewildered look. As if realizing his poor manners, he hastened to add, "I'm Ansel, by the way. Ansel Diggory."

"The hearts keep her young." Gabrielle continued like he

hadn't spoken, nodding in a matter-of-fact way. "*Maman* says I shouldn't speak of such things, but I *know* what I saw, and Bellamy's chest was stitched shut on his pyre—"

"Wait." I felt a bit out of breath myself listening to her. "Slow down. Who's Bellamy?"

"Bellamy was my best friend, but he died last winter. He lost his *maman* a few years before that. His sister was born a white witch, see, so his *maman* sent her to live at the Chateau to have a better life. But then his *maman* went and died of a broken heart because Bellamy wasn't enough for her. He was enough for me, though, until he died too. Now he's not enough at all."

"I'm sor—" Ansel started, but Gabrielle shook her head, sending her auburn hair rippling around her shoulders in an agitated wave.

"Strangers always says that. They always say they're sorry, like they're the ones who killed him, but they didn't kill him. The snow did, and then Nicholina ate his heart." Finally—*finally*—she paused to draw breath, blinking once, twice, three times, as her eyes focused on Ansel at last. "Oh. Hello, Ansel Diggory. Are you related to my brother too?"

Ansel gaped at her. A laugh built in my throat at his gobsmacked expression, at her inquisitive one, and when it finally burst free—brilliant and clear and bright as the moon—Absalon darted into the boughs for cover. Birds in their nests took flight. Even the trees seemed to rustle in agitation.

As for me, however, I felt lighter than I had in weeks.

Still chuckling, I knelt before her. Her brown eyes met mine with familiar intensity. "I cannot *wait* for your brother to meet you, Gabrielle."

She beamed. "You can call me Gaby."

When Nicholina and Ismay returned a moment later—Nicholina trilling about naughty trees—Gaby scoffed and whispered, "I told you she's weird. Too many hearts."

Ansel swallowed hard, casting a dubious look at Nicholina's back as she drifted farther and farther ahead, leaving the rest of us behind. Ismay walked much closer than before. Her rigid spine radiated disapproval.

"You really think she—*eats* hearts?" he asked.

"Why would she do that?" I asked. "And how would they keep her young?"

"Your magic lives outside your body, right?" Gaby asked. "You get it from your ancestors' ashes in the land?" She plowed ahead with her explanation before I could answer. "Our magic is different. It lives within us—right inside our hearts. The heart *is* the physical and emotional center of a blood witch, after all. Everyone knows that."

Ansel nodded, but he didn't seem to know at all. "Because your magic is only accessible through blood?"

"Gabrielle," Ismay said sharply, lurching to a stop. She didn't turn. "Enough. Speak no more of this."

Gaby ignored her. "*Technically*, our magic is in every part of us—our bones, our sweat, our tears—but blood is the easiest way."

"Why?" Ansel asked. "Why blood over the others?"

In a burst of clarity, I remembered the tour he'd given me of

Cathédral Saint-Cécile d'Cesarine. He'd known every detail of that unholy place. And what's more—he'd spent much of our time in the Tower poring over leather-bound books and illuminated manuscripts from the library.

If Gaby's curious nature served, he'd found himself a like-minded friend.

"I said *enough*, Gabrielle." Ismay finally turned, planting her fists on her hips to block our path. She took care not to look at me. "No more. This conversation is inappropriate. If Josephine knew—"

Gaby narrowed her eyes and stepped around her, pulling us along with her. "How much do you know about Dames Blanches' magic, Ansel Diggory?"

Ismay closed her eyes, lips moving as if praying for patience. Ansel gave her an apologetic smile as we passed. "Not much, I'm afraid. Not yet."

"I figured." Tossing her hair over her shoulder, Gaby harrumphed, but a smug smile played on her lips. "Dames Blanches' and Dames Rouges' magic might be different, but it's also the same because each requires balance. When we spill our blood, we weaken our bodies, which limits us. We surrender little pieces of ourselves with each enchantment, and eventually, we *die* from it." She said the last with relish, swinging our hands once more. "Well, if we don't die from exposure first. Or starvation. Or huntsmen."

Ansel frowned, casting me a confused look over her head. I watched as the implication sank in.

Coco.

When I nodded sadly, his face crumpled.

Ismay hurried after us. "Gabrielle, *please*, we cannot discuss such things with—"

"*That* is why blood is the most powerful way," Gaby continued, determinedly ignoring her. "Because we must sacrifice with each cut, and that makes the enchantments stronger."

"*Gabrielle*—"

"Blood is easily given." The words left my mouth before I could catch them. When Gaby peered up at me, surprised, I hesitated. Though she was clearly intelligent, she was also still a child—perhaps only seven or eight years old. And yet . . . she'd also clearly known pain. I repeated the words Coco had told me years ago. "Tears—the pain that causes them—aren't."

They both gazed at me in silence.

"You—" Behind us, Ismay's voice faltered. "You know our magic?"

"Not really." I stopped walking with a sigh, and Ansel and Gabrielle followed suit. They watched with transparent curiosity as I turned to face Ismay. "But I've known Coco for most of my life. When I met her, she was—well, she was trying not to cry." The memory of her six-year-old face flared in my mind's eye: the quivering chin, the determined expression, the crumpled sea lily. She'd clutched it with both hands as she'd recounted the argument with her aunt. "But we were six, and the tears fell anyway. When they touched the ground, they sort of multiplied until we were standing in a pond, ankle-deep in mud."

Ansel stared at me with wide eyes.

At long last, Ismay's hostility seemed to fracture. She sighed and extended a hand to Gabrielle, who took it without complaint. "Long ago, we *did* experiment with tear magic, but it proved too volatile. The tears often overpowered the additives and transformed them into something else entirely. A simple sleeping solution could send the drinker into a peaceful slumber or . . . a more permanent one. We concluded it depended on the *emotions* of the witch when she shed the tears in question."

As fascinating as her conjecture would've been, an inexplicable tugging sensation had started in my chest, distracting me. I glanced around. Nothing seemed amiss. Though we still hadn't found Etienne, there'd been no signs of foul play—no signs of life anywhere, in fact. Except—

A crow alighted on a branch in front of us. It tilted its head, curious, and stared directly at me.

Unease crept down my spine.

"What is it?" Ansel asked, following my gaze. The crow cawed in response, and the sound echoed loudly around us, reverberating through the trees. Through my bones. Frowning, Ismay drew Gabrielle closer. Nicholina had disappeared.

"It's—" I rubbed my chest as the tugging sensation grew stronger. It seemed to be pulling me . . . inward. I dug in my feet, bewildered, and glanced at the sky. Gray light filtered toward us from the east. My heart sank.

Our time was almost up.

In one last effort, I called the patterns back to sight. They

remained as chaotic as ever. In a spectacular show of temper—
or perhaps desperation—I waded through them, determined to
find something, *anything*, that could help locate him before the
sun truly rose. Vaguely, I heard Ansel's concerned voice in the
background, but I ignored it. The pressure in my chest built to a
breaking point. With each pattern I touched, I gasped, startled by
an innate sense of *wrongness*. It felt . . . it felt as if these weren't my
patterns at all. But that was ludicrous, impossible—

A speck of white glinted amidst the golden cords.

As soon as I touched it, a single white cord pulsed to life—
wrapping around my fingers, my wrist, my arm—and my sixth
sense sharpened to crystal clarity. *Finally.* With a sigh of relief, I
whipped my head east once more, gauging the time we had left.

"What's happening?" Ansel asked, alarmed.

"I found him."

Without another word, I tore into the forest, following the
white blaze of light. Racing against the sunrise. The others
crashed after me, and the crow careened from its branch with an
indignant *caw!* Snow flew everywhere. Fiercely hopeful, invigo-
rated, I couldn't help but smile.

"Where is he?" Ismay cried, struggling to keep up.

"How does it work?" Gaby soon outpaced her. "Your—your
pattern?"

Ansel tripped on a root, nearly decapitating himself on a lower
bough. "Why now?"

I ignored them all, ignoring the burn in my lungs and running faster. We had a chance now—a real chance to procure this

alliance. The white pattern continued to pulse, leading me closer and closer to victory, and I nearly crowed in triumph. La Voisin hadn't expected me to find him. I'd prove her wrong, prove them *all* wrong.

My certainty punctured slightly as the trees thinned around us and the first tents of camp came into view.

"He's—he's here?" Face flushed and breath heavy, Ismay looked around wildly. "Where? I don't see him."

I slowed as the pattern wove through the campsite—between firepits and caged animals, past Coco and Babette—before curving down the slope toward . . .

Toward our tent.

I stumbled those last few steps, rounding the corner and skidding to a halt. The pattern burst in a cloud of glittering white dust, and my blood ran cold. Ismay's scream confirmed what I already knew.

Propped against the pole of our tent was the corpse of a young man with auburn hair.

THE FOOL

Reid

"Er—" Toulouse blinked at me the next morning, his baguette still caught between his teeth. Hastily, he tore off a chunk, chewed, and swallowed—then choked. Thierry thumped his back with silent laughter. I still hadn't heard him speak a word. "Come again?"

"Your tattoo," I repeated stiffly. Heat crept up my neck at the awkwardness. I'd never needed to make friends before. I'd never even needed to *get to know* someone. I'd simply always known Célie and Jean Luc. And Lou . . . suffice it to say, there'd never been any awkward silences in our relationship. She always filled them. "What does it mean?"

Toulouse's black eyes still watered. "Straight to the personal questions, eh?"

"It's on your face."

"*Touché.*" He grinned, contorting the tattoo on his cheek. Small. Golden. A rose. It gleamed metallic. When I'd sat next to him and his brother to break my fast, it'd been the first thing I'd seen. The first question out of my mouth. My neck still burned. Perhaps it hadn't been the right question to ask. Perhaps it'd been too . . . *personal*. How could I have known? He'd inked the thing right on his cheek.

Across the fire, Madame Labelle ate her morning meal— cantal cheese and salted ham—with Zenna and Seraphine. Clearly, she hoped to befriend them like she hoped I'd befriend the St. Martins. Her attempts had been met with more enthusiasm than my own; Zenna preened under her praise, swelling like a peacock. Even Seraphine seemed reluctantly pleased at the attention. Behind them, Beau cursed. Deveraux had coerced him into helping with the horses, and it sounded as though he'd just stepped in dung.

My morning could've been worse.

Slightly mollified, I returned my attention to Toulouse and Thierry.

When they'd entered the amber wagon last night, I'd feigned sleep, torn with indecision. It still didn't sit right, my mother's plan. It still felt deceitful to feign friendship. But if deceit would defeat Morgane, if it would help Lou, I could pretend. I could tolerate magic.

I could befriend whoever wielded it here.

Toulouse drew a deck from his pocket, flicking a single card toward me. I caught it instinctively. In thick paints of black, white, and gold, the card depicted a boy standing on a cliff. He held a rose in his hand. A dog stood at his feet.

My first instinct was to recoil. The Church had never tolerated tarot cards. The Archbishop had counseled King Auguste to ban all variety of them from Cesarine years ago. He'd claimed their divination mocked the omniscience of God. He'd claimed those who partook in them would be damned to Hell.

He'd claimed so many things.

I cleared my throat, feigning interest. "What is it?"

"The Fool." Toulouse tapped the rose on his cheek. "First card I ever drew. I inked it as a reminder of my innocence." My eyes honed in on his hands. Black symbols decorated the skin there— one tattoo on each of his knuckles. I vaguely recognized a bolt of lightning. A shield. "The Major Arcana cards," he explained. "Twenty-two in all. Ten on my fingers. Ten on my toes. One on my cheek, and one . . . elsewhere."

He expected a laugh at that. Too late, I forced a chuckle. The sound came out dry, rough, like a cough. He and Thierry exchanged an amused glance at my expense, and I ground my teeth in frustration. I didn't know what to say. Didn't know how to transition smoothly to another topic. God, why wouldn't they *say* something? Another silence threatened to loom. Panicked, I glanced at my mother, who stared at me in disbelief. When she waved her hand impatiently, mouthing, *Go on*, Zenna didn't hide her snicker. Seraphine, however, pulled a Bible from her bag and started reading.

My stomach clenched.

"Uh . . ." I trailed off, not quite sure how to finish. *Are you both witches? How long have you known? Did your powers manifest after brutally killing your patriarch? Will you join us in a battle to the death against*

Morgane? Each question rattled around my brain, but somehow, I didn't think they'd appreciate them. Unfortunately, they didn't seem inclined to end my suffering, either. And their smiles—they were almost *too* benign. Like they enjoyed watching me squirm.

I'd probably tried to kill them at some point.

Turning quickly to Thierry, I blurted, "What's your act?"

Thierry's eyes, black and fathomless, bore into my own. He didn't answer. I cringed in the silence. My voice had been too loud, too curt. A shout instead of a civil question. At least Beau hadn't yet returned to witness my failure. He would've laughed himself hoarse. The mighty Reid Diggory—youngest captain of the Chasseurs, recipient of *four* Medals of Honor for bravery and outstanding service—laid low at last by small talk with strangers. What a joke.

"He doesn't speak," Toulouse said after another painful moment. "Not like you and I do."

I latched onto his answer like a lifeline. "Why not?"

"Curiosity killed the cat, you know." With a flick of his wrist, he cut the cards, shuffling them with lightning speed.

I returned his polite smile with one of my own. "I'm not a cat."

"Fair enough." He bridged the deck together. "My brother and I are resident psychics here at Troupe de Fortune."

"Psychics?"

"That's right. I'm reading your thoughts at this very moment, but I promise not to share. Spilling a person's secrets is a lot like spilling their blood. Once it's done, it's done. There's no going back."

I frowned. They weren't the same thing at all. "Have you ever spilled blood?"

His gaze flicked to Thierry for half a second—less than half a second—but I still saw. He kept smiling. "That's none of your business, friend."

I stared at him. *Psychics.* That sounded like magic to me. My gaze flicked surreptitiously over their clothes. Unlike the others', theirs were dark. Simple. Unremarkable. The clothing of men who didn't want to be remembered. I leaned closer under the pretense of examining Toulouse's deck. This close, I could smell the faint earth on his shirt. The even fainter sweetness on his skin. His hair.

"You admit it, then," I said carefully. The scent itself wasn't proof. It could've lingered on him from another. Claud himself had a peculiar smell. "You use . . . magic."

Toulouse stopped shuffling. If possible, his smile grew—like he'd been waiting for this. Wariness tightened my neck, my shoulders, as he resumed snapping his cards. "An interesting question from a Chasseur."

"I'm not a Chasseur." The tightness built. "Not anymore."

"Really?" He held a card in the air, its face pointed away from me. "Tell me, what card is this?"

I stared at him, confused.

"Your reputation proceeds you, Captain Diggory." He slipped it back into the deck. Still smiling. Always smiling. "I was there, you know. In Gévaudan."

My heart skipped a painful beat.

"Troupe de Fortune had just finished our last performance of the season. There was one boy in the audience—couldn't have been more than sixteen—who just *adored* the cards. He must've visited us—what—three times that night?" He looked to Thierry, who nodded. "He couldn't afford a full spread, so I pulled a single card for him each time. The *same* card for him each time." His smile hardened into a grimace, as did mine. My shoulders ached with tension. In the next second, however, he brightened once more. "I couldn't show it to him, of course. It would've frightened him out of his wits. The next morning, we found him dead along the side of Les Dents, left to rot in the sun like roadkill. A Chasseur had cut off his head. I heard he leveraged it for a pretty captaincy."

"Let me tell you"—Toulouse shook his head, scratched his neck absently—"the Beast of Gévaudan didn't take it well. A friend of mine said you could hear his howls of rage and grief all the way in Cesarine."

I cast a furtive glance at my mother. He still saw.

Leaning forward on his elbows, he spoke softly. "She doesn't know, does she? None of them do. For someone who has never performed, you're doing a fine job of it."

Significance laced his voice. I didn't like his implication.

Thierry watched us impassively.

"They think Blaise will help you kill Morgane," Toulouse said, leaning closer still. "But I don't think Blaise will ever ally with the man who killed his son. Perhaps I'm wrong, though. It's happened before. For instance, I thought only Chasseurs were in the business of killing witches, yet here you are." His eyes fell to the Balisarda still strapped to my chest. "*Not* a Chasseur."

My fingers curled around the hilt protectively. "It's a powerful weapon. It'd be foolish to stop carrying it." The words sounded defensive, even to me. At his superior expression, I added, "And killing Morgane is different. She wants to kill us too."

"So much killing," he mused, flipping the card between his fingers. I still couldn't see its face. Only the gold and black paints on its back. They swirled together into the shape of a skull—a leering skull with roses in its eyes and a snake twined between its teeth. "You say you're no longer a Chasseur. Prove it. What card am I holding in my hand?"

Jaw clenched, I ignored the soft hiss in my ear. "You're the psychic. How should I know?"

Seek us, seek us, seek us.

His smile finally slipped. A cold stare replaced it, chilling me to the bone. "Let me be clear. Claud may trust you, but I don't. It's nothing personal," he added, shrugging. "I don't trust anyone— it's how people like us stay alive, isn't it?"

People like us.

The words hung between us, sentient, and the hiss in my ear grew louder, more insistent. *We have found the lost ones. The lost ones are here. Seek us, seek us, seek us—*

"I know what you want from me," he said, voice hard with finality, "so I'll ask you one last time: What card am I holding?"

"I don't know," I ground out, slamming the door on the voices, retreating from their unholy shrieks. My hands shook with the effort. Sweat beaded my brow.

"Tell me if you figure it out." Toulouse's lips pressed tight in disappointment. He returned the card to his deck, rising to his feet. Thierry shadowed his movements. "Until then, I'd appreciate if you stay away from me, Captain. Oh, and"—he flashed another smile, casting a sly look in my mother's direction— "good luck with your performance."

BLOOD DROPS

Lou

The blood witches called it *pendency*—the time between this life and the next. "The soul remains earthbound until the ashes ascend," Gabrielle murmured, holding a cup of her mother's blood. Identical in their grief, their cheeks were pale, their eyes wet and swollen. I couldn't fathom their pain.

Etienne Gilly hadn't died of exposure or starvation.

His body had been burned beyond recognition, except—

Except for his head.

Ansel had vomited when it'd tumbled from Etienne's charred shoulders, rolling to touch my boots. I'd nearly succumbed as well. The hacked flesh of his throat communicated unspeakable torment, and I didn't want to imagine which horror he'd suffered first—being burned or decapitated alive. Worse still, the witches' horrified whispers had confirmed Etienne hadn't been the first. A handful of similar tales had plagued the countryside since Modraniht, and all the victims shared a common thread: rumors of their mothers once dallying with the king.

Someone was targeting the king's children. Torturing them.

My hands stilled in Gaby's hair, my eyes flicking to where Coco and Babette stood watch over Etienne's pyre. He was little more than ashes now.

Upon finding his body, La Voisin hadn't been kind.

Coco bore the worst of it, though her aunt had made it clear she blamed *me*. After all, Etienne had disappeared when she'd agreed to harbor me. His body had been placed at my tent. And I'd—I'd been led to him, somehow, by the white pattern. In the ensuing chaos—the panic, the screams—I'd quickly realized it wasn't mine. It'd been inside my head, inside my *sight*, yet it hadn't belonged to me. My stomach still rolled at the violation.

This was my mother's handiwork. All of it. But *why*?

The question plagued me, consuming my thoughts. Why here? Why *now*? Had she abandoned her plan to sacrifice me? Had she decided to make the kingdom suffer bit by bit, child by child, instead of killing them all at once?

A small, ugly part of me wept with relief at the possibility, but . . . she'd cut off Etienne's head. She'd burned him and left him at my tent. It couldn't be a coincidence.

It was a message—another sick move in a game I didn't understand.

She'd wanted me to know he'd suffered. She'd wanted me to know it was my fault. *Should you attempt to flee,* she'd told me, *I will butcher your huntsman and feed you his heart.* I hadn't heeded her warning. I'd fled anyway, and I'd taken my huntsman with me. Could this be her retaliation?

Could this heinous evil be less for the king and more for me?

With a deep breath, I resumed braiding Gaby's hair. My questions could wait just a few more hours. *Morgane* could wait. After the ascension this evening, we'd leave to rejoin Reid on the road in the morning—with or without La Voisin's alliance. The plan had changed. If Morgane was actively hunting the king's children, Reid and Beau were in graver danger than we'd anticipated. I needed to find them, tell them her plan, but first . . .

Gaby watched in silence as Ismay dipped a finger into the blood, as she added a strange symbol to the whitewashed pot in her lap. Though I didn't understand the ritual, the marks she painted felt ancient and pure and . . . mournful. No—more than mournful. Anguished. Completely and irrevocably heartbroken. Gaby sniffed, wiping her eyes.

I couldn't leave her. Not yet—and not just because of her grief.

If Reid and Beau were in danger, she was too. Morgane had just proved she could slip through La Voisin's defenses.

Ansel tucked his knees to his chin, watching in silence as Ismay continued to cover the white pot with blood. When they'd finished, Ismay excused herself, and Gaby turned to me. "Did you get your alliance?"

"Gaby, don't worry about—"

"*Did* you?"

I finished her braid, tying it with a scarlet ribbon. "La Voisin hasn't decided."

Her brown eyes were earnest. "But you made a deal."

I didn't have the heart to tell her there'd been quite a bit of gray area in that deal—like whether I'd found her brother dead or alive, for instance. I flicked her braid over her shoulder. "It'll all work out."

Satisfied with my answer, she fixed her attention on Ansel next. "I can read their lips, if you like." Startled from his reverie, he blushed and tore his gaze from Coco. "They aren't talking about anything exciting, though." She leaned forward, pursing her lips in concentration. "Something about Chasseurs burning down a brothel. Whatever that is." Sitting back once more, she patted Ansel's knee. "I like the *princesse*, even though some people don't. I hope she kisses you. That's what you want, isn't it? I only want it to happen if you want it to happen—and if she wants it to happen too. My *maman* says that's called *consent*—"

"Why do some people dislike Coco?" I asked, ignoring Ansel's wide-eyed mortification. Irritation pricked dangerously close to anger at her implication, and I glared at the few blood witches around us. "They should revere her. She's their *princesse*."

Gaby toyed with her ribbon. "Oh, it's because her mother betrayed us, and we've wandered the wilderness ever since. It happened a long time ago, though, before I was born. Probably even before Cosette was born."

A sickening wave of regret swept through me.

In all the years Coco and I had known each other, we'd never spoken of her mother. I'd always assumed the woman was a Dame Blanche—Dames Rouges were incredibly rare, born as unpredictably as those with color blindness or albinism—but I'd never sought her out at the Chateau as a child. I hadn't wanted to look upon a mother who could abandon her own daughter.

The irony of my own situation wasn't lost on me.

"La Voisin always goes on and on about how *we ruled this land from its conception, long before the gods poisoned it with dead magic*," Gaby continued. Her imitation of La Voisin's low voice and rigid calm was uncanny. "I'm assuming that means she's ancient. *I* think she eats the hearts with Nicholina, but *Maman* forbids me from saying so." When she glanced after her mother, her chin wobbled a bit.

"Do it again," I said quickly, hoping to distract her. "Another impression. You were wonderful."

She brightened slightly before twisting her face in an exaggerated scowl. "*Gabrielle*, I do not expect you to understand the *legacy* of *what has always been* and *what will always be*, but *please*, refrain from collaring my auguries and taking them for walks. They are not *pets*."

I stifled a snort and tugged on her braid. "Go on, then. Join your mother. Perhaps she needs a laugh too."

She left with little more convincing, and I laid my head on Ansel's shoulder. His gaze had returned to Coco and Babette. "Chin up," I said softly. "The game isn't over yet. She's just a new piece on the board."

"This isn't the time."

"Why not? Ismay's and Gabrielle's suffering doesn't lessen your own. We need to talk about this."

While we still can, I didn't add.

Resting his head atop my own, he sighed. The sound tugged on my heartstrings. Such naked vulnerability required strength. It required courage. "There are already too many pieces on the board, Lou. And I'm not playing a game," he finished miserably.

"If you don't play, you can't win."

"You also can't lose."

"Now you just sound petulant." I lifted my head to look at him. "Have you told her how you feel?"

"She sees me like a kid brother—"

"*Have you*"—I ducked to catch his eye when he looked away—"*told her*"—I leaned closer—"*how you feel?*"

He huffed another sigh, this one impatient. "She already knows. I haven't hidden it."

"You haven't addressed it, either. If you want her to see you as a man, *act* like a man. Have the conversation."

He glanced again to Coco and Babette, who'd cuddled close together against the cold.

I wasn't surprised. This wasn't the first time Coco had revisited Babette, her oldest friend and lover, for comfort in times of strain. It never ended well, but who was I to question Coco's choices? I'd fallen in love with a Chasseur, for God's sake. Still, I hated this for Ansel. Truly. And though I also hated myself for the part I now played in his eventual heartbreak, I couldn't watch as he pined away from unrequited love. He needed to ask. He needed to know.

"What if she says no?" he breathed, so quietly now that I read his lips rather than heard his voice. He searched my face helplessly.

"You'll have your answer. You move on."

If it was possible to see a heart break, I saw it then in Ansel's eyes. He said nothing more, however, and neither did I. Together, we waited for the sun to set.

The blood witches didn't gather at the pyres all at once; they collected gradually, standing in melancholic silence, joining hands with each new mourner as they came. Ismay and Gabrielle stood at the front, weeping softly.

All wore scarlet—whether a cloak or hat or shirt, as mine.

"To honor their blood," Coco had told Ansel and me before we'd joined the vigil, wrapping a red scarf around his neck. "And its magic."

She and La Voisin had donned thick woolen gowns of scarlet with matching fur-lined cloaks. Though the silhouettes were simple, the ensembles painted them as a striking portrait. Woven circlets adorned their brows, and within the silver vines, drops of rubies glittered. *Blood drops*, Coco had called them. As I watched the two stand together at the pyres—tall, regal, and proud—I could envision the time of which Gaby had spoken. A time when the Dames Rouges had been omnipotent and everlasting. Immortals among men.

We ruled this land from its conception, long before the gods poisoned it with dead magic.

I suppressed a shiver. If La Voisin ate the hearts of the dead to live eternal, it wasn't my business. I was an outsider here. An interloper. This vigil itself proved I didn't understand their customs. I was probably reading too much into her persona, anyway. True, La Voisin could be intimidating, and that book of hers was certainly creepy, but—rumors. That's all they were. Surely this coven would know if their leader harvested hearts. Surely they'd object. Surely Coco would've told me—

Not your business.

I focused on the embers of Etienne's pyre.

But what did *dead* magic mean?

When the sun touched the pines, Ismay and Gaby moved in sync, sweeping the ashes into their whitewashed pot. Gabrielle clutched it to her chest, and a sob escaped her. Though Ismay hugged her tightly, she murmured no words of comfort. Indeed, no one said a word as the two started into the forest. A sort of ritualistic procession formed—first Ismay and Gaby, second La Voisin and Coco, third Nicholina and Babette. The other mourners fell into place behind them until the entire camp trod an unspoken path through the trees—a path they knew well, it seemed. Still no one spoke.

"A soul caught between this life and the next is agitated," Coco had explained. "Confused. They see us here but can't touch us, can't speak with us. We soothe them with silence and lead them to the nearest grove."

A grove. The final resting place of a blood witch.

Ansel and I waited until the last mourner had passed before joining the procession, journeying deeper into the forest. Absalon's tail soon brushed my boots. To my dismay, a black fox joined him. She stalked through the shadows nearest me, her pointed nose swiveling in my direction with every few steps, her amber eyes gleaming. Ansel hadn't noticed her yet, but he soon would. Everyone would.

I'd never heard of a person attracting *two* matagots.

Miserable, I focused on Gaby's auburn braid through a gap in the procession. She and Ismay slowed as we entered a copse of silver birch trees. Snow coated their spindly branches, illuminated by soft white light as feu follet winked into existence around us. Legend claimed they led to the deepest desires of one's heart.

My mother had once told me about a witchling who'd followed them. She'd never been seen again.

Clutching Ansel tighter when he gazed at them, I murmured, "Don't look."

He blinked and halted mid-step, shaking his head. "Thank you."

From the spindly branches of the birch trees, a dozen clay pots blew gently in the wind. Reddish-brown symbols had been painted on each in unique designs, and wind chimes—complete with feathers and beads—hung from most. The few unadorned pots appeared to be so old that their markings had chipped and flaked from the elements. In unison, La Voisin and Coco drew twin daggers from their cloaks, pulled down their collars, and drew the blades across their bare chests, using fresh blood to paint over the faded symbols. When they'd finished, Ismay joined them, accepting a dagger and making an identical cut on her own chest.

I watched in fascination as she painted one last symbol on her son's pot. When she hung it with the others, La Voisin clasped her hands and faced the procession. Every eye turned to her. "His ashes and spirit ascend. Etienne, know peace."

A sob escaped Ismay when La Voisin inclined her head, ending the simple ceremony. Her kin rushed to console her.

Coco extricated herself from the crowd and found us a moment later, her eyes silvered with tears. She rolled them determinedly toward the sky and heaved a great sigh. "I will not cry. I won't."

I offered her my free elbow, and she linked hers through mine, forming a human chain. The cut at her chest still bled freely, staining the neck of her gown. "It's perfectly acceptable to cry at funerals, Coco. Or anytime you like, for that matter."

"That's easy for you to say. Your tears won't set the world on fire."

"That is so badass." She gave a weak chuckle, and warmth spread through me at the sound. It'd been too long since we'd done this. Too long since we'd spoken so simply. "This place is beautiful."

Ansel nodded to Etienne's pot, where Ismay's blood still gleamed against the white clay. "What do the markings mean?"

"They're spells."

"Spells?"

"Yes, Ansel. Spells. They protect our remains from those who'd use them for foul purposes. Our magic lives on with our ashes," she explained at his furrowed brow. "If we scattered them across the land, we'd only strengthen our enemies." Here, she gave me an apologetic look, but I merely shrugged. Our kin might've been enemies, but we were not them.

Fresh tears gathered as her gaze returned to the pots. To Ismay keening beneath them.

"I hardly even knew him," she whispered. "It's just—all of this—" She waved a hand around us and hung her head. Her arm went slack. "It's my fault."

"What?" Dropping Ansel's elbow, I spun to grip her shoulders. "Coco, no. *None* of this is your fault. Your people—they would never blame you for what happened here."

"That's exactly the point, isn't it?" She wiped her eyes furiously. "They should. I abandoned them. *Twice.* They're freezing and starving and *so* afraid, yet their own *princesse* couldn't be bothered to care. I should've been here, Lou. I should've—I don't know—"

"Controlled the weather?" My hands joined hers, wiping at her tears. Though they burned my skin, I didn't pull away, blinking rapidly against the moisture in my own eyes. "Single-handedly defeated Morgane? You didn't know, Coco. Don't blame yourself."

"Yes, I did." She wrenched the crown from her head, glaring at the glittering rubies. "How can I lead them? How can I even *look* at them? I knew their suffering, and I fled anyway, while their conditions only worsened." She tossed the crown into the snow. "I am no *princesse.*"

To my surprise—perhaps because I'd forgotten he still stood with us—Ansel bent to retrieve it. With impossibly gentle hands, he placed it back on her head. "You're here now. That's what matters."

"And you are our *princesse, mon amour,*" Babette said, appearing at her side. She smiled at Ansel, not guileful but genuine, and straightened Coco's crown. "If it wasn't in your blood, it is in your heart. No other cares so much. You are better than us all."

They both stared at her with such warm affection—such *adoration*—that my heart twisted. I did not envy her this choice.

And Beau . . . he wasn't even here to offer his handsome, sneering face as an alternative. Taking pity on her, I turned her shoulders to face me. "They're right. You're doing everything you can to help them now. When Morgane is dead—when I—afterward, your people will be welcome in the Chateau again. We just need to keep focus."

Though she nodded swiftly, instinctively, her face remained grim. "I'm not sure she'll join us, Lou. She—"

A scream overpowered the rest of her words, and Ismay bolted through the crowd, face wild. "Where is Gabrielle? Where is she?" She whirled, shrieking, "*Gabrielle!*" Though hands reached out to her—though La Voisin herself attempted to calm her with steady words and soothing touches—Ismay ignored them all, darting toward me with frantic eyes. She gripped my arms hard enough to bruise. "Have you seen my daughter?"

Panic closed my throat. "I—"

"Could she have followed the feu follet?" Placing a hand on Ismay's, Coco tried and failed to pry me free. "When was the last time you saw her?"

Tears spilled down Ismay's cheeks, peppering the snow with black flowers. Begonias. I'd learned their meaning from a naturalist tutor at the Chateau. "I—I don't remember. She was with me during the procession, but I let go of her hand to finish Etienne's pot."

Beware.

They meant *beware.*

"Don't panic," another witch said. "This isn't the first time

Gabrielle has run off. It won't be the last."

"I'm sure she's fine," another added. "Overwhelmed, perhaps. So much grief is hard on one so young."

"We were all right here," said a third, voicing what everyone else was thinking. "Surely none could have stolen her from the heart of our coven. We would have seen."

"They're right." Coco finally succeeded in loosening Ismay's grip, and blood rushed back into my arms. "We'll find her, Ismay." When she looked at me, however, her eyes said what her mouth did not: *one way or another.*

I only half listened as the blood witches spread out across the grove in search of her.

I knew in my bones what had happened here. Morgane must've rejoiced when she'd discovered not one but *two* of the king's children hidden in this camp. Her timing, as always, had been unerring. She'd planned this.

Twenty-seven children, Madame Labelle had said. The king had sired twenty-seven children at her last count. Surely finding them would be like finding needles in a haystack. But Morgane was nothing if not tenacious. She would find them, she would torture them, and she would kill them. And it was all because of me.

"Look here!" an unfamiliar witch cried after several long moments. Every person in the clearing turned to stare at what she held in her hands.

A scarlet ribbon.

And there—staining the witch's palms on contact—

Blood.

I closed my eyes in defeat. The memory of Etienne's head on my boot soon rose up to meet me, however, forcing them open once more. It would be Gabrielle's head next. Even now—at this very second—Morgane could be mutilating her tiny body. She would shear her auburn braid and slice her pale throat—

Ismay's cries turned hysterical, and the others soon took up her panicked call.

Gabrielle! Gabrielle! Gabrielle!

Her name echoed within the grove, between the trees. Inside my mind. As if in response, the feu follet flickered out one by one, leaving us in darkness. Despite their frantic attempts to conjure a tracking spell, they knew her fate as well as I did. We all knew.

Gabrielle didn't answer.

She never would.

At long last, Ismay fell to her knees, weeping, pounding the snow in anguish.

I wrapped my arms around my waist, doubling over against the nausea, but a hand caught my nape, forcing me upright. Cold, dark eyes met my own. "Compose yourself." La Voisin's grip hardened. When I tried to wriggle away, biting back a cry of pain, she watched me struggle with grim determination. "Your wish has been granted, Louise le Blanc. The Dames Rouges will join you in Cesarine, and I myself will rend your mother's beating heart from her chest."

THE FIRST PERFORMANCE

Reid

Twilight had settled over Domaine-les-Roses when Claud took to his stage the next evening—a cracked fountain in town square, its basin filled with leaves and snow. Ice coated the rim, but he didn't slip as he danced along it. With fingers as deft as his feet, he plucked a mandolin in a lively rhythm. The audience shouted their approval. Some divided into couples, laughing and spinning wildly, while others showered Seraphine's feet with petals. Her voice rose above the crowd. Unearthly. Passionate. Too beautiful to be human.

When I pulled at my leather trousers, sullen, my mother tipped her cup toward me. Inside, a pink-colored liquid swirled. The villagers of Domaine-les-Roses fermented their own rose petal wine. "This might help, you know."

I arched a brow, readjusting my pants again. "I doubt it."

She'd donned a new dress for our performance tonight. Black and white. Garish. The edges of her mask had been trimmed with ludicrous poms. Still, no one had assaulted *her* with kohl. My eyes burned. Itched.

Zenna hadn't told me how to remove it without blinding myself.

Worse still—Deveraux hadn't provided a shirt with my costume. I'd been forced to strap my bandolier to my bare chest. Though I'd thrown on a coat for modesty's sake—and to protect against the bitter wind—I doubted he'd allow it during *The Red Death's* performance.

I told myself it was for the best. If a Chasseur hid in the audience, he wouldn't recognize me. He wouldn't suspect his once great captain of parading shirtless. Of flinging knives or lining his eyes with cosmetics. Of wearing a mask that extended into horns. I was ridiculous. Debased. Heat burned my throat, my ears, as a memory surfaced.

It won't kill you to live a little, you know.

I'm a Chasseur, Lou. We don't . . . frolic.

Glaring out at the festivities from the stoop of a boulangerie, I watched as Beau wove through the audience with a tin can and hooded cloak. In his free hand, he held a wooden scythe. Deveraux had thought it a fitting addition to the sinister costume. In the alley beside us, Toulouse and Thierry had set up a tent to peddle their services. To lure the weak with promises of fame and fortune-filled futures. Women paraded past them, batting their lashes. Blowing kisses. I couldn't fathom it.

"They're handsome," Madame Labelle explained, smirking as Toulouse caught a girl's hand and kissed it. "You can't fault them for that."

I could, and I did. If the villagers' feathered ensembles were any indication, Domaine-les-Roses was a bizarre town.

"Being young and beautiful isn't a crime, Reid." She pointed to the young woman nearest us, who'd been watching me for the last quarter hour. Bold. Blond. Buxom. "You have many admirers yourself."

"I'm not interested."

"Ah, yes." She winked at her own admirers. "For a moment, I forgot I spoke to the inexorable Saint Reid."

"I'm not a saint. I'm married."

"To whom? Louise Larue? I'm afraid the girl doesn't exist."

My fingers stilled around the knife in my hand. "And what's *my* name, *Maman*?" She stiffened at the word, her eyes flying wide. Vicious satisfaction stole through me. "Diggory, Lyon, or Labelle? Should I choose one arbitrarily?" When she didn't answer, opening and closing her mouth—spots of color blooming high on her cheeks—I turned away. Resumed rotating my knife. "A name isn't a person. I don't care what a stupid piece of paper says hers is. I made a vow, and I will honor it. Besides," I muttered, "these girls look like birds."

These girls aren't Lou.

"You think Louise has never worn feathers in her hair?" Madame Labelle returned to herself with a thready laugh. "Those are swan feathers, dear boy, and we wear them to honor the Maiden. See that bonfire? The villagers will light it for Imbolc next month—as Louise has done every year since her birth, I assure you."

My eyes sharpened with newfound interest on the girl, on the revelers near her. They clapped and stamped their feet to Claud's mandolin, shouting praises. Fingers sticky from honey almond fritters. Rosemary biscuits. Seeded rolls. I frowned. The entire square reeked of vitality. *Vitality*—not fear. "They dare celebrate Imbolc?"

"You are far from Cesarine, my dear." She patted my knee. Belatedly, I glanced at the door behind me, at the doors of all the shops lining the street. Not a single wanted poster. Whether Claud or the villagers had removed them, I didn't know. "In the north, the old ways are still more common than you think. But don't fret. Your brethren are too thick-witted to realize what swan feathers and bonfires mean."

"They aren't thick-witted." A knee-jerk response. I ducked my head when she chuckled.

"I had to enlighten *you*, didn't I? How can you condemn your culture if you don't know your culture?"

"I don't want to know my culture."

Sighing heavily, she rolled her eyes. "Mother's tits, you *are* petulant."

I whirled to face her, incredulous. "*What* did you just say?"

She lifted her chin, hands clasped in her lap. The picture of poise and grace. "Mother's tits. It's a common enough expletive at the Chateau. I could tell you all about life there if you'd unclog the wax from your ears."

"I—I don't want to hear about my mother's tits!" Cheeks flaming, I stood, determined to put as much distance between myself and *that* disturbing image as possible.

"Not *mine*, you blathering ingrate. *The* Mother's. As in the *Triple Goddess*. When a woman grows a child in her womb, her breasts swell in preparation for feeding—"

"No." I shook my head vehemently. "No, no, no, no, *no*. We aren't discussing this."

"Honestly, Reid, it's the most natural thing in the world." She patted the spot beside her. "You've been raised in a grossly masculine environment, however, so I'll forgive your immaturity just this—oh, for goodness' sake, *sit*." She caught my wrist as I tried to flee, pulling me down beside her. "I know I'm in dangerous territory, but I've been meaning to discuss this with you."

I forced myself to look at her. "Breasts?"

She rolled her eyes. "No. Louise." At my bewildered expression, she said, "Are you . . . *sure* about her?"

The question—so unexpected, so *absurd*—jarred me to my senses. "You're kidding."

"No, I'm afraid not." Tilting her chin, she seemed to think hard on her next words. A wise decision. She *was* in dangerous territory. "You met only a few months ago. How well can you really know her?"

"Better than you could," I growled.

"I doubt that very much. Morgane was my dearest childhood friend. I loved her, and she loved me. We were closer than sisters."

"So?"

"So I know how alluring the le Blanc women can be." As if sensing the rising tide in me, she plucked my knife away and sheathed it in her boot. "To be near them is to love them. They're wild and free and excessive. Addictive. They consume us. They make us feel *alive*." My hands trembled. I clenched them into fists. "But they're also dangerous. This will always be your life with her—running, hiding, fighting. You will never know peace. You will never know family. You will never grow old with her, son. One way or another, Morgane will not allow it."

Her words knocked the breath from me. A second passed as I regained it. "No. We'll kill Morgane."

"Louise loves her mother, Reid."

I shook my head vehemently. "*No*—"

"*Every* child loves their mother. Even those with complicated relationships." She didn't look at me, intent on sipping her wine. On watching Deveraux dance. His music faded to a dull roar in my ears. "But we aren't discussing Lou and her mother, or her mother and me. We're discussing the two of you. Louise has started her descent. I know the signs." She nodded at my unspoken question. "Yes. The same thing happened to Morgane. You cannot stop it, and you cannot slow it down. It will consume you both if you try."

"You're wrong." Vitriolic anger coated the words, but Madame Labelle didn't recoil. Her voice only strengthened, sharpened.

"I hope so. I don't want this darkness for her—and I certainly don't want it for you. Think hard on your choice, son."

"I've made my choice."

"There are very few choices in life that can't be unmade."

Deveraux and Seraphine ended their song to roars of applause.

A small part of me recognized it was our turn to take the stage, but I didn't move. I wanted to shake her, to make her understand. *There are very few choices in life that can't be unmade*, she'd said. But I'd already killed the Archbishop. That was one choice I couldn't *unmake*—and even if I could, I wouldn't.

I'd lied when I'd said I'd made my choice.

In truth, there'd been no choice at all. There never had been.

I loved her.

And if I had to run, hide, and fight for that love, I would. For the rest of my life, I would.

"I implore you to choose carefully," Madame Labelle repeated, rising to her feet. Her face was grave. "Louise's story does not end in happiness. It ends in death. Whether at her mother's hands or her own, she will not remain the girl with whom you fell in love."

Pressure built behind my eyes. "I'll love her anyway."

"A noble sentiment. But you owe no one unconditional love. Take it from someone who knows—when a person brings you more hurt than happiness, you're allowed to let them go. You do not have to follow them into the dark." She smoothed her skirts before extending a hand to me. Her fingers were warm, steady, as she led me toward the stage. "Let her go, Reid, before she takes you with her."

I managed not to impale my mother.

Sweat curled my hair, slicked my skin, as I threw my last knife, untethered her from the board, and pushed through the horde of women who'd gathered to watch our performance. They giggled. Tittered. The blonde seemed to be following me. Everywhere I turned, she appeared, dragging two friends in tow. Batting her lashes. Angling her body to brush mine. Irritated, I spotted Beau through the crowd and beelined toward him.

"Here." I hooked his arm and wheeled him in their direction. "Distract them."

A roguish chuckle sounded beneath his hood. "With pleasure."

I slipped away before the girls could follow.

Claud had parked the wagons in the alley behind the St. Martins' tent. No one would bother me there. I'd have a moment alone to think, to *change*. To scrub my face. I half listened to Zenna as I wove through the crowd, cursing her and her stick of kohl. At least she hadn't painted my lips blue, as her own. Beneath her extraordinary cloak, a silver dress rippled as she lifted her arms to begin her performance. Bangles glittered on her wrists.

"Herald! Hark! Hold dear ones close!" The cadence of her voice deepened, turned rich and melodic. A hush fell over the audience. "For this, a tale most grandiose of maiden fair and dragon dire—and their love, which ends in fire."

Oi. Verse.

I kept walking. As suspected, Deveraux had confiscated my coat. The wind cut across my bare skin.

"Tarasque, a fearsome beast was he, but Martha, gentler far was she." Enraptured, the crowd stilled as she continued her story. Even the children. I snorted and walked faster, shivering.

"Tarasque a mighty fire sprayed, but Martha closed her eyes and prayed."

At the last, my footsteps slowed. Halted. Against my better judgment, I turned.

Torchlight cast half of Zenna's face in shadow as she tipped her chin to the sky, clasping her hands in prayer. "'Suffer not for me, O Lord, but spare my kin the dragon's hoard!' And as her cry did pierce the sky, Tarasque looked down from kingdom high." Zenna spread her arms wide, fanning the cloak behind her. In this flickering light, the fabric became wings. Even her eyes seemed to glow. "'Who is this morsel, luscious treat, who calls to me with voice so sweet? I shall eat her, bones and all!' And so Tarasque began to fall."

Despite the cold, there was something in her voice, her expression, that held me there. My mother's words echoed around Zenna's. *Toulouse and Thierry St. Martin—probably even Zenna and Seraphine—are not what they appear.*

Like the others, I listened, rapt, as she wove her tale of woe: how Martha's family—crazed with fear—offered her up to the dragon for slaughter, how Tarasque took her as his bride and the two fell in love. How, eventually, Martha longed to return to her homeland, where her father secretly lay in wait with a magic chain. How he used it to fell Tarasque, to hold him while he burned his own daughter at the stake.

At this, Zenna's eyes found mine. Unadulterated hatred simmered within them. I felt it in my own chest.

Her voice grew louder, stronger, as she finished the story.

"Mighty was the dragon's roar, as he broke the magic ore. And from their heads did bodies part, those men who stole his love—his heart." Across the square, the blonde wept into Beau's shoulder. Actually *wept*. And yet—I couldn't scorn her. "To this day, he roves above, still grieving for his lady love. He withers crops and salts the earth and slaughters men, who rue their birth. Herald! Hark! Hold dear ones close, for this a tale of tears and woe, of maiden dead and dragon dire . . . and his wrath, which ends in fire."

She heaved one last, tremendous exhale, and her breath in the cold night air billowed like smoke from her lips. Absolute silence descended in its wake. Undeterred, she swept to the ground in a magnificent bow. Her cloak pooled around her as liquid starlight. She remained that way, posed, until the audience finally found their voice. They erupted in cheers—louder even than they'd given Deveraux and Seraphine.

I gaped at her. What she'd done with her words—it shouldn't have been possible. When she'd told me Claud collected only the exceptional, I hadn't quite believed her. Now I knew. Now I *felt*. Though I didn't examine the emotion too closely, it wasn't a comfortable one. My face burned. My throat tightened. For those brief moments, Tarasque had felt real—more than real. And I'd felt sorry for a monster who'd kidnapped his bride and beheaded her kin.

Her kin who had burned her.

Never before had I thought of the women I'd burned. Not even Estelle. I'd thought only of Lou, who wasn't like them. Lou, who wasn't like other witches. *How convenient*, she'd told me before we'd parted. *You see what you want to see.*

Had I burned my own kin? I had no way of knowing, but even if I did . . . I couldn't handle such knowledge. Couldn't bear the consequences I'd reap, atone for the pain I'd inflicted. For the love I'd stolen. Once I would've argued such creatures weren't capable of love. But Lou had proved otherwise. Madame Labelle and Coco had proved otherwise.

Perhaps Lou *wasn't* like other witches.

Perhaps they were like her.

Unnerved by the realization, I barreled toward the wagons, heedless of those around me. But when I almost knocked a small boy to his knees, I lurched to a halt, catching his collar to steady him. "*Je suis désolé*," I murmured, dusting off his tattered coat. His shoulders felt thin under my hands. Malnourished.

He clutched a wooden doll to his chest and nodded, keeping his eyes downcast.

Reluctant to release him, I asked, "Where are your parents?"

He gestured back toward the fountain, where Zenna had started an encore. "I don't like dragons," he whispered.

"Smart child." I glanced behind him toward Toulouse and Thierry's tent. "Are you . . . in line?"

Again, he nodded. Perhaps not so smart, after all. I let him go.

When I reached the amber wagon, however, I couldn't help but turn to watch him enter their tent. Though I couldn't see Toulouse's face, I could still see the boy's. He requested the crystal ball. When Toulouse set it on the table between them—right next to a pot of incense—I tensed.

The boy clearly had little coin. He shouldn't be spending it on *magic*.

A hand caught my arm before I could intervene. My free hand flew to my bandolier, but I stopped mid-motion, recognizing Thierry. He'd tied his hair away from his face. The style emphasized his harsh cheekbones. His black eyes. With the hint of a smile, he released me, jerking his chin toward the tent. I frowned as the boy handed Toulouse his doll—a wooden carving, I realized. It had horns. Hooves. Peering closer, I vaguely recognized the shape of it from Lou's bottle of wine. I wracked my brain, failing to remember its name.

Toulouse accepted it carefully with one hand. He stroked the crystal ball with his other.

Within the mist of the glass, shapes began to form: the familiar horned man ruling over flora and fauna, a winged woman crowned with clouds. A third woman with fins soon joined them. The boy clapped in delight as she flitted through ocean waves. His laughter, it sounded . . . wholesome.

My frown deepened.

When he scampered from the tent a moment later, he still clutched his coin in hand—no. A *stack* of coins. Toulouse hadn't taken from the boy. He'd *given* to him. I stared, incredulous, as an elderly woman stepped up to the table.

"Why don't you speak, Thierry?" I asked.

He didn't answer me right away, but I felt his eyes upon my face. I sensed his deliberation. I said nothing more, however, watching as Toulouse gestured to the crystal ball. The woman extended her hand instead, and Toulouse traced the lines on her palm. Her withered mouth lifted in a smile.

At long last, Thierry sighed.

Then—impossibly—I heard a voice in my head. An *actual* voice. Like Toulouse's, but softer. Exceedingly gentle.

Toulouse and I grew up in the streets of Amandine.

I should've been surprised, but I wasn't. Not after everything I'd seen. After everything I'd *done*. Part of me rejoiced at having been right—Toulouse and Thierry St. Martin had magic. The other part couldn't celebrate. Couldn't do anything but study the elderly woman in Toulouse's tent. With each stroke of his fingers, the woman seemed to grow younger, though her features never changed. Her skin rosier. Her eyes clearer. Her hair brighter.

We stole what we needed to survive. Thierry too watched his brother help an old woman feel beautiful again. *At first, we were only pickpockets. A* couronne *here and there to purchase food, clothing. But it was never good enough for Toulouse. He eventually set his sights on wealthier marks—comtes, marquises, even a duc or two.*

He gave me a mournful smile. *By then, Toulouse had learned real wealth didn't come from stolen trinkets, but from knowledge. We stole secrets instead of gems, sold them to the highest bidder. It didn't take long for us to gain a reputation. A man named Gris eventually recruited us to join his crew.* He sighed then, looking down at his hands. *Toulouse and Gris got into an argument. Toulouse threatened to spill his secrets, and Gris retaliated by cutting out my tongue.*

I stared at him in horror. "He cut out your tongue."

In response, Thierry slowly opened his mouth, revealing a hollow circle of teeth. At the back of his throat, the stump of his tongue moved uselessly. Bile rose in my own throat. "But you did nothing. Why were you punished?"

The streets are cruel, huntsman. You're lucky you never knew them. They change you. Harden you. The secrets, the lies necessary to survive... they aren't easily unlearned. His eyes flicked back to his brother. *I don't hold Toulouse responsible for what happened. He did what he felt was necessary.*

"He's the reason you don't have a *tongue*."

Gris knew the best way to keep my brother silent was to threaten me. And it worked. The night I lost my voice is the night he lost his. Toulouse has been a secret keeper ever since. And a better man.

Unable to wrap my head around such fortitude—such acceptance, such steady calm—I changed courses. "You said you lost your voice, yet I can hear it clearly in my mind."

We found our magic that night—and I'd already paid the price of silence. Our ancestors allowed me to communicate a different way.

That caught my attention. "You didn't know you had magic?"

To my surprise, it wasn't Thierry who answered. It was Deveraux. He ambled toward us from the scarlet wagon, hands in his pinstriped pockets. His paisley coat gaped open over a shirt riddled with polka dots, and the peacock feather in his hat bounced with each step. "Tell me, Reid, if you'd never seen the color red, would you know what it looks like? Would you recognize it on that cardinal?" He gestured to the roof of the boulangerie, where a crimson bird had perched. As if sensing our attention, it took flight.

"Er . . . no?"

"And do you think it could fly if it spent its entire life believing it couldn't?"

At my frown, he said, "You've spent a lifetime subconsciously repressing your magic, dear boy. Such an undertaking is not easily undone. It seems only the sight of your wife's lifeless body was powerful enough to release it."

My eyes narrowed. "How do you know who I am?"

"You'll soon find out I know a great deal of things I shouldn't. A rather obnoxious corollary of making my acquaintance, I'm afraid."

Thierry's laughter echoed inside my mind. *It's true.*

"And . . . and you?" I asked, throwing caution to the winds. He knew who I was. *What* I was. There was no sense pretending otherwise. "Are *you* a witch, Monsieur Deveraux?"

"From one honest man to another?" He gave a cheery wink and continued toward the square. "I am not. Does that answer your question?"

A nagging sensation pricked the back of my skull as he disappeared into the crowd.

"No, it doesn't," I muttered bitterly. The old woman rose to leave as well, drawing Toulouse into a bone-crushing hug. If I hadn't seen her transformation myself, I would've sworn she was a different person. When he kissed her cheek in return, she blushed. The gesture—so innocent, so *pure*—twisted sharp in my chest. Combined with Deveraux's enigmatic exit, I felt . . . off balance. Adrift. Such magic wasn't done. This—*all* of this—it wasn't right.

Thierry's hand came down on my shoulder. *You see magic as a weapon, Reid, but you're wrong. It simply . . . is. If you wish to use it for harm, it harms, and if you wish to use it to save . . .* Together, we looked to Toulouse, who tucked a flower behind the woman's ear. She beamed at him before rejoining the crowd. *It saves.*

PART II

Quand le vin est tiré, il faut le boire.
When the wine is drawn, one must drink it.
—French proverb

RED DEATH AND HIS BRIDE, SLEEP ETERNAL

Reid

Zenna's necklace—large, gold, its diamond pendant the size of my fist—battered my face as she leaned over my hair. She'd lathered her hands in a putrid paste to style the waves. I pushed her necklace away irritably. Eyes stinging. If I tossed her kohl out of the wagon, would she notice?

"Don't even think about it," she said, swatting my hand away from the death stick.

Beau had conveniently disappeared when Zenna brought forth her pouch of cosmetics. I hadn't seen my mother since we'd parked in this field, either. The villagers of Beauchêne, a hamlet on the outskirts of La Fôret des Yeux, had constructed an actual stage for troupes passing through—much different from the town squares and pubs in which we'd been performing. They'd set it up here this afternoon. Merchant and food carts had followed. As the sun gradually slipped out of sight, laughter and music drifted into the amber wagon.

My chest ached inexplicably. Six days had passed since my

first performance. Beauchêne was the last stop on Troupe de Fortune's official tour. Within Cesarine, Deveraux and his actors would disappear into the catacombs beneath the city, where the privileged of society mingled with the dregs. Uninhibited, wanton, and masked.

La Mascarade des Crânes, Madame Labelle called it.

The Skull Masquerade.

I'd never heard of such a spectacle. She hadn't been surprised.

Deveraux finished buttoning his vest. "A little more volume on top if you please, Zenna. Ah, yes. That's the ticket!" He winked at me. "You look *resplendissant*, Monsieur Red Death. Absolutely *resplendent*—and as you well should! Tonight is a special night, indeed."

"It is?"

Zenna's eyes narrowed to slits. She wore an emerald gown this evening—or perhaps purple. It shimmered iridescent in the candlelight. She'd painted her lips black. "*Every* night is a special night on the stage, huntsman. If you're bored out there, the audience will be able to tell. A bored audience is a tightfisted audience, and if they don't tip *me* because of *you*, I'm going to be upset." She leveled her gilded brush at my face. "You don't want me to be upset, do you?"

I pushed her brush aside slowly. She brought it right back. "You're always upset," I said.

"Oh, no." She flashed a menacing grin. "You haven't seen me upset."

Deveraux chuckled as the voices outside grew louder. The

shadows longer. "I do not imagine *anyone* will be bored tonight, sweet Zenna."

When they shared a meaningful look, I frowned, certain I'd missed something. "Has there been a change of schedule?"

"How very astute." He flicked my horned mask to me, waggling his brows. "As it so happens, dear boy, *you* are the change of schedule. Tonight, you shall replace Seraphine and me as Troupe de Fortune's opening act."

"And you'd better not foul it up," Zenna warned, threatening me with her hairbrush once more.

"What?" I narrowed my eyes as I slipped on my mask. "Why? And where is my mother?"

"Awaiting you, of course. Never fear, I have already alerted her to the change in schedule. Beau is affixing her to the board as we speak." His eyes glittered with mischief. "Shall we?"

"Wait!" Zenna pulled me back to her cot and carefully arranged a lock of hair over my mask. When I stared at her, bewildered, she shoved me toward the door. "You'll thank me later."

Though there was nothing inherently suspicious in her words—in *either* of their words—my stomach rolled and fluttered as I stepped from the wagon. The sun had almost set, and anticipation thrummed in the evening air. It shone in the faces of those nearest me. In how they bounced on their toes, turned to whisper to their neighbors.

My frown deepened.

Tonight was different.

I didn't know why—I didn't know how—but I felt it.

Still grinning like a cat with cream, humming under his breath, Deveraux ushered me to the stage. A wooden square in the center of the field. Lanterns flickered along its perimeter, casting faint light on the hard-packed snow. On the coats and scarves and mittens. Someone had turned my throwing board away from the audience. I couldn't see my mother, but Beau stood slightly apart, bickering with her. I moved to join them.

Deveraux caught my arm. "Ah, ah, ah." He shook his head, spinning me forward and stripping me of my cloak simultaneously. I scowled. Then shivered. Eyes bright with excitement, the crowd watched me expectantly, clutching goblets of mead and spiced wine. "Are you ready?" Deveraux murmured. Instinctively, I checked the knives in my bandolier, the sword strapped down my back. I straightened my mask.

"Yes."

"Excellent." He cleared his throat then, and a hush fell over the field. He spread his arms wide. His smile spread wider. "Lords and ladies, butchers and bakers, plebeians and patricians—*bonsoir*! Salutations! Drink up, drink up, if you please, and allow me to kindly express my deepest gratitude for your hospitality." The crowd cheered. "If you delight in our performances this evening, please consider gifting the actors a small token of appreciation. Your generosity enables Troupe de Fortune to continue providing Beauchêne with that which we all love—unbridled frivolity and wholesome entertainment."

I glanced down at my leather pants.

Wholesome.

As if reading my mind, someone in the crowd catcalled. Ears burning, I squinted in their general direction, but in the semi-darkness, I couldn't discern the culprit. Just shadows. Silhouettes. A shapely woman and lanky man waved back at me. Scoffing, I looked away and—

My eyes flew open.

"Hear me, all, and hear me true!" Deveraux's voice rang out, but I hardly heard him, inching closer to the stage's edge, searching for the familiar woman and man. They'd disappeared. My heartbeat pounded thunderously in my ears. "Honored guests, tonight and tonight only, we shall witness a singular experience on this stage. A wholly and completely *new* act, a saga—a *paragon*—of dangerous intrigue and deadly romance."

New act? Alarmed, I caught his eye, but he only winked, striding past me to the throwing board. Beau grinned and stepped aside. "And now, without further ado, I present to you our very own *Mort Rouge*"—Deveraux gestured to me before wheeling the board around— "and his bride, *Sommeil Éternel*!"

My jaw dropped.

Strapped to the board, Lou grinned back at me. White butterflies—no, *moths*—covered the upper corner of her face, their wings disappearing into her pale hair. But her dress . . . my mouth went dry. It wasn't a dress at all—more like strands of spider silk. Gossamer sleeves trailed down her shoulders. The neckline plunged to the curve of her waist. From there, the delicate fabric of the skirt—sheer, shredded—blew gently in the wind, revealing her legs. Her *bare* legs. I stared at her, transfixed.

Deveraux coughed pointedly.

My face burned at the sound, and I moved without thinking, tearing my cloak from his hands as I went. Lou snorted when I lifted it to shield her, to cover all that smooth, golden skin—

"Hello, Chass."

Blood roared in my ears. "Hello, *wife*."

She glanced behind me, and this close, her grin seemed . . . arranged, somehow. Fixed. At my frown, she smiled all the brighter, lashes fluttering against the silver dust on her cheeks. Perhaps she was just tired. "We have an audience."

"I *know*."

She eyed my hair, following it to the line of my jaw before straying to my throat. My chest. My arms. "I have to admit," she said with a wink, "the eyeliner works for me."

My stomach contracted. Unsure whether I was angry or ecstatic or—or something else—I stepped closer, tossing the cloak aside. Another step. Close enough now to feel the warmth emanating from her skin. I pretended to check the straps on her wrists. Trailed my fingers down the inside of her thighs, her calves, to tighten the ones on her ankles. "*Where* did you get this dress?"

"Zenna, of course. She likes beautiful things."

Of course. *Fucking* Zenna. Still, relief quickly overwhelmed my disbelief. Lou was here. She was *safe*. Slowly, I dragged my gaze up to hers, lingering at her mouth, before rising. "What are you doing here?" When she moved her chin toward Ansel and Coco, who now hovered beside the stage, I shook my head, interrupting.

"No. *You*. What are *you* doing strapped to this board? It's too dangerous."

"I wanted to surprise you." Her smile stretched farther. "And only actors ride in the wagons."

"I can't throw *knives* at you."

"Why not?" When my frown deepened, she wriggled her hips against the board. Distracting me. Always trying to distract me. "Have I exaggerated your prowess?"

Reluctantly, I took a step back. "No."

Her eyes gleamed wicked. "Prove it."

I don't know what made me do it. Perhaps it was the open challenge in her grin. The feverish flush on her cheeks. The hushed whispers of the audience. Unsheathing a knife from my Balisarda, I walked backward, tossing it in the air and catching it with a muted thud. Before I could rethink—before I could hesitate—I hurled it at the board.

It embedded deep in the wood between her legs. The whole board reverberated from the impact.

The crowd roared their delight.

And Lou—she dropped her head back and laughed.

The sound filled me, bolstered me, and the audience fell away. There was only Lou and her laugh. Her smile. Her *dress*. "Is that it?" she called. I drew another knife in response. And another. And another. Flinging them faster and faster as I closed the distance between us, kissing the lines of her body with each blade.

When I'd thrown the last, I rushed forward, breathless with my own adrenaline. I wrenched the knives from the wood amidst the audience's applause. "How did you reach us so quickly?"

She dropped her head on my shoulder. Her own still shook. "Not magic, if that's what you're asking. Your Sleep Eternal hasn't slept in a week."

"And did you—did you get the alliance?"

Lifting her face, she grinned anew. "We did."

"*How?*"

"We—" Something shifted in her eyes, in her smile, and she planted a kiss on the sensitive skin between my neck and shoulder. "It was Coco. You should've seen her. She was brilliant—a natural leader. It took her no time at all to convince her aunt to join us."

"Really?" I paused in pulling another knife free. "La Voisin wouldn't even let me *enter* her camp. How did Coco persuade her to work with us so quickly?"

"She just—the advantages of an alliance outweighed the disadvantages. That's all."

"But she would've known the advantages beforehand." A shard of confusion pierced my thoughts. Too late, I realized Lou had tensed in the straps. "She still refused."

"Maybe she didn't know. Maybe someone enlightened her."

"Who?"

"I already *told* you." Her smile vanished now, and her expression hardened abruptly, all pretenses gone. "It was Coco. *Coco* enlightened her." When I balked at her tone, drawing back, she sighed and looked away. "They're meeting us in Cesarine in two days. I thought you'd be happy."

My brows furrowed. "I am happy, it just—"

It doesn't make sense.

Something had happened at the blood camp. Something Lou wouldn't tell me.

When she finally returned my gaze, her eyes were unreadable. Carefully blank. Controlled. Like she'd pulled shutters between us, blocking me out. She jerked her chin to my knives. "Are we done here?"

As if he'd been listening, Deveraux descended upon us, his gaze darting across the audience. "Is something wrong, poppets?"

I tugged the last knife from the wood, struggling to keep my voice even. "Everything is fine."

"Shall—shall we continue with the grand finale, then?"

Walking backward once more, I drew the sword from its sheath down my spine. "Yes."

A ghost of a smile touched Lou's lips. "Aren't you going to set it on fire?"

"No." I stared at her, thinking hard, as Deveraux wrapped the blindfold around my mask. My eyes. Without my vision, I saw another scene clearly within my mind. The dust. The costumes. The blue velvet. I smelled the cedar wood and oil lamps. I heard her voice. *I'm not hiding anything, Reid.*

It had snowed that evening. Her hair had been damp beneath my fingertips. *If you aren't comfortable enough to tell me, it's my fault, not yours.*

Lou was keeping secrets again.

I forced myself to focus, to listen as Deveraux pulled the

handle, and the board began to move. With each soft *whisk*, I counted its rotation, established its speed, visualized the location of Lou's body in relation to each spin. I'd been nervous throwing this sword at my mother the first time, but I'd known trust was critical to success. I had to trust her, and she had to trust me.

We never missed.

Now—standing before Lou—I visualized the point above her head. Just a few scant inches of wood. Five, to be precise. There was no room for error. Taking a deep breath, I waited. I waited.

I let my sword fly.

The audience gasped, and the sound of sword striking board vibrated in my bones. I tore off my blindfold.

Chest heaving, mouth parted, Lou stared back at me with wide eyes. The sword had lodged not atop her head, but beside it—so close it'd drawn a thin line of blood on her cheek. One of her moth wings fluttered to the stage, severed, as she slowed to a stop. The audience cheered wildly. Their shouts, their praise, their laughter—it made little sense to me.

I'd missed.

And Lou was keeping secrets again.

SHE LOVES ME NOT

Lou

When the last villagers retreated to their homes, bleary-eyed and stumbling, Claud Deveraux broke out the Boisaîné to celebrate our reunion. "We should dance," I murmured, dropping my head to Reid's shoulder. He rested his cheek on my hair. Together, we sat on the amber wagon's steps, huddled beneath a patchwork quilt, and watched as Coco and Ansel joined hands with Zenna and Toulouse. They staggered round and round in a frenzied circle to Deveraux's mandolin. Each tried and failed to remember the lyrics to "Big Titty Liddy." With every bottle of wine at their feet, their laughter grew louder, and their song grew stupider.

I wanted to join them.

When I yawned, however—my eyelids impossibly heavy from exhaustion and wine—Reid brushed a kiss to my temple. "You're exhausted."

"They're butchering Liddy's song."

"*You* butcher Liddy's song."

"Excuse me?" I leaned forward, turning to glare at him. A

smile still tugged at my lips. "Thank you *very* much, but my enthusiasm is everything."

"Except a full vocal range."

Delighted, I widened my eyes in mock outrage. "All right, then. Fine. Let's hear your *full vocal range*." When he said nothing—only smirked—I poked him in the ribs. "Go on. Show me how it's done, O Melodious One. The plebeians await your instruction."

Sighing, he rolled his eyes and scooted away from my finger. "Forget it, Lou. I'm not singing."

"Oh no!" I followed like a plague, poking and prodding every inch of him I could reach. He dodged my attempts, however, and surged to his feet. I bounded to the top step in response, leaning forward until we were nearly nose to nose. The blanket fell to the ground, forgotten. "I'm prepared for shock and awe here, Chass. Your voice had better hypnotize snakes and charm the pants from virgins. It'd better be the love child of Jesus and—"

His kiss swallowed the rest of my words. When we broke apart, he murmured, "I have no interest in charming the pants from virgins."

Smirking, I wound my arms around his neck. He hadn't mentioned our spat onstage or the black fox that slept in our wagon. I hadn't mentioned the cut on my cheek or that said fox's name was Brigitte. "Not even Ansel?" I asked.

After our performance, Coco and Ansel had cornered me, asking how Reid had received the news of his siblings' murders. My ensuing silence had exasperated them. *Their* ensuing silence had exasperated me. It wasn't that I—that I didn't *want* to tell Reid the whole truth, but what purpose would it serve? He didn't *know* Etienne and Gabrielle. Why should he mourn them? Why should he take responsibility for their deaths? And he *would* take responsibility. Of that much, I was certain. If he knew my mother had started targeting his individual siblings, his focus would shift to protecting them instead of defeating Morgane—an illogical strategy, as her death was the *only* way of ensuring their safety.

No, this wasn't a lie. I hadn't *lied* to him. This was just . . . a secret.

Everyone had secrets.

Reid shook his head. "Ansel isn't really my type."

"No?" I pressed closer, the word a breath against his lips, and he climbed the steps slowly, backing me against the wagon door. His hands braced on either side of my face. Caging me there. "What *is* your type?"

He trailed his nose along my shoulder. "I *love* girls who can't sing."

Scoffing, I planted my hands on his chest and shoved. "You *ass*."

"What?" he asked innocently, stumbling backward, nearly busting said ass in the snow. "It's the truth. When your voice cracks on a high note, it gets me—"

"BIG WILLY BILLY TALKED SORT OF SILLY," I bellowed, thrusting a hand on each hip. I stalked toward him, trying and failing to repress my laughter. "BUT HIS KNOB WAS AS LONG AS HIS ARM." When he spluttered, glancing behind toward the others, I said loudly, "Is this what you like, Chass? Does this make you hot?"

The revelry behind us ceased at my words. Every eye fell upon us.

A flush crept up Reid's cheeks, and he lifted a placating hand. "All right, Lou. You've made your point—"

"ITS SHAPE DOWN HIS THIGH SOON CAUGHT LIDDY'S EYE—"

"*Lou.*" Darting forward when Madame Labelle giggled, he attempted to cover my mouth, but I danced out of reach, looping elbows with Beau and spinning wildly.

"—AND IN NINE MONTHS, A NIPPER WAS BORN!" Over my shoulder, I called, "Did you hear that, Reid? A *nipper*. Because *sex*—"

Deveraux clapped his hands together and cackled. "Excellent, excellent! I knew Liddy, you know, and a lovelier creature I will never again meet. Such a vivacious spirit. She would have quite enjoyed knowing she is now beloved by the entire kingdom."

"Wait." I pivoted toward Deveraux, dragging Beau with me as I went. "Big Titty Liddy was a real person?"

"And you *knew* her?" Beau asked incredulously.

"Of course she was. And young William. It's an unfortunate fact the two didn't remain together after the birth of their dear daughter, but such is the nature of relationships nourished solely by appetites of passion."

Reid and I exchanged a glance.

We both looked away quickly.

And *that* is when I saw Coco and Ansel slipping away together.

Unfortunately, Beau saw it too. Scoffing, he shook his head and marched back to the campfire, bending low to snag a bottle of wine as he went. Reid stared after him with an inscrutable expression. As for me, I tried to discern Coco's and Ansel's silhouettes across the field, where they stood near a stream on the edge of the forest. They looked . . . close. *Suspiciously* close. *Alarmingly* close.

Deveraux interrupted my furtive observation. "You fear for your friend's heart."

"I—what?" I tore my gaze from them. "What are you talking about?"

"Your friend." Sagely, he nodded to Ansel. "*La jeunesse éternelle.* He will remain eternally young. There are some who do not appreciate such innocence in a man."

"There are some who are stupid," I said, craning my neck to watch as Ansel—

My eyes widened.

Oh my god.

Oh my god, oh my god, oh my *god.*

They were kissing. They were *kissing.* Coco had—she'd leaned in, and Ansel—he was actually doing it. He was playing the game, making his move. I inched closer, pride and fear swelling within me in equal measure.

Deveraux smirked and arched a brow. "Obviously, there are also some who *do* appreciate it."

Reid dragged me back to his side. "It's none of our business."

I cast him an incredulous look. "You're kidding, right?"

"No—"

But I didn't listen to the rest of his reprimand. Shaking off his hand, I slipped around the wagons. Perhaps it was the wine that compelled me, or perhaps it was the way Coco held herself—stiff and awkward—like . . . like she . . .

Like she was kissing her kid brother. Shit.

She withdrew for one second, two, *three*, before leaning in to try again.

I crept around the stage, hiding within its shadows, close enough to hear her murmur for him to stop. Shaking her head, she wrapped her arms around her waist as if trying to make herself as small as possible. As if trying to disappear. "Ansel, please." She struggled to look at him. "Don't cry. This isn't—I didn't mean—"

Shit, shit, *shit*.

I pressed closer to the stage, straining to hear her whispered explanation. When a hand touched my back, I nearly leapt out of my skin. Reid crouched behind me, radiating disapproval. "I'm serious, Lou," he repeated, voice low. "This is their business, not ours."

"Speak for yourself." Peeking back around the corner of the stage, I watched as Ansel wiped a tear from his cheek. My heart twisted. "Those are my best friends out there. If things get messy between them, I'm the one who'll have to clean it up. It is absolutely my business."

"Lou—"

Coco's head whipped in our direction, and I lurched backward, knocking straight into Reid. He managed to catch himself before he toppled the entire stage, grabbing my shoulders for balance and pulling us both to the ground. I turned my head to whisper against his cheek. "Shhh."

His breath at my ear sent chills down my spine. "This is wrong."

"By all means, then, go back to the wagons."

He didn't, and together, we leaned forward, hanging on Coco's every word.

"I didn't mean for this happen, Ansel." She buried her face in her hands. "I'm so sorry, but this was a mistake. I shouldn't have—I didn't mean for it to happen."

"A mistake?" Ansel's voice broke on the word, and he stepped closer to clutch her hand. Fresh tears trickled down his cheeks. "You kissed me. *You* kissed *me*. How can you say it was a mistake? Why did you kiss me again if it was?"

"Because I needed to know!" Wincing at her outburst, she dropped his hand and started to pace. "Look," she whispered furiously, "I'm a little drunk—"

His face hardened. "You aren't that drunk."

"Yes, I am." She pushed the hair away from her face in agitation. "I'm drunk, and I'm acting like an idiot. I don't want to give you the wrong impression." She clutched his hands then, winging them. "You're a good person, Ansel. Better than me. Better than everyone. You're—you're *perfect*. Anyone would be lucky to have you. I just—I—"

"Don't love me."

"No! I mean *yes*." When he pulled away, turning his face from hers, she visibly wilted. Her voice dropped so low that Reid and I strained forward in our desperation to hear. "I know you think you're in love with me, Ansel, and I—I wanted to be in love with you too. I kissed you because I needed to know if I ever could be. I kissed you again because I needed to be sure."

"You needed to be sure," he repeated. "So . . . each time you touched me . . . made me blush, made me *feel* like you—like you might want me too . . . you didn't know. You gave me hope, but you weren't *sure*."

"Ansel, I—"

"So which is it?" Ansel held himself rigid, his back to us. Though I couldn't see his face, his voice sounded sharper than I'd ever heard it. Meaner. In its pitch, I could almost *see* his anguish, a living thing that tormented them both. "Do you love me or not?"

Coco didn't answer for a long while. Reid and I waited with bated breath, not daring to speak. To even move. Finally, she laid a gentle hand on his back.

"I do love you, Ansel. I just . . . don't love you the same way you love me." When he flinched, violent in his reaction, she dropped her hand and backed away. "I'm so sorry."

Without another word, she turned and fled down the stream.

Ansel's shoulders drooped in her absence, and I moved to approach him—to fold him in my arms and hold him until his tears subsided—but Reid's arms tightened on my waist. "Don't," he said, voice low. "Let him process."

I stilled beneath his touch, listening as Deveraux announced it was time for bed. Ansel wiped his tears, hurrying to help him clean up. "Typical Ansel," I whispered, feeling physically sick. "Why does he have to be so—so—"

At last, Reid released me. "He didn't deserve what she did to him."

Conflicting emotions warred within me. "She didn't *do* anything. Flirtation is hardly a cardinal sin."

"She led him on."

"She—" I struggled to articulate my thoughts. "She can't change the way she feels. She doesn't *owe* him anything."

"It wasn't just harmless flirtation, Lou. She knew Ansel's feelings. She used them to make Beau jealous."

I shook my head. "I don't think she meant to. You have to understand . . . Coco has always been beautiful. She grew up with suitors flocking to her, even as a child, which means she grew up quickly. She's confident and vain and guileful because of it—and I *love* her—but she isn't cruel. She didn't mean to hurt Ansel. She just . . . didn't understand the depth of his emotion."

Reid scoffed and shoved to his feet, extending a hand to me. "No. She didn't."

While the others prepared for bed, dousing the fire and gathering empty bottles of wine, I snuck down the stream to find Coco. It didn't take long. Within a few yards, I found her sitting beside a holly tree, face buried in her arms. I sat next to her without a word. The water trickled gently before us, counting the seconds. It would've been peaceful if not for the snow soaking through my pants.

"I'm a piece of shit," she finally mumbled, not lifting her head.

"Nonsense." In a practiced movement, I parted her hair, dividing each half into three sections near her crown. "You smell much better than shit."

"Did you hear us?"

"Yes."

She groaned and lifted her head, teary-eyed. "Did I ruin everything?"

My fingers maintained their deft movements, adding new strands of hair to each section as I braided. "He'll be fine, Coco. He won't die of a broken heart. It's actually a rite of passage for most." I finished the first braid, leaving the tail loose. "Alec broke mine, and I lived. Babette broke yours. Without them, we wouldn't have found the next one. I wouldn't have found Reid."

She stared out at the water. "You're saying it's fine I broke his heart."

"I'm *saying* if you hadn't done it, someone else would have. Very few of us settle down with our first loves."

She groaned again, tipping her head back in my hands. "Oh, *god*. I was his first love."

"Tragic, isn't it? I suppose there's no accounting for taste." When I finished the second braid, I snapped a sprig of holly from the nearest branch, stripping the berries and tucking them into her hair. She sat in silence while I worked. At last, I crawled around to sit in front of her. "Give him time, Coco. He'll come around."

"No." She shook her head, and her braids came undone. The berries sprinkled the snow around us. "He'll hate me. He might've forgiven the flirtation, but I never should have kissed him."

I said nothing. It would do little good to tell her what she already knew.

"I *wanted* to love him, you know?" She gripped her elbows against the cold, hunching slightly. "That's why I did it. That's why I never shut him down when he *looked* at me like that—all doe-eyed and smitten. It's why I kissed him twice. Maybe I should've tried a third."

"Coco."

"I feel *terrible*." Fresh tears brimmed in her eyes, but she stared determinedly at the sky. Not a single one escaped. "I never wanted to hurt him. Maybe—maybe this ache in my chest means I'm wrong." She looked up abruptly and clutched my hand. "I've never hurt over romance like this in my entire life, not even when Babette abandoned me. Maybe that means I *do* care for him. Maybe—Lou, maybe I'm misinterpreting my feelings!"

"No, I don't think—"

"He's certainly handsome enough." She spoke over me now, her desperation bordering on hysteria. "I *need* someone like him, Lou—someone who's kind and caring and *good*. Why don't I ever like the good ones? *Why?*" Her face crumpled, and her hands relaxed around mine. She dropped her chin in defeat. "We need mothers for this kind of shit."

With a snort, I leaned back on my hands and closed my eyes, savoring the icy bite of snow between my fingers. The moonlight on my cheeks. "Isn't that the truth."

We lapsed into silence, each caught in the tempest of our

thoughts. Though I'd never admitted it to anyone before this moment, I yearned for my mother. Not the scheming Morgane le Blanc. Not the all-powerful La Dame des Sorcières. Just . . . my mother. The one who'd played with me. Listened to me. Wiped my tears when I'd thought I would die of a broken heart.

When I opened my eyes, I caught her staring at the water once more. "Aunt Josephine says I look like her," she said, emotion thick in her voice. "That's why she can't stand the sight of me." She tucked her knees to her chest, resting her chin on them. "She hates me."

I didn't ask her to clarify between La Voisin or her mother. The pain in her eyes would be there with either.

Sensing silence would comfort her more than words, I didn't speak. She'd waited a long time for the right moment to tell me this, I realized. Besides—what words could I possibly offer her? The Dames Blanches' practice of forsaking their children—their sons without magic and their daughters with the wrong kind— was aberrant. No words could ever make it right.

When she finally spoke again, a wistful smile touched her lips. "I can't remember much of her, but sometimes—when I really concentrate—I catch glimpses of blue, or light shining through water. The smell of lilies. I like to think it was her perfume." Her smile faded, and she swallowed hard, as if the pleasant memory had turned sour on her tongue. "It's all ridiculous, of course. I've been with Aunt Josephine since I was six."

"Did she ever visit you? Your mother?"

"Not once." Again, I waited, knowing she had more to say. "On my tenth birthday, I asked Aunt Josephine if *Maman* would come to celebrate." She clutched her knees tighter against the wind. Or perhaps the memory. "I still remember Aunt Josephine's face. I've never seen such loathing before. She . . . she told me my mother was dead."

The confession struck me with unexpected force. I frowned, blinking rapidly against the stinging in my eyes, and looked away to compose myself. "Is she?"

"I don't know. I haven't had the nerve to ask about her since."

"Shit, Coco." Eager to distract her, to distract myself, I shook my head, casting about for a change of subject. *Anything* would be preferable to this distressing conversation. I'd thought Morgane to be cruel. Perspective was a curious thing. "What was the book in your aunt's tent?"

She turned her head to face me, frowning. "Her grimoire."

"Do you know what's in it?"

"Spells, mostly. A record of her experiments. Our family tree."

I repressed a shudder. "What sort of spells? It seemed . . . alive."

She snorted. "That's because it's creepy as hell. I've only flipped through it once in secret, but some of the spells in there are evil—curses, possession, sickness, and the like. Only a fool would cross my aunt."

Now I couldn't repress my shudder, no matter how hard I tried. Mercifully, Claud chose that moment to approach. "*Mes chéries*, though I am loath to interrupt, the hour has grown late. Might I suggest you both retire to the amber wagon? You are undoubtedly exhausted from your travels, and it is unwise to linger alone here at night."

I climbed to my feet. "Where is Reid?"

Claud cleared his throat delicately. "Alas, Monsieur Diggory finds himself otherwise occupied at the moment." At my arched brow, he sighed. "After a poorly timed jest from His Royal Highness, the young master Ansel has succumbed to tears. Reid is comforting him."

Coco sprang to her feet, hissing like an incredulous, angry cat. When she at last found her words, she snarled, "I'm going to kill him." Then she stormed back toward camp with a violent stream of curses. Beau—who spotted her coming across the way—changed directions abruptly, fleeing into a wagon.

"Do it slowly!" I called after her, adding a curse or two of my own. Poor Ansel. Though he'd be mortified if he saw Coco sweeping in to save him, *someone* needed to kick Beau's ass.

Claud chuckled as a shout rent the air behind us. I turned, startled—and perhaps a bit pleased, expecting to see Beau wetting down his leg—and froze.

It wasn't Beau at all.

A half dozen men spilled into the clearing, swords and knives drawn.

AN UNEXPECTED REUNION

Lou

"Get down," Claud ordered, his voice abruptly deeper, more assertive. He pushed me flat to the ground behind him, angling his body to shield mine. But I still peeked beneath his arm, frantically searching for the blue coats of Chasseurs. There were none. Dressed in tattered rags and fraying coats, these men reeked instead of bandits. Literally *reeked*. I could smell them from where we lay, thirty paces away.

Claud had warned us about the danger of the road, but I hadn't taken him seriously. The thought of mere men accosting us had been laughable in light of witches and huntsmen. But that realization wasn't what made me gape. It wasn't what made me struggle to rise, to race *toward* the thieves instead of away from them.

No. It was something else. *Someone* else.

At their back—wielding a blade as black as the dirt on his face—stood Bas.

"*Shit.*" Horrified, I elbowed Claud in the side as Bas's and Reid's eyes met. He didn't budge. "Let me up! Let me up *now*!"

"Do not draw attention to yourself, Louise." He held me down with a single arm, implausibly strong. "Remain still and quiet, or I'll throw you in the creek—a most unpleasant experience, I assure you."

"What the hell are you talking about? That's *Bas*. He's an old friend. He won't harm me, but he and Reid look like they're about to tear each other to pieces—"

"Let them," he said simply.

Helpless, I watched as Reid drew his Balisarda from his bandolier. The last of his knives. The rest remained embedded in his turning board from our performance. Bas's face twisted into a sneer. "*You*," he spat.

His companions continued herding the others into the center of the campsite. We were woefully outnumbered. Though Ansel brandished his knife, they disarmed him within seconds. Four more men erupted from the wagon, dragging Coco and Beau out with them. Already, they'd tied their wrists and ankles with rope, and both struggled in vain to free themselves. Madame Labelle, however, didn't fight her captor. She acquiesced calmly, making casual eye contact with Toulouse and Thierry.

A short man with bone-white skin strolled toward Reid and Bas, picking his teeth with a dagger.

"And just who might this be, eh, Bas?"

"This is the man who killed the Archbishop." Bas's voice was unrecognizable, hard as the steel in his hands. His hair had grown long and matted in the months since I'd last seen him, and a wicked scar forked down his left cheek. He looked . . . sharp.

Hungry. The opposite of the soft, cosseted boy I'd known. "This is the man who killed the Archbishop. Fifty thousand *couronnes* for his capture."

Bone White's eyes lit up in recognition. "Reid Diggory. How 'bout that?" He laughed—a jarring, ugly sound—before slapping one of the wagons in delight. "Dame Fortune's right, innit? Here we was thinking we'd pinch a few coins, maybe cop a touch wit' a pretty actress, and friggin' *Reid Diggory* falls in our lap!"

Another bandit—this one tall and balding—stepped forward, tugging Coco along with him. His knife remained at her throat. "Innit there another one travelin' wit' him, boss? A girl wit' a nasty scar at her throat? Posters say she's a witch."

Shit, shit, *shit*.

"Keep quiet," Claud breathed. "Do not move."

But that was stupid. We were in plain sight. All the idiots had to do was glance down the stream, and they'd spot us—

"Yer right." Bone White scanned the rest of the troupe eagerly. "Hundred thousand *couronnes* for the head o' that one."

Reid's hand tensed on his Balisarda, and Bone White smiled, revealing brown teeth. "I'd hand that over if I was you, sonny. Don't be gettin' no delusions of grandeur." He gestured to Coco, and Baldy tightened his hold. "'Less you wanna see this pretty little thing without her head too."

To my shock, Bas laughed. "Take her head. I'd like to see everything else, though."

"*What* did you just say?" Coco spluttered, indignant. "Did you just—*Bas*. It's *me*. It's Coco."

Grin slipping, he tilted his head to study her. He gripped her chin between his thumb and finger. "How do you know my name, *belle fille*?"

"Unhand her," Beau commanded in a valiant attempt at gallantry. "By order of your crown prince."

Bone White's eyes lit up. "What's this, then? The crown prince?" He crowed with delight. "I didn't recognize yeh, Yer Highness. Yer an awful long way from home."

Beau glared down at him. "My father will hear about this, I assure you. You will be punished."

"Will I, now?" Bone White circled him with a leer. "By my reckonin', I'd wager *yer* the one who'll be punished, Yer Highness. Been gone weeks now, haven' yeh? The city's all in an uproar. Yer dad is tryin' to keep it quiet-like, but rumors spread. His precious boy has taken up with *witches*. Can yeh imagine? No, I don' think I'll be punished for returnin' yeh home to him. I think I'll be rewarded." To Reid, he added, "The *knife*. Hand it over. Now."

Reid didn't move.

Baldy's blade left a thin line of blood at Coco's throat. "Bas—" she said sharply.

"How do you know my *name*?" he repeated.

"Because I know *you*." Coco struggled harder, and the blade bit deeper. Bas's frown deepened inexplicably, as did my own. What was he doing? Why was he pretending not to know her? "We're friends. Now let me *go*."

"D'yeh smell that, then?" Distracted, Bone White stepped toward her, staring at her blood with a peculiar, hungry expression. "Smells like somethin's burnin'." He nodded to himself. A pleased smile stretched across his face. "Y'know I've heard rumors o' a witch o' the blood. They don' cast wit' their hands like the others. Swore I saw one meself once. Smelled it, more like. Nearly singed my nostrils off."

Bas's voice hardened with conviction. "I've never heard of such a thing, and I've never seen this woman before in my life."

Coco's eyes widened. "You *asshole.* We practically lived together for a *year*—"

Baldy clubbed her in the head. Seizing his opportunity, Reid lunged—at the exact same second Coco twisted, trying to coat Baldy's wrist with her blood. Skin sizzling, the man shrieked, and all three collided in a mass of tangled limbs. More men sprang forward amidst the tussle, wrenching away Reid's Balisarda and pinning them both to the ground. Coco's blood hissed where it touched the snow. Smoke curled around her face.

Madame Labelle looked on with an anxious expression, but still she didn't move.

"Well," Bone White said pleasantly, still grinning, "that solves that, then, dinnit? She'll fetch a right nice price wit' the Chasseurs. We passed some o' them just up the road. Smarmy bastards. They've been scourin' the forest for weeks, makin' a right mess for us, haven't they? O'course, I might just keep 'er blood for meself. Near priceless it is, to the right buyer." Bone White scratched his chin thoughtfully before gesturing to Reid. "And this one? How abouts do you be knowin' Reid Diggory, son?"

Bas's grip on his knife tightened. "He arrested me in Cesarine."

Trembling with rage, he knelt beside Reid, sticking his knife in his face. "It's because of you that my cousin disinherited me. It's because of *you* that he left me for dead in the streets."

Reid stared at him impassively. "I didn't murder those guards."

"It was an accident. I only did it because—" Bas spasmed abruptly. Blinking rapidly, he shook his head to clear it. "Because—" He glanced at Coco in confusion. She frowned back at him. "I—why—?"

"Stop yer blatherin', boy, and get to the point!"

"I—I don't . . . remember," Bas finished, brow furrowed. He shook his head once more. "I don't remember."

Baldy regarded Coco warily. "Witchcraft, it is. Eerie stuff."

Bone White snorted in disgust. "I don't give a damn about witchcraft. All I care about is my *couronnes*. Now, Bas, tell me—is the other one here? The one they're all after?" He rubbed his hands together greedily. "Just think what we can do wit' a hundred thousand *couronnes*."

"There are stilts in the wagon, if you're thinking prosthetics." Coco bared her teeth in a smile, jerking her chin toward his diminutive legs. The men tried and failed to force her face into the ground. "I'm sure with the right pants, no one would ever know."

"Shut yer face," Bone White snarled, his cheeks flushing crimson. "A'fore I shut it for you."

Coco's grin vanished. "Please do."

But it seemed Bone White—despite claiming he didn't care about witches—had a healthy respect for them. Or perhaps fear.

He merely grunted and turned back to Bas. "Well? Is she here?"

I held my breath.

"I don't—" Bas's eyes flicked over the troupe members. "I don't know."

"What d'ya mean, *you don't know*? She's supposed to be travelin' wit this one, innit she?" He pointed his knife at Reid.

Bas shrugged weakly. "I've never seen her before."

Relief surged through me, and I closed my eyes, expelling a sigh. Beneath his rather unfortunate new exterior, perhaps Bas was still in there. My old friend. My confidant. I *had* saved his skin in the Tower, after all. It would've been poor repayment for him to watch as his friends chopped off my head. This—this thing with Coco—it was merely an act. He was trying to help us, to save us.

Bone White growled in frustration. "Search the area."

At the command, my eyes snapped open—just in time to see Reid glance in my direction. When Bone White followed his gaze, I suppressed a groan. "Is she hidin' behind that tree, then?" he asked eagerly, pointing his knife straight at us. "Over there, boys! She's over there! Find her!"

"Quiet." Claud's whisper sent a tingle down my spine. The air around us felt heavy, thick with spring rains and storm clouds, pine sap and lichen. "Do not move."

I obeyed his command—hardly daring to breathe—as Bas and one other bandit stalked toward us. The rest remained poised in a circle around the troupe, watching as Baldy began to tie Coco's hands and feet. She eyed his knife as if contemplating whether to impale herself on it. With a bit more blood, these idiots would rue the day they'd been born.

"I don't see nothin'," Bas's companion muttered, circling us with a frown.

Bas peered into the holly branches, his eyes skipping past us as if we weren't there at all. "Me either."

Claud's hand tightened on my shoulder, silently warning me not to move.

"Anythin'?" Bone White called.

"Nothin'!"

"Well, go on and check down the creek then, Knotty! We'll find her."

Bas's companion grunted and hobbled away. Without a backward glance in our direction, Bas rejoined Bone White.

"What was that?" I whispered, confusion heightening to panic. None of this made sense. Even Bas wasn't this good of an actor. He'd stared at me—*through* me—without giving a single indication he saw me. Not a wink or brush of his hand. Not even *eye contact*, for shit's sake. And *why* hadn't Madame Labelle yet trounced these idiots? "What just happened?"

The pressure at my back relented slightly, though Claud still didn't release me. "Illusion."

"What? They—they think we're part of the tree?"

"Yes."

"*How?*"

He fixed me with his gaze, uncharacteristically serious. "Shall I explain now, or shall we wait until the imminent danger has passed?"

I scowled at him, returning my attention to the others. Bas had started helping Baldy with the ropes. When Baldy moved to bind Reid, Bas stopped him with a nasty smile. "I'll take that one."

Reid returned the smile. In the next second, he thrust his head backward—breaking his first captor's nose—and rolled to his back, kicking the second in the knees. I almost cheered. With uncanny speed, he snatched his Balisarda from the howling man and exploded to his feet. Bas reacted with equal swiftness—as if he'd expected the attack—and used Reid's momentum against him.

Though I cried out a warning—though Reid tried to correct—it was too late.

Bas plunged his knife into Reid's belly.

"No," I breathed.

Stunned, Reid staggered sideways, his blood spattering the snow. Bas grinned triumphantly, twisting the knife deeper, slicing upward through skin and muscle and sinew until white glinted through crimson. Bone. Bas had gutted him to the bone.

I moved without thinking.

"Louise!" Claud hissed, but I ignored him, throwing off his arm and scrambling to my feet, racing to where Reid fell to his knees. "Louise, *no*!"

The thieves gawked as I sprinted toward them—probably stupefied at seeing a tree transform into a human—but I couldn't think past the blood roaring in my ears.

If Reid didn't—if Coco couldn't heal—

I would kill Bas. I would *kill* him.

Throwing my dagger at Coco's feet—praying she could reach it—I dropped to my knees in front of Reid. Mayhem erupted around us. Finally, *finally*, Madame Labelle burst free of her ropes. With each flick of her hand, bodies flew. A small part of my brain realized Toulouse and Thierry had joined her, but I couldn't focus, couldn't hear anything but the thieves' panicked cries, couldn't *see* anything but Reid. *Reid.*

Even injured, he still tried to push me behind him. The movement was weak, however. Too much of his blood had been lost. *Decidedly* too many of his innards were on display. "Don't be stupid," I said, trying to hold pieces of his flesh together. Bile rose in my throat as more blood spilled from his mouth. "Keep still. Just—just—"

But the words wouldn't come. I glanced to Coco helplessly, trying to summon a pattern. *Any* pattern. But this wound was mortal. Only another's death would heal it, and I couldn't—I *couldn't* trade Coco. It'd be like ripping out my own heart. And Ansel—

Ansel. Could I—?

Lou is different when she uses magic. Her emotions, her judgment— she's been erratic.

No. I shook my head vehemently against the thought, but it lodged there like a growth, a tumor, poisoning my mind. Reid's blood soaked my front, and he slumped forward in my arms, pressing his Balisarda into my hand. His eyes closed.

No no no—

"Well, looky 'ere." Bone White's snarl sounded behind me.

Too close. His hand fisted in my hair, ripping my head back, and his other tugged aside the ribbon at my throat. He traced my scar. "My little witch has finally come out o' hidin'. Yeh might've changed yer hair, but yeh can' change yer scar. Yer comin' wit' me."

"I don't think so." Coco descended on him like a bat out of Hell, my knife flashing, slashing his wrist.

"You stupid bitch." With a howl, he released my hair and swiped furiously at her. His fingers caught her shirt, and he pulled her to him, forcing her back against his chest. "I'll drain yeh like I drained yer kin, sell all this pretty blood to the highest bidder at the Skull Masquerade—"

Coco's eyes widened, and her face contorted with rage. Bringing her own dagger up sharply, she plunged it deep into his eye. He crumpled instantly, screaming and clutching his face. Blood poured between his fingers. She kicked him once for good measure before dropping to her knees beside Reid. "Can you heal him?" I asked desperately.

"I can try."

BLOOD AND HONEY

Reid

I slammed back into my body with excruciating pain. Gasping for breath, I clung to the first thing I touched—brown hands, scarred. Distantly, the sounds of men shouting and swords clashing met my ears.

"We have to move," Coco said urgently. She pulled at my arms, trying to lift me. Blood trickled from the crook of her elbow, and charred, bitter magic burned my nose. I glanced down to my stomach, where the flesh had begun knitting itself back together. "Come *on*. My blood won't hold it closed without honey. You have to help me. We have to get to the wagons before the Chasseurs show up."

I looked up, disoriented, and took in the field for the first time. Chaos reigned. Someone had freed my throwing knives, and everywhere I turned, actors and thieves battled.

Deveraux chased one into the trees with a bejeweled rapier. Toulouse and Zenna fought back-to-back against three others. Toulouse's hands blurred in the air, and the thieves fell to the ground instantly. Ansel tackled the knees of another—this one descending on Seraphine. When the man disarmed him, Thierry rushed in, but he needn't have. Ansel nearly bit off the man's ear, and Seraphine kicked in his teeth. Madame Labelle and Beau fought together against the others, the former incapacitating them and the latter slitting their throats.

I tried to sit up, stopping short when my elbow met something soft. Warm.

Beside me, their leader lay still with a bloody hole where his eye should've been.

I pushed him away, scoured the scene for Lou. Found her mere feet away.

She and Bas circled each other like wolves. Though blood oozed from Bas's nose, it soon became clear Lou was on the defensive. "I don't want to hurt you, Bas," she hissed, deflecting yet another of his attacks with my Balisarda. "But you *need* to stop being an idiot. It's *me*. It's *Lou*—"

"I've never met you before in my life, *madame*." He lunged once more, and his blade caught her shoulder.

Her mouth flew open in disbelief as she clutched the wound. "Are you *kidding* me? I saved your fucking skin in the Tower, and this is how you repay me?"

"I escaped the Tower on my own—"

With a shriek of rage, she launched herself at him, swinging up and around until she clung to his back. Her legs encircled his waist. Her arms encircled his throat. "This *isn't funny*. We're trouncing your motley crew. It's over. It's finished. There's no reason to keep pretending—"

"*I'm. Not. Pretending.*"

She tightened her hold until his eyes bulged, and he jerked his knife upward, aiming for her eye. Releasing him hastily—too hastily—she fell on her back in the snow. He was on top of her within seconds, his knife poised at her throat.

Again, I struggled to rise, but Coco pinned me in place. "Let me go," I snarled.

"You're too weak." She shook her head, eyes wide as she watched them. "Lou can handle him."

"Bas. Bas, *stop*." Lou's hand closed around his wrist. Her chest rose and fell rapidly, as if fighting back panic. "*How* do you not remember me?" He pressed his knife harder in response. Her arms trembled against his strength. "You're not pretending. Shit. *Shit*."

He hesitated, as if her curses had sparked something in him. A memory. "How do you know me?" he asked fiercely.

"I've known you for years. You're one of my best friends." When she reached up to touch his face, his jaw, his hand eased on the knife. "But I—did I do something to you in the Tower?" Her brows furrowed as she strained to remember. "You were locked away. They were going to kill you unless—" Realization dawned in her turquoise eyes. "Unless you gave them the names of the witches at Tremblay's. That's it."

"You—you know about Tremblay's?"

"I was there."

"You couldn't have been. I would remember."

Finally, she pushed his knife away. He didn't stop her. "Bastien St. Pierre," she said, "we met backstage at Soleil et Lune two summers ago. A rehearsal for *La Barbe Bleue* had just ended, and you hoped to steal a moment or two with the leading lady. You were courting her at the time. A week later, you"—her face contorted with pain against some unseen force, and the scent of fresh magic burst through the air—"you started courting me."

"How do you—?" He lurched away from her abruptly, clutching his head as if she'd cleaved it in two. "Stop it! Stop it, please!"

"I stole your memories from you. I'm simply returning them."

"Whatever you're doing, please, *please* just stop—"

Falling to his knees, Bas begged and pleaded, but Lou did not stop. Soon his wails drew the attention of the others. Madame Labelle—who'd just dispatched the last of the thieves—froze. Her eyes widened. "Louise, stop it. *Stop*," she said sharply, tripping over her skirts in her haste to reach them. "You'll kill yourself!"

But Lou didn't listen. Her and Bas's eyes rolled back simultaneously, and together, they collapsed.

I succeeded in pushing away Coco's hands, in staggering to Lou's side. The smell of incense choked me—sharp and sweet—and I coughed violently. Pain lanced through my stomach at the movement. "Lou." I cupped her neck as Bas regained consciousness. "Can you hear me?"

"Louey?" Bas bolted upright, clutching her hand with sudden urgency. He patted her cheek. "Louey, wake up. *Wake up*."

Nausea churned as her eyes fluttered open, as she blinked up at me. As she turned to face him.

As I realized the truth.

Lou had lied. Again. She *had* rescued her lover from the Tower.

Right under my nose. It shouldn't have surprised me—shouldn't have *mattered*—but the deception still cut deep. Deeper than it should have, deeper than any flesh wound ever could. I felt raw, exposed, cut past muscle and bone to my very soul.

I dropped my hands, collapsing on the ground beside her. Breathing heavily.

With all eyes on us, none saw the thieves' leader climb to his feet behind Coco. None except Lou. She tensed, and I turned to see him raise his knife with deadly intent, aiming for the spot between Coco's shoulders. A death blow.

"Look out!" Bas cried.

Coco whirled, but the man was already upon her, the tip of his blade poised to pierce her chest—

Lou threw my Balisarda.

End over end, it soared between them, but the man moved at the last second, jerking his arm out of its path. And so it continued to fly, unimpeded, straight past. It didn't stop until it sank deep into the tree behind them.

And then the tree ate it.

My mouth fell open. My breath abandoned me. I could do nothing but watch as the whole trunk shuddered, swallowing the precious steel inch by inch until nothing remained. Nothing but the sapphire on its hilt. And the tree—it *changed*. Veins of silver spread through its bark—once black—until the entire tree glinted in the moonlight. Midnight fruit bloomed on stark branches. Thorns enveloped each bud. Sharp. Metallic.

The kites nesting in its boughs took flight with startled cries, shattering the silence.

Coco moved quickly. With brutal efficiency, she stabbed the man in his heart. This time, he didn't rise.

But I did.

"Reid," Lou said placatingly, but I couldn't hear her. A ringing had started in my ears. A numbness had crept through my limbs. Pain should've razed my body with each step, but it didn't. Agony should've destroyed my heart with each beat. *Gone*, it should've thumped. *Gone-gone, gone-gone, gone-gone.* But it didn't.

I felt nothing.

Without my Balisarda, *I* was nothing.

As if floating above, I watched myself reach out to touch the sapphire, but Lou's hand descended on mine. "Don't touch it," she said breathlessly. "The tree could suck you in too." I didn't drop my hand. It kept reaching, reaching, until Lou managed to wrestle it to my side. "Reid, *stop*. It's—it's—it's gone. But don't worry. We'll—we'll get you another one. All right? We'll—" She broke off when I turned to look at her. Pink tinged her cheeks. Her nose. Alarm widened her eyes.

"Let him go, Louise," Madame Labelle said sternly. "You've done quite enough damage for one day."

"Excuse me?" Lou whirled to face her, lip curling. "*You* don't get to speak about damage done."

Coco stepped to Lou's side. "None of this would've happened if you hadn't waited so long to intervene. These men didn't know you had magic. You could've ended this as soon as it began. Why didn't you?"

Madame Labelle lifted her chin. "I do not answer to you."

"Then answer to me."

At my strained words, everyone in the camp turned in my direction. The troupe members huddled close, watching with wide eyes. Deveraux looked aghast. When Ansel took a tentative step forward, Beau pulled him back with a shake of his head. I ignored them all, locking eyes with my mother. She blanched. "I—"

"Isn't it obvious?" Lou's laughter held an ugly edge. "She wants you to use magic, Reid. She waited until the last possible moment to see if your defense mechanisms would kick in. Isn't that right, mother dear?"

I waited for my mother to deny such an outrageous accusation. When she didn't, I felt myself stumble back a step. Away from her. Away from Lou.

Away from my Balisarda.

"I almost died," I said simply.

Madame Labelle's face crumpled, and she stepped closer, lifting a mournful hand. "I never would've let you—"

"You almost didn't have a choice." Turning on my heel, I strode toward the amber wagon. Lou moved behind, but I couldn't look at her. Couldn't trust myself to speak.

"Reid—"

Without a word, I shut the door in her face.

The door couldn't keep Coco away.

She wasted no time in following me, in accosting me with honey. With jerky movements, she pulled the jar of amber liquid from her bag and tossed it to me. "You're bleeding."

My eyes dropped to my stomach, where my wound had pulled open. I hadn't noticed it. Even now—as fresh blood seeped through my shirt—a bone-deep weariness settled within me. Lou's and my mother's voices rose outside. Still arguing. I closed my eyes.

This will always be your life with her—running, hiding, fighting.

No. My eyes snapped open, and I pushed the thought away.

Coco crossed the wagon to kneel at my side. Dipping a bloody finger into the jar of honey, she rubbed the mixture over my wound. The flesh drew together almost instantly.

"Why did your blood burn that man?" I asked, voice hollow.

"A Dame Rouge's blood is poison to her enemies."

"Oh." I nodded mechanically. As if it made sense. "Right."

Finished, she rose to her feet, staring at me as if deliberating. After several awkward seconds, she pressed a fresh vial of blood and honey into my palm. "What happened out there wasn't fair to anyone, least of all you." She closed my fingers around the vial. It was still warm. "Take it. I think you'll need it before all of this is over."

I glanced back at my stomach in confusion. The wound had already healed.

She gave me a grim smile. "It isn't for your flesh. It's for your heart."

DAGGER OF BONE

Lou

Deveraux insisted we keep moving. With bodies piled up outside of Beauchêne, it would only be a matter of time before someone alerted the local authorities. We needed to be far, *far* away before that happened. Fortunately, Deveraux didn't seem to sleep like a normal person, so he harnessed the horses immediately.

Unfortunately, he suggested I join him.

The wagon rocked beneath us as he eased the horses into motion.

One of the twins drove the wagon behind us. The *amber wagon*, Claud had called it. I didn't care about its name. I only cared that Reid was currently inside it, and I was not.

Reid *and* Coco. I should've been grateful they were getting along.

I wasn't.

Burrowing deeper in my blanket, I glared up at the stars. Claud chuckled. "*Couronne* for your thoughts, little one?"

"Do you have a family, Monsieur Deveraux?" The words

popped out of their own volition, and I resisted the urge to clap a hand over my mouth.

With a knowing look—as if he'd been expecting such a question—he coaxed the horses into a trot. "As a matter of fact, I do. Two elder sisters. Terrifying creatures, to be sure."

"And . . . parents?" I asked, curious despite myself.

"If I ever did, I no longer recall them."

"How old are you?"

He chuckled, his eyes cutting to mine. "What an impolite question."

"What a frustratingly vague answer." When his chuckle deepened to a laugh, I switched tactics, narrowing my eyes. "Why are you so interested in me, Deveraux? You know I'm married, right?"

He wiped a tear from his eye. "Dear child, a pervert I am not—"

"What is it, then? Why are you helping us?"

Pursing his lips, he considered. "Perhaps because the world needs a whit less hate and a trifle more love. Does that answer suffice?"

"No." I rolled my eyes, crossing my arms and feeling petulant. A second later, my eyes drifted back to him of their own accord. "Have *you* ever been in love?"

"Ah." He shook his head, eyes turning inward. "Love. The most elusive of mistresses. In all my years, I must confess to finding her only twice. The first was a headstrong young shepherd much like your Reid, and the second . . . well, that wound is not quite healed. It would be foolish to reopen it."

In all my years. It was an odd turn of phrase for someone who appeared to be in his forties.

"How old *are* you?" I asked again, louder this time.

"Very old."

Odd, indeed. I stared at him. "*What* are you?"

He chuckled, his eyes cutting to mine. "I simply . . . am."

"That's not an answer."

"Of course it is. Why must I bind myself to fit your expectations?"

The rest of the conversation—indeed, the rest of the *night*—passed in a similarly frustrating fashion. When the sky had lightened from pitch black to dusky gray to dazzling pink, I was no closer to figuring out the mystery of Claud Deveraux.

"We near Cesarine, little one." He nudged my shoulder and motioned to the east, where wisps of chimney smoke curled into the golden light of dawn. Pulling gently on the reins, he slowed the horses. "I dare venture no closer. Wake your companions. Though her own lodgings have burned, I believe Madame Labelle has contacts within the city. Together, we shall procure a safe place for your return, but we must say *adieu* for now."

For now.

I studied his placid face in bemusement. It made no sense, him helping us. None at all. The suspicious side of my nature cried foul—surely he had hidden motives—but the practical side told it to shut the hell up and thank him.

So I did.

He merely clasped my hand in both of his own, staring me directly in the eye. "Be safe, my darling, while we part. Be safe until we meet again."

I knocked softly on the wagon door.

"Reid?" When he didn't answer, I heaved a sigh, resting my forehead against the wood. "It's time to go."

No response.

Despair threatened to swallow me whole.

Once, when I was a child, my mother took an influential lover—a man from *la noblesse*. When she tired of him, she banished him from the Chateau, but he didn't leave easily. No, this was a man unaccustomed to rejection, with nearly infinite funds and power at his disposal. He soon hired men to haunt the forest, capturing our sisters and torturing them to reveal the Chateau's location. My mother's location.

He was an idiot. I hadn't been sorry when she'd killed him.

I *had* been sorry when she'd cut open his chest and filled him with rocks, dumping his corpse into L'Eau Mélancolique. I'd watched him sink out of sight with a sense of shame. His wife would never know what had happened to him. Or his children.

"Fret not, darling," Morgane had whispered, her bloody fingers squeezing mine in reassurance. "Though a secret is a lie in pretty clothing, some secrets must be kept."

But I hadn't been reassured. I'd been sick.

This silence between Reid and me felt something like that— like leaping into the sea with rocks in my chest, helpless to stop sinking. To stop bleeding. Only it wasn't my mother who had cut me open this time.

It was me.

I knocked harder. "Reid. I know you're there. Can I come in? Please?"

The door finally cracked open, and there he stood, staring down at me. I offered a tentative smile. He didn't return it—which was *fine*. Really. It was. If I kept saying it, maybe it'd become true. After several awkward seconds, Coco swung the door open and stepped outside. Ansel followed. "We'll be right back," she promised, touching my arm as she passed. "We just need to . . . be somewhere else."

Reid closed the door behind me.

"I should pack too," I said, my voice overly bright. Cursing internally, I cleared my throat and adopted a more natural tone. "I mean—there isn't much to pack, but still. The quicker we're on the road again, the better, right? The funeral *is* tomorrow. We only have today to convince Blaise to join us." I cringed into the silence. "If you need more time here, though, one of Claud's horses threw a shoe, so they aren't waiting on *us*, per se. More like Thierry. I think he's the troupe farrier, something about apprenticing for a man up in Amandine . . ." Hunched over his bag, Reid gave no indication he was listening. I kept talking anyway, incapable of stopping. "He might be the only person alive who speaks less than you do." I gave a weak chuckle. "He's quite the brooding hero. Did—did I see him using magic against the bandits last night? Are he and his brother—?"

Reid gave a terse nod.

"And . . . did you *happen* to persuade them into joining us against Morgane?"

Though his entire body tensed, he still didn't turn. "No."

My nausea intensified to something akin to guilt. "Reid . . ." Something in my voice finally made him turn. "Last night was my fault. Sometimes I just *react*—" I blew out a frustrated breath, worrying a strand of my hair. "I didn't mean to lose your Balisarda. I'm so sorry."

For everything.

He caught the strand of my hair, and we both watched it slide through his fingers. I willed him to hold me, to kiss away this tension between us. He handed me a clean shirt instead. "I know."

The rigidity of his shoulders said what he did not.

But it's still gone.

I wanted to shake him. I wanted to scream and rage until I shattered the reproachful silence he cloaked himself in like armor. I wanted to tie us together until we bruised from the binds and *force* him to talk to me.

Of course, I did none of those things.

Whistling low, I trailed my fingers across the lowest shelf. Unable to sit still. Baskets of dried fruit, eggs, and bread cluttered the space, along with wooden toy soldiers and peacock feathers. An odd coalition. "I can't believe you found others so quickly. I'd gone my entire life without meeting a single one." I shrugged and a slid a peacock feather behind my ear. "*True*, most of that life I spent sequestered in the Chateau—where no one would believe such a thing—and the rest I spent thieving in the streets, but still." Whirling to face him, I stuck a feather behind his ear as well. He grumbled irritably but didn't remove it. "I know I'm the first to flip fate the bird, but what are the chances?"

Reid stuffed the last of his clothing in his bag. "Deveraux collects things."

I eyed the cluttered shelves. "I can see that."

"No. He collects *us*."

"Oh." I grimaced. "And no one thinks that's weird?"

"Everything about Deveraux is weird." He cinched his bag shut, throwing it over his shoulder—then stilled, gaze falling to the table. Mine followed. A book lay open there. A journal. We both stared at it for a split second.

Then we lunged.

"Ah ah ah." Snatching the book from beneath his fingers, I cackled and danced away. "You're getting slow, old man. Now—where were we? Ah, yes." I pointed at the leather cover. "Another delicious journal. One would *think* you'd have learned your lesson about leaving these lying about." He sprang at me, but I leapt atop his cot, swinging the pages out of reach. He didn't return my grin. A small voice in my head warned I should stop—warned this behavior, once entertaining, was now decidedly not—even as I opened my mouth to continue. "What shall we find in this one? Sonnets praising my wit and charm? Portraits immortalizing my beauty?"

I was still laughing when a leaf of parchment shook free.

I caught it absently, turning it over to examine it.

It was a drawing of his face—a masterful charcoal portrait of Reid Diggory. Clad in full Chasseur regalia, he stared up at me with an intensity that transcended the page, unnerving in its depth. I leaned closer in fascination. He seemed younger here, the lines of his face smoother, rounder. The cut of his hair short and neat. Save the four angry gashes peeking above his collar, he looked as immaculate as the man I'd married.

"How old were you here?" I traced the captain's medal on his coat, vaguely recognizing it from our time together at the Tower. It'd been nondescript then, a simple piece of his uniform. I'd hardly noticed it. Now, however, it seemed to consume the entire portrait. I couldn't tear my eyes away.

Abruptly, Reid stepped backward, dropping his arms. "I'd just turned sixteen."

"How can you tell?"

"The wounds at my neck."

"Which are from . . . ?"

He tugged the portrait away and shoved it into his bag. "I told you how." His hands moved swiftly now, gathering my own bag and tossing it to me. I caught it without a word. The beginning of a memory took shape in my mind, blurry around the edges. Sharpening with every second.

How did you become captain?

Are you sure you want to know?

Yes.

"Are you ready?" Reid threw his bag over his shoulder, eyes sweeping the clutter of the cot for any forgotten belongings. "If we're going to reach Le Ventre by nightfall, we need to leave now. Les Dents is treacherous, but at least it's a road. We're venturing into the wild."

I stepped down from his cot on wooden legs. "You've been to Le Ventre before, haven't you?"

He nodded tersely.

A few months after I joined the Chasseurs, I found a pack of loup garou outside the city.

"There won't be any bounty hunters or thieves there," he added. "No witches either."

We killed them.

I grew roots at the realization.

Glancing at me over his shoulder, he pushed open the door. "What is it?"

"The werewolves you found outside the city . . . the ones you killed to become captain . . . were they—?"

Reid's expression shuttered. He didn't move for a long moment. Then, curiously, he drew a peculiar knife from his bandolier. Its handle had been carved from bone into the shape of a howling—

The breath left my chest in a rush.

A howling wolf.

"Oh, god," I whispered, acid coating my tongue.

"A gift from the"—Reid's throat bobbed—"from the Archbishop. To celebrate my first kill. He gave it to me at my captain ceremony."

I retreated a step, knocking into the table. The teacups there shuddered. "Tell me that isn't what I think it is, Reid. Tell me that isn't the bone of a *werewolf.*"

"I can't tell you that."

"*Shit*, man." I charged toward him now, reaching behind to wrench the door shut. The others couldn't overhear this. Not when we were moments away from journeying deep into the belly of the beast—a beast that'd be much less amenable to an alliance while we carried around the bones of its *dead*. "Whose bone was it? Fuck. What if it belonged to one of Blaise's relatives? What if he remembers?"

"He will."

"*What?*"

"He'll remember." Reid's voice resumed that irritating steadiness, that deadly calm. "I slaughtered his son."

I gaped at him. "You cannot be serious."

"You think I'd joke about this?"

"I think it'd *better* be a joke. I think a piss poor joke would be a hell of a lot better than a piss poor plan." I sank onto his cot, eyes still wide with disbelief. "I can't believe you. This—this was your plan. *You* were the one who wanted to tear across the kingdom in a mad dash to gather allies. Do you really think Blaise will want to cozy up with the murderer of his child? Why didn't you mention this earlier?"

"Would it have changed anything?"

"Of course it would have!" I pinched the bridge of my nose, squeezing my eyes shut tight. "All right. We'll adapt. We can—we can ride into Cesarine with Claud. Auguste might still join us, and La Voisin has already agreed—"

"No." Though he knelt between my knees, he took care not to touch me. Tension still radiated from his shoulders, his clenched jaw. He hadn't yet forgiven me. "We need Blaise as an ally."

"Now isn't the time for one of your principled stands, Reid."

"I'll accept the consequences of my actions."

I barely resisted the urge to stamp my foot. Just *barely*. "Well, I'm sure he'll appreciate your gallantry. You know—when he's tearing out your throat."

"He won't tear out my throat." Now Reid did touch me, the slightest brush of his fingers across my knee. My skin there tingled. "The werewolves value strength. I'll challenge Blaise to a duel to fulfill my blood debt. He won't be able to resist the opportunity to avenge his son. If I win, we'll have demonstrated we're strong allies—perhaps stronger than even Morgane."

A beat of silence.

"And if you lose?"

"I'll die."

UNTIL ONE OF US IS DEAD

Reid

The forest swallowed us when we left the road. Trees grew thicker, the terrain rugged. In some places, the canopy above blocked all sunlight. Only our footsteps broke the silence. It was slightly warmer here. Muddier. From experience, I knew the farther south we traveled, the wetter the ground would become. With luck, it would be low tide when we reached the cold-water swamp of Le Ventre.

"What an absolute armpit of a place." Beau blew into his hands to warm them. "It's been woefully misnamed."

When no one answered him, he heaved a dramatic sigh.

Coco had taken shelter beside me. Ansel didn't return her covert glances. With the threat of imminent death no longer upon them, their rift had reopened. He hadn't spoken a word since our departure. Neither had Lou. Her silence weighed upon me heavily, but I couldn't bring myself to assuage it. Shame and anger still smoldered deep in my gut.

"It's a real pity," Beau finally muttered, shaking his head and looking at each of us in turn. His eyes shone with disappointment. "I know you're all too preoccupied with your pining to notice, but I just caught my reflection in that last puddle—and *damn*, I look good."

Coco smacked him upside the head. "Do you ever think of anyone but yourself?"

He rubbed the spot ruefully. "Not really, no."

Lou grinned.

"Enough." I hung my bag on a low-lying limb. "We can stop here for midday meal."

"And *eat*." Lou pulled out a hunk of cheese with a moan. Deveraux had kindly supplied us with rations for the journey. Breaking off a piece, she offered it to Ansel. He didn't accept.

"When you're finished," he murmured, sitting on the root beside her, "I thought maybe we could train. We skipped yesterday." To me, he added, "It'll only take a moment."

Lou barked a laugh. "We don't need his permission, Ansel."

Beau helped himself to Lou's cheese instead. "I hope this isn't alluding to his not-so-valiant attempt at swordplay last night."

"He *was* valiant," Lou snapped.

"Don't forget I was there when the men burst into our wagon, Beau," Coco said sweetly. His eyes narrowed. "You almost pissed down your leg."

"Stop it." Voice low, Ansel stared determinedly at Coco's feet. "I don't need you to defend me."

"That's rich." Beau pointed to Ansel's arm. "You're still bleeding. You tripped and cut yourself during the fight, didn't you?

You're lucky the brigands disarmed you."

"Shut your mouth, Beau, before I shut it for you." Lou shoved to her feet, dragging Ansel up as well. She examined the cut on his arm before handing him her knife. "Of course we can train. Just ignore that bastard."

"I don't think *I* am the—"

I interrupted before he could finish. "We don't have time for this. The Chasseurs were near last night. Ansel will be fine. He trained with us in the Tower."

"Yes." Lou knelt over me, tugging another blade from my bandolier. The sheath by my heart remained painfully empty. "That's the problem."

My lip curled of its own volition. "Excuse me?"

"It's just that—how do I put this—" She tilted her head to consider me, puffing air from her cheeks with a crude sound. "Don't be offended, but Chasseurs have a certain reputation for being, well ... archaic. *Gallant*."

"Gallant," I repeated stiffly.

"Don't get me wrong, those injections of yours were a vicious step in the right direction, but historically, your brotherhood seems to suffer from delusions of grandeur. Knight errantry and the like. Protectors of the meek and defenseless, operating under a strict code of moral conduct."

"And that's wrong?" Ansel asked.

"There's no place for morality in a fight, Ansel. Not with bandits or bounty hunters. Not with witches." Her gaze hardened. "And not with Chasseurs, either. You're one of us now.

That means you're no longer meek *or* defenseless. Those men you called brothers won't hesitate to burn you. It's life or death—yours or theirs."

I scoffed. "Ridiculous."

Yes, Lou had cut down the bounty hunters with relative ease. She'd slaughtered the criminals in the smithy and defeated the witch in the Tower. But if she thought she knew better than generations of Chasseurs . . . if she thought she could teach Ansel more than the best fighters in the kingdom . . .

She knew nothing. Trickery might work against bounty hunters and common criminals, but against Chasseurs, skill and strategy were necessary. Fundamentals built upon through years of careful study and training. Patience. Strength. Discipline. For all her skill, Lou possessed none of these. And why would she? She was a witch, trained in darker arts than *patience*. Her time in the streets—clearly her only education in combat—had been short and furtive. She'd spent more time hiding in attics than fighting.

"Ridiculous," I repeated.

"You seem quite confident, Chass." She lifted my knife slowly, angling the blade to reflect the afternoon sunlight. "Perhaps we should give Ansel a demonstration."

"Very funny."

"I'm not laughing."

I stared at her. "I can't fight you. It wouldn't be fair."

Her eyes flashed. "I agree. Not fair in the slightest. But I fear Ansel isn't the only one in need of a lesson today. I would hate for either of you to walk away with the wrong impression."

"No." Rising, I crossed my arms and glared at her. "I won't do it. Don't ask me."

"Why not? You have nothing to fear. You *are* the strongest of us, after all. Aren't you?"

She stepped closer, her chest brushing my stomach, and stroked a finger down my cheek. Her skin flickered, and her voice deepened. Multiplied. Just like it had in the pub. Blood pounded in my ears. Without my Balisarda, I could feel the pull of her magic beneath my skin. Already, my muscles began to relax, my blood to cool. A pleasant numbness crept down my spine.

"You're curious." Her voice was a purr as she circled me, her breath warm against my neck. Ansel, Beau, and Coco watched with wide eyes. "Admit it. You want to know what it feels like. You want to see it—this part of me. This part of *you*. It scares you, but you're curious. So, so curious." Her tongue flicked out, licking the shell of my ear. Heat spiked through my belly. "Don't you trust me?"

She was right. I *did* want to see. I wanted to know. This emptiness on her face was foreign and strange, yet I—

No. I shook my head fiercely. I didn't want to see it at all. Only yesterday, I'd watched her nearly kill herself with magic. She shouldn't do this. *We* shouldn't do this. It wasn't right. It wasn't Lou. It wasn't—

Surrender.

Those strange, unfamiliar voices brushed against my innermost thoughts once more, caressing me. Coaxing me. "Of course I trust you."

"Prove it." She reached up to run her fingers through my

hair. I shuddered at the touch. At the intrusion in my head. "Do as I say."

Surrender.

"I—that's enough. What are you doing?" I tore her hand away and stumbled backward. Knocked my bag from the tree. No one moved to retrieve it. "Stop it!"

But her skin only shone brighter as she reached for me—her eyes full of longing—and suddenly, I wasn't sure I wanted her to stop at all.

Surrender. Touch her.

"Reid." She extended her arms to me in supplication, and I felt myself step forward, felt myself bury my face in her hair. But she smelled wrong. All wrong. Like smoke and fur and—and something else. Something sharp. It pierced through the haze in my mind. "Embrace me, Reid. Embrace *this*. You don't have to be afraid. Let me show you how powerful you can be. Let me show you how weak you are."

Too sharp. Sickly sweet. Burning.

My hands came down on her shoulders, and I forced her back a step, tearing my gaze away. "Stop it. Now." Unwilling to risk her eyes again, I stared instead at her throat. At her scar. Slowly, her skin dimmed beneath my hands. "This isn't you."

She snorted at that, and her skin flickered out abruptly. She shoved away from me. "Quit telling me who I am." When I hazarded a glance at her, she glared back, lips pursed and brows drawn. One hand on her narrow hip. Expectant. "So? Are we doing this or not?"

"Lou . . . ," Ansel warned.

My entire body trembled. "That's twice you've used magic to control me," I said quietly. "Never do it again. Do you understand? *Never.*"

"You're being dramatic."

"You're out of control."

A wicked grin curved her lips. Jezebel incarnate. "So punish me. I prefer chains and a whip, but a sword will do."

Unbelievable. She was—she—

I sucked in a harsh breath. "You really want to do this?"

Her grin widened, feral, and in that instant, I no longer recognized her. She was no longer Lou, but a true white lady. Beautiful, cold, and strange. "I really do."

You met only a few months ago. How well can you really know her? Madame Labelle's words tormented me. Louder and louder they grew. *Louise has started her descent. I know the signs. I've seen it happen before. You cannot stop it, and you cannot slow it down.*

"If I agree to this," I said slowly, "I have a condition."

"I'm listening."

"If I win, no more magic. I'm serious, Lou. You stop using it. I don't want to see it. I don't want to smell it. I don't want to *think* about it until all this is over."

"And if I win?" She trailed a finger across my chest. The unnatural luster returned to her skin. The unfamiliar gleam in her eye. "What then, darling?"

"I learn to use it. I let you teach me."

Her skin guttered abruptly, and her smile slipped. "Deal."

Throat tight, I nodded and stepped back. Finally, we could end this—this madness between us. This tension. This *impasse*. I would disable her quickly, efficiently. Despite her taunting, I didn't wish to harm her. I *never* wished to harm her. I just wanted to protect her. From Morgane. From Auguste.

From herself.

And now I finally could.

Drawing a second knife, I rolled my shoulders back. Stretched my neck. Flexed my wrist.

A sensation akin to giddiness overwhelmed me as we faced each other, as she twirled my knife between her fingers. But I didn't let my emotions betray me. Unlike Lou, I could control them. I could master them. I *would* master them.

"Are you ready?" Her smirk had returned, and her posture remained relaxed. Arrogant. Ansel scrambled to the cover of the nearest tree. Cypress. Even Coco backed away, tugging Beau with her. "Shall we count to three?"

I kept my own grip on my knife light. "One."

She tossed her knife in the air. "Two."

We locked eyes.

"Three," I breathed.

She sprang immediately, surprising me, and attacked with unexpected strength. I blocked her easily enough, countering with a strike of my own. Half force. I just needed to subdue her, not bludgeon her, and she was so small—

Darting around me, she used my momentum to kick the back of my knee and send me sprawling forward. Worse, she half tackled, half rode me to the ground, ensuring I landed face-first in the snow. Her knife touched my throat as my own skidded out of reach. Chuckling, she dug her knees into my back and brushed a kiss to my neck.

"First lesson, Ansel: find your opponent's weaknesses and exploit them."

Furious, I spat snow from my mouth and shoved her knife away. "Get off me."

She laughed again and rolled to the side, freeing me, before springing to her feet. "So, what did Reid do wrong? Besides falling on his face *and* losing his weapon?" Winking, she plucked it from the ground and returned it to me.

Ansel fidgeted under the tree, refusing to make eye contact. "He—he didn't want to hurt you. He held back."

I pushed to my feet. Heat burned up my neck and ears as I beat the snow and mud from my coat, my pants. *Fuck.* "A mistake I won't make twice."

Lou's eyes danced. "Shall we try for round two?"

"Yes."

"On your count."

I took the offensive this time, striking hard and fast. I'd underestimated her quickness before, but not again. Maintaining my momentum and balance, I kept my movements controlled, forceful. She might've been faster, but I was stronger. Much, much stronger.

Her smirk vanished after a particularly powerful blow to her sword arm. I didn't hesitate. Again and again I struck, driving her back toward the cypress tree. Trapping her. *Exploiting her weakness.* Her arms shook with effort, but she could scarcely deflect my attacks, let alone counter. I didn't stop.

With one last strike, I knocked away her knife, pinning her against the tree with my forearm. Panting. Grinning. Triumphant. "Yield."

She bared her teeth and lifted her hands. "Never."

The blast came before I could react. And the smell. The *smell.* It singed my nose and burned my throat, following me as I soared through the air—as I smashed into a branch and slid into the snow. Something warm and wet burst from my crown. I touched the spot gingerly, and my fingers came away red. Bloody.

"You—" My throat tightened with disbelief. With rage. "You cheated."

"Second lesson," she snarled, swooping down to retrieve our fallen knives. "There's no such thing as cheating. Use every weapon in your arsenal."

Ansel watched with wide, terrified eyes. Pale and motionless.

I rose slowly. Deliberately. My voice shook. "Give me a knife."

"No." She lifted her chin, eyes overbright, and slid it through her belt loop. "That's twice you've lost yours. Win it back."

"Lou." Ansel stepped forward tentatively, hands outstretched between us as if placating wild animals. "Maybe—maybe you should just give it—"

His words ended in a cry as I tackled her to the ground. Rolling to my back, I absorbed the worst of the impact, seizing her wrists and tearing her own knife away. She clawed at me, shrieking, but

I kept her hands pinned together with one of my own, using the other to reach—to *search*—

Her teeth sank into my wrist before I could find her belt.

"Shit!" I released her with a snarl, welts forming from the teeth marks. "Are you *crazy*—?"

"*Pathetic.* Surely the great captain can do better than *this*—"

Vaguely, I could hear Ansel shouting something in the distance, but the roaring in my ears drowned out everything but Lou. *Lou.* I rolled, diving for her discarded knife, but she leapt after me.

I reached it first.

Instinctively, I swung out in a wide, vicious arc, defending my back. Lou should've danced out of reach. She should've anticipated the move and countered, ducked beneath my outstretched arm and charged.

But she didn't.

My knife connected.

I watched in slow motion—bile rising in my throat—as the blade tore through her coat, as her mouth widened in a surprised O. As she tripped, clutching her chest, and tumbled to the ground.

"No." I gasped the word before dropping to my knees beside her. The roaring in my ears went abruptly silent. "Lou—"

"Reid!" Ansel's voice shattered the silence as he raced toward us, splattering snow and mud in every direction. He skidded to a stop and fell forward, hands fluttering wildly over the gash in her coat. He sat back with a sigh. "Thank God—"

"Coco," I said.

"But she isn't—"

"COCO!"

A quiet chuckle sounded below us. My vision tunneled on Lou's pale form. A grin touched her lips, wicked, and she rose to her elbows.

"Stay down," I pleaded, my voice cracking. "Please. Coco will heal you—"

But she didn't stay down. No, she continued to rise, lifting her hands in a peculiar gesture. My mind—sluggish and slow with panic—didn't comprehend the movement, didn't understand her intent until it was too late—

The blast lifted me into the air. I didn't stop until my back slammed into the tree once more. Doubling over, I choked and tried to regain my breath.

Another chuckle, this one louder than the last. She strode toward me, opening her coat to reveal her shirt, her skin. Both intact. Not even a scratch. "Third lesson: the fight isn't over until one of you is dead. Even then, check twice. Always kick them when they're down."

A DEBT OF BLOOD

Reid

If the tension between us had been thick before, now it was impassable. Each step a brick between us. Each moment a wall.

We walked for a long time.

Though Lou sent the black fox—*Brigitte*, she had named it—ahead with our request to meet, the Beast of Gévaudan didn't answer.

No one said another word until dusk fell. Cypress trees had gradually replaced pine and birch, and the ground beneath us had softened. It squelched underfoot, more mud now than moss and lichen. Brine flavored the cold winter air, and above us, a lone seagull cawed. Though water soaked my boots, luck was on our side—the tide hadn't yet risen.

"It'll be dark soon," Beau whispered. "Do you know where they live?"

Lou pressed closer to my side. Gooseflesh steepled her skin. "I doubt they invited him in for tea."

I resisted the urge to wrap an arm around her, to hold her

tight. She hadn't apologized this time. I hadn't expected it. "We caught strays unaware last time. I . . . don't know where the pack resides."

"Strays unaware?" Lou looked up at me sharply. "You told me you found the pack."

"I wanted to impress you."

"It doesn't matter." Coco glanced at the sky, at the ghost of the moon in the purple sunset. Full tonight. Growing brighter by the minute. "They'll find us."

Beau followed her gaze, paling. "And until then?"

A howl pierced the night.

Now I did take Lou's hand. "We keep going."

True darkness fell within the hour. With it, deeper shadows materialized, flitting through the trees. "They're here." Voice soft, Lou tipped her head to our left, where a silver wolf slipped out of sight. Another streaked ahead without a sound. More howls echoed the first until a chorus of cries surrounded us. We drew together collectively.

"Stay calm," I breathed. Though anxious to draw a blade, I kept my hand firmly in Lou's. This first moment was critical. If they suspected danger, they wouldn't hesitate. "They haven't attacked yet."

Beau's voice heightened to a squeak. "*Yet?*"

"Everyone kneel." Slowly, warily, I sank into a crouch, bowing my head, guiding Lou down with me. Our fingers threaded together in the mire. With each of her breaths, I synchronized my own. Centered myself. Anticipation corded my neck, my arms. Perhaps Blaise wouldn't listen to me. Despite what I'd told Lou, perhaps he wouldn't accept my challenge. Perhaps he'd just kill us. "Make eye contact with only those you wish to challenge."

As if awaiting my words, the wolves descended. Three dozen of them, at least. They emerged from every direction, as silent as the moon overhead. Surrounding us. Lou's face went white. Beside her, Ansel trembled.

We were outnumbered.

Alarmingly outnumbered.

"What's happening?" Beau asked on a ragged breath. He'd pressed his forehead into Coco's shoulder, clenching his eyes shut.

I struggled to keep my own voice steady. "We're requesting an audience with the alpha."

Directly in front of us, an enormous yellow-eyed wolf stepped into view. I recognized him immediately—his fur the color of smoke, his maw grizzled and misshapen. A chunk of his nose had been torn away. I still remembered the sight of it falling to the ground. The feel, the smell, of his blood on my hands. The sound of his tortured cries.

When he curled his lip, revealing teeth as long as my fingers, I forced myself to speak.

"Blaise. We need to talk."

When I moved to rise, Lou stopped me with a curt shake of her head. She rose instead, addressing Blaise directly. Only I could feel her hand trembling. "My name is Louise le Blanc, and I seek an audience with the Beast of Gévaudan, leader of this pack. Can I assume you're him?"

Blaise snarled softly. He didn't look away from me.

"We're here to negotiate a partnership against La Dame des Sorcières," Lou continued, her voice stronger now. "We don't want to fight."

"You are very brave." A sturdy young woman slipped out from between the trees, dressed in only a shift. Copper skin. Black hair. Deep brown eyes. Behind her, a miniature, male version followed. "Bringing a prince and a Chasseur into Le Ventre."

Beau glanced at me. When I nodded, he too stood. Though cautious, his posture shifted subtly, transforming him before our eyes. He straightened his shoulders. Planted his feet. Gazed down at the woman with an impassive expression. "I'm afraid you have us at the disadvantage, Mademoiselle . . . ?"

She glared at him. "Liana. I am the Beast of Gévaudan's daughter."

Beau nodded. "Mademoiselle Liana. It is a pleasure to meet you." When she didn't return the sentiment, he continued, undeterred. "My companion spoke truth. We are here to make peace with the loup garou. We believe an alliance could benefit all parties involved."

Lou cast him a grateful look.

"And what party do *you* represent?" Liana asked silkily, stalking closer. Beau's eyes shifted as a handful of wolves shadowed her movements. "Your *Highness.*"

Beau gave a strained smile. "Unfortunately, I am not here in an official capacity, though I maintain hope my father is also amenable to an alliance."

"Before or after he sends his huntsmen to slaughter my family?"

"We don't want to fight," Lou repeated.

"That's too bad." Liana grinned, and her incisors lengthened, sharpening to lethal points. "Because we do."

Her little brother—perhaps five years younger than Ansel—bared his teeth. "Take them."

"Wait!" Beau cried, and the wolf nearest him startled, snapping at his hand. He tumbled to the ground with a curse.

"Please, listen!" Lou darted between them, lifting her hands in a placating gesture. Heedless of her pleas, the wolves charged. I scrambled after them, drawing twin knives from my bandolier, preparing to throw—

"We just want to talk!" Her voice rose desperately. "We don't want to fi—"

The first wolf slammed into her, and she staggered back, hand extending to me. Eyes seeking mine. I adjusted my aim instinctively, throwing the knife straight and true. Catching the hilt as it turned, she slashed at the wolf in a single, continuous movement. When it yelped and leapt aside, bleeding, its kin skidded to a halt all around. Snarls and howls filled the night.

"We don't mean any harm." Lou's hand no longer trembled. "But we will defend ourselves if necessary." At her back, I lifted my own knife for emphasis. Coco and Ansel joined with theirs. Even Beau unsheathed his dagger, completing our circle.

"Well," Coco said bitterly. The wolves prowled around us, searching for a weak point to attack. "This spiraled out of control even quicker than I thought it would."

I swung at a wolf who edged too close. "You know what I need to do, Lou."

She shook her head vehemently. "No. No, we can still negotiate—"

"You have an interesting way of *negotiating*," Liana snarled, gesturing to her wounded kin, "bringing knives and enemies into our home and cutting us open."

"I didn't want for that to happen." Another wolf lunged while Lou spoke, hoping to catch her off guard. To her credit, she didn't stab it. She kicked it in the nose. "We have information on your enemy, La Dame des Sorcières. Together, we might finally defeat her."

"Ah. I understand now." A small smile played on Liana's lips. She lifted a hand, and the wolves stopped circling abruptly. "You've come to beg for the pack's help."

"To ask for it," Coco said sharply. She lifted her chin. "We will not beg."

The two stared at each other for several seconds. Neither flinching. Neither looking away. Finally, Liana inclined her head. "I acknowledge your bravery, Cosette Monvoisin, but the pack will never help a prince, a huntsman, and their whore." When she nodded toward Beau, me, and Lou, I saw red. Gripping my knives with deadly intent, I stepped forward. Coco's arm came across my chest. Liana laughed, the sound fierce. Feral. "You shouldn't have come here, Reid Diggory. I'll enjoy tearing out your throat."

"Enough, Liana." Deep and hoarse, Blaise's voice cut through the din of eager growls. I hadn't seen him slip away. He stood before us now as a man, clothed only in a pair of loose-fitting pants. His chest was as scarred as his face. His shoulders as broad as my own. Perhaps broader. Like his wolf's coat, his hair grew long and stormy gray, streaked with silver. "Morgane le Blanc visited us earlier this week with a similar proposition. She spoke of war."

"And freedom from the Chasseurs," Liana spat.

"All we must do is deliver her daughter—your wife"—Blaise's yellow eyes bored into mine, filled with hatred—"and my people's persecution will end."

"She's going to sacrifice me." Lou's hand clenched on her knife. Blaise tracked the movement. Predatory. Assessing any weaknesses, even now. "I'm her *daughter*," Lou continued, her voice rising in pitch. A glance confirmed that her pupils had dilated. Her body was also preparing to fight, even if her mind hadn't yet grasped the danger of our situation. "Yet she only conceived me—raised me—to die. She never loved me. Surely you see how evil that is?"

Blaise bared his teeth at her. His incisors were still sharp. Pointed. "Do not speak to me of family, Louise le Blanc, when you have never known one. Do not talk of killing children. Not with the company you keep."

Lou grimaced, a note of desperation lacing her voice. "He's a changed man—"

"He owes us blood. His debt will be paid."

"We never should've come here," Beau whispered.

He was right. Our plan had been half-assed at best, and this—this had been a suicide mission from the start. The Beast of Gévaudan would never join us. Because of me.

"Morgane won't hesitate to slaughter you after you've fulfilled her purpose." Lou abandoned all attempts at civility, planting her feet wide in front of me. Defending me against an entire pack of werewolves. "Dames Blanches loathe loup garou. They loathe anything different from themselves."

"She can try." Blaise's canines extended past his lip, and his eyes gleamed in the darkness. The wolves around him snarled and began to circle us again. Hackles raised. "But she will quickly discover that loup garou savor the blood of our enemies most. You were foolish to venture into Le Ventre, Louise le Blanc. Now your huntsman will pay with his life." His bones began to crack and shift, and his eyes rolled back in his head. Liana grinned. The wolves inched closer, licking their lips.

Lou lifted her hands once more. This time, the gesture wasn't placating. "You will not touch him."

"Lou." I touched her elbow, shaking my head. "Stop."

She knocked my hand aside and lifted her own higher. "*No, Reid.*"

"I knew what would happen when I came here." Before she could protest, before Blaise could complete his transition to wolf, I took a deep breath and stepped forward. "I challenge you, Blaise, the Beast of Gévaudan and alpha of this pack, to a duel. On your honor, and my own." His bones stopped snapping abruptly, and he stared at me, frozen between two forms. Lupine and humanoid. A grotesque blend of wolf and man. "Just the two of us. One weapon of our choice. If I win, you and your pack will join us in the upcoming battle. You will help us defeat La Dame des Sorcières and her Dames Blanches."

"And if I win?" Blaise's voice was distorted, disjointed, from his elongated mouth. More snarls than words.

"You kill me."

He snorted, his lips pulling back from his teeth. "No."

I blinked. "No?"

"I refuse your challenge, Reid Diggory." He nodded to his daughter and son before surrendering himself to the change completely. Within seconds, he landed on all fours, panting in the cold night air. A wolf once more. Liana stood behind him. In her eyes shone a hatred I recognized. A hatred that had once stolen my own breath and hardened my own heart.

"This time, Captain Diggory," she said softly, "we will hunt you. If you reach the village on the other side of our land, you escape with your life. If not . . ." She inhaled deeply, smiling as if scenting our fear, before extending her arms to her pack members. "Glory to the loup garou who kills you."

Lou's face twisted in horror.

"The village, Gévaudan, is due south from here. We will give you a head start."

"How much of a head start?" Beau asked, eyes tight and anxious.

She only grinned in response.

"Weapons?" Lou asked.

"He may keep the weapons on his person," Liana said. "No more and no less."

I quickly tallied my inventory. Four knives in my bandolier. Two in my boots. One down my spine. Seven teeth of my own. Though I prayed I wouldn't need them, I wasn't naive. This would not end well. It would end bloody.

"If any of *you* intervene in the hunt," her little brother added, looking between Lou, Coco, Ansel, and Beau, "with magic or otherwise, your lives will be forfeit."

"What about Morgane?" Coco asked quickly. "If Reid wins, you'll ally with us against her?"

"Never," Liana snarled.

"This is bullshit!" Lou advanced toward them, hands still lifted, but I caught her arm. To my surprise, so did Beau.

"Little sister," he said, eyes wide as the wolves closed in around us, "I think we ought to play their game."

"He'll *die*."

Coco's eyes darted everywhere as if searching for an escape. There was none. "We'll all die unless he agrees." She looked to me for confirmation. Waiting. In that look, I understood. If I chose not to do this, she would join me in fighting our way out. They all would. But the cost—the risk—

As if pulled by an invisible force, my eyes drifted again to Lou. To her face. I memorized the curve of her nose, the slope of her cheek. The line of her neck. If we fought, they would take her. There were too many of them to kill, even with magic on our side.

They would take her, and she would be gone.

"Don't do this," she said, her distress palpable. My chest ached. "Please."

My thumb brushed her arm. Just once. "I have to."

When I turned back to Liana, she was already halfway through the change. Black fur covered her lupine face, and her lips curled in a horrifying smile. "Run."

THE WOLVES DESCEND

Reid

A sense of calm enveloped me as I entered the swamp. South. Due south. I knew of Gévaudan. The Chasseurs and I had stayed there the night after our werewolf raid—the night before I'd become Captain Diggory. If I remembered the terrain correctly, the river that powered Gévaudan's mill flowed into this estuary. If I could find that river, I could lose my scent in the waters. Traverse them into the village.

If I didn't drown first.

I glanced down. The tide was rising. It'd soon flood the estuary, which would in turn flood the river. The current would be dangerous, especially while I was laden with heavy weaponry. Still—better the devil I knew than the devil I didn't. I'd rather drown than feel Blaise's teeth in my stomach.

Hurtling around the trees—taking care to mark each one with my scent—I doubled back, diluting my trail as much as possible. I dropped to a crouch. Loup garou were faster than regular wolves, faster than even horses. I couldn't outrun them. The water was my only hope. That, and—

Clawing at the ground, I scooped handfuls of mud and slathered them onto my skin. My clothes. My hair. Beyond strength and speed, the werewolves' noses were their greatest weapons. I needed to disappear in every sense.

Somewhere behind me, a howl shattered the silence.

I looked up, the first knot of fear making me hesitate.

My time was up. They were coming.

I cursed silently, sprinting south and listening—*listening*—for the telltale rush of water. Searching for thick trunks and hanging moss amidst the other muted greens and browns of the forest. The river had taken shape within a thick copse of bald cypresses. It had to be near here. I remembered this place. Each landmark that rose up before me refreshed my memory. Jean Luc had stopped to rest against that gnarled trunk. The Archbishop—stubbornly clad in his choral robes—had nearly fallen over that rock.

Which meant the cypresses should be right . . . *there*.

Triumphant, I raced toward them, slipping through the trunks as another howl sounded, breathing a sigh of relief as I finally, *finally* found the—

I stopped short. My relief withered.

There was nothing here.

Where the river had been, only a cluster of ferns remained. Their leaves—brown and dead—fluttered gently in the wind. The ground beneath them was muddy, wet, covered in lichen and moss. But none of the riverbed remained. Not one grain of sand. Not a single river rock. It was as if the entire river had simply . . .

disappeared. As if I'd imagined the whole thing.

My hands curled into fists.

I hadn't imagined anything. I'd drunk from the damn thing myself.

Around me, the trees' branches rustled in the wind, whispering together. Laughing. Watching. Another howl pierced the night—this one closer than the last—and the hair on my neck rose.

The forest is dangerous. My pulse quickened at my mother's words. *The trees have eyes.*

I shook my head—unwilling to acknowledge them—and peered up at the sky to recalculate my bearings. South. Due south. I just had to reach Gévaudan's gate, and the mud on my skin ensured that the werewolves couldn't track me by scent. I could still do this. I could make it.

But when I stepped backward—my boot sinking in a particularly wet pocket of earth—I realized the glaring flaw in my plan. Stopping abruptly, I turned to look behind me. My panic deepened to dread. The werewolves didn't *need* their noses to track me. I'd left them a path of footprints to follow instead. I hadn't calculated the soft terrain into my plan, nor the rising tide. There was no way I could flee for Gévaudan—or the river, or anywhere—without the werewolves seeing exactly where I'd gone.

Come on. My heart beat a frantic rhythm now, thundering inside my head. I forced myself to think around it. Could I magic my way out? I instantly rejected the impulse, unwilling to risk it. The last time I'd used magic, I'd nearly killed myself, freezing to death on the bank of a pool. More than likely, I'd do more harm than good, and I had no room for error now. Lou wasn't here to save me. *Think think think.* I wracked my brain for another plan, another means of hiding my trail. As shitty as Lou was at strategizing, she would've known exactly what to do. She always escaped. Always. But I wasn't her, and I didn't know.

Still . . . I'd chased her long enough to guess what she'd do in this situation. What she did in every situation.

Swallowing hard, I looked up.

Breathe. Just breathe.

Wading back into the cypresses, I heaved myself onto the lowest branch.

Another.

The trees grew close together in this part of the forest. If I could navigate the canopy far enough, I'd break my trail. I climbed faster, forcing my gaze skyward. Not down. Never down.

Another.

When the branches began thinning, I stopped climbing, crawling slowly—too slowly—to the end of the limb. I stood on shaky legs. Counting to three, I leapt onto the next branch as far as I could. It bowed precariously under my weight, and I crumpled, wrapping my arms around it with deep, gasping breaths. My vision swam. I forced myself to crawl forward once more. I couldn't stop. I had to move faster. I'd never reach Gévaudan at this pace, and the wolves grew louder with each howl.

After the third tree, however, my breathing came easier. My muscles relaxed infinitesimally. I moved faster. Faster still. Confident now. The trees still grew thick, and hope swelled in my chest. Again and again I leapt, until—

A splintering crack.

No.

Spine seizing, mind reeling, I swiped desperately at the nearest branch, hurtling toward the ground at alarming speed. The wood snapped under my momentum, and sharp pain lanced up my arm. The next branch smashed into my head. Stars burst behind my eyes, and I landed—hard—on my back. The impact knocked the breath from my throat. Water flooded my ears. I wheezed, blinking rapidly, clutching my bloody palm, and tried to stand.

Blaise stepped over me.

Teeth gleaming, he snarled when I squelched backward—eyes too intelligent, too eager, too *human* for my liking. Slowly, cautiously, I lifted my hands and rose to my feet. His nostrils flared at the scent of my blood. Instinct screamed for me to reach for my knives. To assume the offensive. But if I drew first blood—if I killed the alpha—the werewolves would never join us. Never. And those eyes—

Things had been much simpler when I'd been a Chasseur. When the wolves had been only beasts. Demons.

"It doesn't have to be this way." Head throbbing, I whispered, "Please."

His lips rose over his teeth, and he lunged.

I dodged his strike, circled him as he pivoted. My hands remained outstretched. Conciliatory. "You have a choice. The Chasseurs will kill you, yes, but so will Morgane. After you've served her purpose. After you've helped her murder innocent children."

Mid-charge, Blaise stopped abruptly. He cocked his head, ears twitching.

So Morgane hadn't told him the intricacies of her plan.

"When Lou dies, all of the king's children will die with her." I didn't mention my own death. That would only fortify the were-wolves' resolve to join Morgane. "Dozens of them, most of whom don't even know their father. Should they pay for his sins?"

Shifting his weight, he glanced behind as if uneasy.

"No one else has to die." I hardly dared breathe as I stepped toward him. "Join us. Help us. Together, we can defeat Morgane and restore order—"

Hackles rising, ears flattening, he snapped a warning to stay back. Revulsion twisted my stomach as his bones began to crack. As his joints popped and shifted just enough for him to stand on two legs. Smoky fur still covered his misshapen body. His hands and feet remained elongated, his back hunched. Grotesque. His face contracted in on itself until his mouth could form words.

"Restore order?" he snarled, the words guttural. "You said the Chasseurs will"—he struggled to move his jaw, grimacing in pain—"kill us. How will you defeat them?" Neck straining, he rescinded his teeth farther. "Can you kill—your own brothers? Your own"—another grimace—"father?"

"I'll convince him. I'll convince them all. We can show them another way."

"Too much—hate in their hearts. They'll refuse. What—then?"

I stared at him, thinking quickly.

"As I thought." His teeth snapped again. He started to shift back. "You would watch us—*bleed*—either way. A huntsman—through and through."

Then he lunged.

Though I dove aside, his teeth still caught my arm and buried deep. Tearing muscle. Shredding tendon. I wrenched away with a cry, dizzy with pain, with *anger*. Gold flickered wildly in my mind's eye. It blinded me, disorienting, as voices hissed, *seek us seek us seek us.*

I almost reached for them.

Instinct raged at me to attack, to protect, to tear this wolf's head off by any means necessary. Even magic.

But—no. I couldn't.

When everything is life and death, the stakes are higher, Lou said, chiding me in my memories. *The more we gain, the more we lose.*

I wouldn't.

Blaise readied to spring once more. Gritting my teeth, I leapt straight into the air and caught the branch overhead. My arm screamed in pain, as did my hand. I ignored both, swinging back as he rose to snap at my heels—and kicked him hard in the chest. He yelped and fell to the ground. I dropped beside him, drawing a dagger from my bandolier and stabbing it through his paw into the ground below. His yelps turned to shrieks. The other wolves' answering howls were murderous.

Arm dangling uselessly, I tore at my coat with my good hand. I needed to bind the wound. To stem the bleeding. The mud on my skin wouldn't mask the scent of fresh blood. The others would soon smell my injuries. They'd find me within moments. But my hand refused to cooperate, shaking with pain and fear and adrenaline.

Too late, I realized Blaise's screams had transformed.

Human now, naked, he wrenched the knife from his hand and snarled, "What was his name?"

FROZEN HEART

Lou

My footsteps wore a path in the ground as I paced. I hated this feeling—this *helplessness*. Reid was in there, fleeing for his *life*, and there was nothing I could do to help him. The three wolves Blaise had left to guard us—one of them Blaise's own son, Terrance—made sure of that. Judging by their size, Terrance's companions were equally young. Each of them stared at the tree line, giving us their backs, and whined softly. Their rigid shoulders and pinned ears said what they no longer could.

They wanted to join the hunt.

I wanted to skin them alive and wear their fur like a mantle.

"We have to do something," I muttered to Coco, glaring at Terrance's dark back. Though he and the others were smaller than the rest, I had no doubt their teeth were still sharp. "How will we know if he reaches Gévaudan? What if Blaise kills him anyway?"

I felt Coco's gaze, but I didn't look away from the wolves, longing to embed my knife in their rib cages. Restless energy hummed beneath my skin. "We don't have a choice," she murmured. "We just have to wait."

"There's always a choice. For example, we could *choose* to slit these little imps' throats and be on our way."

"Can they understand us?" Ansel whispered anxiously from beside Beau. "You know"—he dropped his voice further—"in their wolf form?"

"I don't give a shit."

Coco snorted, and I glanced at her. She smiled without humor. Her eyes were as drawn as mine, her skin paler than usual. It seemed I wasn't the only one worried about Reid. The thought warmed me unexpectedly. "Trust him, Lou. He can do this."

"I *know*," I snapped, said warmth freezing as I whirled to face her. "If anyone can out-beast the Beast of Gévaudan, it's Reid. But what if something goes wrong? What if they ambush him? Wolves hunt as a pack. It's highly unlikely they'll attack unless they have him outnumbered, and the idiot spurns magic—"

"He's armed to the teeth with knives," Beau reminded me.

"He was a Chasseur, Lou." Coco's voice gentled, so unbearably patient that I wanted to scream. "He knows how to hunt, which means he also knows how to hide. He'll cover his tracks."

Ansel nodded in agreement.

But Ansel—bless him—was a *child*, and neither he nor Coco knew what the hell they were talking about.

"Reid isn't the type to hide." I resumed pacing, cursing bitterly at the thick mud coating my boots. Water sloshed up my legs. "And even if he was, this entire godforsaken place is knee-deep in mud—"

Beau chuckled. "Better than snow—"

"Says who?" His eyes narrowed at my tone, and I scoffed,

kicking at the water angrily. "Stop looking at me like that. They're equally shitty, okay? The only real advantage in the middle of winter would be ice, but *of course* the dogs live in a goddamn swamp."

Howls erupted in the distance—eager now, tainted with unmistakable purpose—and our guards stood, panting with feverish excitement. Terrance licked his lips in anticipation. Horror twisted my chest like a vise. "They've found him."

"We don't know that," Coco said quickly. "Don't do anything stupid—"

Reid's cry rent the night.

"Lou." Eyes wide, Ansel swiped for my wrist. "Lou, he doesn't want you to—"

I slammed my palm into the ground.

Ice shot from my fingertips across the swamp floor, the very ground crackling with hoarfrost. I urged it onward, faster, *faster*, even as tendrils of bone-deep cold latched around my heart. My pulse slowed. My breathing faltered. I didn't care. I stabbed my fingers deeper into the spongy soil, urging the ice as far as the pattern would take it. Farther still. The gold cord around my body pulsed—attacking my mind, my body, my very *soul* with deep and boundless cold—but I didn't release it.

Vaguely, I heard Coco shouting behind me, heard Beau cursing, but I couldn't distinguish individual sounds. Black edged my vision, and the wolves in front of me faded to three snarling shadows. The world tilted. The ground rushed up to meet me. Still I held on. I would freeze the entire sea to ice—the entire world—before I let go. Because Reid needed help. Reid needed . . .

Frozen ground. He needed frozen ground. Ice. It would . . . it would give him . . . something. Advantage. It would give him . . . an advantage. Advantage against . . .

But delicious numbness crept through my body, stealing my thoughts, and I couldn't remember. Couldn't remember his name. Couldn't remember my own. I blinked once, twice, and everything went black.

Pain cracked across my cheek, and I jerked awake with a start.

"Holy hell." Coco dragged me to my feet before slipping on something and plummeting back to the ground. We landed in an angry heap. Swearing viciously, she rolled me off her. I felt . . . odd. "You're lucky you aren't *dead*. I don't know how you did it. You *should* be dead." She struggled upward once more. "What the hell were you *thinking?*"

I rubbed my face, wincing slightly at the sharp scent of magic. It burned my nose, brought tears to my eyes. I hadn't smelled it this concentrated since the temple at Modraniht. "What do you mean?"

"Ice, Lou," Coco said, gesturing around us. "*Ice.*"

Thick, crystalline rime coated every inch of our surroundings, from the blades of dead grass, ferns, and lichen on the forest floor to the boughs of cypress in the canopy. I gasped. As far as the eye could see, Le Ventre was no longer green. No longer wet and heavy and *alive*. No. Now it was white, hard, and glistening, even in darkness. I took a step, testing the ice under my foot. It didn't yield beneath my weight. When I stepped again, checking behind, my footprint left no impression on its surface.

I smiled.

A snarl to my left jerked me back to attention. A wolf had just launched himself at Beau and Ansel, who lifted his knife in an attempt to defend them. Coco darted forward to help, dodging Terrance, who slid right past her in his haste. The third wolf loped toward me, teeth first.

I grinned wider. It seemed I'd broken the rules.

With a snort of amusement, I twirled my fingers, and the wolf spun out of control on the ice. The pattern dissolved into golden dust. I wobbled but kept my feet, fighting a rush of vertigo. When the sensation passed, the wolf regained his footing. I bounced a finger off his nose as he careened past once more, slipped, and fell in a tangled heap.

Though my vision swam, I laughed—then clenched my fist, guiding the ice up and over his paws.

He yelped as it devoured his legs, his chest, edging steadily toward his throat. I watched in fascination, even as my laughter turned colder. Chilling.

More more more.

I wanted to watch the light leave his eyes.

"Lou!" Coco cried. "Look out!"

With hollow compulsion, I turned and flicked my wrist—catching a pattern easily—as Terrance leapt for my throat. The bones on the right side of his body shattered, and he fell to the ice with a piercing cry. But I felt no pain. Stepping over him, I lifted my hands toward his remaining companion. He backed away from Ansel and Coco slowly.

"You will leave my friends alone," I said, following him with a smile. Gold winked all around me with infinite possibilities—so many more now than ever before. So much pain. So much suffering. The wolf deserved it. He would've killed them.

His kin might've already killed Reid, a voice whispered.

My smile vanished.

Ansel stepped in front of me, looking alarmed. "What are you doing?"

"Ansel." Coco eased between us, gripping his hand and maneuvering him behind her. "Stay back." Her eyes never left mine. "Enough, Lou. You control your magic. It doesn't control you." When I didn't answer, when I didn't lower my hands, she stepped closer still. "This ice. Melt it. The price was too much."

"But Reid needs the ice. He'll die without it."

She grasped my hands gently, guiding them down between us. "There are worse things than death. Undo it, Lou. Come back to us. Don't continue down this path."

I stared at her.

Witches willing to sacrifice everything are powerful, the voice reminded me.

And dangerous, a distant corner of my mind argued. *And changed*.

"You aren't your mother," Coco whispered.

"I'm not my mother," I repeated, uncertain. Ansel and Beau watched with wide eyes.

She nodded and touched my cheek. "Undo it."

My ancestors kept silent now, waiting. Despite what Coco thought, they wouldn't urge me to do anything I didn't want to do. They only amplified my desires, carried me away in order to fulfill them. But desire was a heady thing, as addictive as it was deadly.

Reid's voice reverberated from that distant corner. *Reckless.*

"This isn't you, Lou," Coco said, coaxing. "Undo it."

If I'd trusted her any less, I might not have listened. But that distant corner of my mind seemed to believe her words. Kneeling, I placed my hand on the ground. A single pattern arose in my mind's eye, drifting out from the frozen wasteland of my chest toward the ice. I took a shuddering breath.

And a blue-tipped arrow nicked my leg.

"No!" Coco cried, flinging herself over me. "Stop! Don't shoot!"

But it was too late.

We passed some o' them just up the road. Bone White's eyes had gleamed with hunger. *Smarmy bastards. They've been scourin' the forest for weeks, makin' a right mess for us, haven't they?*

Reid's face now, drawn with fatigue. *The Chasseurs were near last night.*

Nearer than we'd thought, it seemed. Pushing Coco aside, I rose to my feet. My body thrummed with anticipation. My fingers flexed. It'd only been a matter of time before they found us—and what spectacular timing too.

At last, they were here.

Chasseurs.

Bows and Balisardas drawn, Jean Luc led a squadron from behind the trees. Surprise lit his eyes when he saw me, replaced quickly with resolve. Lifting a hand to halt the others, he approached slowly. "If it isn't Louise le Blanc. You can't imagine how pleased I am to see you."

I smiled, staring at his Balisarda. "Likewise, Jean Luc. What took you so long?"

"We buried the corpses you left on the road." Those pale eyes took in the ice around us before flicking to my face, my hair. He whistled low. "The facade has cracked, I see. The surface finally reflects the rot within." He gestured to the half-frozen wolf. "Though I'll thank you for making our jobs easier. Blaise's pack has never been easily tracked. His Majesty will be pleased."

I bowed low, extending my arms. "We are ever his servants."

Jean Luc spotted Beau then. "Your Highness. I should've known you'd be here. Your father has been in an uproar for weeks."

Though he still looked uneasy, Beau rose to his full height, staring down his nose at him. "Because you told him about my involvement on Modraniht."

Jean Luc sneered. "Your indiscretions shall not go unpunished. Truly, it disgusts me to one day call you king."

"Never fear. You won't be alive to witness that crowning achievement. Not if you continue to threaten my friends."

"Your *friends*." Jean Luc stepped closer, his knuckles white on silver and sapphire. I grinned. I'd told Reid I'd get him another Balisarda. How *delightful* that Balisarda would be Jean Luc's.

"Understand me, Your Highness. This time, there will be no escape. These witches"—he jerked his chin toward Coco and me—"and their conspirators will burn. *Your friends* will burn. I will light their pyres myself when we return to Cesarine. One for Cosette Monvoisin. One for Louise le Blanc. One for Ansel Diggory"—he bared his teeth—"and one for Reid Diggory."

He was wrong, of course. So very, very wrong.

"A fitting way to honor our late forefather. Don't you agree?"

"Célie will hate you if you burn Reid," Beau spat.

I twirled a lock of hair around my finger. "Tell me, Jean, have you fucked her yet?"

A beat of silence, then—

"I don't—" His eyes flew wide, and he spluttered incoherently. "What—"

"That's a yes, then." I sauntered closer, just out of his blade's reach. "Reid never fucked her himself, in case you were wondering. Poor girl. He did love her, but I suppose he took his vows seriously." My grin widened. "That, or he was saving himself for marriage."

He lashed out with his Balisarda. "Shut your mouth—"

I met him with a blade of ice. The other men tensed, edging closer, and Coco, Ansel, and Beau lifted their knives in turn.

"I can't imagine he'll be pleased when he learns his best friend loved his girlfriend in secret for all those years. So *naughty* of you, Jean. Did you at least wait to sow your seed until Reid moved to greener pastures?"

He jutted his face over our clashed blades. "Do not speak of Célie."

I continued undeterred. "One can't help but notice your new circumstances with Reid out of the picture. He always had the life you wanted, didn't he? Now you get to pretend at his. Secondhand title, secondhand power." I shrugged with a saccharine grin, sliding my blade along his slowly. The ice touched his hand. "Secondhand girl."

With a snarl, he pushed away from me. A vein throbbed in his forehead. "Where is Reid?"

"How disappointed she must be now. Though I suppose a secondhand girl deserves a secondhand boy—"

He launched himself at me again. I sidestepped easily. "That *murderer* didn't deserve to breathe her air. When she heard what he'd done, it nearly killed her. She's been in seclusion for *weeks* because of some misplaced emotion for him. If not for me, he would've *ruined* her. Just as you've ruined him. Now *where is he?*"

"Not here," I sang, still smiling sweetly as we circled each other. Beneath me, the ice thickened, and the foliage cracked audibly. "You're a thief, Jean Luc—a damn good one, of course—but I'm better. You have something I need."

"Witch, tell me where he is, or I'll—"

"You'll what? If your history is any indication, soon you'll be begging me to ruin *you* too."

With a snarl, he signaled to his men, but I jerked my hand upward before they could reach us. Shards of ice spiked up behind him, around him, until we stood in a circle of jagged icicles. Trapped, he shouted panicked orders—eyes darting, searching for a gap—while the Chasseurs hit and hacked at the ice.

"Cut it down!"

"Captain!"

"Get him *out*—"

One of the icicles shattered, raining ice on our heads. Capitalizing on the distraction, I lunged, slicing Jean Luc's sword hand. He cried out but kept hold of his Balisarda. His other hand seized my wrist, twisting, and that—well, that just wouldn't do.

I spat directly in his eye.

Rearing back, he loosened his hold on me, and I dug my fingers into his wound, pulling and tearing the skin there. He roared with pain. "You *bitch*—"

"Oh dear." I flipped his Balisarda into my hand, the ice sword poised at his throat. Then I laughed. Laughed and laughed until Coco, Ansel, and Beau joined the Chasseurs in beating against the ice. *Lou Lou Lou* came their anxious cries, reverberating around me. Through me. The moon reflected in Jean Luc's wide eyes. He backed away slowly. "It seems you've misplaced something, Captain." I hurled the ice sword into the icicle by his head before raising my free hand. "This is going to be fun."

SANCTUARY

Reid

"His—his name?"

Blaise bared his teeth, the first flicker of emotion flashing through his eyes. Blood dripped down his hand. "My *son.* Do you even know his name?"

I unsheathed a second blade, shame congealing in my gut. Though he made no further move to attack, I would not be caught unaware. "No."

"Adrien." He said the word on a whisper. Reverential. "His name was Adrien. My eldest son. I still remember the moment I first held him in my arms." He paused. "Do you have children, Captain Diggory?"

Distinctly uncomfortable now, I shook my head. Gripped my knives tighter.

"I thought not." He stepped closer. I stepped back. "Most loup garou mate with progeny in mind. We cherish our pups. They are everything." Another pause, longer this time. "My mate and I were no different, but we were incapable of reproduction. He came from a pack across the sea." Another step. We stood nearly nose to nose now. "When your brethren slew Adrien's biological parents, we adopted him as our own. When you slew Adrien, my mate took his own life." His eyes—once unbearably soft, lost in memory—now hardened. "He never met Liana or Terrance. He would've loved them. They *deserved* his love."

Self-loathing burned up my throat. I opened my mouth to say something—to say anything—but closed it just as quickly, fighting the urge to vomit. No words could ever erase what I'd done to him. What I'd taken.

"So you see," Blaise said, voice rough with emotion, "you owe me blood."

I still couldn't speak. When he began to shift once more, however, I choked, "I don't want to fight you."

"Nor I you," he growled, bones shuddering, "but fight we shall."

He'd just fallen back to all fours when the temperature plummeted, and ice—*ice*—shot across the ground beneath us. Stumbling, I stared as it devoured the path ahead, engulfing each tree and ravaging each leaf. Each needle. When it reached the tip of the tallest branches, it burst into a cloud of white, showering us with snow that stank of magic. Of *rage*. Blaise yelped in surprise and lost his footing.

Horror gripped my heart in a fist.

What had Lou done?

"Powerful—isn't she?" Blaise's body continued to snap and twist, his eyes gleaming in the darkness. His teeth glinting. "Her mother's daughter, after all."

A piercing howl erupted over the trees then. Higher than the others. Anguished. Blaise's head snapped up, and he gave a panicked whine. "Terrance." The word was garbled, barely discernible through his maw. He bolted without finishing his transition.

Lou.

Knives in hand, I hurried after him, slipping and sliding on the ice. It didn't matter. I didn't stop. Neither did Blaise. When we finally burst through the trees at the edge of the loup garou territory, I lurched to a halt at the sight before me.

A handful of Chasseurs hung midair, revolving slowly—necks taut, muscles seizing—while even more loup garou struggled to free themselves from the ice trapping their paws. Their legs. The Chasseurs and wolves who weren't debilitated hacked at one another with steel and teeth. When the bodies shifted—revealing a slight, pale-haired figure in the center of a shattered ice cage— my heart dropped like a stone.

Lou.

Eyes hollow, smile cold, she contorted her fingers like a maestro. Coco shouted beside her, tugging fruitlessly on her arms, while Beau and Ansel tried their best to defend them. Tears spilled down Ansel's cheeks. Blaise lunged forward with a snarl. I tackled him from behind, wrapping my arms around his ribs, and we rolled.

"Lou!" My shout made Lou pause. Made her turn. My blood ran cold at her grin. "Lou, stop!"

"I know I lost your Balisarda, Reid," she called, her voice sickeningly sweet, "but I found you a new one."

She lifted a bloody Balisarda into the air.

Jean Luc—I did a double take—*Jean Luc* dove at her.

"Watch out!" I cried, and she spun gracefully, lifting him with the sweep of her hand. He landed hard on a shard of ice, nearly impaling himself. Realization dawned swift and brutal.

She'd taken his Balisarda.

Spotting his father, Terrance whined and tried to drag himself toward us. Half of his body looked—limp. The angles wrong. Distorted. Blaise thrashed in my arms, twisting around to bite the wound on my arm, and I dropped him. He shot forward like a flash, gripping Terrance's ruff between his teeth and dragging him to safety.

I dodged around a Chasseur, sprinting toward Lou. When I took her in my arms, she cackled. And the look in her eyes . . . I squeezed her tighter. "What is this?"

"She has to melt the ice!" Coco cried, now locked in battle with Jean Luc. He fought viciously despite his injuries—or perhaps because of them. Within seconds, I realized he didn't just want to hurt Coco. He wanted to kill her. "She won't listen to—" She ducked as he swung a piece of ice savagely, but it still caught her chest. Her words ended in a gasp.

Bewildered, still horrified—torn between helping Coco or Lou—I took Lou's face in my hands. "Hello, you," she breathed, leaning into my embrace. Her eyes were still horribly empty. "Did the ice save you?"

"Yes, it did," I lied quickly, "but now you need to melt it. Can you do that for me? Can you melt the ice?"

She tilted her head, and confusion stirred within those lifeless eyes. I held my breath. "Of course." She blinked. "I'll do anything for the ones I love, Reid. You know that."

The words, spoken so simply, sent a chill down my spine. Yes, I did know that. I knew she would freeze to death to put breath in my lungs, twist up her very memory to give my body heat.

I knew she would sacrifice her warmth—her humanity—to protect me from loup garou.

"Melt the ice, Lou," I said. "Do it now."

Nodding, she sank to her knees. When she pressed her hands against the ground, I moved to defend her back. Punched a Chasseur who came too close. Prayed the pattern was reversible. That it wasn't too late.

The world seemed to still as Lou closed her eyes, and warmth pulsed outward in a wave. The ground melted to mud beneath her fingers. The suspended Chasseurs drifted back to their feet, and the trapped werewolves licked their newly freed paws. I prayed. I prayed and prayed and prayed.

Bring her back. Please.

Seek us.

When she rose, shaking her head, I crushed her in my arms. "Lou."

"What—" She leaned back, eyes widening at the carnage around us. The Chasseurs and werewolves watched her warily, unsure how to proceed without orders. No one appeared eager to approach her again. Not even those with Balisardas. Jean Luc's hung limp at Lou's side. "What happened?"

"You saved us," Coco said firmly. Though she swayed on her feet—face ashen, shirt bloody—she still looked better than Jean Luc. He'd collapsed, panting, at her boots. When he struggled to rise, she kicked him in the face. "And you will never . . . *ever* do it again. Do you hear me? I don't care if Reid is . . . bound and gagged . . . at the stake—" She broke off with a wince, applying pressure to her wound.

Lou sprang forward just in time, and Coco collapsed in her arms.

"I'm fine," Coco said, voice faint. "It'll heal. Don't use your magic."

"You stupid—bitches." Clutching his nose, Jean Luc crawled toward them. Blood poured through his fingers. "I'm going to cut you both to pieces. Give it back to me. Give me back my Balisarda—"

"Enough." Blaise's deep, terrible voice preceded him into view, and the werewolves shifted anxiously. In his arms, he held Terrance. Sweat coated the boy's brow, and his breathing came quick. Labored. He'd shifted back. In this form, it was clear his entire right side had collapsed. A brown wolf near Ansel yelped sharply. After the telltale crack of bones, Liana raced forward. Though I averted my eyes from her naked skin, I couldn't ignore her cries.

"Terrance! No, no, *no*. Mother moon, please. *Terrance.*"

Blaise's yellow eyes flashed from the Chasseurs to Lou. "Who did this?"

Jean Luc spat blood. "*Magic.*"

Every eye in the vicinity turned to Lou. She paled.

"I can heal him." Coco lifted her head from Lou's shoulders. Her eyes were glazed. Pained. "Bring him here."

"No." I stepped in front of them, and Blaise snarled. "Peace, Blaise. I—I can heal your son." Reaching into my pocket, I withdrew the vial of blood and honey.

A ghost of a smile touched Coco's lips. She nodded. "His injuries are internal. He needs to drink it."

Blaise didn't stop me when I approached. He didn't halt my wrist when I lifted the vial to Terrance's lips.

"Drink," I urged, tipping the liquid down the boy's throat. He struggled weakly against me, but Blaise held him firm. When he swallowed the last of it, we all waited. Even Jean Luc. He watched with an expression of fascination and disgust as Terrance's breathing grew stronger. As the color returned to his cheeks. One by one, the bones of his ribs snapped back into their proper places. Though he gasped in pain, Blaise stroked his hair, whispering comforts.

Tears poured down the old man's cheeks.

"*Père?*" Terrance's eyes fluttered open, and Blaise wept harder.

"Yes, son. I am here."

The boy groaned. "The witch, she—"

"Will not be harmed," I finished. Blaise and I locked eyes. After a tense moment, he dipped his chin in a nod.

"You have saved my son's life, Reid Diggory. I am indebted to you."

"No. I am indebted to you." My gaze dropped to Terrance, and my gut twisted once more. "I know it changes nothing, but

I am sorry. Truly. I wish—" I swallowed hard and looked away. Lou clutched my hand. "I wish I could bring Adrien back."

"Oh, good Lord." Jean Luc rolled his eyes and motioned to the Chasseurs from his position on the ground. "I've heard enough. Round them all up—even the Beast. They can bond in the Tower dungeon before they burn." He turned his glare on Lou. "Kill that one now."

Blaise's lip curled. He stepped beside me, and the wolves stepped beside him. Growls built deep in their throats. Their hackles rose. I drew my own knives, as did Ansel, and though her face was still pale, Lou lifted her free hand. The other supported Coco. "I think not," Blaise said.

Beau sauntered in front of us. "Consider me on their side. And as my father isn't here to throw his weight, I'll speak for him too. Which means . . . I outrank you." He grinned and nodded curtly to the Chasseurs. "Stand down, men. That's an order."

Jean Luc glared at him, trembling with rage. "They don't answer to you."

"Without your Balisarda, they don't answer to you either."

The Chasseurs hesitated.

"We have a proposition," Lou said.

I tensed, wary once more. We'd just defused the greatest danger. A single word from Lou could exacerbate it again.

At the sound of her voice, Blaise's lip curled over his teeth. One of the werewolves growled. Lou ignored them both, focusing only on Jean Luc. He laughed bitterly. "Does it end with you on the stake?"

"It ends with Morgane on one."

Surprise stole the scowl from his face. "What?"

"We know where she is."

His eyes narrowed. "Why should I believe you?"

"I hardly have reason to lie." She gestured around us with his Balisarda. "It's not like you're in any position to arrest me now. You're outnumbered. Vulnerable. But if you return to Cesarine with us, you'll have a good chance of finishing what you started on Modraniht. Just think—she's still injured. If she dies, King Auguste is safe, and *you* become the kingdom's new hero."

"Morgane is in Cesarine?" Jean Luc asked sharply.

"Yes." She glanced at me. "We . . . think she's planning an attack during the Archbishop's funeral."

Heavy silence descended. At last, Blaise asked coldly, "Why do you think this?"

"We received a note." She bent to retrieve it from her boot. "It's in my mother's handwriting, and it mentions a pall, and tears."

Blaise regarded her with suspicion. "If your mother delivered this note, why did she not take you then?"

"She's playing with us. Baiting us. This is her idea of a game. It's also why we believe she'll strike amidst the Archbishop's funeral—to make a statement. To rub salt in the wound of the kingdom's grief. La Voisin and the Dames Rouges have already agreed to stand with us. With all of your help, we can finally defeat her."

"We need your help, *frère*." I hesitated before finally extending a hand to him. "You're . . . you're a captain of the Chasseurs now.

Your support might sway King Auguste to our cause."

He knocked my hand away. Bared his teeth. "You are no brother of mine. My brother died with my father. My *brother* would not defend one witch to condemn another—he would kill them both. And you're a fool to believe the king will ever join your *cause.*"

"I'm still the same person, Jean. I'm still *me.* Help us. We can be as we were once more. We can honor our father *together.*"

He stared at me a beat.

Then he punched me in the face.

I staggered backward, eyes and nose streaming, as Lou snarled and tried to leap forward, caught beneath Coco. Ansel and Beau stepped to my side instead. The former attempted to subdue Jean, who lunged for another attack, while the latter bent to check my nose. "It's not broken," he muttered.

"I *will* honor our father"—Jean Luc struggled to free himself from Ansel, who held him with surprising strength—"when I lash you to the stake for conspiracy. As God is my witness, you will burn for what you've done. I will light your pyre myself."

Blood poured down my mouth, my chin. "Jean—"

He finally shoved Ansel away. "How disappointed he would be to see how far you've fallen, Reid. His golden son."

"Oh, get over it, Jean Luc," Lou snapped. "You can't win a dead man's affection. Even alive, the Archbishop saw you for the sniveling little rat you are—"

He launched himself at her now, completely out of control, but Blaise rose up to meet him, his expression hard as flint. Liana,

Terrance, and a handful of others closed in behind him. Some bared their teeth, incisors sharp and gleaming. Others shifted their eyes yellow. "I have offered Reid Diggory and his companions sanctuary," Blaise said, voice steady. Calm. "Leave now in peace, or do not leave at all."

Lou shook her head vehemently, eyes wide. "Blaise, no. They can't leave—"

Jean Luc swiped at her. "*Give me my Balisarda*—"

The wolves around us growled in agitation. In anticipation.

"Captain . . ." A Chasseur I didn't recognize touched Jean Luc's elbow. "Perhaps we should go."

"I will not leave without—"

"Yes," Blaise said, lifting a hand to his wolves. They pressed closer. Too close now. Close enough to bite. To kill. Their snarls multiplied to a din. "You will."

The Chasseurs needed no further encouragement. Eyes darting, they seized Jean Luc before he could damn them all. Though he roared his protests, they pulled him backward. They kept pulling. His shouts echoed through the trees even after they'd disappeared.

Lou whirled to face Blaise. "What have you done?"

"I have saved you."

"No." Lou stared at him in horror. "You let them *go*. You let them go after we told them our plan. They know now we're traveling to Cesarine. They know we're planning to visit the king. If Jean Luc tips him off, Auguste will arrest us the moment we step foot in the castle."

Grimacing, Coco readjusted her arm on Lou's shoulders. "She's right. Auguste won't want to listen. We've just lost the element of surprise."

"Maybe"—Lou's eyes swept the pack—"maybe if we show up in numbers, we can *make* him listen."

But Blaise shook his head. "Your fight is not our fight. Reid Diggory saved my second son after taking the life of my first. He has fulfilled his debt. My kin will no longer hunt him, and you will leave our homeland in peace. I do not owe him an alliance. I do not owe him anything."

Lou stabbed the air with her finger. "That's horseshit, and you know it—"

His eyes narrowed. "After what you've done, be grateful I do not demand *your* blood, Louise le Blanc."

"He's right." I took her hand in mine, squeezing gently when she opened her mouth to argue. "And we need to leave now if we have any hope of beating Jean Luc to Cesarine."

"What? But—"

"Wait." To my surprise, Liana stepped forward. She'd set her chin in a determined expression. "You may owe him nothing, *Père*, but he saved my brother's life. I owe him everything."

"As do I." Terrance joined her. Though young, his flinty countenance reflected his father's as he nodded in my direction. He didn't make eye contact. "We will join you."

"No." With the curt shake of his head, Blaise lowered his voice to a whisper. "Children, I have already told you, our debt is fulfilled—"

Liana clasped his hands together, holding them between her own. "Our debt is not yours. Adrien was your son, *Père*, but we didn't know him. He's a stranger to Terrance and to me. We must honor this debt—especially now, beneath the face of our mother." She glanced up at the full moon. "Would you have us spurn this obligation? Would you disavow Terrance's life so quickly after she restored him to us?"

Blaise stared down at them both for several seconds. Finally, his facade cracked, and beneath it, his resolve crumbled. He kissed both their foreheads with tears in his eyes. "Yours are the brightest of souls. Of course you must go, and I—I will join you. Though my debt as a man is fulfilled, my duties as a father are not." His eyes cut to mine. "My pack will remain here. You will never step foot in our lands again."

I nodded curtly. "Understood."

We turned and raced toward Cesarine.

A PROMISE

Reid

Blaise, Liana, and Terrance outdistanced us by the next morning, promising to return with reconnaissance of the city landscape. When they found us again—a mere mile outside of Cesarine, hidden within the trees near Les Dents—they delivered our worst fear: the Chasseurs had formed a blockade to enter the city. They checked each wagon, each cart, without bothering to hide their intentions.

"They're searching for you." Liana emerged from behind a juniper in fresh clothes. She joined her father and brother with a grim expression. "I recognized some of them, but I didn't see Jean Luc. He isn't here."

"I assume he went straight to my father." Beau readjusted the hood of his cloak, eyeing the thick congestion of the road. Though his expression remained cool and unaffected, his hands shook. "Hence the blockade."

Lou kicked the juniper's branches in frustration. When snow fell into her boots, she cursed viciously. "That sniveling little *shit*.

Of course he isn't here. He wouldn't want an audience to watch him piss down his leg when he sees me. An appropriate response, mind you."

Despite her brazen words, this crowd made me uncomfortable. It'd grown worse the nearer we'd drawn to the city, as Les Dents was the only road into Cesarine. Part of me rejoiced so many had come to honor the Archbishop. The rest didn't know how to feel. Here—with every face and every voice a reminder—I couldn't properly dissociate. The doors to my fortress rattled. The walls shook. But I couldn't focus on that now. Couldn't focus on anything but Lou. "Are you all right?" she'd whispered earlier when we'd hidden amongst these trees.

I'd studied her face. It seemed she'd reversed her disastrous pattern, yes, but appearances could be deceiving. Memory lasted forever. I'd certainly never forget the sight of her braced within that frozen swamp, fingers contorted, expression cold and hard as the ice at her feet. I doubted she would either. "Are *you*?" I'd whispered back.

She hadn't answered.

She whispered to her matagots now. A third had joined us overnight. A black rat. It perched on her shoulder, eyes beady and bright. No one mentioned it. No one dared look in its direction—as if our willful disregard could somehow make it less real. But the set of Coco's shoulders said the words she didn't, as did the shadow in Ansel's eyes. Even Beau cast me a worried glance.

As for the wolves, they wouldn't go near them. Blaise's lip curled when Absalon sauntered too close.

"What is it?" Taking her hand, I pulled her apart from the others. The matagots followed like shadows. If I knocked the rat from her shoulder—if I wrapped my hands around the necks of the cat and fox—would they leave her in peace? Would they haunt me instead?

"I'm sending word to Claud," she said, and the fox disappeared in a cloud of smoke. "He might know how to get through this blockade undetected."

Beau craned his neck, eavesdropping unapologetically. "That's your plan?" Skepticism laced his voice. "I know Claud somehow . . . shielded you in Beauchêne, but these aren't bandits."

"You're right." An edge clipped Lou's voice as she faced him. "These are huntsmen armed with Balisardas. I got lucky with Jean Luc—I knew his buttons, and I pressed them. I distracted him, disarmed him. His men didn't dare hurt me while he was under my power. But he isn't here now, and I doubt I'll be able to disarm all two dozen of them without quite literally setting the world on fire." She exhaled impatiently, stroking the rat's nose, as if to—as if to calm down. My stomach twisted. "Even then, we're trying *not* to raise the alarm. We need a quick and quiet entrance."

"They'll be expecting magic," I hurried to add. Anything to keep her from changing strategy. Anything to keep her from the alternative. "And Claud Deveraux hid us along Les Dents. Maybe he can hide us here too."

Beau threw his hands in the air. "This is a completely different situation! These men *know* we're here. They're searching every wagon. For Claud Deveraux to hide us, he'd need to *quite literally* make us disappear."

"Do you have another plan?" Both Lou and the rat glared at him. "If so, by all means, please share with the class." When he didn't answer, she scoffed bitterly. "That's what I thought. Now can you do everyone a favor and shut the hell up? We're anxious enough as it is."

"Lou," Coco admonished in a low voice, but Lou only turned away, crossing her arms and scowling at the snow. Of their own volition, my feet moved—my body angled—to shield her from the others' disapproving looks. She might've deserved them. I didn't care.

"If you're going to reprimand me, you can piss off too." Though she wiped furiously at her eyes, a tear still escaped. I brushed it away with my thumb. Instinctive. "Don't." She jerked, swatting my hand, and turned her back on me too. Absalon hissed at her feet. "I'm *fine.*"

I didn't move. Didn't react. Inside, however, I reeled as if she'd struck me—as if the two of us hurtled toward a cliff, heedless, each pulling at the other. Each pushing. Both desperate to save ourselves, and both helpless to stop our trajectory. We were careening toward that edge, Lou and I.

I'd never felt so powerless in my life.

"I'm sorry," I whispered, but she didn't acknowledge me, instead shoving Jean Luc's Balisarda into my hand.

"We didn't have time earlier, but while we're waiting . . . I stole it for you. To replace the one I lost." She pressed it harder. My fingers curled around the hilt reflexively. The silver felt different. Wrong. Though Jean Luc had clearly cared for the blade—it'd been recently cleaned and sharpened—it wasn't *mine*. It didn't smooth the jagged edge in my chest. Didn't fill the empty hole there. I slid it into my bandolier anyway, unsure of what else to do. She continued without enthusiasm. "I know I might've gotten a little carried away in the process. With—with the ice. I'm sorry. I promise it won't happen again."

I promise.

For days I'd waited to hear those words, yet now they rang hollow in my ears. Empty. She didn't understand the meaning of them. Perhaps couldn't. They implied truth, trust. I doubted she'd ever known either. Still—I wanted to believe her. Desperately. And an apology from her didn't come lightly.

I swallowed against the sudden tightness in my throat. "Thank you."

We stayed quiet for a long time after that. Though the sun crept across the sky, the queue hardly moved. And the others' eyes—I felt them on us. Especially the wolves'. Heat prickled along my neck. My ears. I didn't like the way they looked at Lou. They knew her only as she was now. They didn't know her warmth, her compassion. Her love.

After what you've done, be grateful I do not demand your *blood, Louise le Blanc.*

Though I trusted they wouldn't harm *me*, they'd made no such promise to her. Whatever madness this day inevitably brought, I wouldn't leave them alone with her. I would give them no opportunity to retaliate. Forlorn, I traced the curve of Lou's neck with my gaze. She'd knotted her white hair at her nape. Tied another ribbon around her throat. All at once so familiar yet so different.

I had to fix her.

When the sun crested the trees, the fox at last returned to us. She nosed Lou's boot, staring up at her intently. Communicating silently with her eyes. "Does she . . . speak to you?" I asked.

Lou frowned. "Not with words. It's more like a feeling. Like— like her consciousness touches mine, and I *understand*." Her head snapped up. "Toulouse and Thierry are coming."

Within minutes, two familiar black heads parted the crowd, proving her right. With a crutch under his arm, Toulouse whistled one of Deveraux's tunes. He grinned at Liana, tipping his hat, before grasping my shoulder.

"*Bonjour à vous*," he told her. "Good morrow, good morrow. And fancy meeting you here, Monsieur Diggory."

"Shhh." I ducked my head, but no one on the road paid us any notice. "Are you daft?"

"Some days." His gaze fell behind us to the werewolves, and he grinned wider. "I see I was mistaken. How unexpected. I'll admit, I doubted your powers of persuasion, but I've never been more pleased to be wrong." He elbowed Thierry with a chuckle. "Perhaps I should try it more often, eh, brother?" His grin faded slightly as he turned back to me. "Would you like to try that card now?"

I nodded to his crutch instead. "Are you injured?"

"Of course not." He tossed it to me. "I'm fit as Deveraux's fiddle. That's one of his stilts, by the way. He sends his assistance."

Thierry swung a bag from his shoulder and handed it to Lou.

"Spectacles?" Beau leaned over her, incredulous, withdrawing a pair of wire frames. She pushed him away. "Mustaches? Wigs? *This* is his assistance? Costumery?"

"Without magic, there's little other way to trick the huntsmen, is there?" Toulouse's eyes gleamed with mischief. "I mistook you for intelligent along Les Dents, Beauregard. It seems I'm wrong *twice* in one day. It's absolutely thrilling."

I ignored them both as Thierry's voice resounded in my head. *I am sorry. Claud wishes he could've come himself, but he won't leave Zenna and Seraphine alone.*

My thoughts sharpened. *Has something happened to them?*

It's dangerous inside the city, Reid. Worse even than usual. Jean Luc warned the king of Morgane's threat, and the Chasseurs have arrested three women this morning alone. The rest guard him and his daughters inside the castle. Toulouse has requested we not assist you further.

I startled. *What?*

The card, Reid. Prove him wrong a third time.

What does the card *have to do with anything?*

Everything. He sighed as Lou pushed Beau out of her personal space again, shaking his head. *I like you, huntsman, so I will help you one last time: Morgane can't touch the king in his castle, but he will join the funeral procession this afternoon. It's his duty as sovereign to honor the Holy Father. If Morgane is to strike, it will be then. Though Jean Luc resides with him, he no longer holds his Balisarda.* His black eyes dipped to the sapphire in my bandolier. *A dozen others are new. Inexperienced. They took their vows only this morning.*

The tournament. I closed my eyes in resignation. Amidst the horrors of Les Dents, I'd forgotten about the Chasseurs' tournament. If there'd been any doubt Morgane would attack at the funeral, it vanished with the realization. The brotherhood had never been weaker. The crowd had never been larger. And the stakes—they'd never been higher. It was the perfect stage for Morgane, grander even than that on Saint Nicolas Day. We needed to get into the city. Now. *Is there nothing else Claud can do?*

You do not need Claud. You need only trust yourself.

My gaze cut to Lou. She still bickered with Beau. Toulouse looked on with amusement. *If you're suggesting I use magic, I won't.*

It is not your enemy, Reid.

It's not a friend, either.

Your fear is irrational. You are not Louise. You are reason, where she is impulse. You are earth. She is fire.

Anger sparked. More riddles. More convolution. *What are you talking about?*

Your choices are not her choices, friend. Do not condemn yourself to her fate. My brother and I have used magic for years, and we remain in control of ourselves. So too does Cosette. With temperance, magic is a powerful ally.

But I heard only some of his words. *Her fate?*

As if in answer, Beau muttered, "I never thought I'd die dressed as a hag. I suppose there are less interesting ways to go." He made to throw the spectacles back into the bag, raising his voice at my uncertain glance. "What? You know how this ends. We're arming ourselves with scraps of lace against blades of steel. We're—we're playing dress-up, for Christ's sake. The Chasseurs will kill us out of spite for the insult."

"You forget I sprinkle spite into my tea every morning." Lou snatched the spectacles from his hand and shoved them on her nose. "Besides, playing dress-up hasn't failed me yet. What could possibly go wrong?"

TRIAL BY FIRE

Reid

Everything went wrong.

"That wagon there." Crouched in the boughs of a pine, Lou pointed to a wagon apart from the crowd. Its horse was bony. Old. A middle-aged man held the reins. His leathery skin and gnarled hands marked him a farmer, and his gaunt face marked him poor. Hungry.

"No." I shook my head abruptly, voice brusque. "I won't prey on the weak."

"You will if you want to live." At my silence, she sighed impatiently. "Look, those are the only two covered transports within a mile. I'll be preying on that one"—she pointed to the gilded carriage in front of the farmer's wagon—"so I'll be close, in case you need help. Just give me a shout, but remember—it's Lucida, not Lou."

"This is madness." My chest constricted at the thought of what I was about to do. "It'll never work."

"Not with that attitude!" Gripping my shoulders, she turned

me to face her. Nausea rolled through my stomach. Disguised in Deveraux's velvet suit and hat, she looked at me from behind gold spectacles. An aristocrat's scholarly son on his return home from Amandine. "Remember your story. You were set upon by bandits, and they broke your nose." She adjusted the bloody bandage on my face for good measure. "And your leg." She tapped the make-shift crutch we'd fashioned out of the stilt. "Just knock on the door. The wife will take pity on you after one look."

"And if she doesn't?"

"Knock her out. Drag her inside. Enchant her." She didn't flinch at the prospect of bludgeoning an innocent woman. "Do whatever is necessary to get inside that wagon."

"I thought you said no magic."

She snorted impatiently. "This isn't the time for a principled stand, Reid. We can't risk magic out in the open, but within the confines of her wagon, do whatever is necessary. If even one person recognizes us, we're dead."

"And when the Chasseur arrives to search the wagon?"

"You're in a wig. Your face is covered. You might be worrying for nothing. But if he recognizes you—if he suspects—you'll have to disarm him while keeping him conscious. Otherwise he can't wave you through the blockade."

"Even if I threaten to slit his throat, a Chasseur will never wave me through that blockade."

"He will if he's enchanted." I opened my mouth to refuse—or to vomit—but she continued, undeterred. "Whatever you do, don't cause a scene. Be quick and quiet. That's the only way we survive this."

Saliva coated my mouth, and I struggled to breathe, clutching my bandolier for support. I didn't fear meeting my brethren. I didn't fear exchanging blows or obtaining injury. I didn't even fear capture, but if that happened—if the Chasseurs arrested me here—Lou would intervene. They'd call in reinforcements. They would hunt her, and this time, she wouldn't escape.

That could not happen.

Even if—even if that meant using magic.

It is not your enemy, Reid.

With temperance, magic is a powerful ally.

"I won't. I *can't*." I nearly choked on the words. "Someone will smell it. They'll know we're here."

She tugged my coat closed over my bandolier. "Maybe. But this road is teeming with people. It'll take them time to distinguish who's casting it. You can force the enchanted Chasseur to wave you through before they figure it out."

"Lou." The word was desperate, pleading, but I didn't care. "There are too many things that could go wrong—"

She kissed my cheek swiftly. "You can do this. And if you can't—if something *does* go wrong—just punch the Chasseur in the nose and run like hell."

"Great plan."

She chuckled, but the sound was strained. "It worked for Coco and Ansel."

Pretending to be newlyweds, they'd already slipped through the convoy on foot. The Chasseur who'd inspected them had been new, and they'd passed into Cesarine unscathed. Beau had forgone costume completely, instead finding a pretty young widow to smuggle him inside. She'd nearly fainted at the sight of his royal face. Blaise and his kin hadn't revealed how they planned to slip into the city. As there'd been no commotion, I assumed they made it in undetected.

I doubted Lou and I would be so lucky.

"Reid. *Reid.*" I snapped to attention. Lou spoke faster now. "The enchantment should come naturally, but if you need a pattern, focus with specific intent. Visualize your objectives. And remember, it's always, *always* about balance."

"Nothing about magic comes easily to me."

Liar.

"Because you're incapacitating yourself with hate," Lou said. "Open yourself up to your magic. Accept it, welcome it, and it'll come to you. Are you ready?"

Seek us.

My lips were numb. "No."

But there was little time to argue. The wagon and carriage were almost upon us.

She squeezed my hand, tearing her gaze from the carriage to look at me. "I know things have changed between us. But I want *you* to know that I love you. Nothing can ever change that. And if you die today, I will find you in the afterlife and kick your ass for leaving me. Understand?"

My voice was weak. "I—"

"Good."

And then she was gone, tugging a book from her pack and dashing toward the carriage. "*Excusez-moi, monsieur!*" she called to the driver, pushing her spectacles up her nose. "But my horse has thrown a shoe...."

A hollow pit opened in my stomach as her voice faded into the crowd.

I love you. Nothing can ever change that.

Damn it.

I didn't get to say it back.

Adopting a limp, leaning heavily on my crutch, I navigated the crowd to the wagon. The convoy was at a standstill, and the farmer—preoccupied with a dirty child throwing rocks at his horse—didn't see me. I knocked once, twice, on the frame. Nothing. I knocked louder.

"What d'yeh want?" A reedy woman with sharp cheekbones and horselike teeth finally poked her head out. A cross dangled from her throat, and a cap covered her hair. Pious, then. Probably traveling to Cesarine to pay her respects. Hope swelled in my chest. Perhaps she *would* take pity on me. It was the mandate of our Lord to help the helpless.

Her scowl quickly punctured that hope. "We don't 'ave no food fer beggars, so clear off!"

"Apologies, *madame*," I said hastily, catching the flap when she moved to yank it shut, "but I don't need food. Bandits set upon me down the road"—I rapped my crutch against the wagon for emphasis—"and I cannot continue my journey on foot. Do you have room in your wagon for one more?"

"No," she snapped, trying to wrestle the flap from my hand.

No hesitation. No remorse. "Not fer the likes o' you. Yer the third one oo's come knockin' at our wagon this mornin', and I'll be tellin' you the same as I told them: we won't be takin' no chances wif strange folk today. Not wif His Eminence's funeral this evenin'." She clutched the cross at her throat with spindly fingers and closed her eyes. "May God keep 'is soul." When she cracked an eye open and saw me still standing there, she added, "Now shove off."

The wagon inched forward, but I held firm, forcing myself to remain calm. To think like Lou would think. To lie. "I'm not a witch, *madame*, and I'm in desperate need of aid."

Her mouth—deeply lined—twisted in confusion. "O course yer not a witch. D'yeh think I'm daft? Everyone knows menfolk can't have magic."

At the word, those nearest us turned to stare. Eyes wide and wary.

I cursed inwardly.

"Bernadette?" The farmer's voice rose above the din of the crowd. More heads swiveled in our direction. "Is this lad botherin' you?"

Before she could answer—before she could seal my fate—I hissed, "'He that despiseth his neighbor sinneth, but he that hath mercy on the poor, happy is he.'"

Her eyes narrowed. "What did you just say?"

"'He that giveth unto the poor shall not lack: but he that hideth his eyes shall have many a curse.'"

"Are you quotin' scripture at me, boy?"

"'Withhold not good from them to whom it is due, when it is in the power of thine hand to do it.'"

"Bernadette!" The farmer stood from his box. "Did you hear me, love? Shall I fetch a Chasseur?"

"Should I continue?" White-knuckled on the wagon flap, my fingers trembled. I fisted them tighter, glaring at her. "For as the Lord commands—"

"That's enough o' you." Though her wrinkled lip curled, she surveyed me with grudging appreciation. "I don't be needin' no lessons in 'oliness from guttersnipes." To her husband, she called, "Everythin's fine, Lyle! This one 'ere busted 'is ankle and needs a lift is all."

"Well, tell 'im we don't want no—"

"I'll tell 'im what I want to tell him!" Jerking her head behind her, she drew the wagon flap aside. "Come inside, then, Yer Holiness, a'fore I change me mind."

The inside of Bernadette's wagon looked nothing like the inside of Troupe de Fortune's. Every inch of the troupe's wagons had been crammed full. Trunks of costumes and trinkets. Crates of food. Props. Lanterns. Cots and bedrolls.

This wagon was bare save a single blanket and a near empty satchel of food. A lonely pot sat beside it.

"Like I said," Bernadette muttered, hunkering down on the floor. "No food fer beggars here."

We waited in stony silence as the wagon crept closer to the Chasseurs. "You look familiar," she said after several moments. She peered at me suspiciously, eyes sharper than I would've liked.

They studied my black wig, my charcoal-dark eyebrows. The bloody bandage on my nose. I readjusted it involuntarily. "Ave we met a'fore?"

"No."

"Why is you goin' to Cesarine, then?"

I stared at my hands without seeing them. *To attend the funeral of the man I killed. To fraternize with blood witches and werewolves. To kill the mother of the woman I love.* "Same as you."

"You don't strike me as the religious type."

I pinned her with a glare. "Likewise."

She harrumphed and crossed her arms. "Mouthy lit'le imp, isn't you? Ungrateful too. Should've made you walk like all the rest, busted ankle an' all."

"We're comin' up on 'em now!" Lyle called from outside. "City's straight ahead!"

Bernadette rose and marched to the front of the wagon, sticking her head out once more. I strode after her.

Framed by the gray skyline of Cesarine, a dozen Chasseurs rode through the crowd, slowing traffic. Some inspected the faces of those on foot. Some dismounted to check wagons and carriages intermittently. I recognized eight of them. Eight out of twelve. When one of those eight—Philippe—started toward our wagon, I cursed.

"Watch yer mouth!" Bernadette said in outrage, elbowing me sharply. "And budge over, would you—" She stopped short when she saw my face. "Yer white as a sheet, you are."

Philippe's deep voice rumbled through the procession, and he pointed toward us. "Have we cleared this one yet?"

Older than me by several decades, he wore a beard streaked through with silver. It did nothing to diminish the breadth of his chest or heavy muscle of his arms. A scar still disfigured his throat from his battle with Adrien's kin in the werewolf raid.

He'd hated me for stealing his glory that day. For stealing his advancement.

Shit.

Jean Luc's Balisarda weighed heavier than the other knives in my bandolier. If Philippe recognized me, I'd need to kill or disarm him. And I couldn't kill him. I couldn't kill another brother. But if I disarmed him instead, I'd have to—

No. My mind raged against the thought.

This isn't the time for a principled stand, Reid, Lou had said. *If even one person recognizes us, we're dead.*

She was right. Of course she was right. And even if it made me a hypocrite—even if it condemned me to Hell—I would channel those insidious voices. I would hang myself with their golden patterns. If it meant Lou would live, I would do it. Damn the consequences. I would do it.

But how?

Open yourself up to your magic. Accept it, welcome it, and it'll come to you.

I hadn't welcomed anything on Modraniht, yet the pattern had still appeared. The same had happened at the pool near the Hollow. In both situations, I'd been desperate. Hopeless. Morgane had just cut Lou's throat, and I'd watched as her blood poured into the basin, draining her life by the second. The golden cord had risen from my pit of despair, and I'd reacted instinctively. There hadn't been time for anything else. And—and at the pool—

The memory of Lou's blue lips surfaced. Her ashen skin.

But this wasn't like that. Lou wasn't dying in front of me now. I tried to summon the same sense of urgency. If Philippe caught me, Lou *would* die. Surely that possibility should trigger something. I waited anxiously for the floodgates to burst open, for gold to explode in my vision.

It didn't.

It seemed imagining Lou dying wasn't the same as watching it happen.

Philippe continued toward us, close enough now to touch the horses. I nearly roared in frustration. What was I supposed to *do?*

You could ask. A small, sinister voice echoed through my thoughts at last, reverberating as if legion. The hair on my neck rose. *You need only seek us, lost one, and you shall find.*

Panicking, I shoved at it instinctively.

An unearthly chuckle. *You cannot escape us, Reid Labelle. We are part of you.* As if to prove its words, it latched tighter, the pressure in my head building—painful now—as tendrils of gold snaked outward, stabbing deep and taking root. Into my mind. My heart. My lungs. I choked on them, struggling to breathe, but they only pressed closer. Consuming me. *For so long we have slept in the darkness, but now, we are awake. We will protect you. We will not let you go. Seek us.*

Black threatened the edges of my vision. My panic intensified. I had to get out, had to stop this—

Staggering backward, I faintly registered Bernadette and Lyle's alarm. "What's the matter wif you, eh?" Bernadette asked. When I didn't answer—couldn't answer—she moved slowly to her bag. My eyes struggled to focus on her, to remain open. I dropped to my knees, fighting desperately to repress this growing *thing* inside me—this monster clawing through my skin. Inexplicable light flickered around us.

He approaches, child. He is coming. The voice turned hungry now. Anticipatory. The pressure in my head built with each word. Blinding me. Tormenting me. My nightmares made flesh. I clutched my head against the pain, a scream rising in my throat. *He will burn us if you let him.*

"What's happenin' wif yer head?"

No. My mind warred against itself. The pain cleaved me in two. *This isn't right. This isn't—*

"I'm talkin' to you, imp!"

He will burn Louise.

No—

"Oi!" A whistle cut through the air, and fresh pain exploded behind my ear. I crumpled to the wagon floor. Groaning softly, I could just distinguish Bernadette's blurred form above me. She lifted her frying pan to strike again. "Bleedin' mad, aren't yeh? I knew it. And today o' all days—"

"Wait." I held up a weak hand. The peculiar light shone brighter now. "Please."

She lurched backward, face twisting in alarm. "What's this happenin' with yer skin, then, eh? What's goin' on?"

"I don't—" My vision sharpened on my hand. On the soft light emanating from it. Hideous despair swept through me. Hideous relief.

Seek us seek us seek us.

"P-Put down the frying pan, *madame.*"

She shook her head frantically, struggling to keep her arm raised. "Wha' witchcraft is this?"

I tried again, louder now. A strange humming filled my ears, and the inexplicable desire to soothe her overwhelmed me—to soothe and be soothed. "It's going to be all right." My voice sounded strange, even to my own ears. Layered. Resonant. Part of me still raged against it, but that part was useless now. I left it behind. "Put down the frying pan."

The frying pan fell to the floor.

"Lyle!" Her eyes boggled from her head, and her nostrils flared. "Lyle, help—!"

The wagon flap burst open in response. We turned as one to see Philippe standing in the entrance, his Balisarda drawn. Despite the bandage—the wig, the cosmetics—he recognized me immediately. Hatred burned in his eyes. "Reid Diggory."

Kill him.

This time, I heeded the voice without hesitation.

With lethal speed, I charged, seizing his wrist and dragging him into the wagon. His eyes widened—shocked—for a split second. Then he attacked. I laughed, evading his blade easily.

When the sound reverberated through the wagon, infectious and strange, he recoiled.

"It can't be," he breathed. "You can't be a—a—"

He lunged, but again, I moved too quick, sidestepping at the last moment. He barreled into Bernadette instead, and the two careened into the wall of the wagon. My skin erupted with light at her shrieks.

Silence her!

"Be quiet!" The words tore through me of their own volition, and she slumped—mercifully quiet—with her mouth closed and her eyes glazed. Philippe launched to his feet just as Lyle entered the wagon, bellowing at the top of his lungs.

"Bernadette! Bernadette!"

I struggled to look at him, prying Philippe's fingers from my throat with one hand and holding his Balisarda off with the other. My wig tumbled to the floor. "Qui—et—" I said, voice strangled, as Philippe and I crashed through the wagon. But Lyle didn't quiet. He continued shouting, lunging forward to grab Bernadette beneath the arms and drag her from the wagon.

"Wait!" I flung a hand out blindly to stop him, but no patterns emerged. Not even a flicker. Anger erupted at my own ineptitude, and the light emanating from my skin vanished abruptly. "Stop!"

"Help us!" Lyle dove from the wagon. "It's Reid Diggory! He's a witch! HELP!"

New voices sounded outside as Chasseurs converged. Blood roaring in my ears—the voices in my mind damnably silent—I wrenched away from Philippe, flinging the blanket in his face. A quiet entrance into the city was no longer possible. I had to flee. To *run*. Disentangling himself from the blanket, he slipped on the food satchel and flailed backward. I dove for the frying pan.

Before he could regain his footing—before I could reconsider—I swung it at his head.

The crack reverberated through my bones, and he toppled to the wagon floor, unconscious. I dropped to make sure his chest moved. Up and down. Up and down. The other Chasseurs tore aside the wagon's flap just as I leapt through the front, vaulting over the box to the horse's back. It reared, braying indignantly, and the wagon's front wheels lifted from the ground, tipping the structure precariously. Inside, the Chasseurs shouted in alarm. Their bodies thudded into the canvas.

I fumbled with the horse's harness, cursing as more Chasseurs sprinted toward me. Slick with sweat, my fingers slipped over the buckles. I cursed and tried again.

"It's Reid Diggory!" someone shouted. More voices took up the call. Blood roared in my ears.

"Murderer!"

"Witch!"

"Arrest him!"

"ARREST HIM!"

Losing any semblance of control, I tore at the last buckle with frantic fingers. A Chasseur I didn't recognize reached me first. I kicked him in the face—finally, *finally* loosening the clasp—and urged the horse forward with a violent squeeze of my legs. It bolted, and I held on for dear life.

"Out of the way!" I roared. People dove sideways, dragging children with them, as the horse careened toward the city. One man was too slow, and a hoof caught his leg, breaking it. The Chasseurs on horseback pounded after me. They gained ground quickly. Theirs were stallions, bred for speed and strength, and mine was an emaciated mare on her last leg. I urged her on anyway.

If I could clear the city limits, perhaps I could lose them in the streets—

The crowd thickened as the road narrowed, transitioning from dirt to cobblestone. The first buildings rose up to swallow me. Above, a shadow leapt lithely from rooftop to rooftop, following the shouts that chased me. It pointed frantically to the dormer looming ahead.

I nearly wept with relief.

Lou.

Then I realized what she wanted me to do.

No. No, I couldn't—

"Got you!" A Chasseur's hand snaked out and caught the back of my coat. The others closed in behind him. Legs cinching the mare like a vise, I twisted to break his grip, but the mare had had enough.

Braying wildly, she reared once more, and I saw my opportunity.

Climbing up her neck—praying to whoever might be listening—I caught the metal sign overhead with the tips of my fingers. It splintered under my weight, but I kicked hard, leveraging myself against the mare's back and leaping onto the dormer. The mare and Chasseurs' stallions cantered past below.

"STOP HIM!"

Gasping for air, I scrabbled for purchase against the rooftop. My vision pitched and rolled.

"Just keep climbing!" Lou's voice rang out above me, and my head snapped up. She leaned over the roof's edge, fingers splayed and straining to reach me. But her hand was so small. So far away. "Don't look down! Just look at me, Reid! Keep looking at me!"

Below, the Chasseurs roared orders, urging the crowd to part as they turned their horses around.

"AT ME, REID!"

Right. Swallowing hard, I set to finding pockmarks in the stone wall. I inched higher. My head spun.

Higher.

My breath caught.

Higher.

My muscles seized.

Higher.

The Chasseurs had maneuvered back to me. I heard them dismounting. Heard them starting to climb.

Lou's hand caught my wrist and heaved. I focused on her face, on her freckles. Through sheer willpower alone, I clambered over the eave and collapsed. But we didn't have time to relax. She pulled me to my feet, already sprinting for the next rooftop. "What *happened?*"

I followed her. Concentrated on my breathing. It was easier now, with her here. "Your plan was shit."

She had the gall to laugh, but quickly stopped when an arrow whizzed past her face. "C'mon. I'll lose these jackasses within three blocks."

I didn't reply. It was best I kept my mouth closed.

THE DROWNING

Lou

Always aiming to please, I lost them in two.

Their voices faded as we ran, dipping into shadowy alcoves and dropping behind ramshackle dormers. The key was breaking their line of sight. Once that happened, it was too easy to slip into the boundlessness of the city.

No one could disappear like I could.

No one had the practice.

I dropped to a forgotten backstreet in East End. Reid landed a second later, collapsing against me. Though I tried to hold him steady, we both tumbled to the dirty cobblestones. He kept his arms locked around my waist, however, and buried his face in my lap. His heart pulsed a frantic rhythm against my thigh. "I can't do that again."

Throat suddenly thick, I stroked his hair. "That's fine. They're gone." His breathing gradually slowed, and finally, he sat up. I let him go reluctantly. "Before your fiasco, I sent Charles to find Madame Labelle. She booked us rooms at an inn called Léviathan."

"Charles?"

"The rat."

He expelled a harsh breath. "Oh."

Shame—now familiar—washed through me all over again. Though sharp words rose to my tongue in response, I bit down on them hard, drawing blood, and offered him a hand. "I already sent Absalon and Brigitte to fetch Coco, Ansel, and Beau. Charles went to the werewolves and blood witches. We'll all need to strategize before the funeral this afternoon."

We climbed to our feet together, and he kissed the back of my hand before releasing it. "It'll be difficult to gain an audience with the king. Thierry said all Chasseurs who aren't at the blockade are inside the castle. Maybe Beau can—"

"Wait." Though I forced a chuckle, there was nothing funny about that obstinate gleam in his eyes. "You can't seriously mean to still speak with Auguste? Jean Luc tipped him off. He knows you're coming. He—he knows Madame Labelle's a witch, and if those Chasseurs' shouts were any indication, he'll soon know *you're* one too." Reid's face blanched at the last. *Ah.* It seemed he hadn't yet drawn *that* conclusion. I hurried to press my advantage. "He knows you're a witch," I repeated. "He won't help you. He certainly won't help me. We don't *need* him, Reid. The Dames Rouges and loup garou are powerful allies."

His lips pursed as he considered this—his jaw clenched— and I waited for him to see the sense in my plan. But he shook his head and muttered, "No. I'll still speak with him. We need a united front against Morgane."

I gaped at him. "Reid—"

A group of children raced past our alley at that moment, chasing a snarling cat. The slowest of them hesitated when he saw us. I jerked my brim lower on my forehead, and Reid hastily retied the bandage over his eye. "We need to get off the streets," he said. "Our entrance into the city wasn't exactly subtle—"

"Thanks for that—"

"And East End will be crawling with Chasseurs and constabulary soon."

I waved to the child, who grinned and took off after his friends, before slipping my elbow through Reid's. I poked my head into the street. It was less crowded here, the majority of funeral visitors congregating in the wealthier West district. The shops lining the streets were closed. "Léviathan is a few blocks past Soleil et Lune."

Reid quickened his pace, adopting a limp once more. "Given our history, the theater will be the first place the Chasseurs look."

Something in his voice made me pause. I frowned up at him. "That wasn't intentional, by the way. My little stunt in the theater. I don't think I ever told you."

"You're kidding."

"I'm not." With nonchalance, I tipped my hat to a nearby woman. Her mouth parted at my velvet suit. Not exactly mourning attire, but at least it was a nice deep shade of aubergine. Knowing Claud, it could've been canary yellow. "Completely accidental, but what could I do? It's not my fault you couldn't keep your hands off my breasts." When he sputtered indignantly, I pressed on, smirking. "I don't blame you in the slightest."

Careful to keep my brim low, I kept a sharp eye on passersby. A familiar air of trepidation hung heavy and thick overhead, as it always did when a crowd this size gathered in Cesarine. People from every walk of life had come to honor the late Archbishop: aristocrats, clergymen, and peasants held vigil together as we neared the cathedral, where the Archbishop's body waited to receive burial rites. Dressed all in black, they leeched the color from an already dreary city. Even the sky was overcast today, as if it too mourned the fate of the wrong man.

The Archbishop didn't deserve anyone's grief.

The only color in the streets came from the fanfare. The usual Lyon flags had been replaced with brilliant red banners depicting the Archbishop's coat of arms: a bear spouting a fountain of stars. Drops of blood in a sea of black and gray.

"Stop." Reid's eyes widened with horror at something in the distance. He pivoted in front of me, clutching my arms as if to shield me from it. "Turn around. Let's go a different way—"

I shook him off, rising to my toes to see over the crowd.

There, at the base of the cathedral, stood three wooden stakes. And chained to those stakes—

"Oh my god," I breathed.

Chained to those stakes were three charred bodies.

Limbs crumbling—hair gone—the corpses were near indistinguishable. Behind them, ash coated the cathedral steps, thicker than the snow on the street. Bile rose in my throat. There had been others before these women. Many others. And recently. The wind hadn't yet carried away their ashes.

But true witches were careful and clever. Surely so many hadn't been caught since Modraniht.

"These women"—I shook my head in disbelief—"they can't all have been witches."

"No." Cradling the back of my head, Reid pulled me to his chest. I inhaled deeply, ignoring the sting of pain in my eyes. "No, they probably weren't."

"Then what—?"

"After the Archbishop, the king would've needed a show of power. He would've needed to reestablish control. Anyone suspicious would have burned."

"Without proof?" I leaned back, searching his face for answers. His eyes were pained. "Without trial?"

He clenched his jaw, looking back at the blackened corpses. "He doesn't need proof. He's the king."

I spotted her the moment Reid and I turned away—thin as a reed with ebony skin and onyx eyes, standing so still she could've been the statue of Saint-Cécile if not for her hair blowing in the breeze. Though I'd known her my entire life, I couldn't read the emotion in her eyes as she stared at the women's remains.

As she turned on her heel and fled into the crowd.

Manon.

"Léviathan is that way." I craned my neck to keep her in my sights, jerking my chin westward. A golden-haired man had followed her, catching her hand and spinning her into his arms. Instead of protesting—of spitting in his face—she gave him a tight smile. That arcane emotion in her eyes melted to unmistakable warmth as she gazed at him. Just as unmistakable, however, was her sorrow. As if trying to banish the emotion, he peppered her cheeks with kisses. When the two started forward once more, I hurried after them. "I'll meet you there in a quarter hour."

"Hold on." Reid seized my arm with an incredulous expression. "We aren't separating."

"I'll be fine. If you keep to the side streets and maybe hunch a bit, you will be too—"

"Not a chance, Lou." His eyes followed mine, narrowing as they searched the crowd, and he slid his grip from my elbow to my hand. "What is it? What did you see?"

"You are the most obstinate—" I stopped short with an impatient huff. "*Fine.* Come with me. But stay low and stay quiet." Without another word, fingers still entwined with his, I slipped through the crowd. No one spared us a second glance, their eyes rapt on the three burning women. Their fascination sickened me.

Manon appeared to be leading the golden-haired man to a less congested area. We followed as quickly and noiselessly as we could, but twice we were forced to duck out of sight to avoid Chasseurs. By the time we found them again, Manon had steered the man down a deserted alley. Smoke from a nearby trash pile nearly obscured its entrance. If not for the man's panicked cry, we might've walked straight past.

"You don't have to do this," he said, voice cracking. Exchanging a wary glance, Reid and I crouched behind the trash and peered through the smoke. Manon had cornered him against a wall. Hands raised, she wept openly, her tears flowing so thick and so fast that she struggled to breathe. "We can find another way."

"You don't understand." Though her entire body spasmed, she lifted her hands higher. "Three more burned this morning. She'll be wild—crazed. And if she finds out about us—"

"How can she?"

"She has eyes everywhere, Gilles! If she even suspects I'm attached to you, she'll—she'll do horrible things. She tortured the others for no other reason than their parentage. She'll do worse to you. She'll *enjoy* it. And if—if I return to her again today empty-handed, she'll know. She'll come for you herself, and I would rather *die* than see you in her hands." She pulled a blade from her cloak. "I promise you won't suffer."

He extended his hands, beseeching, reaching to hold her even as she threatened his life. "So we run away. We leave this place. I have some money saved from cobbling. We can sail to Lustere or—or anywhere. We can build a new life far, far away from here. Somewhere Morgane's influence doesn't reach."

At my mother's name, Reid stiffened. I glanced at him, watching as he finally placed Manon's face.

Head thrashing, she wept harder. "No. No, stop. Please. I *can't*."

"You *can*, Manon. *We* can. Together."

"She gave me orders, Gilles. If—if I don't do this, she will."

"Manon, please—"

"This wasn't supposed to happen." Her hands shook around the blade. "*None* of this was supposed to happen. I—I was supposed to find you and kill you. I wasn't supposed to—to—" A strangled sound tore from her throat as she stepped closer. "They killed my sister, Gilles. They killed her. I—I swore on her pyre I'd avenge her death. I swore to *end* this. I—I—" Her face crumpled, and she lifted the blade to his throat. "I love you."

To his credit, Gilles didn't flinch. He merely dropped his hands, eyes tracing her face as if trying to memorize it, and brushed his lips to her forehead. "I love you too."

They stared at each other. "Turn around," Manon whispered.

"I have to stop her." Tension radiated from every muscle in Reid's body. Unsheathing Jean Luc's Balisarda, he rose to charge forward, but I leapt in front of him—tears streaming down my own cheeks—and pressed my hands against his chest. Manon couldn't know he was here. I had to hide him. I had to make sure she never saw. "What are you doing?" he asked, incredulity twisting his face, but I only shoved him backward.

"Move, Reid." Panic stole the heat from my voice, made it breathless, desperate. I pushed him harder. "*Please*. You have to move. You have to go—"

"*No*." His hands pried my wrists away. "I have to *help*—"

Behind us, something thudded to the ground. It was a horrible, final sound.

Too late—locked in our own sick embrace—we turned as one to see Gilles lying facedown on the cobblestones. Manon's knife protruded from the base of his skull.

My breath left me in a painful rush, and suddenly, only Reid's hands kept me upright. Blood roared in my ears. "Oh my god."

Manon sank to her knees, pulling him into her lap and closing her eyes. His blood soaked her dress. Her hands. She cradled him to her neck anyway. Though her tears had finally stopped, she gasped as she rocked him, as she slid the knife free of his flesh and dropped it to the ground. It landed in the pool of Gilles's blood. "This isn't God, Louise." Her voice was wooden. Hollow. "This isn't Goddess, either. No divinity smiles upon us now."

I stepped toward her despite myself, but Reid held me back. "Manon—"

"Morgane says sacrifice is necessary." She clutched Gilles tighter, shoulders shaking and fresh tears spilling down her cheeks. "She says we must give before we receive, but my sister is still dead."

Acid coated my tongue. I said the words anyway. "Did killing him bring her back?"

Her eyes snapped to mine. Instead of fury, they filled with a hopelessness so deep I could've drowned in it. I *wanted* to drown in it—to sink beneath its depths and never resurface, to leave this hell behind. But I couldn't, and neither could she. Reaching slowly for the knife, her fingers swam instead through her lover's blood. "Run, Louise. Run far and run fast, so we never find you."

MADAME SAUVAGE'S CABINET OF CURIOSITIES

Lou

Heart still racing from Manon's warning, I dragged Reid down the nearest alleyway—through a narrow, shadowed arch—and into the first shop I saw. If Manon had followed us, we couldn't risk staying on the street. A bell tinkled at our entrance, and the sign above the door swayed.

MADAME SAUVAGE'S CABINET OF CURIOSITIES

I skidded to a halt, regarding the little shop warily. Stuffed rats danced in the window display, alongside glass beetles and dusty books with gold-painted edges. The shelves nearest us—teetering between black-and-white floors and starry ceilings—had been crammed with a motley assortment of animal skulls, gemstones, pointed teeth, and amber bottles. Pinned along the far wall, barely visible beneath all the clutter, were cerulean-blue butterfly wings.

Reid's silence cracked at the queerness of the place. "What . . . what is this?"

"It's an emporium." My voice came out a whisper, yet it still seemed to echo all around us. The hair on my neck rose. If we left now, Manon might see us—or worse, follow us to Léviathan. Grabbing a brown wig from a particularly hideous marionette, I tossed it to him. "Put this on. The Chasseurs recognized you earlier. You need a new disguise."

He crumpled the wig in his fist. "Your disguises don't work, Lou. They never have."

I paused in rifling through a basket of woven fabrics. "Would you prefer we use magic instead? I noticed you used it earlier to get yourself out of that little bind with the Chasseurs. How does that work? You're allowed to use it when you deem necessary, but I'm not?"

He clenched his jaw, refusing to look at me. "I used it responsibly."

They were the simplest words—perhaps spoken innocently—yet anger cracked open in my stomach all the same, like a rotten egg that'd been waiting to hatch. I felt it rising to my cheeks, enflaming me. I didn't care that we were standing in a house of horrors. I didn't care that the clerk was probably listening out of sight, that Manon was likely closing in at this very moment.

Slowly, I removed my spectacles and placed them on the shelf. "Say what you need to say, Reid, and say it now."

He didn't hesitate. "Who was the man, Lou? Why didn't you let me save him?"

My heart dropped like a stone. Though I'd expected the question—though I'd known this conversation to be inevitable after what we'd witnessed—I was less prepared to address it now than I'd been in Beauchêne. I swallowed hard, tugging on my cravat, trying and failing to articulate the situation without causing irreparable damage. I didn't want to lie. I *certainly* didn't want to tell the truth. "We've been fighting for days, Reid," I deflected. "Those aren't the right questions."

"Answer them anyway."

I opened my mouth to do exactly that—unsure what words would spill out—but an elderly woman with deep, leathery skin hobbled toward us, swathed in a burgundy cloak three times her size. Golden rings glinted on her every finger, and a maroon scarf enveloped her hair. She smiled at us, brown eyes crinkling at the corners. "Hello, dearies. Welcome to my cabinet of curiosities. How may I serve you today?"

I willed the old woman to go away with every fiber of my being. "We're just browsing."

She laughed, the sound throaty and rich, and began rifling through the shelf nearest her. This one held a collection of buttons and pins, with the occasional shrunken head. "Are you quite sure? I couldn't help but overhear terse words." She plucked two dried flowers from a bin. "Might I interest you in calla lilies? They're said to symbolize humility and devotion. The perfect blooms to end any lovers' quarrel."

Reid accepted his in a reflexive movement, too polite to decline. I knocked it from his hand to the floor. "They also mean death."

"Ah." Her dark eyes glittered with mischief. "Yes, I suppose that is one interpretation."

"We're sorry if we disturbed you, *madame*," Reid muttered, his lips hardly moving, his jaw still clenched. He stooped to retrieve the flower and handed it back to her. "We'll leave now."

"Nonsense, Reid." She winked cheerily, returning the lilies to the shelf. "Manon won't find you here. You and Louise may stay as long as you like—though *do* lock the door when you're finished, won't you?"

We both stared at her, alarmed, but she simply spun with unnatural grace and ... *vanished.*

I turned to Reid incredulously, mouth parted, but he'd resumed glaring at me with a single-minded intensity that immediately roused my defenses.

"What?" I asked warily.

"Who was that?" He articulated the words slowly, precisely, as if expending extraordinary effort to keep his temper in check. "And how do you know her? How does she know us?"

When I opened my mouth to answer him—to tell him I hadn't the faintest idea—he cut across me abruptly, voice harsh. "Don't lie to me."

I blinked. The implication of his words stung more than I cared to admit, rekindling my anger. I'd only lied to him when absolutely necessary—like when the alternative had been him burning me alive. Or Morgane chopping off his head. *Don't lie to me,* he said. Just as sanctimonious and arrogant as he'd always been. As if *I* were the problem. As if *I* were the one who'd spent the last fortnight lying to myself about who and what I was.

"You can't handle the truth, Reid." I stalked past him toward the door, a flush creeping up my cheeks. "You couldn't handle it then, and you can't handle it now."

His hand caught my arm. "Let me decide that."

"Why? You don't have a problem making decisions for me." Jerking away, I pressed a hand against the door, fighting to prevent the words from spilling out of me. To swallow the bitter vitriol that had settled in my bones after weeks of his disapproval. His hatred. *Aberrant*, he'd called me. *Like a sickness. A poison.* And his face—after I'd saved his ass with the ice in Le Ventre—

"I'm clearly not making decisions for you," he said dryly, dropping my arm. "Or we wouldn't be in this mess."

Hateful tears welled in my eyes. "You're right. You'd be dead at the bottom of a pool with a frozen dick." My hand curled into a fist against the wood. "Or you'd be dead in the remains of a pub with a burnt one. Or bleeding out in La Fôret des Yeux from a thief's blade. Or in Le Ventre from werewolves' teeth." I laughed then—wild, perhaps hysterical—my nails biting into the door hard enough to leave marks in the wood. "Let's pick a death, shall we? God forbid I take the decision away from you."

He pressed forward, so close now I felt his chest against my back. "What happened in the blood camp, Lou?"

I couldn't look at him. Wouldn't look at him. Never before had I felt so stupid—so stupid and callow and unappreciated. "A funeral," I said, voice wooden. "For Etienne Gilly."

"A funeral," he repeated softly, planting his hand on the wood above my head, "for Etienne Gilly."

"Yes."

"Why didn't you tell me?"

"Because you didn't need to know."

His head dropped to my shoulder. "Lou—"

"Forgive me, husband, for trying to keep you *happy*—"

Snapping his head up, he snarled, "If you want to make me *happy*, you'd treat me like your partner. Your *spouse*. You wouldn't keep secrets from me like a foolish child. You wouldn't play with memories or steal Balisardas. You wouldn't turn yourself to *ice*. Are you—are you *trying* to get yourself killed? I don't—I just—" He pushed away, and I turned, watching him drag a hand through his hair. "What is it going to *take*, Lou? When are you going to *see* how reckless you're being—"

"You churlish *ass*." My voice rose, and I fought the urge to pound my fists and stomp my feet, to *show* him what a foolish child I could be. "I have sacrificed *everything* to keep your ungrateful ass alive, and you've scorned me at every turn."

"I never asked you to sacrifice anything—"

I lifted my hands to his face. "Perhaps I can find a pattern to reverse time. Is that what you want? Would you rather have died in that pool than lived to see me become who I truly am? I'm a *witch*, Reid. A *witch*. I have the power to protect the ones I love, and I will sacrifice *anything* for them. If that makes me a monster—if that makes me *aberrant*—I'll don the teeth and claws to make it easier for you. I'll get worse, if that justifies your twisted rhetoric. Much, much worse."

"Goddamn it, I'm trying to *protect* you," he said angrily, flinging my hands out of his face. "Don't turn this into something it's not. I *love* you, Lou. I *know* you're not a monster. Look around." He extended his arms, eyes widening. "I'm still here. But if you don't stop sacrificing pieces of yourself to save us, there won't be anything left. You don't owe us those pieces—not me, not Coco, not Ansel. We don't want them. We want *you*."

"You can cut the shit, Reid."

"It's not shit."

"No? Tell me something, then—that night when I robbed Tremblay's townhouse, you thought I was a criminal, not a witch. Why?"

"Because you *were* a criminal."

"Answer the question."

"I don't know." He scoffed, the sound harsh and jarring in the stillness of the shop. "You were wearing a suit three sizes too big and a mustache, for God's sake. You looked like a little girl playing dress-up."

"So that's it. I was too human. You couldn't fathom me being a witch because I wasn't inherently evil enough. I wore pants and ate sticky buns and sang pub songs, and a witch could never do those things. But you knew, didn't you? Deep down, you *knew* what I was. All the signs were there. I called the witch at Tremblay's a friend. And Estelle—I mourned her. I knew more about magic than anyone in the Tower, loathed the books in the library that denounced it. I bathed twice a day to wash away the scent, and our room smelled permanently of the candles I stole from the sanctuary. But your prejudices ran deep. Too deep. You didn't want to see it—didn't want to admit that you were falling in love with a witch."

He shook his head in vehement denial. It was as good as a condemnation.

A sick sort of satisfaction swept through me. I was right, after all. My magic hadn't twisted *me*; it'd twisted *him*, taking root in the space between us and wrapping around his heart. "After everything, I thought you could change—could learn, could grow—but I was wrong. You're still the same as you were then— a scared little boy who thinks all things that roam the night are monsters, and all things that rule the day are gods."

"That's not true. You *know* that's not true—"

But with one realization came another. This one bit deeper, its thorns drawing blood. "You're never going to accept me." I stared up at him. "No matter how hard I try, no matter how much I wish it weren't so . . . you're not my husband, and I'm not your wife. Our marriage—our entire relationship—it was a lie. A hoax. A trick. We're natural enemies, Reid. You'll always be a witch hunter. I'll always be a witch. And we'll always bring each other pain."

A beat of silence passed, as deep and dark as the pit opening in my chest. The mother-of-pearl ring burned a circle of fire into my finger, and I tore at the golden band, desperately trying to remove it—to *return* it. It wasn't mine. It'd never been mine. Reid hadn't been the only one playing pretend.

He marched forward, ignoring my struggle and gripping my face between his hands. "Stop this. Stop. You need to listen to me."

"Stop telling me what I *need* to do." Why wouldn't he just admit it? Why couldn't he say the words that would set me free? That would set *him* free? It wasn't fair to either of us to continue this way, aching and yearning and pining after something that could never be. Not like this.

"You're doing it again." His thumbs stroked my cheeks anxiously, desperately, as my hysteria built. "Don't make a rash decision. Stop and think, Lou. Feel the truth in my words. I'm here. I'm not leaving."

My gaze sharpened on his face, and I reached deep, searching for something—anything—that'd force him to admit he thought me a monster. To admit the *truth*. I thrust the ring into his pocket. "You wanted to know about the man. Gilles." Though somewhere inside that pit a voice warned me to stop, I couldn't. It *hurt*. That revulsion in his eyes when he'd seen me in Le Ventre—I could never forget it. I'd done *everything* for him, and now I—I was scared. Scared he was right. Scared he wasn't.

Scared I'd get worse before I got better. Much, much worse.

Reid's thumbs stilled on my cheeks. I forced myself to meet his eyes, to speak each word to them.

"He was your brother, Reid. Gilles was your brother. Morgane has been hunting your siblings, torturing them to send me a message. She murdered two more at the blood camp while I was there—Etienne and Gabrielle Gilly. *That* is why La Voisin joined us—because Morgane murdered your brother and sister. I didn't tell you because I didn't want to distract you from our plan. I didn't want you to feel pain—*guilt*—for two people you've never known. I stopped you from saving Gilles because it didn't matter if he died, so long as you lived. I did it for the greater good—*my* greater good. Do you understand now? Does that make me a monster?"

He stared at me for a long moment, white-faced and trembling. At last, he dropped his hands and stepped back. The anguish in his eyes cleaved my chest in two, and fresh tears trickled down my cheeks. "No," he finally murmured, brushing them away one last time. A farewell. "It makes you your mother."

I waited several minutes after Reid left the shop to break down. To sob and scream and smash the glass beetles from their shelves, crush the calla lilies beneath my boot. When I finally cracked the door open a half hour later, the shadows of the alley had vanished in the afternoon sun, and he was nowhere in sight. Instead, Charles waited at the threshold. I breathed a sigh of relief—then stopped short.

A small piece of paper had been tacked to the door. It fluttered in the breeze.

Pretty porcelain, pretty doll, forgotten and alone,
Trapped within a mirrored grave, she wears a mask of bone.

I tore it from the door with shaking fingers, peering down the alley behind me. Whoever had left this here had done it while I was still inside the shop—either when Reid and I had argued or after Reid had left. Perhaps Manon had found me, after all. I didn't question why she hadn't attacked, however. I didn't question the morbid words of her riddle. It didn't matter. They didn't matter.

Nothing mattered at all.

A CHANGE OF PLANS

Reid

My heart beat a painful rhythm outside Léviathan. Though I could hear the others inside, I paused at the back entrance, hidden from the street beyond. Breathing heavily. Light-headed with words. They careened into my defenses like bats out of Hell, wings tipped with steel. With razors. Bit by bit, they sliced.

Lou is going to get worse before she gets better. Much, much worse.

Deeper now. They found each crack and cut deeper.

This will always be your life with her—running, hiding, fighting. You will never know peace.

We were supposed to be partners.

Louise has started her descent. You cannot stop it, and you cannot slow it down. It will consume you both if you try.

God, I'd tried.

She will not remain the girl with whom you fell in love.

My hands curled into fists.

I'll don the teeth and claws to make it easier for you. I'll get worse, if that justifies your twisted rhetoric. Much, much worse.

Tendrils of anger curled around the words now, charring them. Setting fire to their sharp tips. I welcomed each flame. Relished them. The smoke didn't damage the fortress—it added to it. Swathed it in heat and darkness. Time and time again, I'd trusted her. And time and time again, she'd proven herself unworthy of my trust.

Did I not deserve her respect?

Did she truly think so little of me?

I'd given her everything. *Everything.* My protection, my love, my *life.* And she'd tossed each aside as if they meant nothing. She'd stripped me of my name, my identity. My *family.* Every word from her mouth since the day we'd met had been a lie—who she was, *what* she was, her relationship with Coco, with Bas. I'd thought I'd moved past them. I'd thought I'd forgiven her. But that hole . . . it hadn't healed quite right. The skin had grown over infection. And hiding my siblings from me, preventing me from saving them . . .

She'd torn me back open.

I couldn't trust her. She obviously didn't trust me.

Our entire relationship had been built on lies.

The fury, the betrayal, burned up my throat. This anger was visceral, a living thing clawing from my chest—

I pounded a fist against the stone wall, sinking to my knees. The others—they couldn't see me like this. Alliance or not, if they scented blood in the water, they'd attack. I had to master myself. I had to—to—

You are in control. Another voice—this one unbidden, still painful—echoed through my mind. *This anger cannot govern you, Reid.*

I'd—I'd killed the Archbishop to save her, for Christ's sake. How could she say I'd scorned her?

Breathing deeply, I knelt in silence for another moment. The anger still burned. The betrayal still ached. But a deadly sense of purpose overpowered both of them. Lou no longer wanted me. She'd made that perfectly clear. I still loved her—I always would—but she'd been right: we could not continue as we were now. Though ironic, though cruel, we'd fit together as witch and witch hunter. As husband and wife. But she'd changed. *I'd* changed.

I wanted to help her. Desperately. But I couldn't force her to help herself.

On steadier feet, I rose, pushing open the door to Léviathan.

What I *could* do was kill a witch. It's what I knew. It's what I'd trained for my entire life. At this very moment, Morgane hid within the city. She hunted my family. If I did nothing—if I sat in this alley and wept over things I could not change—Morgane would find them. She would torture them. She would kill them.

I would kill her first.

To do that, I needed to visit my father.

When I stepped over the threshold, Charles, Brigitte, and Absalon turned and fled upstairs. She was here, then. Lou. As if reading my thoughts, Madame Labelle touched my forearm and murmured, "She came in a few moments before you did. Coco and Ansel followed her up."

Something in her eyes spoke further, but I didn't ask. Didn't want to know.

Small and unremarkable—contrary to its namesake—Léviathan sat tucked within the farthest reach of Cesarine, overlooking the cemetery. Gaps in the floorboards. Cobwebs in the corners. Cauldron in the hearth.

No patrons beyond our own group.

At the bar, Deveraux sat with Toulouse and Thierry. Déjà vu swept through me at the sight of them together. Of another time and another place. Another tavern. That one hadn't housed blood witches and werewolves, though. It'd caught fire instead. "There's a joke here somewhere," Beau muttered, nursing a pint at the table nearest me. His hood still shadowed his face. Beside him sat Nicholina and a woman I didn't recognize. No—a woman I *did*. Tall and striking, she had Coco's face. But her eyes gleamed with unfamiliar malice. She held her spine rigid. Her mouth pursed.

"Good evening, Captain." She inclined her neck stiffly. "At last we meet."

"La Voisin."

At the name, Blaise and his children bared their teeth, snarling softly.

Heedless of the tense silence—of the palpable antagonism—Deveraux laughed and waved me over. "Reid, how *splendid* to see you again! Come hither, come hither!"

"What are you doing here?"

"La Mascarade des Crânes, dear boy! Surely you haven't forgotten? One of the entrances lies below this very—"

I turned away, ignoring the rest of his words. I didn't have time for a happy reunion. Didn't have time to make peace between blood witches and werewolves. To entertain them.

"We're lucky he's here," Madame Labelle murmured, though her voice held more strain than reproach. "After Auguste burned the Bellerose, my contacts in the city are too frightened to speak with me. I would've had a devil of a time procuring a safe place for us if Claud hadn't stepped in. Apparently, the innkeeper owes him a favor. We're the only patrons of Léviathan tonight."

I didn't care. Instead of answering, I nodded to Beau, who plunked his tankard down with a sigh. He joined Madame Labelle and me at the door. "If you're still planning what I think you're planning, you're an idiot of the highest order—"

"What's the timetable?" I asked brusquely.

He blinked at me. "I assume the priests are finishing preparation of the body now. They'll administer last rites soon. Mass will commence in under an hour, and afterward, the Chasseurs will escort my family in the burial procession. They'll lay it to rest around four o'clock this afternoon."

It. The implication of the word stung. *It.* Not *him.*

I forced the thought away. "That gives us an hour to breach the castle. Where will Auguste be?"

Though Beau and Madame Labelle shared an anxious look, neither protested further. "The throne room," he said. "He, my mother, and my sisters will be in the throne room. It's tradition to hold court before ceremonial events."

"Can you get us in?"

He nodded. "Like Claud said, there is a system of tunnels that span the entire city. I used to play in them as a child. They connect the castle, the catacombs, the cathedral—"

"The Bellerose," Madame Labelle added, arching a wry brow. "This pub."

Beau dipped his head with a chuckle. "There's also a passage behind a tapestry in the throne room. You and your mother can hide while I approach my father. After Jean Luc's explanation of events in Le Ventre—and your own rather unfortunate entrance to the city—I think it best I speak with him first. It'll prevent him from arresting you on sight." He leaned in, lowering his voice. "But word will have spread, Reid. He'll know you're a witch now. They all will. I don't know what he'll do. Approaching him on the day of the Archbishop's funeral is a huge risk, especially since you're—" He broke off with an apologetic sigh. "Since you're the one who killed him."

Emotion choked my throat, but I swallowed it down. I could not dwell. I had to move forward. "I understand."

"If I judge him to be amenable, I'll summon you forth. If I don't, you'll run like hell." He looked me in the eye then, squaring his shoulders. "I won't concede that point, brother. If I tell you to run, you will run."

"Perhaps you should have a code word for when things go wrong." With a skeletal grin, Nicholina slipped her face between Beau's and mine. "I suggest flibbertigibbet. Or bumfuzzle. *Bumfuzzle, bumfuzzle, meaning to puzzle—*"

Beau pushed her face away without hesitation. "If for some reason we're separated, take the left-hand tunnel at each fork you meet. It'll take you to La Mascarade des Crânes. Find Claud, and he'll lead you back here."

My brow furrowed. "Won't taking the left-hand tunnel lead us in a circle?"

"Not underground it won't. The left-hand tunnel is the only way to reach the Skull Masquerade." He nodded again, this time to himself. "Right. The entrance is in the storeroom behind the bar, and the castle is a twenty-minute walk from here. If we're going to do this, we need to leave now."

"What's this, then?" Nicholina's brows wriggled as she circled us. Her girlish voice pitched higher. "*To the castle, to the snare, you rush to save your lady fair*—"

"Would you *shut up*, woman?" Beau whirled, incredulous, and tried to shoo her back toward La Voisin. "She's been doing this since I arrived." To her, he added, "Go on, now. Go. Back to your—your master, or whoever—"

Nicholina giggled. "Flibbertigibbet."

"What an odd creature," Madame Labelle murmured, staring after her with a frown. "Quite touched in the head. She called Louise a *mouse* earlier. Do you have any idea what that means?"

I ignored her, signaling for Beau to lead the way. He hesitated. "Should someone—fetch her? Lou? I thought she'd planned on joining us?"

And I thought she'd planned on loving me forever.

I stepped around him, around the counter, disregarding the barkeep's objections. "Plans change."

THE KING'S COURT

Reid

I had a rock in my boot.

It'd lodged there immediately upon entering the tunnels. Small enough for me to endure. Large enough for me to fixate. With each step, it jostled against my foot. Curling my toes. Setting my teeth on edge.

Or perhaps that was Beau.

He'd thrown back his hood in the semidarkness, and he strolled through the earthen tunnels with hands in his pockets. Torchlight flickered over his smirk. "So many rendezvous down here. So many memories."

The rock slid under my heel. I shook my foot irritably. "I don't want to know."

Apparently, however, Madame Labelle did. She arched a brow. Lifted her skirt to step over a divot in the earth. "Come now, Your Highness. I've heard rumors your exploits are *grossly* exaggerated."

His eyes widened. "Excuse me?"

"I owned a brothel." She fixed him with a pointed look. "Word spread."

"*What* word?"

"I don't want to hear," I repeated.

It was her turn to smirk. "You forget I knew you as a child, Beauregard. I remember the gap in your teeth and the spots on your chin. And then—when you developed that unfortunate stutter—"

Cheeks flushing, he thrust out his chest, nearly stumbling on another rock. I hoped it found quarter in *his* heel. "I didn't develop a stutter," he said, indignant. "That was a complete and utter misunderstanding—"

I kicked at the air surreptitiously, and the rock caught between my toes. "You had a stutter?"

"*No*—"

Madame Labelle cackled. "Tell him the story, dear. I'd quite like to hear it again."

"How do you—?"

"I told you—brothels are hotbeds of information." She winked at him. "And I *do* intend that pun."

He looked mutinous. Though pink still tinged his cheeks, he expelled a breath, blowing a limp strand of hair from his eye. Madame Labelle's smile broadened with expectation. "Fine," he snapped. "As I'm sure you heard the *incorrect* story, I will set the matter straight. I lost my virginity to a psellismophiliac."

I stared at him, the rock in my boot forgotten. "A what?"

"A psellismophiliac," he repeated irritably. "Someone who is *aroused* by *stuttering*. Her name was Apollinia. She was a chamber-maid in the castle and several years older than me, the beautiful hag."

I blinked once. Twice. Madame Labelle cackled louder. Glee-ful. "Go on," she said.

He glared at her. "You can imagine how our encounter pro-ceeded. I thought her fetish normal. I thought *everyone* enjoyed stuttering in the bedchamber." Recognizing the horror in my eyes, he nodded fervently. "Yes. You see the problem, don't you? When I found my next lover—a *peer* in my father's court—I'm sure you can imagine how *that* encounter proceeded, as well." He lifted a hand to his eyes. "God. I've never been so mortified in my entire life. I was forced to flee to these very tunnels to escape his laughter. I couldn't look him in the eye for a year." He snapped his hand to his side in agitation. "A *year*."

An unfamiliar tickle built in my throat. I pursed my lips against it. Bit my cheek.

It escaped anyway, and I laughed, sharp and clear, for the first time in a long time.

"It's *not funny*," Beau snapped as Madame Labelle joined in. She bent double, clutching her ribs, her shoulders shaking. "Stop laughing! Stop it now!"

At long last, she wiped a tear from her eye. "Oh, *Your Majesty*. I shall never tire of that story—which is, in fact, the story my girls thought so amusing. If it soothes your wounded pride, I'll con-fess I too have experienced my share of humiliating encounters. I often perused these tunnels myself as a younger woman. Why, there was a time your father spirited me down here—"

"No." Beau shook his head swiftly, waving a hand. "No. Do not finish that sentence."

"—but there was a feral cat." She chuckled to herself, lost in memory. "We didn't notice him until it was too late. He, ah, *mistook* part of your father's anatomy—or rather, *two* parts of your father's anatomy—"

The laughter died in my own throat. "Stop."

"—for a plaything! Oh, you should've heard Auguste's shrieks. One would've thought the cat had gutted his liver instead of scratched his—"

"*Enough.*" Horrified, wide-eyed with disbelief, Beau physically clapped a hand over her mouth. She snorted against his fingers. "Never, *ever* tell that story again. Do you understand me? *Ever.*" He shook his head sharply, clenching his eyes shut. "The psychological *scars* you've just inflicted, woman. I cannot unsee what my mind's eye has conjured."

She knocked his hand away, still laughing. "Don't be such a prude, Beauregard. Surely you understand your father's extra-curricular activities, given the situation we're all—" Her smile slipped, and the playful atmosphere between us vanished instantly. She cleared her throat. "What I mean to say is—"

"We shouldn't talk anymore." With a grim expression, mouth drawn, Beau pointed ahead to a northward tunnel. "We're near-ing the castle. Listen."

Sure enough, in the quiet that followed, muffled footsteps could be heard overhead. Right. I knelt to wrench off my boot. Shook the damn rock free and replaced it. No more distrac-tions. Though I appreciated Madame Labelle's attempt to lift our spirits, this wasn't the time or the place.

It hadn't been the time or place in weeks.

We walked the rest of the way in silence. As the tunnel sloped gradually upward, the voices grew louder. As did my heartbeat. I shouldn't have been nervous. I'd seen the king before. Seen him, talked to him, dined with him. But I'd been a huntsman then, esteemed, celebrated, and he'd been my king. Everything had changed.

Now I was a witch—reviled—and he was my father.

"Everything will be fine," Madame Labelle whispered as if reading my thoughts. She nodded to me. To herself. "You are his child. He will not harm you. Even the Archbishop did not burn his child, and Auguste is twice the man the Archbishop was."

I flinched at the words, but she'd already turned to the cavernous fissure in the wall. The warp and weft of a muted tapestry covered it. I recognized it from my brief time in the castle—a man and a woman in the Garden of Eden, naked, fallen before the Tree of the Knowledge of Good and Evil. In their hands, each held a golden fruit. Above them, a giant serpent coiled.

I stared at the reverse of its black coils now, feeling sick.

"Watch through here," Beau breathed, pointing to a thin gap between the wall and tapestry. Less than an inch. Bodies shifted beyond it. Aristocrats and clergymen from all over the kingdom—all over the world. An assemblage of black caps, veils, and lace. Their low voices reverberated in a steady hum. And there—raised on a stone dais, draped over a colossal throne—sat Auguste Lyon.

From the window directly behind, a shaft of sunlight traced

his silhouette. His gilded crown and golden hair. His fur cape and broad shoulders. The placement of the window, the throne . . . they'd been arranged intentionally. An optical illusion to trick the eye into believing his very body emitted light.

Backlit, however, his face remained shadowed.

But I could still see his smile. He laughed with three young women, heedless of Queen Oliana beside him. She stared determinedly at nothing, expression as stony as the steps beneath her. In the corner of the room, a handful of aristocrats in foreign clothing shared her features. Shared her anger. Theirs were the only sober faces in the room.

Resentment prickled beneath my skin as I took in the bards, the wine, the food.

These people did not mourn the Archbishop. How dare they mock his death with their revelry? How dare they speak idly beneath black hoods? No mourning veil could hide their apathy. Their hedonism. These people—these *animals*—did not deserve to grieve him.

On the heels of that thought, however, came another. Shame burned away my righteousness.

Neither did I.

Beau beat the dust from his cloak, smoothed his hair as best he could. It did little to help his travel-worn appearance. "Right. I'll enter the proper way and request an audience. If he's amenable—"

"You'll call us forward," I finished, mouth dry.

"Right." He nodded. Kept nodding. "Right. And if he's not . . . ?" He waited expectantly, brows climbing upward each second I didn't answer. "I need to hear a confirmation, Reid."

My lips barely moved. "We run."

Madame Labelle clasped my forearms. "Everything will be fine," she repeated. Beau didn't look convinced. With one last nod, he strode in the opposite direction from whence we'd come. Unconsciously, I stepped closer to the gap between wall and tapestry. Waited for him to reappear. Watched as two familiar figures cut toward the dais.

Pierre Tremblay and Jean Luc.

Expression drawn, stricken, Jean Luc pushed Tremblay forward with inappropriate force. Those nearest the king stilled. Tremblay was a *vicomte*. Jean Luc assaulting him—in public, no less—was a punishable offense. Frowning, Auguste waved the women away, and the two climbed the dais steps. They leaned close to whisper in Auguste's ear. Though I couldn't hear their hasty words, I watched as Auguste's frown deepened. As Oliana leaned forward, concerned.

The throne room doors burst open a moment later, and Beau strode in.

Audible gasps filled the chamber. All conversation ceased. One woman even emitted a small shriek. He winked at her. "*Bonjour*, everyone. I am sorry if I kept you waiting." To his mother's family in the corner, he added in a softer voice, "*Ia orana.*"

Tears filled Oliana's eyes as she leapt to her feet. "Arava."

"*Metua vahine.*" Upon seeing her, Beau's smile warmed to something genuine. He tilted his head to peer behind her at someone I couldn't see. "*Mau tuahine iti.*" When delighted squeals answered him, my heart stuttered painfully. Two someones. Violette and Victoire. I pressed closer, trying in vain to see them, but Madame Labelle pulled me back.

Auguste stiffened visibly at his son's arrival. His eyes never left Beau's face. "The prodigal son returns."

"*Père.*" Beau's smirk reappeared. His armor, I realized. "Did you miss me?"

Absolute silence reigned as Auguste studied his son's rumpled hair, his filthy clothes. "You disappoint me."

"I assure you, the sentiment is mutual."

Auguste smiled. It held more promise than a knife. "Do you think you're clever?" he asked softly. He still didn't bother to rise. "Do you mean to embarrass me with this tawdry display?" With a lazy flick of his wrist, he gestured around the chamber. "By all means, do continue. Your audience is rapt. Tell them of how disappointed you are in your father, the man who ravaged the countryside for weeks to find his son. Tell them of how your mother wept herself to sleep all those nights, waiting for word. Tell them of how she prayed to her gods and mine for your return." Now he did stand. "*Tell them,* Beauregard, of how your sisters slipped out of the castle to find you, how a witch nearly cut off their heads."

Fresh gasps sounded as Beau's eyes widened.

Auguste descended the steps slowly. "They're all waiting to hear, son. Tell them of your new companions. Tell them of the witches and werewolves you call *friends.* Perhaps they're already acquainted. Perhaps your companions have murdered their families." His lip curled. "Tell them of how you abandoned *your* family to help the daughter of La Dame des Sorcières—the daughter whose blood could kill not only you, but also your sisters. Tell them of how you freed her." He reached Beau at last, and the two stared at each other. For a second. For an eternity. Auguste's voice quieted. "I have long tolerated your *indiscretions*, but this time, you go too far."

Beau tried to sneer. "You haven't tolerated them. You've ignored them. Your opinion means less to me now than it ever has—"

"My *opinion*," Auguste snarled, fisting the front of Beau's shirt, "is the only reason you haven't been lashed to a stake. You dare to dismiss me? You dare to challenge your father for the sake of a witch's dirty cunt?" Auguste shoved him away, and Beau stumbled, blanching. No one lifted a hand to steady him.

"It isn't like that—"

"You are a *child*." At the venom in Auguste's voice, the aristocrats drew back further. "A cosseted child in a gilded tower, who has never tasted the blood of war or smelled the stench of death. Do you fancy yourself a hero now, son? After a fortnight of playing pretend with your friends, do you call yourself a warrior? Do you plan to *save* us?" He shoved him again. "Have you ever seen a loup garou feast on the intestines of a soldier?" And again. "Have you ever watched a Dame Blanche desiccate a newborn babe?"

Beau struggled to his feet. "They—they wouldn't do that. Lou wouldn't—"

"You are a child *and* a fool," Auguste said coldly, "and you have humiliated me for the last time." Expelling a hard breath from his nose, he straightened to his full height. *My* height. "But I am not without mercy. Captain Toussaint told me of your grand plan to defeat La Dame des Sorcières. Tell me the location of her daughter, and all will be forgiven."

No. Panic caught in my throat. I forgot to breathe. To think. I could only watch as Beau's eyes widened. As he yielded a step to his father. "I can't do that."

Auguste's face hardened. "You will tell me where she is, or I will strip you of your title and inheritance." Shocked whispers erupted, but Auguste ignored them, his voice growing louder with each word. With each step. Oliana touched a hand to her mouth in horror. "I will banish you from my castle and my life. I will condemn you as a criminal, a conspirator, and when you burn beside your friends, I will think of you no more."

"Father," Beau said, aghast, but Auguste did not stop.

"*Where is she?*"

"I—" Beau's gaze darted helplessly to his mother, but she merely closed her eyes, weeping softly. He cleared his throat and tried again. I held my breath. "I can't tell you where she is because I—I don't know."

"*Frère!*" From behind Oliana, a beautiful girl with Beau's black hair and tawny skin darted forward. My chest seized as she wrung her hands, as Auguste swept her backward, away from Beau. "*Frère*, please, tell him where she is. Tell him!"

Her twin raced to join them. Though she glared, her chin quivered. "You don't need to *beg*, Violette. Of course he'll tell him. The witches tried to *kill* us."

Beau's voice turned strangled. "Victoire—"

Auguste's eyes narrowed. "You would protect a witch over your own sisters?"

"We should go." Madame Labelle tugged fruitlessly on my arm, her breathing shallow. Panicked. "This was a mistake. Clearly Auguste won't help us."

"We can't just *leave* him—"

Beau lifted his hands, gesturing to the aristocrats. "It doesn't have to *be* this way. They aren't all evil. If you'd just *help* us, we can eliminate Morgane. She's in the city—here, *now*—and she's planning something terrible for the Archbishop's funeral—"

Madame Labelle pulled more insistently. "Reid—"

"You truly are a fool." Auguste wrapped a possessive arm around each of his daughters, dragging them backward. "I must confess, however, I am not surprised. Though you loathe me, I know you, son. I know your habits. I know your haunts. For fear of losing your newfound friends, I knew you would visit me on this foolish errand."

Vaguely, I recognized the sound of footsteps behind me. Of voices. Madame Labelle clawed at my arm now, shouting my name, but my mind followed too slow, sluggish. The realization came too late. I turned just as Auguste said, "And I knew you would use the tunnels to do it."

"Flibbertigibbet!" Beau's shouts filled the chamber as he whirled toward us with wild eyes. "Bumfuzzle!"

The hilt of a Balisarda smashed into my temple, and I saw no more.

PRIDE GOETH BEFORE THE FALL

Lou

He'd left without me. I stared into my whiskey, tipping it side-ways, pouring it slowly onto the wooden bar. Coco took the tumbler from me without missing a beat in her conversation with Liana. Across the tavern, Ansel sat between Toulouse and Thierry. They all laughed at a joke I couldn't hear.

One big, happy family.

Except they all stared at me, whispering, like I was a cannon about to explode.

And that bastard had left without a word.

I don't know what I'd expected—I'd practically doused *him* in whiskey and lit the match. But I hadn't lied. I hadn't said anything *untrue*. That's what he'd wanted, right? He'd wanted the *truth*.

Don't lie to me, he'd said.

I shoved away from the bar, stalking to the filthy window up front and staring through its dirt-streaked panes. He should've been back by now. If he'd left when Deveraux said he'd left— when I'd been sulking upstairs in misery—he should've climbed back through the tunnel a half hour ago. Something must've happened. Perhaps he'd found trouble—

Do you understand now? Does that make me a monster?

No. It makes you your mother.

A fresh wave of anger washed over me. Perhaps he *had* found trouble. And—this time—perhaps he could sort it out without me. Without magic.

Breath tickled my neck, and I whirled, coming face-to-face with Nicholina. When she grinned at me, I scowled. Blood had stained her teeth yellow. Indeed, her paper-thin skin was now her palest feature, brighter and whiter than the moon. I shouldered past her to an empty table in the corner. "I want to be alone, Nicholina."

"Shouldn't be too hard, *souris*." She drifted around me, whispering, gesturing to Coco and Ansel, to Blaise and Liana, to Toulouse and Thierry. "*They* certainly don't want our company." She leaned closer. Her lips brushed my ear. "We make them uncomfortable."

I swatted her away. "Don't touch me."

When I plunked down, turning my back to her, she floated to the chair opposite. She didn't sit, however. I supposed wraiths didn't sit. One couldn't look sinister and uncanny with one's ass on a barstool. "We aren't so very different," she breathed. "People don't like us either."

"People like me just fine," I snapped.

"Do they?" Her colorless eyes flicked to Blaise, where he watched me from the bar. "We can sense his thoughts, oh yes, and he hasn't forgotten how you crushed his son's bones. He longs to feast on your flesh, make you whimper and groan."

My own gaze cut to his. His lip curled over sharp incisors. Fuck.

"But you won't whimper, will you?" Nicholina canted her face closer to mine. "You'll fight, and you'll bite with teeth of your own." She laughed then—the sound skittered down my spine—and repeated, "We aren't so very different. For years, our people have been persecuted, and *we* have been persecuted among even them."

For some reason, I doubted she referred to *we* as her and me, the two of us. No. It seemed Nicholina wasn't the only one living inside her head these days. Perhaps there were ... others. *I told you she's weird*, Gabrielle had confided. *Too many hearts*. My own heart twisted at the memory. Poor Gaby. I hoped she hadn't suffered.

Ismay sat at a table with La Voisin, eyes red-rimmed and glassy. A handful of their sisters joined them. Babette had remained in the blood camp to care for those too young, too old, too weak, or too sick to fight.

They hadn't recovered Gaby's body.

"We'll tell you a secret, little mouse," Nicholina whispered, drawing my attention back to her. "It isn't on us to make them comfortable. No, no, no it's not. It's not, it's not, it's not. It's on *them*."

I stared at her. "How did you become like this, Nicholina?"

She grinned again—a too-wide grin that nearly split her face in half. "How did *you* become like this, Louise? We all make choices. We all suffer consequences."

"I'm done with this conversation." Expelling a harsh breath, I returned Blaise's glare with one of my own. If he didn't blink soon, he'd lose an eye. Nicholina—though clearly demented—was right about one thing: I *would* bite back. When Terrance murmured in his ear, he finally shifted his gaze away from me toward the storeroom door. I tensed immediately. Had they heard something I hadn't? Had Reid returned?

Without hesitating, I curled a finger, and my eyesight clouded. My hearing, however, heightened, and Terrance's low voice echoed as if he stood beside me. "Do you think he's dead? The huntsman?"

Blaise shook his head. "Perhaps. There is no peace in the human king's heart. Reid was foolish to approach him."

"If he *is* dead . . . when can we leave this place?" Terrance cast a sidelong look at La Voisin and Ismay, at the blood witches around them. "We owe these demons no loyalty."

A twitch started in my cheek. Before I realized my feet had moved, I was standing, pressing my fists against the table. The pattern dissolved. "It seems you owe Reid no loyalty either." They both looked up, startled—angry—but theirs was a flicker to my rage. Nicholina clapped her hands together in delight. Coco, Ansel, and Claud all rose tentatively. "If you suspect he's in danger, why are you still here?" My voice rose, grew into something beyond me. Though I heard myself speaking, I did not form these words. "You owe him a life debt, you mangy *dogs*. Or would you like me to reclaim Terrance's?" I lifted my hands.

Blaise's teeth flashed as he rose from his chair. "You dare threaten us?"

"Louise . . . ," Claud said, his voice conciliatory. "What are you doing?"

"They think Reid is dead," I spat. "They're debating when they can leave us."

Though La Voisin chuckled, her eyes remained flat and cold. "Of course they are. At the first sign of trouble, they tuck their tails and flee back to their swamp. They're cowards. I told you not to trust them, Louise."

When Liana moved toward the door, I slammed it shut with an easy flick of my wrist. My eyes never left Blaise's. "You aren't going anywhere. Not until you bring him back to me."

Snarling, Blaise's face began to shift. "You do not control the loup garou, witch. We did not harm you for your mate's sake. If he dies, so too does our benevolence. Be very careful."

La Voisin stepped to my side, hands clasped. "Perhaps it is *you* who should be careful, Blaise. If you invoke the wrath of this witch, you invoke the wrath of us all." She lifted a hand, and the blood witches stood as one—at least a dozen of them. Four times as many as Blaise, Liana, and Terrance, who edged back-to-back, growling low in their throats. Their fingernails extended to lethal points.

"We will leave here in peace." Despite his words, Blaise met La Voisin's gaze in open challenge. "No blood must be drawn."

"How easily you forget." La Voisin smiled, and it was a cruel, chilling thing. When she lowered her collar, revealing three jagged scars across her chest—claw marks—the blood witches hummed with anticipation. And so did I. *God*, so did I. "We *like* blood. Especially our own."

Tension in the room taut to explode, they stared at each other.

Ansel started to step between them—*Ansel*, of all people—but Claud stopped him with a hand on his shoulder. "Stand down, lad. Before you get hurt." To La Voisin and Blaise, he said, "Let us not forget the grander purpose here. We have a common enemy. We can all play nice until Monsieur Diggory returns, can't we?" With a pointed glance first at Blaise, then at me, he added, "Because he *will* return."

Not a breath sounded in the long, tense silence that followed. We all waited for someone to move. To strike.

At last, Blaise sighed heavily. "You speak wisdom, Claud Deveraux. We will await Monsieur Diggory's return. If he does not, my children and I will leave this place—and its inhabitants"—his yellow eyes found mine—"unharmed. You have my word."

"Ah, excellent—"

But La Voisin only smirked. "Coward."

That was all it took.

With a snarl, Terrance launched himself at her, but Nicholina appeared, seizing his half-shifted throat and twisting. He yelped, flying through the air, and landed at Blaise's feet. Liana had already shifted. She tore after Nicholina. Blaise quickly followed, as did Ansel and Claud when they realized the blood witches were after, well—*blood*. Knives in hand, Ismay and her sisters attacked the wolves' jugulars, but the wolves moved faster, leaping atop the bar to gain higher ground. Though cornered, though outnumbered, Terrance managed to knock away Ismay's knife, pinning her beneath his paw. When his other slashed open her face, she screamed. Coco rushed to intervene.

And I . . . I touched a finger to the whiskey on the bar. Just a finger. One simple spark—so similar, yet so different from that pub fire long ago. Had it only been a fortnight?

It felt like years.

The flames chased the whiskey down the bar to where Terrance—

No. Not Terrance. I tilted my head, bemused, as the flames instead found another, climbing up her feet, her legs, her chest. Soon she screamed in terror, in pain—trying desperately to draw blood, to claw magic from her wrists—but I only laughed. I laughed and laughed until my eyes stung and my throat ached, laughed until her voice finally pierced the smoke in my mind. Until I realized to whom that voice belonged.

"Coco," I breathed.

I stared at her in disbelief, releasing the pattern. The flames died instantly, and she crumpled to the floor. Smoke curled from her clothing, her *skin*, and she gasped between sobs, struggling to catch her breath. The rest of the room came back in pieces— Ansel's horrified expression, Terrance's frantic shout, Ismay's mad dash to find honey. When I stumbled forward to help her, a hand caught my throat.

"No closer," La Voisin snarled, her nails biting into my skin.

"Enough, Josephine." Deveraux loomed over us, graver than I'd ever seen him. "Release her."

La Voisin's eyes bulged slightly as she glared at him, but—one by one—her fingers gradually loosened. I sucked in a harsh breath and staggered forward. "*Coco.*"

But both blood witches and werewolves shielded her as I approached, and I could see little more than her eye above Ansel's arm. He too had positioned himself between us. My breath caught at the hostility in their gazes. At the fear. "Coco, I'm so sorry—"

She struggled to rise. "I'll be fine, Lou," she said weakly.

"It was an accident. You have to believe me." My voice broke on the last, but my heart—it broke at the tears welling in her eyes as she looked at me. She pressed a hand to her mouth to stem her sobs. "Coco, please. You *know* I never would've—would've never intentionally—"

Behind her, Nicholina grinned. Her inflection deepened, changed, as she said, "The Lord doth say, 'Come, heed him, all. Pride goeth before the fall.'"

The finality of what I'd done cleaved through me, and I heard his voice. Felt his soft touch on my hair.

You haven't been yourself.

You see what you want to see.

Do you think I want to see you as—

As what? As evil?

Burying my face in my hands, I sank to my knees and wept.

PROPER KNIGHTS

Reid

A face.

I woke to a face. Though mere inches from my own, I struggled to bring its features into focus. They remained shapeless, dark, as if I stood in heavy fog. But I wasn't standing. I couldn't move my limbs. They felt heavier than normal—impossibly heavy and cold. Except my wrists. My wrists burned with black fire.

Eyes closing, opening—lethargic, each blink enormous effort—I tried to lift my head. It slumped uselessly against my shoulder. I thought the shape of lips might've moved. Thought a voice might've rumbled. I closed my eyes again. Someone pried my jaw apart, forced something bitter down my throat. I vomited instantly.

I vomited until my head pounded. My throat ached.

When something hard struck my face, I spat blood. The taste of copper, of salt, jarred my senses. Blinking faster now, I shook my head to clear it. The room swam. At last, the face before me took shape. Golden hair and gray eyes—like a wolf—with straight nose and chiseled jaw.

"You're awake," Auguste said. "Good."

Beside me, Madame Labelle sat with her wrists bound behind her chair. It forced her shoulders out of socket. Though blood trickled from a puncture at the side of her throat, her eyes remained clear. It was then I noticed the metal syringes in Auguste's hand. The bloody quills.

Injections.

He'd drugged us—drugged *me*—like I was a—a—

Bile burned up my throat.

Like I was a witch.

Madame Labelle struggled against her binds. "Really, Auguste, this isn't necessary—"

"You dare address His Majesty so informally?" Oliana asked. Her voice pitched and rolled with my consciousness.

"Forgive me," Madame Labelle snapped. "After birthing a man's child—and all that predicates such a happy occasion—I assumed formalities would cease. An egregious mistake."

I vomited again, unable to hear Oliana's reply.

When I reopened my eyes, the room sharpened. Mahogany shelves filled with books. A carved mantel. Portraits of stern-lipped kings and embroidered carpet beneath booted feet. I blinked, vision honing in on the Chasseurs lining the walls. At least a dozen. Each held a hand to the Balisarda at his waist.

Except the Chasseur who stood behind me. He held his at my throat.

A second moved to stand behind Madame Labelle. His blade

drew blood, and she stilled. "At least clean him up," she said weakly. "He isn't an animal. He is your *son*."

"You insult me, Helene." Auguste crouched before me, tracking a hand in front of my face. My eyes struggled to follow it. "As if I'd allow even my hounds to sit in their own spew." He snapped his fingers. "I need you to focus, Reid. Mass starts in a quarter hour, and I cannot be late. The kingdom expects me to mourn that sanctimonious prick. I shan't disappoint them."

Hatred burned through the haze of my thoughts.

"But you understand the importance of keeping up pretenses, don't you?" He arched a golden brow. "You had all of us fooled, after all. Including him." My stomach heaved again, but he leapt backward just in time, lip curling. "Between the two of us, I'm pleased you killed him. I cannot count the times that filthy hypocrite presumed to admonish me—*me*—when all this time, he'd stuck his cock in Morgane le Blanc."

"Yes, a filthy hypocrite," Madame Labelle echoed pointedly. The Chasseur behind her ripped her hair backward, pressing his blade deeper into her throat. She said no more.

Auguste ignored her, tilting his head to study me. "Your body reacted to the injection. I suppose that proves Philippe's claim. You are a witch."

I forced my head upright through sheer power of will. For one second. Two seconds. "I would like to see . . . *your* body . . . react to hemlock . . . Your Majesty."

"You poisoned them?" Beau asked in disbelief. Another Chasseur held him in the corner of the room. Though his mother shook her head desperately, he didn't acknowledge her. "You put *hemlock* in those injections?"

"A fucking gilded tower." Auguste rolled his eyes. "I have little patience for your voice at the moment, Beauregard—or yours, Oliana," he added when she tried to interrupt. "If either of you speak again, you will regret it." To me, he said, "Now, tell me. How is it possible? How did you come to exist, Reid Diggory?"

A grin rose, unbidden, and I heard Lou's voice in my head. Even then—trapped backstage with two of her mortal enemies— she'd been fearless. Or perhaps stupid. Either way, she hadn't known how right she was. "I believe," I gasped, "when a man and a . . . witch . . . love each other very much—"

I anticipated his strike. When it came, my head thudded against the chair and stayed there. A laugh bubbled from my lips, and he stared at me like I was an insect. Something to quash beneath his boot. Perhaps I was. I laughed again at the irony. How many times had I drugged a witch? How many times had I worn his exact expression?

He grabbed my chin, crushing it between his fingers. "Tell me where she is, and I promise you a quick death."

My grin receded slowly. I said nothing.

His fingers bit harder. Hard enough to bruise. "Are you fond of rats, Reid Diggory? They're ugly little creatures, to be sure, but beneath their beastly hides, I must admit to sharing a certain kinship with them."

"I'm not surprised."

He smiled then. It was cold. "They're intelligent, rats.

Resourceful. They value their own survival. Perhaps you should heed their good instinct." When still I said nothing, his smile grew. "It's a curious thing when you trap a rat atop a man's stomach— let's say, for example, with a pot. Now, when you apply heat to said pot, do you know how the rat responds?" He shook my head for me when I didn't answer. "It burrows through the man's stomach, Reid Diggory. It bites and claws through skin and flesh and bone to escape the heat. It *kills* the man, so it might survive."

At last, he released me, standing and flicking a handkerchief from his pocket. He wiped the vomit from his fingers in distaste. "Unless you desire to be that man, I suggest you answer my question."

We stared at each other. The shape of his face wavered. "I won't," I said simply.

The words echoed in the silence of the room.

"Hmm." He picked something up from his desk. Small. Black. Cast iron. "I see."

A pot, I realized.

I should've felt fear. Perhaps the hemlock prevented it. Perhaps the rolling nausea or splitting headache. He *wanted* me to fear him. I could see it in his eyes. In his smile. He wanted me to tremble, to beg. This was a man who relished dominance. Control. I'd helped him, once. As his huntsman. I'd sought his approval as my king. Even after—when I'd learned his role in my conception, my suffering—I'd wanted to know him, deep down.

I'd dreamed up a version of him from my mother's stories. I'd accepted her rose glasses. But this man was not him.

This man was real.

This man was ugly.

And—looking at him now—all I felt was disappointment.

Slowly, he placed the pot on a rack above the fire. "I shall ask you one more time—where is Louise le Blanc?"

"Father—" Beau started, pleading, but with the wave of Auguste's hand, the Chasseur struck him in the head. When he slumped, dazed, Oliana's shrieks filled the cabinet. She rushed toward him, but Auguste caught her around the waist, flinging her against his desk. She collapsed to the ground with a sob.

"I said *be silent*," Auguste snarled.

Madame Labelle's eyes widened.

"Who are you?" Her voice climbed higher with disbelief. "The man I loved would *never* have treated his family this way. That is your *wife*. These are your *sons*—"

"They are no sons of mine." Auguste's face flushed as he gripped the arms of Madame Labelle's chair. As he bent low in her face, eyes burning with wild intensity. "And I shall have another son, Helene. I shall have a *hundred* more sons to spite that heinous, white-haired bitch. My legacy will live on. Do you understand me? I don't care if I have to fuck every woman in this godforsaken spit of land, I will not yield." He lifted a hand to her face, but he didn't touch her. His fingers clenched with hatred. With longing. "You beautiful, fucking *liar*. What am I going to do with you?"

"Please, stop this. It's me. It's Helene—"

"You think I loved you, *Helene*? You think you're any different from the others?"

"I know I was." Her eyes shone with fierce conviction. "I could not tell you I was a witch—and for that, I apologize—but you knew me, Auguste. As one soul knows another, you *knew* me, and I knew you. What we shared was real. Our child was born from love, not from lust or—or obligation. You must rethink this blind hatred and remember. I am the same now as I was then. *See* me, *mon amour*, and see him. He needs our help—"

Auguste did touch her now, twisting her lips between his fingers. He pulled them a hair's breadth from his own. "Perhaps I shall torture you too," he whispered. "Perhaps I shall see which of you breaks first."

When she glared back at him, resolute, pride swelled in my chest.

Love.

"Why doesn't the hemlock work on you, *mon amour*?" He released her lips to stroke her cheek. They could've been the only two people in the room. "How do you remain unaffected?"

She lifted her chin. "I've injected myself with hemlock every day since the day we met."

"Ah." His fingers tightened, clawing her skin. "So much for it being real."

The door to the cabinet burst open, and a liveried man swept in. "Your Majesty, I've delayed the priests as long as possible. They insist we begin Mass immediately."

Auguste stared at my mother for a second longer. With a sigh, he released her and straightened his coat. Smoothed back his hair. "Alas, it seems our conversation must wait until after the festivities." Donning black gloves with practiced efficiency, he slid his mask back into place. His persona. "I shall call for the two of you when they're over—if she hasn't arrived by then."

"We've told you." I closed my eyes to stop the spinning. To stop the nausea. When the darkness made it worse, I forced them open once more. "Morgane is already in the city."

"I speak not of Morgane, but of her daughter." His smile emanated through the room, casting shadows in my heart. The first flicker of fear. "If you love her as you say, she will come for you. And I"—he patted my cheek as he strode past—"I will be waiting."

If possible, the dungeons were colder than even the air outside. Icicles had formed in the corner of our cell where water had dripped down the stone. Pooled on the earthen floor. I slumped against the iron bars, muscles weak and useless. Though Madame Labelle's hands remained bound, she rubbed her sleeve against the ice to wet the fabric. Knelt beside me to clean my face as best she could.

"With the emetic and your body mass," she said, trying and failing to soothe, "the effects of the injection should wane soon. You'll be fit as a fiddle when Louise comes to rescue us. We can only hope she realizes what has happened before we're eaten by rats."

"She isn't coming." My voice rang hollow. Dull. "We had a fight. I told her she was like her mother."

Beau broke off an icicle and shattered it against the wall. "Brilliant. That's just *brilliant*. Well done, brother. I can't wait to see how your spleen looks when a rat opens you up." He whirled to

Madame Labelle. "Can't you—I don't know—magic us out of here somehow? I know you're bound, but all it takes is a twitch of your finger, right?"

"They've coated our irons in some sort of numbing agent. I can't move my hands."

"Can you use your elbow instead? Perhaps a toe?"

"Of course I could, but the magic would be clumsy. I'd likely do more harm than good if I attempted it."

"What are you talking about?"

"Manipulating patterns requires dexterity, Your Highness. Imagine tying a knot with your elbows or toes, and you might grasp the difficulty. Our hands—our fingers—enable us to signify intent with much greater specificity." Color rose on her cheeks as she scrubbed my own. "Also, though it has *clearly* escaped your great mental prowess, there are four huntsmen standing guard at the end of this corridor."

He prowled the cell like an angry cat. Hackles raised. "So?"

"Mother's tits." She dragged her forehead across her shoulder in exasperation. "*So* I realize that I've accomplished *many* extraordinary magical feats in our time together, Beauregard, but even I must admit defeat when confronted with escaping prison, defeating four huntsmen, and fleeing the city with only my damned *elbow*."

"Well, what are we supposed to do, then?" Beau flung his hands in the air. "Sit here and wait for my father to feed us to his rats? Excellent plan, approaching him, by the way," he added with a snarl. "*He loved me once*, my ass."

"Beau," I said when Madame Labelle flinched. "Shut up."

"He isn't going to feed *you* to his rats, Your Highness," she said. "Despite his bluster, I don't think he means you any real harm. You're his only legitimate heir. The law dictates he cannot pass the kingdom to Violette or Victoire."

Beau whirled to face the corridor, crossing his arms angrily. "Yes, well, forgive me for no longer trusting your instincts." I stared at his profile as the pieces clicked into place. Her rose-colored glasses. He'd worn them too. Despite their unhappy relationship, Beau had still dreamed of more with his father. Those dreams had publicly shattered on the floor of the throne room.

I'd lost the idea of my father. Beau had lost the real thing.

"Hang on." Beau gripped the bars abruptly, his eyes fixating on something at the end of the corridor. I turned my head. Eased myself up the bars as panicked cries resounded from behind the door. Hope swelled, sharp and unexpected. Could it be . . . ? Had Lou come for us, after all? Beau grinned. "I know that voice. Those little *shits*."

Footsteps pounded away from us, and with them, the shouts faded. The corridor door creaked open.

A mischievous face poked through. Violette. I didn't know *how* I knew it was her rather than her sister, but I did. Instinctively. She skipped down the corridor toward us with a smirk. In her hand, she swung the guards' keys. "Hello, *taeae*. Did you miss me?"

"Violette." Beau thrust his face between the bars. "How are you here? Why aren't you at Mass?"

She rolled her eyes. "Like Papa would let us outside the castle with Morgane on the loose."

"Thank God for small mercies. Right. We need to hurry." He held his hand out insistently. "The huntsmen could be back any second. Give me the keys."

She settled a hand on her narrow hip. "They *won't* be back any second. I told them Victoire accidentally impaled herself on her blade, and the idiots dashed upstairs to help her." She scoffed. "As if Victoire would ever *accidentally* impale someone."

"Yes," he said impatiently, "but when they don't find Victoire bleeding to death, they'll know you tricked them. They'll come back down—"

"No, they won't. There's quite a bit of blood."

"*What?*"

"We snuck into the apothecary's stores and stole his lamb's blood. Victoire was a bit heavy-handed with it on the carpets, but she has several more vials. She's leading the huntsmen on a wild-goose chase. It should keep them busy for a few moments at least."

"You gave Victoire blood?" Beau blinked at her. "You just . . . gave it to her? To play with?"

Violette shrugged. "Couldn't be helped. Now"—she dangled the keys in front of his nose—"do you want to be rescued or not?" When he swiped for them, she snatched them out of reach. "Ah, ah, ah. Not so fast. You owe us an apology."

"Yes." A second voice joined hers, and Victoire materialized. Her eyes gleamed in the semidarkness, and blood coated her hands. She extended her sword to the tip of Beau's nose. "Apologize for leaving us, *taeae*, and we shall free you." Her nose wrinkled when she looked at me. At Madame Labelle. "*You*. Not them. Papa says they deserve to burn."

Beau swung for the keys again. Missed. "Do me a favor, girls. When Father opens his mouth, close your ears. His voice will rot your brains."

"I think it's awfully romantic." Violette tilted her head to study me in an eerie impression of Auguste. Whereas his gaze had been cold, however—calculating—hers was shyly curious. "*Metua vahine* said he sacrificed everything to save the girl he loves. She doesn't like you much," she added to me, "or your *maman*, but I think she respects you."

"It's not romantic. It's *stupid*." Victoire kicked the bar closest to me before turning to Beau. "How could you choose this son of a whore over us?"

"Don't say that word," Beau said sharply. "Don't say it ever again."

She ducked her head, glowering but chastised. "You left us, *taeae*. You didn't tell us where you'd gone. We could've come with you. We could've fought the witches by your side."

He lifted her chin with his finger. "Not all witches are bad, *tuahine, tou*. I found some good ones. I intend to help them."

"But Papa said he'd disinherit you!" Violette interjected.

"Then I suppose you'll be queen."

Her eyes widened.

"I'm sorry I didn't say goodbye," Beau said softly, "but I'm not sorry I left. I have a chance to be part of something extraordinary. Together, all of us—humans, witches, werewolves, maybe even mermaids—we have a chance to change the world."

Violette gasped. "Mermaids?"

"Oh, shut it, Violette." Victoire snatched the keys from her and tossed them to Beau. "Do it." She nodded to him curtly. "Break it. Make it better. And at the end of it—when you put the pieces back together—I want to be a huntsman."

"Oh, me too!" Violette cried. "Except I want to wear a dress."

Beau fumbled to unlock the cell. "Huntsmen will be part of the broken pieces, girls."

"No." Victoire shook her head. "Not a huntsman like they are now. We want to be huntsmen like they should be—proper knights, riding forth to vanquish the forces of evil. *True* evil." She waved a hand at me—at the sick covering my front—as Beau slid the cell open. "Not whatever this is."

I couldn't help but grin.

To my surprise, she grinned back. Small. Hesitant. But still there. Emotion reared at the sight, and I stumbled at the strength of it. Violette wrapped an arm around my waist to steady me. To lead me down the corridor. "You stink, *taeae*. And proper knights don't stink. How can you rescue your fair maiden if she can't stand the smell of you?"

Fighting her own grin, Madame Labelle braced my other side. "Perhaps his fair maiden doesn't need rescuing."

"Perhaps *she* will rescue him," Victoire called over her shoulder.

"Perhaps *they* will rescue each other," Violette snapped back.

"Perhaps we will," I murmured, feeling lighter than I'd felt in ages. Perhaps we could. Together. In a swift burst of realization, I saw things clearly for perhaps the first time: she wasn't the only broken one. I'd closed my eyes to hide from the monsters—*my* monsters—hoping they couldn't see me. Hoping if I buried them deep enough, they'd disappear.

But they hadn't disappeared, and I'd hidden long enough.

Anxious now, I walked faster, ignored the pounding in my head. I had to find Lou. I had to find her, to *talk* to her—

Then several things happened at once.

The door flew open with a cataclysmic *bang*, and the four huntsmen charged back into the corridor. Madame Labelle yelled "RUN!" at the same time Victoire sliced through her binds. Chaos reigned. With the pulse of Madame Labelle's hands, rock from the ceiling rained on the Chasseurs' heads. A stone the size of my fists connected with one, and he collapsed. The others shouted in panic—in *fury*—trying to coordinate, to subdue her. Two tackled her while the third leapt in front of us. Shrieking a battle cry, Victoire stomped on his toes. When he reeled backward, swinging the blade of his Balisarda away from her, Violette punched him in the nose.

"Get out of here!" Victoire shoved him, and—already off balance—he tumbled to the floor. Beau cut his binds on her sword. "Before it's too late!"

I struggled to reach Madame Labelle. "I can't leave her—"

"GO!" Madame Labelle flung an arm out beneath the

Chasseurs' bodies, blasting the door apart. "NOW!"

Beau didn't give me a choice. Flinging his arms around me, he dragged my weakened, useless body down the corridor. More footsteps pounded above us, but we took a sharp left down another corridor, disappearing within a half-concealed crag in the wall. "Hurry," Beau said desperately, pulling me faster. "Mass has started, but the Chasseurs who remained in the castle will be here soon. They'll search these tunnels. Come on, *come on.*"

"But my mother, our *sisters*—"

"Our sisters will be fine. He'll never hurt them—"

Still I struggled. "And Madame Labelle?"

He didn't hesitate, forcing me down another tunnel. "She can take care of herself."

"NO—"

"*Reid.*" He spun me to face him, gripping my arms when I thrashed. His eyes were wide. Wild. "She made a choice, all right? She chose to save you. If you go back now, you won't be helping her. You'll be spiting her." He shook me harder. "Live today, Reid, so you can fight tomorrow. We'll get her back. If I have to burn down this castle myself, we *will* get her back. Do you trust me?"

I felt myself nod, felt him pull me along once more.

Behind us, her screams echoed in the distance.

WHEN A SNAKE SHEDS HER SKIN

Lou

Wrapping my arms around my legs, I rested my chin on my knees and gazed up at the afternoon sky. Thick, heavy clouds had gathered overhead, shrouding the sunshine and promising precipitation. Though my eyes still stung, I postponed closing them just a little longer. Below me, Coco and Ansel waited in my room. I could hear their murmurs from where I sat atop the roof.

At least something good had come from this nightmarish day.

At least they were speaking again—even if it was about me.

"What can we do?" Ansel said anxiously.

"We can't do anything." Coco's voice was hoarse from tears—or perhaps smoke. The honey had healed her burns, but it hadn't repaired the bar. Claud had promised to pay the innkeeper for damages. "At least she knows now. She'll be more careful."

"And Reid?"

"He'll come back to her. He always does."

I didn't deserve any of them.

As if trying to lift my spirits, the wind caressed my face,

grasping tendrils of my hair in its wintry grip. Or maybe it wasn't the wind at all. Maybe it was something else. *Someone* else. Feeling slightly ridiculous, I looked to the vast, ubiquitous clouds and whispered, "I need your help."

The wind stopped teasing my hair.

Encouraged, I sat up and squared my shoulders, letting my feet dangle from the eave. "Fathers shouldn't abandon their children. Mine was a shitty excuse for a human being—give him a kick from me if he's up there—but even he tried to protect me in his own twisted way. You, though . . . you should do better. You're supposed to be the father of all fathers, aren't you? Or maybe—maybe you're the mother of all mothers, and it's like my own *maman* said." I shook my head, defeated. "Maybe she's right. Maybe you *do* want me dead."

A bird shot from a window below me with a startled cry, and I tensed, peering down the edge of the building, searching for what had disturbed it. There was nothing. All was quiet and calm. Remnants of the last snowfall still clung to the corners of the rooftop, but now the sky couldn't seem to decide between snow and rain. Aimless flakes drifted through the air. Though a few mourners gathered in the damp, narrow street below, most wouldn't arrive until they finished with Requiem Mass.

Coco's and Ansel's voices had tapered off a few moments ago. Perhaps they'd gone to her room to resolve their own problems. I hoped they did. Whether together or apart, they each deserved happiness.

"Reid says I'm . . . lost," I breathed. Though the words unfurled gently, softly, I couldn't have stemmed them if I'd tried. It's as if they'd been floating just beneath my skin, waiting patiently for this moment. For this last, desperate window of opportunity to open. For this . . . prayer. "He says I'm changing—that I'm different. And maybe he's right. Maybe I just don't want to see it, or—or maybe I can't. I've certainly made a piss poor mess here. The werewolves left, and if my mother doesn't kill me, they will. Worse, La Voisin keeps—keeps *watching* me like she's waiting for something, Nicholina thinks we're great pals, and I—I don't know what to do. I don't have the answers. That's supposed to be your job."

I snorted and turned away, anger spiking sharp and sudden in my heart. The words spewed faster. Less a trickle, more a torrent. "I read your book, you know. You said you knitted us together in our mothers' wombs. If that's true, I guess that joke was on me, huh? I really am the arrow in her hand. She wants to use me to destroy the world. She thinks it's my purpose to die at the altar, and you—you *gave* me to her. I'm not innocent now, but I was once. I was a baby. A *child*. You gave me to a woman who would kill me, to a woman who would never love me—" I broke off, breathing hard and grinding my palms against my eyes, trying to relieve the building pressure. "And now I'm trying not to break, but I *am*. I'm broken. I don't know how to fix it—to fix me or Reid or *us*. And he—he *hates* me—" Again, I choked on the words. An absurd bubble of laughter rose in my throat.

"I don't even know if you're real," I whispered, laughing and crying and feeling infinitely foolish. My hands trembled. "I'm probably talking to myself right now like a madwoman. And maybe I am mad. But—but if you *are* real, if you *are* listening, please, *please*..."

I dropped my head and closed my eyes. "Don't abandon me."

I sat there, head bowed, for several long minutes. Long enough for my tears to freeze on my cheeks. Long enough for my fingers to stop trembling. Long enough for that window in my soul to slowly, quietly click closed. Was I waiting for something? I didn't know. Either way, the only answer I received was silence.

Time slipped away from me. Only Claud Deveraux's whistle— it preceded him to the rooftop—drew me from my reverie. I almost laughed. Almost. I'd never met a person so attuned to melancholy; at the first sign of introspection, he seemed to just *appear* like a starving man before a buffet of pastries and sweets. "I could not help but overhear," he said lightly, dropping to the eave beside me, "your rather magnificent conversation with the celestial sphere."

I rolled my eyes. "You absolutely could've."

"You're right. I'm a filthy eavesdropper, and I have no intention of apologizing." He nudged my shoulder with a small smile. "I thought you should know Reid just arrived, whole if not unharmed."

A beat passed as his words sank in.

Whole if not unharmed.

Lurching to my feet, I nearly slipped and fell to my death in my haste to reach the stairwell. When Claud caught my hand with the gentle shake of his head, my heart plummeted. "Give him a few moments to collect himself, *chérie*. He's been through an ordeal."

"What happened?" I demanded, snatching my hand away.

"I did not ask. He will tell us when he's ready."

"Oh." That one simple word echoed my heartache better than a hundred others ever could. I was part of that *us* now, an outsider, no longer privy to his innermost thoughts or secrets. I'd pushed him away, frightened—no, nearly crazed—that he would do it first. He hadn't, of course, but the effect remained the same. And it was my fault—*all* my fault. Slowly, I sank back onto the eave. "I see."

Claud raised a brow. "Do you?"

"No," I said miserably. "But you already knew that."

A moment passed as I watched mourners—the poor and bereft, mostly, with their tattered black clothes—trickle into the street. The bell tower had chimed half past a quarter hour ago. Soon, Requiem Mass would end, and the burial procession would wind through these streets, allowing commoners to say their goodbyes. The Archbishop's body would pass directly beneath us on its way to the cemetery, to the Church's tomb in the catacombs and its final resting place. Though I still didn't *like* Madame Labelle, I appreciated her forethought in this location. If there was one person in the entire kingdom who'd loved the Archbishop, it was Reid. He should've been the one to prepare the body this morning. He should've been the one to speak over it. Even now, he should've been the one holding vigil beside it.

Instead, he was forced to hide in a dirty inn.

He would miss the Archbishop's last rites. He would miss lowering his forefather into the earth. He would miss his final goodbye. I forced the thought away, tears threatening once more. It seemed all I did was cry these days.

At least here, Reid would have one last glimpse of him.

If Morgane didn't kill us all first.

I felt rather than saw Claud studying me. He had the air of someone trapped in paralyzing indecision. Taking pity on him, I turned to tell him to stop, to tell him it was okay, but his resolve seemed to harden at something in my eyes. He removed his top hat with a sigh. "I know you are troubled. Though I have long debated the time and place to tell you this, perhaps I might ease your conscience by freeing my own." He looked to the sky with a wistful expression. "I knew your mother, and you are nothing like her."

I blinked at him. Of all the things I'd been expecting, that wasn't one. "What?"

"You're the best parts of her, of course. The vitality. The cleverness. The charm. But you are not her, Louise."

"How do you know her?"

"I don't know her. Not anymore." The wistfulness in his gaze faded, replaced by something akin to sorrow. "In a different time—a thousand years ago, it seems—I loved her with a passion unequal to any I've ever known. I thought she loved me too."

"Holy hell." I lifted a hand to my brow and closed my eyes. It made sense now, his strange and unsettling fascination with me.

The white hair probably hadn't helped. "Look, Claud, if you're about to tell me you—you empathize with her, or you still love her, or you've been secretly plotting with her all along, can you wait? I've had the shittiest of all days, and I don't think I can handle a betrayal right now."

His chuckle did little to reassure me. "Dear girl, do you really think I'd admit such a connection if I were in league with her? No, no, no. I knew Morgane before she . . . changed."

"Oh." There was that word again. It plagued me, full of unspoken pain and unacknowledged truths. "No offense, but you're hardly my mother's type."

He laughed then, louder and more genuine than before. "Appearances can be deceiving, child."

I fixed him with a pointed look and repeated my earlier question. It seemed important now. "What *are* you, Claud?"

He didn't hesitate. His brown eyes—warm, concerned— might've pierced my soul. "What are *you*, Louise?"

I stared at my hands, deliberating. I'd been called many impolite things in my life. Most didn't bear repeating, but one had stuck with me, slipping beneath my skin and moldering my flesh. He'd called me a liar. He'd called me—

"A snake," I replied, breath hitching. "I suppose . . . I'm a snake. A liar. A deceiver. Cursed to crawl on my belly and eat dust all the days of my life."

"Ah." To my surprise, Claud's face didn't twist in disgust or revulsion. He nodded instead, a knowing smile playing on his lips. "Yes, I would agree with that assessment."

Humiliation hung my head. "Right. Thanks."

"Louise." A single finger lifted my chin, forcing me to look at him. Those eyes, once warm, now blazed with intensity, with conviction. "What you are now is not what you've always been, nor is it what you always will be. You *are* a snake. Shed your skin if it no longer serves you. Transform into something different. Something better."

He tapped my nose before rising and offering me his hand. "Both blood witch and werewolf will stay until after the funeral. Cosette spoke rather passionately to the former on your behalf, and with Reid's return, the latter are eager to repay their blood debt. However, I wouldn't expect a bouquet of roses from either party in the foreseeable future, and—well, I might also avoid Le Ventre for the entirety of my life if I were you."

I accepted his hand, rising heavily. "Reid."

"Ah, yes. Reid. I'm afraid I might have omitted the teensiest, tiniest of details in his regard."

"What? What do you—"

He pressed a kiss to my forehead. Though the gesture should've been jarring in its intimacy, it felt . . . comforting. Like a kiss my father might've given if . . . well, if things had been different. "He asked for you. Quite insistently, in fact, but our stalwart Cosette insisted he bathe before seeing you. He was covered in vomit, of all things."

"Vomit?" Each rapid blink only heightened my confusion. "But—"

The door to the stairwell burst open, and there—filling up

every inch of the frame—stood Reid.

"Lou." His face crumpled when he looked at me, and he crossed the rooftop in two strides, crushing me into his arms. I buried my face in his coat, fresh tears dampening the fabric, and held him tighter still. His frame trembled. "They took her, Lou. They took my mother, and she's not coming back."

THE FUNERAL

Reid

The first drops of rain signaled the start of the burial procession. The droplets stung my hand. Icy. Sharp. Like tiny knives. Lou had flung open our room's window to watch as the crowd thickened. A sea of black. Of tears. Few bothered with umbrellas, even as the rain fell harder. Faster.

Constabulary lined the street in somber uniforms, their faces and weapons drawn. Chasseurs swathed in black stood rigid among them. Some I recognized. Others I didn't.

Somewhere down there, the Dames Blanches and loup garou lay in wait for any sign of Morgane. Toulouse and Thierry hadn't joined them. My fault. My own stubborn pride. Deveraux, however, had insisted on helping. He'd also insisted Lou and I remain out of sight. Though he claimed our absence might dissuade her from foolish action, I knew better. He'd gifted us privacy—*me* privacy—to watch the procession. To . . . mourn.

"Therewithal," he'd said, matter-of-fact, "we can't very well allow the king or Chasseurs to spot you in the crowd. Chaos would ensue, and our dear Lady *thrives* in chaos."

In the room beside us, water gurgled through the pipes. I assumed it was for Coco's bath. Like us, Deveraux had banished her, Beau, and Ansel to their rooms, asserting, "Your faces are known." It felt silly, after everything, to hide away while the others endangered themselves. This hadn't been part of the plan.

I couldn't bring myself to protest.

Ansel probably watched the procession from his window. I hoped he did. He wasn't a Chasseur, but he might have been, once. He might've grown to love the Archbishop. If not loved . . . he certainly would've respected him. Feared him.

I wondered if anyone below had truly loved our patriarch.

He'd had no siblings, no parents. No wife. At least, not in the legal sense. In the biblical, however, his had been a woman who'd tricked him into bed, into conceiving a child destined to destroy him—

No. I stopped the thought before it could form. Morgane was to blame, yes, but so was he. She hadn't forced him. He'd made a decision. He wasn't perfect.

As if reading my thoughts, Lou squeezed my hand. "Sometimes it hurts to remember the dead as who they were, rather than who we wanted them to be."

I returned the pressure but said nothing. Though I knew she longed for a bath—for a change of clothes—the tub remained empty. The fresh clothing Deveraux had procured for her remained folded on the bed. Untouched. Instead, she stood beside me, with me, staring down at the street below. Listening to the rain, to the faint chants of liturgy from Saint-Cécile. Waiting for the procession to pass through East End to the cemetery beyond.

I couldn't imagine what she felt. Did she too mourn him? Did she too feel the keen loss of a father?

Will there be a funeral?

Yes.

But . . . he was my father. I remembered her wide eyes back in the Hollow. Her hesitance. Her guilt. Yes, she'd felt something. Not grief, exactly, but perhaps . . . regret.

He slept with La Dame des Sorcières. A witch.

I couldn't blame her. I couldn't hate her for what had happened. I'd made a choice, same as the Archbishop. Lou might've lied. She might've deceived me. But when I'd followed her to the Chateau, I'd chosen my fate, and I'd done it with my eyes wide open. I'd chosen this life. This love. And with my fingers trembling in hers, with her heart beating alongside mine, I still chose it.

I still chose her.

The king can't possibly honor him.

Once, I would've agreed with her. A man tainted by witchcraft deserved no honor. He deserved only judgment—only hatred. But now . . . now I tired of hating that man. Of hating myself. That hatred could crush a person. Even now, it weighed heavily, a millstone around my neck. Strangling me. I couldn't hold it much longer. I didn't want to.

Perhaps . . . perhaps Lou had been right. Perhaps a small part of me *did* resent her magic. My magic. The small part of me still connected to the man below. After seeing what I'd seen, it'd be easy to disparage magic. I couldn't deny its effects on Lou. And yet . . . Lou had proven time and time again she wasn't evil. Despite those changes, despite the hurt between us, she was still here—holding my hand, comforting me—as I mourned the father she'd never know. The father I'd taken from her.

Magic was just one part of her.

It was part of me.

And we would find a way forward together.

The voices outside grew louder, rising over the crowd, and an assemblage of clergymen turned down our street. They moved slowly, regally, and incanted the Song of Farewell, their holy vestments soaked through from rain. Behind them, a small army of Chasseurs surrounded the royal carriage. Auguste and Oliana had changed into full mourning regalia. Their faces solemn. False.

Between just the two of us, I'm pleased you killed him.

More carriages rounded the corner, bringing with them notable members of the aristocracy. At the end of the line, the Tremblay carriage appeared. The grief on Pierre's face seemed genuine, at least. I couldn't see beyond him to Célie, but her tears would've been too. The Archbishop had doted on her.

"Reid." Lou's voice lowered to a whisper, and she stared at the last carriage as it appeared around the corner. "It's him."

Crafted from gold brighter than even the king's crown—engraved with angels and skulls and crossbones, his name and reign of service—the Archbishop's casket remained closed. Of course it did. My chest ached. He'd been unrecognizable, in the end. I didn't want to imagine him, didn't want to remember—

My hand slips, and Morgane hisses as blood trickles down her throat. The ebony witch steps closer. "Let her go, or he dies."

"Manon," Lou pleads. "Don't do this. Please—"

"Be quiet, Lou." Her eyes glow manic and crazed—beyond reason. The Archbishop continues screaming. The veins beneath his skin blacken, as do his nails and tongue. I stare at him in horror.

No. I shook my head, dropping Lou's hand and reeling backward. He'd once been immortal in my eyes. Strong and unbreakable. A god in himself.

"I know it hurts," Lou whispered. "But you need to grieve him, Reid, or you'll never be able to let him go. You need to *feel*."

At her words, another memory surfaced, uninvited:

Blood drips from my nose. Father Thomas says I'm a hateful child for brawling with the local street rats. They resent me for my situation in the Church, for the hot food in my belly and the soft bed in my room. Father Thomas says I was found in the trash. He says I should've been one of them, should've grown up in their hovel of poverty and violence. But I didn't, and the Church's hot food made me tall and the Church's soft bed made me strong.

And I taught them for attacking when my back was turned.

"Come back here!" Father Thomas chases me through the cathedral with a switch. But he's old and slow, and I outrun him, laughing. He doubles

over to catch his breath. *"Wicked boy, I shall inform the Archbishop this time, mark my words!"*

"Inform me of what?"

That voice makes me stumble, makes me fall. When I look up, the Archbishop looms over me. I've only seen him from afar. From the pulpit. After the priests force me to wash my hands and face. After they thrash my backside so I can't sit during Mass.

I sit anyway.

Father Thomas draws himself up, struggles to breathe. *"The boy nearly crippled a child in East End this morning, Your Eminence."*

"I was provoked!" I wipe the blood from my nose, glaring at them. I am not afraid of the switch. I am not afraid of anything. *"He and his friends ambushed me."*

The Archbishop raises a brow at my insolence. At my defiance. *"And you dealt their punishment?"*

"They deserved what they got."

"Indeed." He circles me now, assessing. Despite my anger, I am uneasy. I've heard of his soldiers. His huntsmen. Perhaps I have grown too tall. Too strong. *"'Let justice roll on like a river, and righteousness like a never-failing stream.'"*

I blink at him. *"What?"*

"What is your name, young man?"

"Reid Diggory."

He repeats my name. Tastes it. *"You have a very bright future ahead of you, Reid Diggory."* To Father Thomas, he nods curtly. *"After you've finished with the boy, bring him to my study. We begin his training immediately."*

In the street below, Jean Luc marched in my place beside the casket. Beside the Archbishop. Even from afar—even in the rain—I could see his eyes were red. Raw. Hot tears spilled down my own cheeks. I wiped them away furiously. Once, we would've comforted each other. We would've mourned together. But no longer.

"Again, Reid."

The Archbishop's voice cuts through the din of the training yard. I pick up my sword and face my friend. Jean Luc nods encouragingly. "You can do it," he whispers, lifting his sword again. But I can't do it. My arm trembles. My fingers ache. Blood runs from a cut on my shoulder.

Jean Luc is better than me.

Part of me wonders why we're here. The initiates around us are older. They are men, and we are boys. And fourteen-year-olds have no hope of becoming Chasseurs.

"But you're growing stronger every day." Inside my head, the Archbishop reminds me. "Channel your anger. Sharpen it. Hone it into a weapon."

Anger. Yes. Jean Luc and I are very angry.

This morning, Julien cornered us in the commissary. Captain Aurand had left with the others. We were alone.

"I don't care if you are the Archbishop's pet," he said, lifting his blade to my throat. Though he's several years older than Jean Luc and me, his head only brushes my chin. "When Chasseur Delcour retires, his position is mine. No trash boy will carry a Balisarda."

Trash boy. That is my name in this place.

Jean Luc punched him in the stomach, and we ran.

Now, I turn my blade on Jean Luc, determined. I am no trash boy. I am worthy of the Archbishop's attention. Of his love. I am worthy of the Chasseurs. And I will show them all.

Small hands touched my shoulder, easing me onto the bed. I sat without thinking. My lips trembled, but I fought viciously against the despair rising inside me. The hopelessness. He was gone. The Archbishop was gone, and he was never coming back.

I'd killed him.

The crowd's cheers drown out Jean Luc's roar of pain. I do not stop. I do not hesitate. Despite my too-small coat, the bile on my tongue, I strike swift and sure, knocking his sword from his hand. Disabling him. "Yield," I say, lifting my boot to his chest. Adrenaline makes me dizzy. Clouds my thoughts.

I have won.

Jean Luc bares his teeth, clutching his wounded leg. "I yield."

Captain Aurand steps between us. Lifts my arm. "The winner!"

The crowd goes wild, and Célie cheers loudest of all.

I think I love her.

"Congratulations," the Archbishop says, striding into the arena. He draws me into a tight embrace. "I am so proud of you, my son."

My son.

The pride in his eyes makes my own prick and sting. My heart threatens to burst. I am no longer trash boy. I am the Archbishop's son—Chasseur Diggory—and I belong. I hug him so tightly that he gasps, laughing.

"Thank you, Father."

Behind us, Jean Luc spits blood.

"I killed my father," I whispered.

Lou stroked my back. "I know."

Heat washes over me as her lips touch mine. Slowly, at first, and tentative. As if fearful of my reaction. But she has nothing to fear from me. "Célie," I breathe, looking at her in wonder.

She smiles, and the entire world lurches to a halt at her beauty. "I love you, Reid."

When her lips descend once more, I forget the bench in this dark confessional. I forget the empty sanctuary beyond. There is only Célie. Célie, standing between my legs. Célie, twining her fingers in my hair. Célie—

The door bursts open, and we break apart.

"What is going on here?" the Archbishop asks, appalled.

With a horrified squeak, Célie covers her mouth and ducks beneath his arm, fleeing into the sanctuary and out of sight. The Archbishop watches her go incredulously. Finally, he turns back to me. Scrutinizes my rumpled hair. My flushed cheeks. My swollen lips.

Sighing, he extends a hand to help me up. "Come, Reid. It seems we have much to discuss."

He was the only man who'd ever cared for me. The tears fell faster now, soaking my shirt. My hands. My tarnished, *ugly* hands. Gently, Lou wrapped her arms around me.

The loup garou's blood coats the grass in the clearing. It stains the wildflower petals, the riverbank. My Balisarda. My hands. I rub them on my pants as inconspicuously as possible, but he still sees. He approaches warily. My brothers part for him, bowing low.

"To mourn them would be a waste of your compassion, son."

I stare at the corpse at my feet. The body, once lupine, reverted back to humanoid after death. His dark eyes stare at the summer sky without seeing. "He's my age."

"It," the Archbishop corrects me, voice gentle. "It was your age. These creatures are not as you and me."

The next morning, he presses a medal into my palm. Though the red is gone, the blood remains. "You have done the kingdom a great service," he says. "Captain Diggory."

"I'm sorry, Reid." Despite my shaking shoulders, Lou held me tightly. Tears streamed down her own cheeks. I crushed her against me, breath shuddering—each gasp painful, burning—as I buried my face in the crook of her neck. As I finally, *finally* allowed the grief to win. To consume me. In great, heaving sobs, it burst forth—a torrent of hurt and bitterness, of shame and regret—and I choked on it, helpless to stop its wrath. Helpless to do anything but cling to Lou. My friend. My shelter. My home. "I'm so sorry."

I don't hesitate. I don't think. Moving quickly, I sweep a second knife from my bandolier and charge past Morgane. She lifts her hands—fire lashing from her fingertips—but I don't feel the flames. The gold light wraps around my skin, protecting me. But my thoughts scatter. Whatever strength my body claimed, my mind now forfeits. I stumble, but the gold cord marks my path. I vault over the altar after it.

The Archbishop's eyes fly open as he realizes my intent. A small, pleading noise escapes him, but he can do little else before I fall upon him.

Before I drive my knife home in his heart.

The Archbishop's eyes are still wide—confused—as he slumps forward in my arms.

"I did it all for you too, Lou."

And with that—as his casket faded from view in the cemetery beyond, as the crowd swallowed up my last memory of him—I let the Archbishop go.

SOMETHING NEW

Lou

I didn't know how much time passed as Reid and I held each other on that bed. Though my limbs ached from sitting still for so long—from the cold creeping into the room—I didn't dare let go. He needed this. He needed someone to love him. To comfort him. To honor and keep him. I would've laughed at the irony of the situation if it hadn't been so heartbreaking.

How many people in this world had truly loved Reid? A lost little boy in a trash can grown into a hardened young man in a uniform. Two? Maybe three? I knew I loved him. I knew Ansel did too. Madame Labelle was his mother, and Jean Luc had cared once. But our love was fleeting, all things considered. Ansel had only grown to love him in the last few months. Madame Labelle had abandoned him. Jean Luc had grown to resent him. And I . . . I'd given up on him at the first opportunity. No, for all his hypocrisy and hatred, the Archbishop had loved him most and loved him longest. And I would always be grateful to him for it—that he'd been a father to Reid when he hadn't been one to me.

But now he was dead.

Reid's shoulders stopped shaking as the sun dipped below the windowsill—his sobs gradually quieting—but still he didn't loosen his grip. "He would've hated me," he finally said. More tears leaked onto my shoulder. "If he'd known, he would've hated me."

I stroked his back. "It wouldn't have been possible for him to hate you, Reid. He adored you."

A beat of silence passed.

"He hated himself."

"Yes," I said grimly. "I think he did."

"I'm not like him, Lou." He leaned back to look at me, though his arms didn't leave my waist. His poor face was splotched with color, and his eyes were nearly swollen shut. Tears clung to his lashes. But there—resolving behind the sorrow—was a hope so keen and sharp I might've cut my finger on it. "I don't hate myself. I don't hate you either."

I gave him a wary smile but said nothing.

Releasing my waist, he lifted a hand to cup my jaw, brushing a tentative thumb across my lips. "You still don't believe me."

I opened my mouth to argue, but the words died in my throat when he lifted his hand to the open window. The temperature had fallen with the sun, and the raindrops had solidified to snow-flakes. They drifted into the room on a gentle breeze. At the coaxing of his fingers, they transformed into fireflies.

I exhaled in delight as they floated toward me, as they landed on my hair. "How are you . . . ?"

"You said it yourself." Their glow reflected in his eyes. "Magic isn't good or evil. It heeds those who summon it. When life is a choice between fighting or fleeing—every moment life or death—everything becomes a weapon. It doesn't matter who holds them. Weapons harm. I've seen it. I've experienced it first-hand."

He touched the dingy, floral paper on the walls, and the blooms exploded upward, *outward*, until he reached up to pluck one, tucking it behind my ear. The scent of winter jasmine filled the room. "But life is more than those moments, Lou. We're more than those moments."

When he dropped his hands, the flowers returned to their paper, and the fireflies dimmed, white and wet once more. But I didn't feel the cold. I stared at him for a while, memorizing the lines of his face with a sense of wonder. I'd been wrong about him. About everything. I'd been so very, very wrong.

A tremble of my lips betrayed me. "I'm sorry, Reid. I *am* out of control. I—I set Coco on fire this afternoon. Maybe ... maybe you were right, and I shouldn't use magic at all."

"I spoke with Coco earlier. She told me what happened. She also said she'd exsanguinate me if I judged you for it." He brushed the snow from my hair, swallowing hard. "Not that I ever would. Lou ... we've both made mistakes. You're a witch. I shouldn't have resented you using magic. Just—don't let it take you somewhere I can't follow." When he glanced out the window, my gaze followed instinctively, and I saw what he saw.

A cemetery.

He shook his head. "Where you go, I go, remember? You're all I have now. I can't lose you too."

I crept into his lap. "What am I, Reid? Say it again."

"You're a witch."

"And what are you?"

He didn't hesitate, and my heart swelled. "I am too."

"Only partly right, I'm afraid." My smile—now genuine—grew at his confusion, and I leaned forward, rubbing my nose against his. He closed his eyes. "Allow me to fill in the gaps for you." I kissed his nose. "You are a huntsman." Though he recoiled slightly, I didn't let him escape, kissing his cheek. "You are a son." I kissed his other cheek. "You are a brother." His forehead. "You are a husband." His eyelids and his chin. "You are brave and strong and *good*." And, finally, his lips. "But most important, you are *loved*."

A fresh tear trickled down his face. I kissed it too. "You're also sanctimonious and stubborn and short-tempered." His eyes flicked open, and he frowned. I kissed his lips again. Gentle and slow. "Not to mention brooding, with a shit sense of humor." When he opened his mouth to argue, I spoke over him. "But despite all that, you aren't alone, Reid. You'll never be alone."

He stared at me for a long moment.

And then he was kissing me.

"I'm sorry too," he breathed, hands cradling my face as he lowered me to the bed. Gently. So, so gently. But those hands burned as they trailed down my throat, down my chest. Burned and trembled. "I'm so sorry—"

I caught them before they could reach my belt. "Reid. Reid, we don't have to do this. If it's too soon—"

"Please." When he looked at me, the longing in his eyes made my breath catch in my throat. I'd never seen anything so beautiful. "I can't—I've never been good with words. Just—please. Let me touch you. Let me *show* you."

Swallowing hard, I released his hands.

Slowly—so slowly I wanted to scream—he slid the velvet jacket from my shoulders, untucking my shirt and inching it up my torso, revealing the skin of my belly. My ribs. My chest. When I lifted my arms for him to continue, however, he carefully rolled the hem over my eyes and left it there. Blinding me. Trapping my arms in the sleeves.

When I wriggled in protest, he splayed a hand across my hip, stilling me. His lips moved lightly against my neck. "Don't you trust me?"

The word rose to my lips, unbidden. "Always."

"Prove it."

I stopped straining abruptly. A chill swept through my entire body, lifting the hair on my arms, my neck, as I remembered.

Do as I say.

"Embrace me, Lou," he repeated my own words back to me, trailing feather-light kisses on my throat, catching my earlobe gently in his teeth. I gasped. Though his body pinned mine to the mattress, he was careful to support his weight with his elbows. I wished he wouldn't. I wanted to feel him. All of him. "Embrace *us.*"

Let me show you how powerful you could be. My hateful words seemed to echo around us. *Let me show you how weak you are.*

"You don't have to be afraid." If possible, his touch—his lips— turned even gentler. He trailed a finger between my breasts, and fresh gooseflesh erupted in his wake. I shivered, my knees shaking. "Let me show you how much you mean to me. Let me show you how loved *you* are." His lips followed after his hand, each kiss reverent. Each a vow. "I'll never take you for granted. I'll want you every day for the rest of my life, and I'll love you even after."

"Reid—"

"Do you want to kiss me?" His finger stilled on my waistband, and I nodded, breathless. I knew the next words before he spoke them. I reveled in them. "Show me."

In a single, smooth motion, he pulled the shirt over my head.

I was on him in a second. He landed on his back with a soft laugh, which I captured in a kiss. He laughed again at my enthusiasm, arms tightening around me, before rising up to his elbows to help me tear his shirt from his pants. I shucked it over his head and to the floor, pushed him back against the bed and straddled his waist.

"Have I told you," I said, bending low to whisper in his ear, "how beautiful you are when you smile?"

He smiled then, the kind of smile that dimpled his cheek and set my heart on fire. "Tell me."

"Sometimes when I look at you, I can't breathe." My hand moved to his belt. "I can't think. I can't function until you look back. And when you give me this smile"—I brushed my knuckle against his dimple—"it's like a secret just for the two of us. I don't think I ever love you more than when you smile at me."

He chuckled in disbelief at the words, but the sound faded into nothing as we stared at each other. As he slowly realized their truth. And they *were* true. Each of Reid's smiles—so rare, so genuine—was a gift to me. He couldn't know how much I cherished them, how I wished I could keep them in my pocket to pull out whenever he felt sad. He felt sad so often.

After all this was over, I'd make sure he never felt sad again.

He ran his fingertips down my ribs, lingering on my waist. "I want to know all your secrets."

"My secrets are ugly, Reid."

"Not to me." He swallowed hard when I inched my hand beneath his belt. Lower still. "I meant what I said after Modraniht. I've never met anyone like you. You make me feel alive, and I just"—he gasped at my touch—"I want to share everything with you."

I pressed my free fingers to his lips. "And you will."

I released him only to ease his pants down his hips, his thighs, his ankles, trailing kisses down every inch of pale skin I revealed. He shuddered beneath me but mostly kept still . . . until I took him in my mouth. His hips bucked involuntarily then, and he lurched upright. "Lou—"

I placed a hand against his chest to still him. "Do you want me to stop?"

He groaned, falling backward and clenching his eyes shut. "No."

"Then open your eyes. Don't hide from me."

Though he seemed to have difficulty drawing breath, he did as I asked. Slowly, his eyes fluttering open and shut, he flexed into me. Every muscle in his body went taut. He flexed again. A fine sheen of sweat coated his skin. Again. His throat worked, and his mouth parted. Again and again and again. He fisted his hands in the bedsheets and threw his head back, breathing ragged, body on the edge of losing control—

Lunging forward suddenly, he yanked at my pants, and I twisted to oblige, helping him drag them down my legs. When they caught on my shoes, he made a low, impatient sound, and my stomach knotted with anticipation. I shucked each boot off hastily, ignoring the notes that fluttered to the floor. Ignoring everything but his hard body on mine. When we fell back to the bed, tangled in every possible way, I clung to him, reveling in the way he moved, in the way his hips fitted between my legs and his hands braced against the headboard. In the heat of his skin. Of his gaze.

He didn't hide from me.

Each emotion played in his eyes, uninhibited, and I consumed them all, kissing every part of his damp face between breaths, between gasps. Desire. Joy. Wonder. He moved faster, determined—chasing each raw emotion as it came—and I followed, digging my fingertips into the hard muscle of his back. Though I was desperate to close my eyes—to revel in the sensation—I couldn't stop looking at him. He couldn't stop looking at me. Trapped in each other's eyes, helpless to stop ourselves, we built and built until we shattered, baring ourselves to each other at last.

Not just our bodies.

Our souls.

And in that moment when we fell apart . . . we came together again as something new.

PART III

Qui vivra verra.
He who lives, shall see.
—French proverb

THE LAST NOTE

Lou

I descended the steps that night feeling lighter than I'd felt in weeks—and perhaps a bit foolish. Coco had knocked on our door only moments ago to tell us there'd been no sign of Morgane during the procession. Not a single sighting. Not even a hint of magic on the breeze. It seemed after everything—after suffering blood camps and cold swamps, Les Dents and Le Ventre—we'd come here for nothing. I couldn't say I was exactly *disappointed* she hadn't wreaked havoc and mayhem. Indeed, her inaction had quite made my night. Her notes burned holes in my boot, but I ignored them, pinching Reid's backside as we entered the bar.

Though I knew he still grieved—as he should, as he would for the rest of his life—he shot me an indulgent, slightly exasperated smile before looping his arm around my neck and kissing my temple. "Insatiable as ever, *mademoiselle*."

"That's Madame Diggory to you."

His free hand slipped into his pocket. "About that. I think we should—"

"At last!" At a table near the stairs, Claud applauded as we arrived. The dim candlelight couldn't conceal the impatience on La Voisin's and Blaise's faces. Both sat with their respective parties as far from one another as the small room allowed. Coco, Ansel, Toulouse, and Thierry acted as a buffer between them— as did Zenna and Seraphine. They'd donned glittering costumes quite at odds with the others' travel clothing. "The lovebirds have flown. How wonderful, how *marvelous*—"

"Where's Beau?" I interrupted, scanning the room again.

"He stepped out for a moment." Coco's expression turned grim. "He said he needed air."

I frowned but Reid shook his head and murmured, "I'll explain later."

"You lied to us." La Voisin didn't raise her voice, despite the wrath in her eyes. It seemed she hadn't yet forgiven me for Coco's sake. "You said Morgane would attack today. I brought my people here to claim vengeance, yet all we've received"—those eyes flicked to Blaise—"is disrespect and disappointment."

I hurried to correct her. "We didn't lie. We said we *thought* Morgane would attack today—"

"We too have been disrespected." Blaise stood, and Liana and Terrance followed. "Though our debt remains unfulfilled, we will leave this place. Nothing more can be done."

When both parties looked to us expectantly, Reid and I shared a surreptitious glance.

What do we do now? his eyes seemed to ask.

The hell if I know, mine replied.

Before either of us could bumble a plea, Coco spoke instead. Bless her. "Clearly, we misinterpreted the notes, but that doesn't mean our window of opportunity has passed. Manon is in the city, which means Morgane likely is too. Perhaps we shouldn't have hidden Lou and Reid away. Maybe we could use them to draw her out—"

"No, no." Deveraux shook his head vehemently. Tonight, his clothes were uncharacteristically simple in head-to-toe black. Even the paint on his fingernails and kohl around his eyes matched. His lips, however, he'd daubed with bloodred rouge. "'Tis never a good idea to play cat and mouse with Morgane. She is never the mouse. Inherently feline, that one—"

Coco's eyes narrowed. "Then what do you suggest?"

"I suggest"—he pulled a white mask from his cloak and tied it around his face—"that you all take a breath and attend our performance tonight. Yes, even you, Josephine. Some levity in La Mascarade des Crânes might do wonders for those crinkles between your brows."

I froze, staring at him.

His mask was shaped like a skull.

Though Claud continued to babble about Dame Fortune, delighted when La Voisin snapped back, Reid didn't miss the abrupt change in my manner. "What is it?" he asked. With cold fingers, I reached down into my boot, and his smile faltered. "What are you—?"

Without a word, I handed him the scraps of paper I'd hastily replaced after my bath this evening. He accepted them with a frown. I watched his lips shape the words to himself.

Pretty porcelain, pretty doll, with hair as black as night,
She cries alone within her pall, her tears so green and bright.

Pretty porcelain, pretty doll, forgotten and alone,
Trapped within a mirrored grave, she wears a mask of bone.

"I don't understand." Reid's eyes shot to mine, searching, as Claud finally stopped talking. As he stood to read the lines over Reid's shoulder. "We still don't know what these mean—"

"Mask of bone," I whispered. "La Mascarade des Crânes. It can't be coincidence."

"*What* can't be a coincidence?" He took my face in his hands. The papers fluttered to the dirty floor. "These are just bits of gibberish, Lou. We came to the Archbishop's funeral. She wasn't—"

"Oh dear." Claud's eyes widened as he bent to retrieve them, finally catching sight of the ominous words. "Feline, indeed."

Reid spun to face him, but a knock sounded on Léviathan's door. Frowning, I crossed the room to pull it open, but Reid stopped me with a hand on my arm. Straightening his coat, Claud opened the door instead. A small, unfamiliar girl stood on the threshold. "For you, *mademoiselle*," she said, stuffing a third scrap of paper in my palm before scurrying away. I unfolded it cautiously, dread seeping into my stomach.

Pretty porcelain, pretty doll, your pretty clock doth start

Come rescue her by midnight, or I shall eat her heart.

All my love,
Maman

With shaking fingers, I showed the note to Reid. He skimmed it quickly, face paling, before hurtling after the girl. Blaise followed with a snarl.

"Oh dear," Claud said again, taking the note from me. He shook his head, reading through it once, twice, three times. "Oh dear, oh dear, oh dear. Who is this poor soul? This—this porcelain doll?"

I stared at him in dawning horror.

Yes. We'd misinterpreted the notes.

Mistaking my silence, he patted my shoulder consolingly. "Not to worry, dear. We shall solve this mystery. Now, it seems to me the greatest clues to learning her identity lie in this first note . . ."

"What's going on?" Coco joined us now, Ansel following on her heels. She plucked the note from Claud, skimming the words before passing it to Liana, who in turn handed it to Terrance. La Voisin stood behind them, watching with an inscrutable expression. Nicholina, as always, smiled.

"Perhaps her skin could be described as porcelain?" Claud mused, stroking his beard. "Her features doll-like? The black hair is quite clear, but the—"

"Green tears?" Terrance scoffed. "No one has green tears."

"It's symbolic," Ismay said, rolling her eyes. "Green is a meta-phor for envy."

Oh no.

I took the note from her, rereading the lines and thinking hard—praying, *praying* I was wrong. But no. It was all here. Porcelain skin. Black hair. Envious tears. Forgotten, alone . . . even the goddamn *pall* fit. How could we have missed it? How could we have been so *stupid?*

But that last line . . . eating her *heart* . . .

Feeling sick, I glanced at La Voisin and Nicholina, but Reid soon emerged beside me—red-faced and panting—and scattered my train of thought. "She's gone. She just—vanished."

"Of course she did," Coco muttered bitterly. "Morgane wouldn't have wanted her to stick around and play."

"Who was taken?" Blaise asked, voice deep and insistent. "Who is the girl?"

A commotion sounded at the door, and Jean Luc plowed inside, holding Beau by the collar. The former's eyes were wild, crazed, as they found mine. Found Reid's. He pushed toward us with single-minded determination. "Reid! Where is she? *Where?*"

When she heard what he'd done, it nearly killed her. She's been in seclusion for weeks—weeks—and all because of some misplaced emotion for him.

Lips numb, I crumpled the note in my fist, taking a deep breath and steeling myself for the pain to come—for the emotions I'd see in Reid's uncharacteristically open expression, in those newly vulnerable eyes. I could've kicked myself. I'd encouraged him to stop hiding, to *feel*. And now he would. And now I didn't want to see.

And my mother had known exactly how to play with us.

I turned toward him anyway.

"It's Célie, Reid. She's taken Célie."

COCO'S VISION

Lou

Until the day I died, I'd never forget the look on Reid's face.

The disbelief.

The horror.

The rage.

And in that moment, I knew—deep down in my bones—that I would save Célie's life or die trying.

Our motley crew glanced back and forth between where I paced at the window and Reid stood at the door. Heedless of the chairs, Claud had plunked down on the floor by the bar, crossing his legs as if he intended to stay awhile. But we didn't have awhile. Already our clock had started. *Come rescue her by midnight, or I shall eat her heart.*

Reid stared at his hands, transfixed and unmoving.

"She's trying to lure you out," Beau insisted. "Don't let her."

"She'll kill Célie," Jean Luc snarled, still clutching the notes I'd handed him. When Monsieur Tremblay had finally revealed Célie's *weeks of seclusion* hadn't been seclusion at all, but abduction,

Jean Luc had combed through every inch of East End to find us after the funeral. It'd been a happy coincidence indeed that Beau had stepped out tonight, or Jean Luc never might've found us. What a tragedy that would've been. "We have to rescue her."

"*You* do not speak." La Voisin's eyes held vicious promise. "Make no mistake, huntsman. Your holy stick will not prevent me from cutting out your tongue."

"*How does he taste, he taste, he taste?*" Nicholina edged forward, licking her lips. "*Let's tear off his face, his face, his face.*"

Blaise growled low in agreement.

Claud persuading the innkeeper to let his rooms to witches and werewolves had been nothing. Claud persuading the blood witches and werewolves not to tear a huntsman limb from limb, however, was proving more difficult. Jean Luc didn't seem to realize the precariousness of his situation—especially as his *holy stick* remained tucked out of sight in Reid's bandolier. To Reid's credit, he didn't reveal his old friend's secret. If the blood witches suspected Jean Luc defenseless, they wouldn't hesitate to attack.

Terrance knew, however. His lip curled in anticipation as he looked between Reid and Jean Luc.

"And where *is* she, exactly?" Coco had gravitated back to her kin, standing between La Voisin and Nicholina. "Have you managed to divine her location from Morgane's riddles?"

Jean Luc gestured to the rumpled papers. "She's—she's in the tunnels. In this Skull Masquerade."

"The tunnels are vast, Captain." Claud turned a tarot card over in his fingers again and again. At my repeated glances, he extended it to me. It wasn't a tarot card at all. Upon closer inspection, this card was crimson, not black, and painted with a leering skull. Gold letters that read *Nous Tombons Tous* curled into the shape of its mouth and teeth. At the top, *Claud Deveraux and his Troupe de Fortune* had been inked in meticulous calligraphy. An invitation. I handed it back with an ominous feeling. "They traverse the entire city," Claud continued. "Our search will continue long after midnight without proper direction."

"She's given us direction," Zenna pointed out. "*She cries alone within her pall* and *trapped within a mirrored grave* couldn't be more obvious. She's in the catacombs."

The catacombs. Shit.

"She has given *us* nothing," Claud said sharply. When Zenna's eyes flashed, his voice softened. "Alas, we must cancel our performance, *mes chers*. The world below is not safe tonight. I fear you must return to your rooms, where you might escape Morgane's notice. Toulouse and Thierry will join you there."

Zenna's eyes flashed. "The witch does not scare me."

Claud's face grew grave. "She should." To Seraphine, he added, "Perhaps you could . . . ruminate on the situation."

She clutched the cross at her throat, staring at him with wide eyes.

Once again, I turned to Reid, but he remained as if carved from stone. A statue. I sighed. "The catacombs will still take several hours to search. Does anyone have the time?"

Deveraux pulled out his pocket watch—a silly, gilded contraption. "Just shy of nine o'clock in the evening."

"Three hours." I nodded to myself, trying to infuse optimism into my words. "We can find her in three hours."

"I can perhaps buy you an extra hour or two," Claud offered, "if I find Morgane before we find this Célie. We have much to debate, La Dame des Sorcières and I." He ambled to his feet, abruptly relaxed once more—as if we discussed the weather and not abduction and murder. "The hour draws late, Monsieur Diggory. It is clear none wish to proceed without your blessing. A decision must be made. Will we ignore La Dame des Sorcières' threat, or will we venture into La Mascarade des Crânes to rescue your lady fair? All paths involve considerable risk to those you love."

Your lady fair. I couldn't help a grimace. *Those you love.*

Reid's eyes snapped to mine, not missing the movement. Neither did Jean Luc. He pressed closer to Reid, unwilling or unable to hide his desperation. "Reid." He touched a hand to Reid's chest, tapping insistently. "Reid, this is Célie. You aren't going to leave her in the hands of that madwoman, are you?"

If Reid wondered about Jean Luc's sudden interest in Célie, he didn't show it. Perhaps he'd known. Perhaps he'd known all along. He didn't break eye contact with me. "No."

"Thank God." Jean Luc allowed himself a brief second of relief before nodding. "We haven't a moment to lose. Let's go—"

Reid stepped around him to face me. I forced myself to return his gaze, knowing his next words before he even opened his mouth. "Lou, I . . . I don't think you should come. This is a trap."

"Of course it's a trap. It's always been a trap."

At last, La Voisin broke her silence. "If you need reassurance of her safety, huntsman, I can provide it." If Nicholina had been capable, she might've bounced on the balls of her feet. As it was, she tittered girlishly. "A bit of Louise's blood will show me her future." She extended her hand to me with an inscrutable expression. "If she dares."

The werewolves looked on uneasily, shifting their feet. Though they remained in their human forms, their nails had sharpened amidst the panic. An instinctive reaction, I presumed.

"No." Coco slapped her aunt's hand away—actually *slapped* it—and stepped in front of her. "If *anyone* tastes Lou's blood, it'll be me."

La Voisin's lip curled. "You do not have my skill with divination, niece."

"I don't care." Coco squared her shoulders before asking me silent permission with her eyes. If I said no, she wouldn't ask again. She wouldn't let the others ask either. She'd accept my decision, and we would find another way forward. "It's me or no one."

Inexplicably nervous, I placed my hand in hers. I didn't fear Coco. She wouldn't abuse my blood in her system. She wouldn't attempt to control me. No, I feared what she might see. When she lifted my finger to her mouth, the blood witches—even the werewolves—seemed to press closer in response. In anticipation. Reid seized my wrist. "You don't have to do this." Panic laced his voice. "Whatever *this* is."

I gave a grim smile. "It's better to know, isn't it?"

"Rarely," Claud cautioned.

"Just do it," I said.

Without another word, Coco pierced the pad of my finger with her incisor, drawing a single bead of blood into her mouth. I didn't turn to see the others' reactions, instead watching as Coco closed her eyes in concentration. After several tense seconds, I whispered, "Coco?"

Her eyes snapped open, rolling to the back of her head. Though I'd seen her scour the future countless times before, I still shivered at the way those white, sightless eyes studied my face. At least I'd been prepared for it. The others gasped audibly—some cursing, some retching—as Ansel darted forward. His hands fluttered around her, helpless, as if he was unsure whether or not he could touch her. "What's happening? What's wrong?"

"Shut up, and she'll tell us," Beau said, watching her with rapt attention.

"Lou . . ." Reid edged closer, his hand slipping into mine. "What is this?"

"She's fine." I glanced back at the werewolves, who—standing in the tavern of a dirty inn, watching a witch divine the future—seemed to be questioning their life choices. Jean Luc's face contorted with disgust. "Just give her a moment."

When Coco touched my cheek, everyone drew a collective breath. "I see death," she said, voice deep and strange.

A beat passed as we all stared at her.

"I see death," she repeated, tilting her head, "but not your own." Reid exhaled in a sigh of relief. The movement attracted

Coco. Her eerie gaze flicked between us, through us. My chest tightened at that look. This wasn't over. This wasn't good, and Reid didn't seem to understand—

"By the stroke of midnight, a man close to your heart will die."

My hand slipped from Reid's.

"What?" Ansel whispered, horrified.

"Who?" Pushing past us, Beau gripped Coco's shoulder with sudden urgency. "What man?"

"I cannot see his face."

"Damn it, Coco—"

"Let her go." Through numb lips, I forced the words out, remembering her explanation from so long ago. Before the heist. Before Reid. Before everything. "All she can see is what my blood shows her."

Beau stumbled back, crestfallen, before whirling to look at Reid. "We don't know it's you. It could be Ansel or Deveraux or—or that Bas fellow. Or the heart could be symbolic," he added quickly, nodding. "*You* are her heart. Maybe—maybe it could mean a man close to *you* like—like Jean Luc or our father, or—"

"Or you," Reid admitted quietly.

Beau whirled to face me. "Are there any other ex-boyfriends who—"

"Beau." I shook my head, and he broke off, staring at his boots. I swallowed hard. My throat ached with unshed emotion, but only a fool cried over what hadn't yet happened—what *would not* happen. A small voice in my head warned it unwise to poke fate in the nose, so I gave her the finger instead. Because I wouldn't allow this. I wouldn't accept it.

"Can you see anything else, Cosette?" More than one head turned at the cool, detached voice of La Voisin. She surveyed Coco dispassionately. "Ground yourself in the vision. Touch it. Taste it. Hone your focus however you can."

But Coco's hand merely fell from my cheek. Her eyelids fluttered shut. "You will lose the one you love."

Absolute silence descended as Coco gradually came back to herself.

Though Beau dropped his head in defeat, Reid turned me to face him with gentle hands. "Are you . . . okay? Lou?"

You will lose the one you love.

I supposed that cleared it up nicely.

"Of course. Why wouldn't I be?" At his concerned look, I said, "Oh, I won't be losing you anytime soon. Coco's visions are changeable, subjective to the user's current path. You see?"

"I—" He glanced at Coco, whose eyes sharpened as they returned to normal. Ansel held her steady. "No, I don't."

"It's simple, really. If I continue on the path as planned, you'll die, but if I change my path, you'll live. Which means you aren't coming with me."

Reid fixed me with a flat, incredulous look, while Deveraux tilted his head. "I'm not sure that logic tracks, my dear. He can expire in this inn quite as easily as he can expire in the tunnels."

"Yes, but Morgane is down there," Beau insisted. Our eyes locked in understanding. "At least he has a chance up here."

I stared at the door to the storeroom, unable to meet anyone's eye.

Blaise shook his head. "We cannot afford for Reid to hide

above. We need numbers in this battle. Strength."

"You owe him a *life debt*," Beau said, uncharacteristically emphatic. "How can you fulfill it if he dies?"

"She said *someone* would die." Liana crossed her arms, shooting an unapologetic look in my direction. "You were right. We don't know if it'll be Reid."

Beau threw his hands in the air. "Except Coco then followed with—and I quote—*you will lose the one you love.* How the hell are we supposed to interpret that? Morgane told her once that she'd cut out his heart. How do we know that won't happen tonight?"

Coco clamped her jaw and exhaled hard through her nose. "We don't know. We don't know what's going to happen down in those tunnels. But I *do* know that my visions are rarely what they seem. I had one before we robbed Tremblay too. I thought it meant something ominous, but Angelica's Ring ended up saving Lou's ass—"

Jean Luc looked likely to die from apoplexy then and there. "I don't care about rings and blood visions. Célie is down there now—trapped in a *crypt*—and we're wasting time."

"You *do not speak*—" La Voisin hissed.

"He's right," Reid said curtly. "I'm going into those tunnels. The more people searching, the faster we'll find her." Though he gave me a cursory glance, lips pursed with genuine remorse, his voice brooked no argument. Heart pounding, still numb, I felt myself nod.

Beau slumped in his chair, defeated, and cursed bitterly. "The crypts are nearly as expansive as the tunnels—and they're creepy as shit, in case you were wondering."

Reid nodded. "We'll split into groups to cover more ground." With a subtle change in posture, he shifted seamlessly into captain once more. Jean Luc didn't even gnash his teeth. "Josephine, divide your kin into groups of three. You can search the northern and eastern crypts. Blaise, you and your children can take the southern. Deveraux and his troupe can take the Skull Masquerade."

Ansel stepped forward tentatively. "What about me? Where should I go?"

"I need you to stay here, Ansel. The patrons of La Mascarade des Crânes won't know the danger that awaits them. If anyone enters Léviathan seeking this entrance through the tunnels, warn them away."

It was a thinly veiled excuse, and Ansel knew it. His face fell. There would be no patrons in Léviathan tonight. Claud had assured it. Though Reid sighed, he continued, undeterred. "Coco and I will take the western crypts . . ."

His voice dimmed into background noise as Nicholina caught my eye from behind him. She looked pointedly to the storeroom door. For once, she wasn't smiling. I stared at her. She couldn't possibly be helping me. She couldn't possibly care. . . .

Soon we'll taste the noises on his tongue, oh yes, each moan and sigh and grunt.

A sharp pain spiked through my chest.

Perhaps she didn't want Reid to die either.

I didn't stop to consider her nefarious purposes for wanting him alive. When she glided toward him, weightless, I shifted subtly, making room for her beside him. She took full advantage, draping herself across his chest. "Do you wish to die, Monsieur Diggory?" He shot me an anxious glance, but I shrugged, adopting my best nonplussed expression. *"Death comes swiftly on this night,"* she sang sweetly, *"cloaked not in black, but eerie white."*

I inched backward.

Coco scowled. "Get off him, Nicholina—"

"She is his bride, his maiden fair, who feasts upon flesh and despair."

"Just ignore her," Beau said, rolling his eyes. "I do."

The wood of the storeroom door touched my fingertips as he tried to push her away. His hands couldn't quite connect, however, as if her form consisted of more vapor than flesh. It clung to him like mist.

"As she eats, her bridegroom moans, come to gather skin and bones—"

I turned the handle. Reid struggled helplessly as Nicholina brought her lips toward his.

Swallowing bile, I hesitated, but La Voisin slid into place before the door, blocking me from view. She didn't look at me. The slight dip of her chin was my only indication she'd seen me at all.

With one last, lingering look at Reid's back—the breadth of his shoulders, the coppery waves at his neck—I slipped through the door and out of sight. This was the only way. Though they'd deliberated, Coco's vision had been clear: *you will lose the one you love.* I let the words flow through me, strengthening my resolve, as I glanced around the storeroom, searching for the tunnel entrance.

A thick layer of dust coated the rotting shelves, the amber bottles, and the oaken barrels. I stepped carefully over shards of shattered glass, my boots sticking to the tacky floor around them. A single lantern bathed everything in flickering, eerie light. But—*there*.

I rolled a whiskey cask away from the darkest corner, revealing a trapdoor. Its hinges made not a sound as I swung it open. They were well oiled, then. Well used. Beneath the trapdoor, a narrow staircase disappeared into complete and utter darkness. I peered into it warily. The only things missing were weeping and gnashing of teeth.

After bending to retrieve the dagger from my boot, I stepped down, closed the door overhead, and shoved the blade through the handle. I pushed up once experimentally. It didn't budge.

Good.

I turned away. He couldn't follow me—not easily, at least. Not without magic.

When life is a choice between fighting or fleeing—every moment life or death—everything becomes a weapon. It doesn't matter who holds them. Weapons harm.

Weapons harm.

If we lived through this, I refused to be a weapon any longer.

But until then . . . I glanced up at the trapdoor, torn with indecision.

You're a witch. I shouldn't have resented you using magic. Just—don't let it take you somewhere I can't follow.

This time, however, that was exactly what I needed to do. A

simple knife wouldn't keep Reid away. Despite Coco's vision, he would do everything in his power to follow, to protect me from Morgane. From myself. If ever there was a moment of life and death, this was it—and it was mine.

I slipped my dagger from the handle, sheathing it in my boot once more. Then I lifted trembling hands. "Just once more," I promised him, taking a deep breath. "One last time."

I heard their shouts—the storeroom door rattle—as I turned and descended into Hell.

NOUS TOMBONS TOUS

Reid

"Lou! LOU!" I pounded on the trapdoor, roaring her name, but she didn't answer. There was only silence. Silence and panic— raw, visceral panic that closed my throat. Narrowed my vision. I beat on the door again. Tore at the handle. "Don't do this, Lou. Let us in. LET US IN."

Deveraux, Beau, Coco, and Ansel gathered around me. The others watched from the tavern door. "If you're determined to continue on this rather fruitless course of action, I will not stop you." Deveraux touched a gentle hand to my forearm. "I will, however, point out this door has been barred with magic and suggest we journey to a secondary entrance. The closest resides within the cemetery, perhaps a quarter hour walk from here."

Jean Luc pushed past Nicholina, who stroked a pale hand down his back. He leapt away. "East End is brimming with Chasseurs. The rest are down those tunnels. If we're seen, I can't protect you. I won't."

"Your loyalty inspires," Liana snapped.

"I'm not *loyal* to any of you. I'm *loyal* to Célie—"

"Jean Luc," Beau said, clapping a hand to his shoulder. Bracing. "Everyone here wants to kill or possibly eat you. Shut up, good man, before you lose your spleen."

Jean Luc fell into mutinous silence. I turned to Coco. "Open the door. Please."

She stared at me for several tense seconds. "No," she said at last. "You could die. I know you don't care, but Lou does. To everyone's surprise, *I* do. I won't supersede her efforts to protect you—and even if I wanted to, I can't open this door. No one can but the witch who cast the enchantment."

A snarl to rival the werewolves' tore from my throat. "I'll do it myself."

When I willed the patterns to emerge, however, none did. Not a single strand of gold. Not a single voice in my head. Furious, desperate, I turned to Toulouse, ripping the tarot deck from his shirt pocket. I shoved a card into his chest, and now, *now*, gold finally flared in my vision.

To know the unknown, you must unknow the known, the voices whispered.

Nonsense. Riddles. I didn't care. Choosing a pattern at random, I watched as it exploded into dust. "Reverse Strength," I snapped, and Toulouse grinned, glancing down at the card. "It means intense anger. Fear. A lack of confidence in one's own abilities, a loss of faith in oneself. In some cases—"

"—it is a loss of one's identity altogether." He chuckled and flipped the card to face me, revealing an upside-down woman and lion. Despite the horrific circumstances, triumph burst in my chest. Toulouse's grin spread. "It's about time too. You had me worried for a moment."

I jerked my chin toward the door. "Can you help me?"

His eyes dimmed. "Only Lou can open that door. I'm sorry."

Fuck.

"On to the cemetery, is it?" Deveraux clapped his hands. "Marvelous! Might I suggest we tarry forth? Time continues slipping away from us."

I nodded, breathing deeply. Forcing myself to calm. He was right. Each moment I'd bickered was a moment wasted—a moment Morgane tormented Célie, a moment Lou slipped farther away. Two desperate problems. One potential solution? I wracked my brain, thinking quickly. Analytically.

Lou would find Célie. Of that, I was sure. She had a head start. She had knowledge. She had incentive. No, there wasn't a force in Heaven or Hell—including Morgane—that would prevent her from succeeding in this. I didn't need to find Célie. If I found Lou, I'd find them both.

Lou was the target.

And if a small part of me hesitated, remembering Coco's premonition, I ignored it. I moved forward. I threw an arm across Ansel's chest when he followed the others to the door, shaking my head. "I told you to guard the tunnel."

His brows furrowed. "But the tunnel is locked. No one is going through it."

"Just stay here." Impatience sharpened my voice. I didn't care to soften it. Too much was at stake. At Modraniht, he'd proved more hindrance than help, and now we'd allied with enemies. Any one of them could turn on us in the tunnels. Ansel proved the easiest prey. I tried again. "Look, Zenna and Seraphine are staying behind too. Look after them. Keep them safe."

Ansel's chest caved, and he turned his burning gaze to the ground. Pink tinged his cheeks, his ears. Though he looked as if he wanted to protest, I was out of time. I could humor him no longer. Without another word, I turned on my heel and left.

There was nothing stiller than a cemetery at night. This one was small, the oldest in the city. The Church had stopped burying citizens in its soil long ago, favoring the newer, larger plot beyond Saint-Cécile. Now only the most powerful and affluent members of the aristocracy rested here—but even they weren't buried, instead joining their ancestors in the catacombs below.

"The entrance is there." Deveraux nodded to a statue of an angel. Moss grew on half her face. The wind had effaced her nose, the feathers on her wings. Still, she was beautiful. Words engraved onto the crypt beside her read *Nous Tombons Tous*. I didn't know what it meant. Fortunately, Deveraux did. "We all fall down," he said softly.

When I swung open the door, a gust of stale air rose to meet me. A single torch lit the narrow, earthen steps.

Beau stepped too close behind, peering into the darkness with unabashed apprehension. "Does the plan remain the same? Do we separate?"

Instead of looking below, Deveraux gazed upward at the night sky. Moonless tonight. "I don't think that's wise."

"We'll cover more ground if we do," Jean Luc insisted.

Foreboding lifted the hair on my neck as I climbed down the first step. "We stay together. Blaise, Liana, and Terrance can lead us to Lou. They know her scent. She'll be with Célie."

"You place an awful lot of confidence in that witch." Jean Luc shoved past me, tugging the torch from the wall and lifting it higher. Illuminating the path. The ceiling pressed down on us, forcing me to stoop. "What makes you so sure she'll find her?"

"She will."

Behind me, Beau and Coco struggled to walk side by side. "Let's hope the Chasseurs don't find *her*," she muttered.

The rest filed in after them, their footsteps the only sounds in the silence. So many footsteps. Jean Luc. Coco and Beau. Deveraux, Toulouse, and Thierry. La Voisin and her blood witches. Blaise and his children. Each equipped. Each powerful. Each ready and willing to destroy Morgane.

A tendril of hope unfurled in my chest. Perhaps that would be enough.

The first passage wore on interminably. Though I thought the tight space inconvenient, it didn't bring the sweat to my skin as it did Jean Luc. It didn't make my hands tremble, my breath catch. He refused to slow, however, walking faster and faster until we reached our first split in the tunnel. He hesitated. "Which way?"

"The crypts should be just past the eastern tunnel," Beau whispered.

"Why are you whispering?" Despite her objection, Coco whispered too. "And which direction is that?"

"East."

"*Left* or *right*, jackass?"

"Cosette," Beau said in mock surprise, "do you not know your—?"

A sudden wind doused the torch, plunging us into absolute darkness. Panicked voices rose. Swiftly, I reached for the wall, but it wasn't where it should've been. It wasn't *there*. "What the hell is going on?" Beau cried, but Liana interrupted, cursing violently.

"Something just *cut* me. Someone—"

Nicholina's scream splintered the tunnel.

"*Nicholina*." La Voisin's voice pitched high and sharp. My own throat felt tight. When I brushed wool in front of me—Jean Luc's coat—his fingers seized my arm and held on. "Nicholina, where are you?"

"Everyone stay calm," Deveraux commanded. "There is strange magic here. It plays tricks—"

The torch sprang back to life abruptly.

Blood spattered the tunnel floor. A handful of panicked faces blinked back at me in the light. Too few. *Far* too few.

"Where is Nicholina?" La Voisin seized Blaise's coat and slammed him against the wall, baring her teeth. I'd never seen her exhibit such uncontrolled emotion. Such fear. "*Where is she?*"

Blaise shoved her away with a snap of his teeth, charging down the tunnel and shouting for Liana and Terrance. A quick glance confirmed they too had vanished—along with the majority of blood witches. I searched the remaining faces, weak with relief when Beau and Coco nodded back at me, clutching each other. With a start, I realized Jean Luc still held my arm. He released me at the same instant.

Deveraux's face was drawn. "Thierry has disappeared as well."

"I swear I saw—" Toulouse started, but the torch extinguished again. His voice went with it. Forcibly. When Deveraux called after him, he didn't answer. Blaise's snarls echoed through the narrow tunnel, amplifying, heightening our frenzy, and something—something snarled *back*. La Voisin shouted, but I couldn't hear over the blood roaring in my ears, my own shouts for Beau and Coco—

Then she and Deveraux went silent too.

Forcing myself to focus, I summoned the patterns. Sifted through them on instinct, discarded them at the slightest touch. I needed fire. Not as a weapon. As *light*. Anger, hatred, bitter words—they'd all provide the expedient. I cast them aside without hesitation, searching for that single spark of energy. Something simple. Something . . . physical?

There.

I chafed my palms together—just once, with just enough pressure. Heat sparked. A flame flickered to life, illuminating the newfound blister on my finger. Like I'd rubbed actual kindling instead of skin. The air took care of the rest, and the fire grew in my hand.

Only Beau, Coco, Blaise, and Jean Luc remained in the tunnel with me.

The latter stared at the fire with an inscrutable expression. He hadn't seen it yet. My magic.

"They're gone." Beau loosened his grip on Coco, face pale. "They're just *gone*." He glanced up and down the tunnel with wide eyes, hesitating at the blood by our feet. "What do we do?"

Jean Luc answered for me, relighting his torch with my fire. Turning to the eastern tunnel. "We continue."

PARADISE LOST

Lou

Torches lined the earthen passages, casting the faces of passersby in shadow. Fortunately, few wandered this part, and those who did walked purposefully toward something—La Mascarade des Crânes, if their jewel-toned masks were any indication. They took the left-hand tunnels. On a whim, I took the right. The floors sloped gradually at first—the stone below smooth and slippery from the tread of many feet—before dipping unexpectedly. I stumbled, and a man lurched from the shadows, knocking into me and clutching my shoulders. I let out an undignified squeak.

"Where's your mask, pretty lady?" he slurred, his breath nearly burning the hair from my nose. His own mask covered the upper part of his face, jutting out in a cruel black beak. A crow. In the center of his forehead, a third eye stared down at me. It couldn't have been coincidence.

And I swore it just blinked.

Scowling—face hot with embarrassment, shoulders tense with unease—I pushed him away. "I'm already wearing one. Can't you tell?" I resisted the urge to flick my wrist, to lengthen my nails into razor-edged knives and score the porcelain at his cheek. Though the magic to lock Reid out physically had also locked him out emotionally—temporarily, until I lifted the pattern—I still heard his voice within my mind, if not my heart. I needn't harm this man. I needn't harm myself. Forcing a wicked grin instead, I whispered, "It's the skin of my enemies. Shall I add yours?"

He yelped and scrambled away.

Exhaling hard, I continued.

The tunnels wound in a labyrinth of stone. I wandered them in silence for several more minutes, my heart pounding a wild beat in my chest. It grew louder with each step. I walked faster, the hair on my neck lifting. Someone watched me. I could feel it. "Come out, come out, wherever you are," I breathed, hoping to bolster myself.

At my words, however, a strange wind rose in the tunnel, blowing out the torches and plunging me into darkness. Familiar laughter echoed from everywhere at once. Cursing, I grappled for my knife and tried to find a wall, tried to anchor myself in this insidious darkness—

When my fingertips brushed stone, the torchlight sprang back to life.

A flash of white hair disappeared around the bend.

I tore after it like a fool, unwilling to be caught alone in that darkness again, but it was gone. I kept running. When I burst into a long, shadowed room lined with coffins, I stopped short, panting and examining the nearest one in relief. "Father Lionnel Clément," I said, reading the faded name scratched into the stone. A yellow skull sat on a ledge above it. I glanced at the next name. *Father Jacques Fontaine.* "Clergymen."

I crept forward, pausing every so often to listen.

"Célie?" Though soft, my voice echoed unnaturally in the tomb. Unlike the absolute silence of the tunnels, this silence seemed to live and breathe, whispering against my neck, urging me to flee, flee, *flee.* I grew increasingly jumpy as the moments wore on, as the rooms grew in size. I didn't know what to look for—didn't know where even to start. Célie could've been in any one of these caskets, unconscious or worse, and I never would've known. Still . . . I couldn't shake the feeling Morgane *wanted* me to find Célie. There was less fun in a game I had no chance of winning. Morgane wouldn't have liked that. She wouldn't have just chosen an arbitrary grave, either. Her games were methodical, every move striking hard and true. Her notes had led me this far, each phrase a riddle, a clue, leading me deeper into her game.

Forlorn within her pall . . . alone but not alone.
Trapped within a mirrored grave, she wears a mask of bone.

It all pointed to *here*, now, this place. Only her use of the word *mirrored* made me pause.

Lost in thought—certain I'd missed something—I nearly didn't notice the dais in the next room, where hundreds of candles illuminated a gilded coffin. Winged angels and horned demons flickered in shadow on the lid, locked in an eternal embrace, while roses and skulls wove together in macabre beauty on each side. It was a masterpiece. A work of art.

Unbidden, I stepped closer, trailing my fingers along the cruel face of an angel. The petals of a rose. The letters of his name.

HIS EMINENCE, FLORIN CARDINAL CLÉMENT, ARCHBISHOP OF BELTERRA

Verily I say unto thee, today shalt thou be with me in Paradise

Florin Clément. I'd laughed at the name once, not knowing it belonged to me. In a different world, I might've been Louise Clément, daughter of Florin and Morgane. Perhaps they would've loved each other, adored each other, filling our home in East End with sticky buns and potted eucalyptus—and children. Lots and lots of children. An entire house of them, little brothers and sisters with freckles and blue-green eyes. Just like me. I could've taught them how to climb trees and braid hair, how to sing off pitch outside our parents' room at dawn. We could've been happy. We could've been a family.

Now that—*that*—would've been Paradise.

With a wistful sigh, I lowered my hand and turned away.

It did little good to imagine such a life for myself. My wine had been drawn long ago, and it was not a bouquet of hearth and home, nor friends and family. No, mine smelled of death. Of secrets. Of rot. "Are you in there with him, Célie?" I asked bitterly, mostly to distract myself from such wallowing thoughts.

"Seems like the sort of thing Morgane would—" Gasping, I whirled around, eyes wide. "Mirrored grave," I whispered. *An entire house of them, little brothers and sisters with freckles and blue-green eyes. Just like me.*

Holy hell.

I knew where she was.

A NECESSARY EVIL

Reid

The others' disappearances became a presence of its own. It hung over us like a rope, tightening with each small noise. When Beau kicked a pebble, Jean Luc tensed. When Coco inhaled too sharply, Blaise growled. He'd half shifted, eyes glowing luminous in the semidarkness, to better scent Lou—and to better fight whatever roamed these tunnels.

"This doesn't end with Célie and Lou," Coco had said fiercely when he'd tried to leave, to search for his missing children. Curiously, he hadn't been able to smell where they'd gone. Where *any* of them had gone. They'd just . . . vanished. "It ends with Morgane. This has her clawed hands all over it. Wherever she is, Liana and Terrance will be too. Trust me."

No one voiced what that meant. Everyone knew.

Even a moment spent under Morgane's mercy was too long. Too late.

"*Are* her hands clawed?" Beau had muttered a few moments later.

Coco had raised her brows at him. "You were at Modraniht. You saw them."

"They weren't clawed."

"They should've been. She should have a wart and a hunchback too, the hackneyed bitch."

Even Jean Luc cracked a grin. His Balisarda weighed heavy against my chest. At last—when I could stand it no more—I unsheathed it, handing it to him. "Here. Take it."

His smile slipped, and he missed a step. "Why—why would you give this back to me?"

I curled his fingers around the hilt. "It's yours. Mine is gone." When I shrugged, the movement didn't feel forced. It felt . . . right. *Light*. A weight lifted from my shoulders. "Perhaps it's for the best. I'm not a huntsman anymore."

He stared at me. Then the dam broke. "You're a witch. You killed the Archbishop with . . . magic." His voice dripped with accusation. With betrayal. But there, in his eye, was a sliver of hope. He wanted me to deny it. He wanted to blame someone else—anyone else—for what had happened to our forefather. In that sliver, I recognized my old friend. He was still in there. Despite everything, he still wanted to trust me. The thought should've warmed me, but it didn't.

That sliver was a lie.

"Yes." I watched as his hope shriveled, as he physically recoiled from me. Blaise's gaze touched my cheek, curious—studying—but I ignored him. "I won't deny it, and I won't explain myself. I am a witch, and I killed our forefather. The Archbishop didn't deserve it, but he also wasn't the man we thought he was."

Visibly deflating, he scrubbed a hand down his face.

"Mother of God." When he looked up again, he met my gaze with not camaraderie, exactly, but a sense of resignation. "Have you known all this time?"

"No."

"Did you enchant him to receive your position?"

"Of course not."

"And does it . . . feel different?" At this, he swallowed visibly, but he did not look away. In that small act of defiance, I remembered the boy who'd befriended me, cared for me, the one who'd always pulled me up when I fell. The one who'd punched Julien for calling me trash boy. Before the greed had hardened us to each other. Before the envy.

"I'm not the same person I was, Jean." The words, so different than before—so true—fell heavy from my lips. Final. "But neither are you. We'll never be what we were. But here, now, I'm not asking for your friendship. Morgane is near, and together—regardless of our past—we have a real chance to finish her."

"You thought she'd attack at the funeral. You were wrong."

Unbidden, more truth spilled forth. I felt lighter with each word. "I thought whatever I needed to think to attend the Archbishop's funeral." I hadn't realized it at the time. Perhaps *couldn't* have realized it. And though I'd thought wrong, I didn't regret it. I couldn't. He started to argue, but I pushed forward before the next words died in my throat. Forced myself to meet his gaze directly. "Jean. I . . . I never knew about Célie."

He stiffened.

"If I'd known how you felt, I would've..." What? Not accepted her love? Not accepted the Archbishop's? Would I not have fought him in the tournament or taken my oath? Would I have given up my dreams because he wanted them too? "I'm sorry," I said simply.

And I was. I was sorry life had dealt us the same cards. I was sorry for his pain, for the suffering I'd inadvertently caused him. I couldn't take it away, but I could acknowledge it. I could open the door for us. I couldn't, however, force him to step through it.

A tense moment passed before he dipped his chin, but I recognized that nod for what it was—a single step.

Without another word, we continued our search. It took another half hour for Blaise to catch Lou's scent. "She is close." He frowned, creeping toward the tunnel ahead. "But there are others. I can hear their heartbeats, their breaths—" He skidded backward abruptly, eyes wide as he turned. "*Run.*"

Chasseurs rounded the corner.

Balisardas lifted, they recognized me immediately and charged. Philippe led them. When Jean Luc leapt in front of us, however—shoving me backward, out of their line of fire—they staggered to a halt. "What is this?" Philippe snarled. He didn't lower his blade. His eyes fell to Jean Luc's own Balisarda. "Where did you...?"

"Reid returned it to me."

Those behind Philippe shifted uncomfortably. They disliked this new information. I was a witch. A murderer. Confusion, unease flitted across their faces as they took in Jean's protective stance. "Why are you here, Captain?" Philippe jerked his chin toward me. "He is our enemy. They all are."

"A necessary evil." After a single, hesitant look in my direction, Jean Luc straightened his shoulders. "We have new orders, men. Morgane is here. We find her, and we kill her."

THE MIRRORED GRAVE

Lou

In the middle of the catacombs, I found the Tremblay family tomb.

Never before had I hoped I was wrong as fervently as I did now—and never before had I felt so sick. As with the other tombs, skulls lined the shelves here, marking each ancestor's final resting place. It was a custom I'd never understood. Witches didn't decapitate their dead. Did one remove the deceased's head before or after decomposition? Or—or did they do it during the embalming process? And for that matter, *who* was responsible for doing it in the first place? Surely not the family. My stomach churned at the thought of sawing through a loved one's bones, and I decided I didn't want to know the answers after all.

My steps grew heavier, leaden, the farther I crept into the room until finally—*finally*—I found her name carved into a pretty rosewood casket.

FILIPPA ALLOUETTE TREMBLAY
Beloved daughter and sister

"Célie? Are you in there?"

There was no answer.

At least Filippa's skull hadn't yet been displayed.

Muscles straining, I pried at the casket's lid, but it didn't budge. After several moments of struggling in vain, I panted, "I don't know if you can hear me—and I really hope you're not in there, in which case I apologize *profusely* to your sister—but this isn't working. The damn thing is too heavy. I'll have to magic you out."

A rock skittered across the ground behind me, and I whirled, hands lifted.

"*Ansel?*" Mouth falling open, I dropped my hands. "What are you doing here? How did you *find* me?"

He took in the skulls with wide eyes. "When the others left, I tried the trapdoor again. I had a hunch." He gave me a tentative smile. "After what happened with Coco, I knew you'd try to be more careful with your magic, with the patterns you could safely maintain, and sealing the door against just Reid . . . it seemed simpler than sealing it against everyone else or sealing it permanently. I was right. When it opened, I followed the first tunnel. It led me straight here."

"That's impossible." I stared at him incredulously. "That tunnel is a dead end. You must've gotten turned around in the dark. Where are the others?"

"They went to a cemetery entrance."

"A cemetery entrance." Instinctively, I released the pattern keeping hold of my heart, and all the love I felt for Reid—all the despair, all the *panic*—surged through me in a disorienting wave. I stumbled slightly under its magnitude. "*Shit*. Did Reid—?"

He shrugged helplessly. "I don't know. He told me to stay behind, but I—I couldn't. I had to help you somehow. Please don't be mad."

"Mad? I'm not—" A sudden, terrible thought caught my throat in its fist. No. I shook my head, reeling at the complete absurdity of it. Choking with laughter. To him, to myself, I said, "No, no, no. I'm not mad."

No, no, no, my thoughts echoed, repeating the word like a talisman.

Pasting on a bright smile, I looped my elbow through his and tugged him to my side. "There's absolutely nothing to worry about. I just think, under the circumstances, Reid might've been right. It'd be better if you returned to the tavern and waited—"

He pulled away, eyes flashing with hurt. "It's almost midnight, and you haven't found Célie. I can help."

"Actually, I might've found her—"

"Where is she?" He glanced at the skulls and caskets, anxiety creasing his brow. "Is she alive?"

"I think so, but I'm having a little trouble—"

"Whatever it is, I can help."

"No, I think it's better if you—"

"What's the problem?" His voice rose. "Do you not think I can do it?"

"You *know* that's not what I—"

"Then what is it? I can help. I *want* to help."

"I know you do, but—"

"I'm not a *child*, Lou, and I'm sick and tired of everyone treating me like one! I'm almost *seventeen*! That's a year older than you were when you saved the kingdom—"

"When I *fled*," I said sharply, losing my patience. "Ansel, I *fled*, and now I'm asking you to do the same—"

"*Why?*" he exploded, throwing his hands in the air. Color bloomed on his cheeks, and his eyes burned overbright. "You once told me I'm not worthless, but I still don't believe you. I can't fight. I can't cast enchantments. Let me prove I can do *something*—"

I swore loudly. "How many times do I have to tell you, Ansel? You don't need to prove *anything* to me."

"Then let me prove it to myself." Voice breaking on the word, he cringed and dropped his gaze. Stared dejectedly at his fists. "Please."

My heart broke at the sight of him. He thought he was worthless. No, he *believed* it, deep down in his bones, and I—I could do nothing about it. Not now. Not with his life at stake. Perhaps he wasn't worth much to the world, to himself, but to me... to me, he was precious beyond value. If there was even a chance...

A man close to your heart will die.

I loathed myself for what I was about to do.

"You're right, Ansel." My voice hardened. If I told him the truth, he would balk. He'd refuse to leave. I needed to hurt him badly enough that he wouldn't—*couldn't*—stay. I nodded and crossed my arms. "You want me to say it? You're right. You wreck everything you touch. You can't even *walk* without stumbling, let alone wield a sword. You can't talk to a woman without blushing, so how could you save one? Honestly, it's—it's *tragic* how helpless you are."

With each word, he crumbled more, tears sparkling in his eyes, but I wasn't finished.

"You say you're not a child, Ansel, but you are. You *are*. It's like—you're a little boy playing pretend, dressing up with our coats and boots. We've let you tag along for laughs, but now the time for games is done. A woman's life is in danger—*my* life is in danger. We can't afford for you to mess this up. I'm sorry."

Face ashen, he said nothing.

"Now," I said, forcing myself to continue, to *breathe*, "you're going to turn around and march back up the tunnel. You're going to return to the tavern, and you're going to hide in your room until it's *safe*. Do you understand?"

He stared at me, pressing his lips together to stop their trembling. "No."

"No, you don't understand?"

"No." He stood a little taller, wiping an errant tear from his cheek. "I will not."

"Excuse me?"

"I said *no*, I will—"

My eyes narrowed. "I heard what you said. I'm giving you a chance to reconsider."

"What are you going to do?" He laughed scornfully, and the sound was so sad, so unnatural, it cut me at my core. "Freeze my heart? Shatter my bones? Make me forget I ever knew you?"

I brushed the rosewood with my fingertips, deliberating. This magic would hurt us both, but at least he'd be hurt and *alive*. "If you make me."

We stared at each other—him looking fiercer than I'd ever seen him—until something thumped beside us. We turned to look at Filippa's coffin, and I closed my eyes in shame. I'd forgotten about Célie.

"Is someone—" Ansel's lips parted on a horrified breath. "Is Célie in there? *Alive?*"

"Yes," I whispered, the fight leaving me abruptly. Coco had said her visions were rarely what they seemed. Perhaps this one could still play out differently. The future was fickle. If I sent him away, he could meet his death in the tunnels instead. At my side, perhaps I could . . . protect him, somehow. "Stay close to me, Ansel."

Between the two of us, we managed to slide Filippa's coffin to the floor. Opening the lid was another story. It took magic to unseal it. But I knew all about breaking locks, however, and fortunately for me, I'd just broken a relationship.

Another round in Morgane's game.

The lid opened easily after that.

When we saw Célie lying, unconscious, among her sister's remains, Ansel promptly vomited up the contents of his stomach. I nearly joined him, pressing a fist to my mouth to stem the bile. Filippa's corpse had not yet fully decomposed, and her rotted flesh oozed against Célie's skin. And the smell, it—

I vomited on Monique Priscille Tremblay's skull.

"She'll never recover from this," I said, wiping my mouth on my sleeve. "This—this is sick, even for Morgane."

At the sound of my voice, Célie lurched upright at the waist, her eyes snapping open. Tears spilled down her cheeks as she turned to stare at me. "Célie," I breathed, dropping down beside her. "I am so sorry—"

"You found me."

I wiped the slime from her face and hair the best I could. "Of course I did."

"I d-didn't think you'd c-come. I've been down here for w-weeks." Though she shivered violently, she didn't rise from the coffin. I slipped my cloak around her shoulders. "She—she visited me sometimes. Taunted me. S-said that I'd d-d-die here. Said—said Reid had f-forgotten about me."

"Shhh. You're safe now. Reid is the one who sent me. We'll get you out of here, and—"

"I can't leave." She sobbed harder when Ansel and I tried to lift her, but her body remained firmly in the coffin. We tugged harder. She didn't budge. "I c-c-can't m-move. Not unless I take you to—to her. She e-enchanted me." I smelled it then, the magic, almost indiscernible beneath the stench of decay. "If I d-don't, I'll have to s-s-stay here with—with Filippa—" A keening wail rose from her throat, and I hugged her closer, wishing desperately Reid were here. He'd know what to do. He'd know how to comfort her—

No. I slammed the door shut on the thought.

I hoped Reid *wasn't* here. Though I couldn't lock Ansel away—not alone in the catacombs with only Filippa's corpse for company—I could still prevent Reid from finding us, from following us to Morgane. In my mind, if I kept them separate, he'd be fine. I could still pray Coco's vision had been wrong, and everyone would survive the night.

"Can you stand at all?" I asked.

"I d-don't think so."

"Can you try? Ansel and I will help you."

She cringed away as if just realizing I'd been touching her. "N-No. You—you t-*took* Reid from me. She t-told me you *enchanted* him."

I tried to remain calm. This wasn't Célie's fault. It was Morgane's. If I knew my mother at all, everything she'd told Célie in their time together had been a lie. Once Célie's shock wore off, it'd be impossible to persuade her into leaving with me. I was the enemy. I was the witch who'd stolen Reid's heart. "We can't sit on this floor forever, Célie. Eventually, we have to move."

"Where's Reid?" Her breathing hitched once more, and she looked around wildly. "Where is he? I want Reid!"

"I can take you to him," I said patiently, motioning for Ansel to join me on the floor. She'd started keening again, rocking back and forth and clutching her face. "But I need you to step out of the coffin."

As predicted, her wailing ceased when she spotted Ansel through her fingers. "You," she whispered, clutching the edge of the casket. "I—I saw you in the Tower. You're an initiate."

Thank God Ansel had enough sense to lie. "Yes," he said smoothly, taking her hand. "I am. And I need you to trust me. I won't let anyone harm you, Célie, especially a witch."

She leaned closer. "You don't understand. I can f-feel her magic pulling at me. Right here." She tapped her chest, the movement fitful, frantic. Blood caked beneath her fingernails, as if she'd tried to scratch her way through the rosewood. "If I get up, I won't have a choice. S-She's *waiting* for us."

"Can you break the enchantment?" Ansel asked me.

"It doesn't work like that. I don't know how Reid did it at Modraniht, but it must've taken extraordinary focus, maybe a powerful surge of emotion while Morgane was distracted, and right now, I can't—" Faint voices echoed down the tunnel. Though I couldn't discern the words, the cadences, it wouldn't do for anyone to find us here. Especially Reid.

"Get up," I snapped to Célie. "Get up, and take us to Morgane before this night goes to complete hell." When she stared, dumbfounded at my sudden outburst, I tugged fiercely on her hand. It was no use. I couldn't break this bind. Célie would have to choose to rise herself. Which she did, after I grabbed her face and hissed, "If you don't get up, Reid will die."

LA MASCARADE DES CRÂNES

Lou

No longer in control of her body, Célie walked with mechanical footsteps down each left-hand tunnel, leading us into La Mascarade des Crânes. I nearly clipped her heels twice in my haste. Any second, Reid could march around the bend. I needed to deal with Morgane before that happened.

My mind raged against me, presenting fresh problems with each step—fresh problems and stale solutions. As usual, Morgane had played one move ahead. I'd gathered my allies—*and snuck away to face Morgane without them*, my mind sneered—persuaded powerful pieces onto the board, waited for her to strike. But she hadn't struck. At least, not in the way I'd planned. I stared at Célie's frail back, her soiled mourning gown. Now I was trapped like a rat in the sewers with only Ansel and Célie for help. Even if I hadn't vowed to keep both out of the fray, my chances of walking away from this encounter were nonexistent.

This was a disaster.

The path widened as we crept onward, more lanterns

illuminating this tunnel than the others. We'd walked for only a minute or so before voices echoed up the tunnel—many voices this time, carousing and loud. Unfamiliar. Some rose together in song, accompanied by the merry twang of mandolins, the dulcet chords of a harp, even the sharper notes of a rebec. When we rounded the corner, the first painted stalls rose to meet us. Here, masked merchants crooned to scandalously clad maidens, promising more than sweetmeat and pies, while others hawked wares such as bottled dreams and fairy dust. Bards wove through the shoppers. To the applause of passersby, a contortionist twisted his limbs into impossible shapes. Everywhere I looked, revelers danced, laughed, shouted, spilling wine on the tunnel floors. Coins spilled just as freely.

When a dirty-faced child—a cutpurse—slipped her hand into my pocket, I seized her wrist, clucking my tongue. "I think you'll find better luck over there," I whispered, pointing to a drunken couple who sat beside a cart of powdered *bugne*. The girl nodded appreciatively and crept toward them.

We couldn't stop to enjoy the sights, however, as Célie marched onward, weaving through the revelers like a snake being charmed. We hurried to keep up.

She ignored the infinite side tunnels and their unknown delights, keeping instead to the main path. Others joined us, whispering excitedly, their faces obscured by elaborate costumes: lions and lionesses with thick fur headpieces and claws of diamond; horned dragons with painted-on scales that gleamed metallic in the torchlight; peacocks with teal, gold, and turquoise feathers, their glittering masks carved into fashionable beaks. Even the poorer attendants had spared no expense, donning their finest suits and painting their faces. The man nearest me resembled the devil with his red face and black horns.

Each glanced at our bare faces curiously, but none commented. My apprehension mounted with each step. Morgane was nearby. She had to be. I could almost feel her breath on my neck now, hear her voice calling my name.

Sensing my distress, Ansel slipped his hand into mine and squeezed. "I'm here, Lou."

I returned the pressure with numb fingers. Perhaps I hadn't broken our relationship beyond repair. The thought bolstered me enough to whisper, "I'm scared, Ansel."

"So am I."

Too soon, the tunnel opened to cavernous, empty space—like the inside of a mountain growing down into earth instead of up into sky. Crude stone benches lined the sloping walls like rows of teeth, and steep stairs led down, down, down to an earthen mouth.

And there, in the center of that primitive stage, stood my mother.

She looked resplendent in robes of black velvet. Her arms remained bare despite the underground chill, and her moonbeam hair waved loose down her back. An intricate golden circlet sat atop her head, but the corpses floating above her in a circle— peaceful, eyes closed and hands clasped—they formed her true crown. Though I couldn't see the details of their faces, I *could* see their slashed throats. My stomach dropped with understanding. With dread. I shifted Ansel and Célie ever so subtly behind me.

She spread her arms wide, smiled broadly, and called, "Darling, welcome! I'm so happy you could join us!"

Around us, hundreds of people sat unnaturally still on the benches, silent and staring behind their masks. Magic coated the air, so thick and heavy my eyes watered, and I knew instinctively they couldn't move. The eyes of those who'd entered with us emptied, and without a word, they walked promptly to their seats. Seized by sudden panic, I searched for Reid, Coco, and Beau amidst the audience, but they were nowhere to be seen. I breathed a short-lived sigh of relief.

"Hello, *Maman*."

Her smile grew at my defensive stance. "You look beautiful. I must admit, I *did* chuckle when you melted your hair—classic mistake, darling—but I think you'll agree the new color suits you. Do come closer, so I might see it better."

My feet grew roots. "I'm here. Let Célie go."

"Oh, I don't think so. She'll miss all the fun." Flicking the train of her robes behind her, she stepped forward, revealing another body at her feet. My heart dropped. Even from afar, I recognized the slight build, the auburn curls.

"Gabrielle," I whispered in horror.

Ansel stiffened beside me. "Is she . . . ?"

"Dead?" Morgane supplied helpfully, nudging Gaby's face with her boot. Gaby moaned in response. "Not yet, but soon. With my daughter's help, of course." She stepped on Gabrielle's hand as she continued across the stage. "Where is your hunts-man, Louise? I had hoped he would join you. I have *much* to discuss with him, you see. A male witch! You cannot imagine my surprise after the little trick he pulled at Modraniht. Trading the Archbishop's life for yours? It was inspired."

I squared my shoulders. "Your note said you'd let her go."

"No. My note said I'd eat her heart if you didn't rescue her by midnight, which"—she licked her teeth salaciously—"is now. Perhaps you can offer a distraction in the meantime."

"But I rescued her—"

"No, Louise." Morgane's grin darkened. "You haven't. Now," she said, matter-of-fact, "tell me, are there more like your hunts-man? Perhaps I was foolish in sending away our sons. It has proved near impossible to track them, and those we found . . . well, they're quite terrified of me. It seems not *all* sons inherit our gifts." She looked lovingly to the corpses above her. "But I am not without reward. My labor yielded different fruit."

"We found no one," I lied, but she knew. She smiled.

"Come here, sweeting." She crooked a finger at Célie, who stood so close behind me I could feel her body shake. "Such a lovely little doll. Come here, so I may shatter you."

"Please," Célie whispered, clutching my arm as her feet moved of their own accord. "Please, help me."

I caught her hand and held it there. "Leave her alone, Mor-gane. You've tormented her enough."

Morgane cocked her head as if considering. "Perhaps you're right. It would be much less satisfying to simply kill her, wouldn't it?" She clapped her hands together and laughed. "Oh, how delightfully cruel you are. I must say I'm impressed. With her dead sister's flesh still fouling her skin, *of course* we must condemn her to live—to live and to never forget. The *torment*, as you say, will be delicious."

Tasting bile, I released Célie's hand. When her feet continued forward, however, she let out a sob. "What are you doing?" I snarled, leaping down the steps after her.

"Please, Louise," Morgane crooned, "I *desire* for you to come closer. Follow the doll." To Ansel, she added, "From the way you flit at her side, I assume you're some kind of pet. A bird, perhaps. Remain where you are, lest I pluck your feathers for a hat."

Ansel reached for the knife at his belt. I waved him back, hissing, "Stay here. Don't give her more reason to notice you."

His doe-like eyes blinked, confused. He still hadn't connected the dots.

"I'm waiting," she sang, her voice dripping with honey.

Witches lined the steps, watching as Célie and I descended. More than I'd expected. More than I recognized. Manon stood near the bottom, but she refused to look at me. Indifference smoothed her pointed features, turned her ebony face into a hard mask. But—she swallowed hard as I passed, mask cracking as her eyes flicked to one of the corpses.

It was the handsome, golden-haired man from earlier. Gilles.

Beside him, two girls with equally fair complexions drifted, their glassy eyes just as blue. An older brunette hovered on his other side, and a toddler—he couldn't have been older than three—completed the circle. Five bodies in all. Five perfect corpses.

"Do not let their expressions deceive you," Morgane murmured. This close, I could see the angry red scar on her chest from Jean Luc's blade. "Their deaths were not peaceful. They were not pretty or pleasant. But you know that already, don't you? You saw our sweet Etienne." Another smile twisted her lips. "You should've heard him scream, Louise. It was beautiful. Transcendent. And all because of you."

With the curl of her fingers, the bodies lowered, still circling, until they surrounded me at eye level. Their toes brushed the earth, and their heads—I swallowed a gag.

Their heads were clearly kept intact by magic.

Numb, I rose to my toes, closing first the toddler's eyes—his head wavered at the contact—then the brunette's, the twins', and finally, the handsome stranger's. Manon shifted in my peripheral vision. "You're sick, *Maman*," I said. "You've been sick for a long time."

"You would know, darling. You can't imagine my delight watching you these past weeks. I've never been so proud. Finally, my daughter realizes what must be done. She's on the wrong side, of course, but her sacrifices are still commendable. She has become the *weapon* I conceived her to be."

Bile rose in my throat at her emphasis, and I prayed—*prayed*—she hadn't been spying on us earlier, hadn't overheard Reid's words in our room at Léviathan. Our *bedroom*. Her presence would poison those moments between us.

Please, not those.

Her finger—cold and sharp—lifted my chin. But her eyes were colder. Her eyes were sharper. "Did you think you could save them?" When I said nothing, only stared, she pinched my chin harder. "You humiliated me on Modraniht. In front of all our sisters. In front of the Goddess herself. After you fled, I realized how blind I'd been. How fixated. I sent your sisters into the kingdom in search of Auguste's spawn." She backhanded Gilles's face, rupturing his skin. Stagnant blood oozed out of him. It dripped onto Gaby's hair. She moaned again. "And I found them—not all of them, no, not yet. But soon. You see, I do not need your wretched throat to exact my vengeance, Louise. My will shall be done, with or without you.

"Make no mistake," she added, seizing my chin once more, "you *will* die. But should you escape again, I will not chase you. Never again will I chase you. Instead, I will cherish dismembering your huntsman's brothers and sisters, and I will send you each piece. I will bottle their screams and poison your dreams. Each time you close your eyes, you will witness the end of their miserable lives. And—after the last child is slain—I will come for your huntsman, and I will cut the secrets from his mind, butchering him in front of you. Only *then* will I kill you, daughter. Only when you *beg* for death."

I stared at her. My mother. She was mad, wholly and completely crazed. She'd always been passionate, volatile, but this . . . this was different. In her quest for vengeance, she'd given away too much. *All those pieces you're giving up—I want them,* Reid had said. *I want you. Whole and unharmed.* I searched her face for any sign of the woman who'd raised me—who'd danced with me on the beach and taught me to value my worth—but there was nothing left. She was gone.

Do you think you'll be able to kill your own mother?

She hasn't given me a choice.

It hadn't been an answer then. It was now.

"Well?" She released my chin, her eyes blazing with fury. "Have you nothing to say?"

My hands were heavy, leaden, but I forced them upward anyway. "I think . . . if you plan to dismember *all* of his children, one by one . . . I have quite a bit of time to stop you." She bared her teeth, and I grinned at her, faking bravado. That stretch of my mouth cost everything. It also provided a distraction for the half step I took in Gabrielle's direction. "And I *will* stop you, *Maman*—especially if you blather about your plans every time we meet. You really love the sound of your voice, don't you? I never took you for narcissistic. Deranged and fanatical, yes, at times even vain, but never narciss—"

Morgane hauled Gaby to her feet before I could finish, and I cursed mentally. When she twisted a hand, a ball of fire bloomed atop her palm. "I had thought to offer you an ultimatum, *darling*, between Célie and Gabrielle—just a bit of fun—but it seems you've quite tested my patience. Now I will kill them both. Though I know you prefer ice, I'm partial to fire. It's rather poetic, don't you think?"

Célie whimpered behind me.

Shit.

At the stroke of Morgane's finger, Gaby's eyes snapped open—then widened, darting around us. "Lou." Her voice cracked on my name, and she thrashed in Morgane's arms. "Lou, she's a maniac. She and—"

She stopped talking on a scream when Morgane swept the fire against her face—when Morgane swept and kept sweeping, drawing the flames down her throat, her chest, her arms. Though she screamed and screamed, thrashing anew, Morgane didn't release her. Panicked, I cast about for a pattern, for *the* pattern, but before I could commit, a blade sliced through the air, through Morgane's *hand*.

Howling in outrage, she dropped Gaby and jerked toward—

My breath caught in my throat.

Ansel. She jerked toward Ansel.

He'd followed me again.

Eyes narrowing, she looked at him—*really* looked at him—for the first time. Her blood dripped onto the hem of her robes. One drop. Two drops. Three. "I remember you." When she smiled, her face twisted into something ugly and dark. She didn't stop Gaby as she scrambled backward, away from us, and disappeared into the tunnel below the aisles. "You were at Modraniht. Such a pretty little bird. You've finally found your wings."

He gripped his knives tighter, jaw set, and widened his stance, planting his feet and preparing to use both his upper- and lower-body strength. Pride and terror warred inside my heart. He'd saved Gaby. He'd drawn Morgane's blood.

He'd been marked.

The patterns came without hesitation as I stepped to his side. When I raised my hands, determined, he nudged the knife in my boot instead. I drew it swiftly. "First lesson," he breathed. "Find your opponent's weaknesses and exploit them."

"What are you whispering?" she hissed, drawing another fireball into her hand.

She'd chosen fire to make a statement, but fire could be stoked. It meant passion. *Emotions.* In combat, she'd react swiftly, without forethought, and that impulsivity could be her undoing. We'd have to be careful, quick. "I knew you'd choose fire." I smirked, tossing the blade in my hand with casual nonchalance. "You're growing predictable in your old age, *Maman.* And wrinkled." When she launched the first fireball, Ansel ducked swiftly. "It's a good thing your hair is naturally white. It hides the gray, yes?"

With a scream of indignation, she flung the second. This time, however, I moved swifter still, catching the flames on my blade and hurling them back at her. "Second lesson," I said, laughing as her cloak caught fire. "There's no such thing as cheating. Use every weapon in your arsenal."

"You think you're clever, don't you?" Morgane flung her cloak to the ground, panting. It smoldered gently, sending clouds of smoke to curl around her. "But I taught you how to fight, Louise. *Me.*" Barely discernible through the smoke, she gathered a third ball of fire between her palms, eyes glittering with malice. "Third lesson: the fight isn't over until one of you is dead." When she threw the fireball, it grew into a sword—a pillar—and neither Ansel nor I could move swiftly enough. It razed our skin as it passed, knocking us from our feet, and Morgane lunged.

Anticipating the movement—body screaming in pain—I swiped Ansel's knife and rolled over him, slashing his blade at her face. Her upper half reared backward, but the movement propelled her lower half toward me—toward *my* knife, which I drove through her stomach. She gasped. The flames vanished, and the bodies floating above thudded to the ground. Horrified gasps rose from the audience as her spell lifted. With Ansel's blade, I moved to finish the job, watching her every movement, every emotion, as if time had slowed. Memorizing her face. Her brows as they dipped in confusion. Her eyes as they widened in surprise. Her lips as they parted in fear.

Fear.

It was one emotion I'd never seen on my mother's face.

And it made me hesitate.

Above us, footsteps thundered, and Reid's shout splintered the silence.

No.

Faster than humanly possible, Morgane's hand snaked out, catching my wrist and twisting. The world rushed back into focus with vivid clarity, and I dropped the knife with a cry.

"You tried to kill me," she whispered. "*Me.* Your *mother.*" Wild, cackling laughter stole her breath, even as—as *Chasseurs* descended. Reid and Jean Luc led them with Blaise snarling behind, fully shifted. "And what if you'd succeeded, daughter? Is that why you came here? Did you think you'd become queen?"

She twisted brutally, and I heard my bone snap. Pain radiated up my arm, consuming everything, and I screamed. "A queen must do what is necessary, Louise. You were almost there, but you stopped. Shall I show you the path to continue? Shall I show you everything you lack?"

She dropped my wrist, and I staggered backward, watching through tears as Reid sprinted toward us, pulling away from the rest, knives drawn. I couldn't move fast enough. I couldn't stop him. "Reid, *NO*—!"

Morgane hurled a fourth and final ball of fire, and it exploded against his chest.

THE WOODWOSE

Reid

Smoke engulfed me, thick and billowing. It smothered my nose, my mouth, my eyes. Though I couldn't see her, I could still hear Lou as she screamed, as she raged against her mother, who laughed. Who laughed and laughed and laughed. I waded through the smoke to reach her, to tell her I was fine—

"Reid!" Ansel bellowed. Jean Luc's voice soon joined his, shouting over the din as audience members fled for safety. As witches shrieked and footsteps pounded, thick as the smoke in the air.

But where was the fire?

I patted my chest, searching for the sharp heat of flames, but there were none. Instead, there was—there was—

Claud Deveraux stood beside me, offering me a sly smile. In his hands, he held the ball of flames—shrinking now, smoking wildly—and in his eyes . . . I blinked rapidly through the smoke. For just a moment, his eyes seemed to flicker with something ancient and wild. Something *green*. I yielded a step in astonishment. The faint earthiness I'd smelled within Troupe de Fortune's wagons had returned tenfold. It overwhelmed the smoke, doused the cavern in the scent of pine sap and lichen, fresh soil and hay. "I thought—you said you weren't a witch."

"And I'm still not, dear boy."

"We couldn't find you. In the tunnels, we couldn't—"

"My ducklings had gone missing, hadn't they?" He straightened my coat with a tight smile. "Never fear. I *shall* find them." Beyond the smoke, Lou still screamed. It filled my ears, hindering all other thought. "And though *sweet* Zenna knew better, the temptation of violence proved too much to resist—such bloodlust in that one. I found her in the tunnels while I searched for the others. Poor Seraphine had no choice but to follow, and I couldn't very well leave them unprotected. I *had* hoped to return before the situation here escalated—better to prevent than to heal, you know—but alas." He looked over his shoulder toward Morgane's laughter. "Her sickness may consume us all. If you'll excuse me."

He parted the smoke with the flick of his wrist.

Lou and Morgane materialized, circling each other with their hands raised. Past them, Ansel shielded Célie in his arms, and Jean Luc and Coco fought back-to-back against a trio of witches. Above us, Beau ushered panicked revelers to the exits. The body of a witch cooled at Blaise's feet, throat torn open, but another had cornered him. Her hands contorted wildly.

Two Chasseurs reached her first.

When Deveraux stepped out of the smoke, Lou and Morgane both froze. I followed behind.

"*You*," Morgane snarled at him, and she stumbled—actually *stumbled*—backward.

Deveraux sighed. "Yes, darling. Me."

And with those words, Claud Deveraux began to change. Growing taller, broader, his form stretched over even me. Cloven hooves burst from his polished shoes. Stag antlers erupted from his styled curls. A crown of oaken branches wove around them. Pupils narrowing abruptly to slits, his eyes gleamed in the darkness like a cat's. He stared down at us in silence for several seconds.

I took a shaky breath.

"Holy *shit*." Lou gaped up at him in disbelief. In confusion. I edged toward her. "You're . . . you're the Woodwose."

Winking, he tipped his hat to her. It vanished in a burst of lilacs, which he presented to her with a flourish. "'Tis a pleasure to meet you, little one." His voice was deeper now, ancient, as if it hailed from the earth itself. "I do apologize for not revealing myself sooner, but these are strange and difficult times."

"But you aren't *real*. You're a goddamn *fairy tale*."

"As are you, Louise." His yellow eyes crinkled. "As are you."

"You shouldn't have come here, Henri," Morgane said through tight lips. She still hadn't lowered her hands. "I'll kill all of them to spite you."

He smiled without warmth, revealing pointed fangs. "Tread carefully, darling. I am not a dog who must obey his master's summons." His voice grew harder, fiercer, at Morgane's grimace. "I am the Wild. I am all that inhabits the land, all things that are made and unmade. In my hand is the life of every creature and the breath of all mankind. The mountains bow to my whim. The wild animals honor me. I am the shepherd and the flock."

Despite herself, Morgane yielded a step. "You—you know the Old Laws. You cannot intervene."

"I cannot *directly* intervene." He drew to his full height, looming over her—over us all—his catlike eyes flashing. "But my sister . . . she is displeased with your recent exploits, Morgane. Very displeased."

"Your sister," Lou repeated faintly.

Morgan paled. "Everything I've done, I've done for her. Soon, her children will be free—"

"And your child will be dead." Frowning, he reached down to touch her cheek. She didn't recoil. Instead, she leaned into his touch. I wanted to look away. I couldn't. Not when profound sadness welled in this strange being's eyes, not when it slid as a tear down Morgane's cheek. "What has happened to you, my love? What evil poisons your spirit?"

Now she did recoil. The tear curled into smoke on her cheek. "You *left* me."

The word broke something in her, and she leapt into movement, thrusting her hands toward him. Lou lifted her own instinctively. I followed a second too late, dropping one of my knives, cursing as it skidded across the ground past Morgane. She didn't see it, thrusting her hands at Deveraux again and again. He only flicked his wrist and sighed. The sharp scent of cedar wood engulfed us.

"You know that won't work on me, darling," he said irritably. With another flick, Morgane sailed directly upward, suspended as if pinned to a tree. Her palms snapped together. The tumult around us quieted as everyone turned to stare. "I *am* the land. Your magic comes from *me*."

When she screamed in frustration, flailing wildly, he ignored her. "But you're right," he continued. "I never should've left. It is a mistake I will not make twice." He paced before a line of corpses, growing steadily taller with each step. Nausea pitched violently in my stomach when I looked closer. When I recognized my mouth on one face. My nose on another. My jaw. My eyes.

Deveraux spotted the toddler, and his voice darkened. "For too long, I've sat quietly—watching you drown others, watching you founder yourself—but no longer. I will not let you do this, *ma chanson*." He glanced at Lou, and the terrible fury in his eyes softened. "She could have been ours."

"But she's *not*," Morgane spat, throat bulging with strain. "She's not mine, and she's not yours. She is *his*. She is *theirs*." She pointed to me, to Ansel, to Coco and Jean Luc, to Beau and Blaise. "She was *never* mine. She has chosen her side. If it's the last thing I do, I will make her suffer as her sisters have suffered."

Several witches crept toward the main tunnel now. Blaise— face bloody, mouth dripping—blocked the entrance, but he numbered only one. When the witches engaged, streaking past, the Chasseurs gave chase, deserting us. Ansel edged back to guard the smaller actors' tunnel. Trembling beside the corpses, Célie stood alone. When she turned to look at me—alive, *terrified*—I beckoned her over. The slightest twitch of my fingers. Her face crumpled, and she raced toward us. Lou caught her, and I wrapped my arms around them both.

We would survive this. All of us. I didn't care what Coco's vision said.

Deveraux watched us for a moment, his expression wistful, before turning back to Morgane. He shook his head. "You are a fool, my love. She is your daughter. Of course she could have been yours." With the wave of his hand, Morgane floated back to the ground. Her hands broke apart. "This game is over. My sister has grown rather fond of Louise."

My arms tightened around her, and—shuddering with relief—she dropped her head to my shoulder. To my surprise, Célie stroked her hair. Just once. A simple gesture of comfort. Of hope. The unlikeliness of it startled me, shattered me, and warm relief swept in. My knees buckled. We really *would* survive this. All of us. With Deveraux and his sister on our side—a *god* and *goddess*—Morgane's hands were tied. For all her power, she was human. She couldn't hope to fight this war and win.

Panting and flexing her wrists, she glared at Deveraux with pure animosity. "Your sister is the fool."

His eyes flattened, and he motioned for Blaise and Ansel to step away from the tunnel entrances. "You try my patience, love. Leave now, before I change my mind. Undo what can be undone. Do not attempt to harm Louise again, or feel my sister's wrath—and mine. This is your final warning."

Morgane backed toward the tunnel slowly. Her eyes darted

upward, watching the last witches flee from sight and the last huntsmen follow. Deveraux let them go. Morgane would never surrender with an audience. Now the auditorium was nearly empty. Only our own remained—and Manon. She stared at Gilles's empty face, her own equally lifeless. Lou looked as if she might approach her, but I squeezed her waist. *Not yet.*

"My final warning," Morgane breathed. "The wrath of a goddess." When she lifted her hands, everyone tensed, but she only brought them together in applause. Each clap echoed in the empty auditorium. A truly frightening grin split her face. "Well done, Louise. It seems you have powerful pieces in our game, but do not forgot I have mine. You have outplayed me . . . for now."

Lou stepped away from Célie and me, swallowing hard. "I was never playing, *Maman.* I loved you."

"Oh, darling. Didn't I tell you love makes you weak?" A wild gleam lit Morgane's eyes as she inched backward. She was close to the tunnel now. Close to escape. Ansel hovered nearby with an anxious expression. It mirrored my own. I glanced to Deveraux, praying he'd change his mind—capture her—but he didn't move. He trusted her to leave, to obey her goddess's command. I didn't. "But the game isn't over yet. The rules have simply changed. That's all. I cannot use magic, not here. I cannot touch *you*, but . . ."

I realized her intent too late. We all did.

Cackling, she swooped up my fallen knife and lunged, driving it into the base of Ansel's skull.

THE END OF THE WORLD

Lou

The world didn't end in a scream.
   It ended in a gasp. A single, startled exhalation. And then—
   Nothing.
   Nothing but silence.

SOMETHING DARK AND ANCIENT

Lou

I could do nothing but watch him fall.

He dropped to his knees first—eyes wide, unseeing—before falling forward. There was no one to catch him, no one to stop his face from hitting the ground with a sickening, definitive thud. He did not move again.

Ringing silence filled my ears, my mind, my *heart* as blood surrounded him in a scarlet halo. My feet wouldn't move. My eyes wouldn't blink. There was only Ansel and his crown, his beautiful limbs draped behind him as if—as if he were just sleeping—

By midnight, a man close to your heart will die.

A scream pierced the silence.

It was mine.

The world rushed back into focus then, and everyone was shouting, running, slipping in Ansel's blood—

Coco tore her arm open with one of Reid's knives, and her own blood spilled on Ansel's face. They turned him over on

Reid's lap, forcing his lips apart. His head lolled. Already, his skin had lost its color. It didn't matter how they shook him, how they sobbed. He wouldn't wake.

"Help him!" Coco lurched to her feet and took Claud by the coat. Tears streamed down her face, burning everything they touched, sparking tendrils of flame at our feet. And still they fell. She was breathless now, no longer shaking him, but clutching his shoulders. Keening. Drowning. "Please, *please*, bring him back—"

Claud removed her hands gently with a shake of his head. "I am sorry. I cannot interfere. He is . . . gone."

Gone.

Ansel was gone.

Gone gone gone. The word swirled around me, through me, whispering with finality. *Ansel is gone.*

Coco sank to the ground, and her tears fell thicker, faster. Fire curled around her like molten petals. I relished the heat. The pain. This place would burn for what it'd taken. I hoped the witches were still here. I hoped the red-faced devil and his friends had not yet escaped. Blowing each shimmering pattern, I fanned the flames higher, hotter. They would all die with Ansel. Each one of them would die.

Laughter echoed from the darkness of the tunnel.

With a guttural roar, I tore after it. Jean Luc said I'd rotted, but that wasn't true. Magic didn't rot. It cracked, like a splintering mirror. With each brush of magic, those cracks in the glass deepened. The slightest touch might shatter it. I hadn't corrected him at the time. I hadn't wanted to acknowledge what was happening to me—what we'd all known. But now—

"Did you *love* him, Louise?" Morgane's voice echoed in the darkness. "Did you watch as the light left those pretty brown eyes?"

Now I shattered.

Light exploded from my skin in every direction, illuminating the entire tunnel. The walls shook, the ceiling cracking and raining stones, collapsing beneath my wrath. I pushed harder, wrenching patterns blindly. I would bring the tunnel down on her head. I would break the world and tear down the sky to punish her for what she'd done. For what *I* had done. At a gap in the passage, Morgane stood frozen, mouth parted in surprise—in delight. "You are magnificent," she breathed. "*Finally.* We can have some fun."

Closing my eyes, I tipped my head back, holding all of their lives in my fingers. Reid. Coco. Claud. Beau. Célie. Jean Luc. Manon. I tested the weights of each one, searching for a thread to match Morgane's. She had to die. Whatever the cost.

And if another must die in return? the voice whispered.

So be it.

Before I could pluck the thread, however, a body slammed into me. Blood soaked his shirt. I tasted it in my mouth as he trapped me against the wall, as he lifted my hands above my head. "Stop, Lou. Don't do this."

"Let me *go*!" Half screaming, half sobbing, I fought Reid with all my strength. I spat out Ansel's blood. "It's my fault. I killed him. I told him he was *worthless*—he was *nothing*—"

At the mouth of the tunnel, Claud, Beau, and Jean Luc struggled to contain Coco. She must've followed me in. By her feral expression, she'd planned a similar fate for my mother. Fire roared behind her.

When I turned back to Morgane, she'd disappeared.

"Let her go," Reid pleaded. Tears and soot streaked his face. "You'll get another chance. We have to move, or this whole place will come down on top of us."

I slumped in his arms, defeated, and he exhaled hard, pressing me into his chest. "You don't get to leave me. Do you understand?" Cupping my face, he wrenched me backward and kissed me hard. His voice was fierce. His eyes were fiercer. They burned into mine, angry and anguished and *afraid*. "You don't get to do this alone. If you retreat into your mind—into your magic—I'll follow you, Lou." He shook me slightly, tears glistening in those frightened eyes. "I'll follow you into that darkness, and I'll bring you back. Do you hear me? Where *you* go, *I* will go."

I looked back to the auditorium. The flames burned too high now for us to retrieve Ansel's body. He would burn here. This dirty, deplorable place would be his pyre. I closed my eyes, expecting the pain to come, but there was only emptiness. I was hollow. Vacant. No matter what Reid claimed . . . this time, he wouldn't be able to bring me back.

Something dark and ancient slithered out of that pit.

OLD MAGIC

Lou

Late afternoon sunlight shone through the dusty window, illuminating the warm woods and thick carpets of Léviathan's dining room. La Voisin and Nicholina stared at me from across the table. They looked out of place in this ordinary, mundane room. With their scarred skin and haunting eyes, they were two creatures of a horror story who'd escaped their pages.

I would bring their horror story to life.

The innkeeper had assured me that we wouldn't be disturbed here.

"Where were you?"

"The tunnels separated us." La Voisin met my gaze impassively. We still hadn't found the others. Though Blaise and Claud searched relentlessly, Liana, Terrance, Toulouse, and Thierry remained lost. I assumed Morgane had killed them. I couldn't bring myself to care. "When we reached the Skull Masquerade, Cosette had already set it on fire. I instructed my kin to flee."

"*Sea of tears and lake of fire.*" Nicholina rocked back and forth on her chair. Her silver eyes never left mine. "*To drown our foes on their pyres.*"

"My niece tells me you've had a change of heart." La Voisin glanced toward the door, where the others waited in the tavern. All except one. "She says you wish to march on Chateau le Blanc."

I met Nicholina's unflinching stare with one of my own. "I don't want to march on Chateau le Blanc. I want to burn it to the ground."

La Voisin lifted her brows. "You must see how that upsets my agenda. Without the Chateau, my people remain homeless."

"Build a new home. Build it on my sisters' ashes."

A peculiar glint entered La Voisin's eyes. A smile touched her lips. "If we agree . . . if we burn your mother and sisters inside their ancestral home . . . it does not solve the larger problem. Though your mother's methods have grown erratic, we are still hunted. The royal family will not rest until every one of us is dead. Even now, Helene Labelle remains captive."

"So we kill them too." My voice sounded hollow to my own ears. "We kill them all."

La Voisin and Nicholina exchanged a glance, and La Voisin's smile grew. Nodding—as if I'd passed some sort of unspoken test—she drew her grimoire from her cloak and placed it on the table. "How . . . cruel."

Nicholina licked her teeth.

"They want death," I said simply. "I'll give them death."

La Voisin rested her hand atop her grimoire. "I appreciate your commitment, Louise, but such a feat is easier said than done.

The king has numbers in his Chasseurs, and the Chasseurs have strength in their Balisardas. Morgane is omniscient. She has . . . powerful pieces on her board."

It seems you have powerful pieces in our game, but do not forgot I have mine. I frowned at the turn of phrase.

"Did you never wonder how she found you in Cesarine?" La Voisin stood, and Nicholina followed. I rose with them, unease prickling my neck. The door behind them remained shut. Locked. "How she slipped a note into my own camp? How she knew you traveled with Troupe de Fortune? How she followed you to this very inn?"

"She has spies everywhere," I whispered.

"Yes." La Voisin nodded, moving around the table. I fought to remain still. I would not flee. I would not cower. "Yes, she does." When she stood only a hair's breadth from my shoulder, she stopped, staring down at me. "I warned Coco against her friendship with you. She knew I disliked you. She was always so careful to protect you from me, never revealing even a scrap of information about your whereabouts." Tilting her head, she considered me with predatory focus. "When she heard of your marriage to the Chasseur, she panicked. It made her careless. Reckless. We followed her trail back to Cesarine, and lo and behold—there you were. After two years of searching, we had found you."

I swallowed hard. "We?"

"Yes, Louise. We."

I bolted then, but Nicholina flashed in front of the door. In a sickeningly familiar movement, she pushed me into the wall, yanking my hands above my head with inhuman strength. When I smashed my forehead into her nose, she simply leaned closer, inhaling against the skin of my neck. Her blood sizzled against my skin, and I screamed. "Reid! REID! *COCO!*"

"They can't hear you." La Voisin flipped through the pages of her grimoire. "We've enchanted the door."

I watched, horrified, as Nicholina's nose shifted back into place. "It's the mice," she breathed, grinning like a fiend. "The mice, the mice, the mice. They keep us young, keep us *strong*."

"What the *hell* are you always talking about? Do you eat mice?"

"Don't be silly." She giggled and brushed her nose against mine. Her blood continued to boil my face. I thrashed away from her—from the pain—but she held strong. "We eat *hearts*."

"Oh my god." I retched violently, gasping for breath. "Gaby was right. You eat your dead."

La Voisin didn't look up from her grimoire. "Just their hearts. The heart is the core of a blood witch's power, and it lives on after one dies. The dead have no need for magic. We do." She pulled a bundle of herbs from her cloak next, setting each beside her grimoire and calling them by name. "Bayberry for illusion, eyebright for control, and belladonna"—she lifted the dried leaves to inspect them—"for spiritual projection."

Spiritual projection.

What was the book in your aunt's tent?

Her grimoire.

Do you know what's in it?

Curses, possession, sickness, and the like. Only a fool would cross my aunt.

Oh shit.

"Fang of an adder," Nicholina chanted, still leering at me. "Eye of an owl."

La Voisin set to crushing the herbs, the fang, the *eye* into powder on the table.

"Why are you doing this?" I kneed Nicholina in the stomach, but she pressed closer, laughing. "I agreed to *help* you. We want the same things, we want—"

"You are easier to kill than Morgane. Though the plan was to deliver you to La Mascarade des Crânes, we are flexible. We will deliver you to Chateau le Blanc instead."

I watched in horror as she slit her wrist open, as her blood poured into a goblet. When she added the powder, a plume of black smoke curled from the foul liquid. "So kill me, then," I choked. "Don't—don't do *this*. Please."

"By decree of the Goddess, Morgane can no longer hunt you. She cannot force you to do anything against your will. You must go to her willingly. You must *sacrifice* yourself willingly. I would simply feed you my blood to assume control, but the pure, unadulterated blood of an enemy kills." She gestured to Nicholina's blood on my face, to my ravaged skin. "Fortunately, I have an alternate solution. It's all thanks to you, Louise. The rules of old magic are absolute. An impure spirit such as Nicholina's cannot touch a pure one. This darkness in your heart . . . it calls to us."

Nicholina tapped my nose. "Pretty mouse. We shall taste your huntsman. We shall have our kiss."

I bared my teeth at her. "*You* won't."

She cackled as La Voisin crossed the room to lift the goblet to her lips. Drinking greedily, she relaxed her hands, and I bucked away from her, lunging for the door—

La Voisin caught my injured wrist. I arched away, screaming—screaming for Reid, for Coco, for *anyone*—but she caught my hair and forced my head back. My mouth open. When the black liquid touched my lips, I collapsed and saw no more.

EVIL SEEKS A FOOTHOLD

Reid

Deveraux's face was unusually grim as he sat down across the table in Léviathan. At least it was *human*. The Woodwose's face had been . . . unsettling. I shook my head, staring into my tankard of beer. It'd gone flat an hour ago. Jean Luc brought me another one. "Drink up. I have to leave soon. The king wants us in the catacombs within the hour."

"What will you tell him?" Deveraux asked.

"The truth." He chugged his own tankard before nodding to Beau, who'd draped an arm around Coco at the next table. Her eyes were red-rimmed and swollen, and she turned a glass of wine in her hand without seeing it. Beau coaxed her into taking a sip. "He's already after all of you," Jean Luc continued. "This changes nothing."

Deveraux frowned. "And your men? They won't reveal your involvement?"

"Which was what, exactly?" Jean Luc's eyes narrowed. "I took advantage of a poor situation to rescue the daughter of an aristocrat." He plunked his glass on the table and stood, straightening his coat. "Make no mistake—we are not allies. If you aren't gone by the time I return, I will arrest all of you, and I will lose no sleep tonight."

Deveraux looked down to conceal his grin. "Why not now? We are here. You are here."

Jean Luc scowled, leaning closer and lowering his voice. "Do not make me regret this, old man. After what I saw down there, I could see you burned. It is the fate that awaits every witch. You are no different."

"After what you saw down there," Deveraux mused, still examining his fingernails, "I assume you have many questions." When Jean Luc opened his mouth to argue, Deveraux spoke over him. "Your men certainly will. Make no mistake. Are you prepared to answer them? Are you prepared to paint us all with the same stroke as Morgane?"

"I—"

"Louise risked her life to save an innocent young woman last night, and she paid dearly for it."

As one, they turned to look at Célie. She sat beside me at the table, pale and trembling. She hadn't spoken since we'd left La Mascarade des Crânes. When I'd kindly suggested she return home, she'd broken down in tears. I hadn't mentioned it since. Still, I didn't know what to do with her. She couldn't stay with us. Her parents must've been worried sick, and even if they weren't ... the road ahead would be dangerous. It was no place for someone like Célie.

She blushed under Deveraux's and Jean Luc's gazes, folding

her hands in her lap. Dirt still stained her mourning dress. And something else. Something—putrid.

I still didn't know what had happened to her down there. Lou had refused to tell me, and Ansel—

My mind viciously rejected the thought.

"Louise is the *reason* Célie was kidnapped," Jean Luc said through gritted teeth. "And I cannot discuss the matter any further. I must go. Célie"—he extended a hand toward her, face softening—"can you stand? I will escort you home. Your parents are waiting." Fresh tears welled in her eyes, but she wiped them away. Straightening her shoulders, she placed her trembling hand in his. Jean Luc moved to leave but stopped short, clutching my shoulder at the last second. His eyes were impenetrable. "I genuinely hope I don't see you again, Reid. Leave the kingdom. Take Louise and Coco with you if you must. Take the prince. Just—" Sighing heavily, he turned away. "Take care of yourself."

I watched the two of them walk out the door with a strange, pinching sensation. Though I no longer loved Célie romantically, it was . . . odd. Seeing her hand in Jean Luc's. Uncomfortable. Still, I wished them every happiness. Someone should have it.

"How is she?" Deveraux said after a moment. No one asked who he meant. "*Where* is she?"

I took my time answering, contemplating my beer again. After one enormous swallow and another, I wiped my mouth. "She's in the dining room with La Voisin and Nicholina. They're . . . planning."

"La Voisin? Nicholina?" Deveraux blinked between Coco and me, appalled. "These are the same women who abandoned us in the tunnels, are they not? What in the wilderness is Lou *planning* with them?"

Coco didn't look up from her wine. "Lou wants to march on Chateau le Blanc. It's all she's talked about since we escaped. She says she needs to kill Morgane."

"Oh dear." Deveraux's eyes widened, and he blew out a breath. "Oh dear, oh dear, oh dear. I must admit, that is . . . troubling."

Coco's hand tightened around her glass. Her eyes snapped up, burning with unshed emotion. "Why? We all want vengeance. She's taking the steps to get us there."

Deveraux appeared to choose his next words carefully. "Thoughts such as these could invite something very dark into your lives, Cosette. Something very dark, indeed. Evil always seeks a foothold. We must not give it one."

The stem of her glass snapped between her fingers, and a tear sizzled against the table. "She snuffed him out like a *candle*. You were there. You *saw*. And he—he—" She closed her eyes to regain her composure. When she opened them again, they were nearly black. Beau watched her with a wooden expression. Emotionless. Blank. "He was the best of us. Evil has more than a foothold here, Claud—thanks to you. You set it loose last night. You let it roam free. Now we all must suffer the consequences."

The door to the dining room flew open, and Lou stepped out. When her eyes met mine, she grinned and started toward me. I frowned. I hadn't seen her grin since—since—

Without a word, she swept me into a passionate kiss.

ACKNOWLEDGMENTS

People warned me about second books. They said the sophomore novel, whether sequel or standalone, was an entirely different beast than a debut. After a rather intense revision period with *Serpent & Dove*, I thought I could handle whatever *Blood & Honey* threw at me. Life doesn't come with voice-over narration, but if it did, my narrator would've laughed at this point—perhaps Jim would've deadpanned to the camera—and said, "How very wrong she was." For whatever reason, this book demanded my blood and sweat and tears. It gave me nightmares; my first panic attack. I nearly had a psychotic break in the coffee aisle of the grocery store. (I don't drink coffee. I started drinking coffee while rewriting this book.) Now, on the other side, I can't help but feel proud of this story. It's proof we're capable of doing hard things, even if we need to ask for help with them sometimes—which I did while writing this book. A lot.

RJ, I don't think I'll ever forgive you for the airball reference, but also, like . . . you made me laugh when I wanted to cry. That's a gift. It's also why I married you. Thanks for being a single parent the last few months while I wrote and rewrote and revised and re-revised. I love you.

Beau, James, and Rose, I hope when you read this someday, you'll know that while you don't owe anyone unconditional love, you certainly have mine. Even when you argue. Even when you scream. Even when you paint the bathroom with my favorite lipstick on the morning of my 7 o'clock flight.

Mom and Dad, words don't suffice when I think of how to thank you. Even as a writer, I can't quite describe the swell of emotions in my chest at everything you've done for me, so I won't even try. Just know I pretty much hero-worship both of you.

There's a passage near the end of *Blood & Honey* where Lou describes her childhood paradise as being surrounded by family and laughter. Jacob, Brooke, Justin, Chelsy, and Lewie, you guys inspired that paradise. I lived it then, and I live it now.

Pattie and Beth, those days you spent with the kids were invaluable. You gave a lot of time and energy—and probably food—for me to write this book, and I appreciate it. Truly.

Jordan, Spencer, Meghan, Aaron, Courtney, Austin, Adrianne, Chelsea, Jake, Jillian, Riley, Jon, and Aaron, writing has become a large part of my life, but you've never begrudged me it. You've kept me grounded while simultaneously allowing me to grow, all without judgment. Even for the black lipstick. I couldn't do life without you guys.

Jordan, if there's a single person I need to thank for helping me write *Blood & Honey*, it's you. The time and energy you've poured into both me and this story . . . honestly, it chokes me up a little. Thank you for listening as I cried in the coffee aisle of the grocery store. Thank you for talking me through my panic attack, for suggesting Beau's next joke, for loving these characters like I do, for sending TikTok videos to make me laugh, for enduring hours upon hours of Voxer messages when I just couldn't crack the plot. Most important, however, thank you for being so much more than my critique partner. I cherish our friendship.

Katie and Carolyn, your support through the years means more than you know. Buckle up. I'm never letting either of you go.

Isabel, thank you for welcoming me into your home—and life—with open arms. Also for feeding me delicious food. Adalyn, you've become both the angel and the devil on my shoulders, whispering my worth in both ears. Your Instagram feed looks great too. Adrienne, your drive and work ethic and knowledge inspire me daily. Like, you literally inspired me to order a carrot stick for my eyes the other day. That doesn't just happen. Kristin, you have great hair. And skin. And fierce, badger-like loyalty to the people you love. I'm so lucky to have you in my corner. Rachel, the support you've given me—someone you've never met who crashed the group chat on a random Tuesday—is overwhelming. I can't wait to crash your next writing retreat, too.

Agent extraordinaire, Sarah, none of this would be possible without your knowledge, guidance, and warmth. Erica, your vision for this series remains unerring. Thank you for keeping

Lou, Reid, and me in line, especially when we tend to stray in the middle. You have the patience of a saint. Louisa Currigan, Alison Donalty, Jessie Gang, Alexandra Rakaczki, Gwen Morton, Mitch Thorpe, Michael D'Angelo, Ebony LaDelle, Tyler Breitfeller, Jane Lee, and everyone else at HarperTeen, if someone would've asked what my dream team looked like before I sold *Serpent & Dove*, that team would've looked exactly like you. I can't thank you enough for the time and energy you've given to this series.

TURN THE PAGE FOR A
SNEAK PEEK AT THE NEXT
BOOK IN THE SERIES.

A LOVE THAT WILL BURN FOR ETERNITY

Gods

Monsters

NEW YORK TIMES BESTSELLING AUTHOR OF *BLOOD & HONEY*
SHELBY MAHURIN

A NEST OF MICE

Nicholina

Bayberry, eyebright, belladonna
Fang of an adder, eye of an owl
Sprinkle of flora, spray of fauna
For purpose fair or possession foul.

Ichor of friend and ichor of foe
A soul stained black as starless night
For in the dark dost spirits flow
One to another in seamless flight.

The spell is familiar, oh yes, familiar indeed. Our favorite. She lets us read it often. The grimoire. The page. The spell. Our fingers trace each pen stroke, each faded letter, and they tingle with promise. They promise we'll never be alone, and we believe them. We believe *her*. Because we aren't alone—we're never alone—and mice live in nests with dozens of other mice, with *scores* of them. They burrow together to raise their pups, their children, and they find warm, dry nooks with plenty of food and magic. They find crannies without sickness, without death.

Our fingers curl on the parchment, gouging fresh tracks.

Death. Death, death, *death*, our friend and foe, as sure as breath, comes for us all.

But not me.

The dead should not remember. Beware the night they dream.

We tear at the paper now, shredding it to pieces. To angry bits. It scatters like ash in the snow. Like memory.

Mice burrow together, yes—they keep each other safe and warm—but when a pup in the litter sickens, the mice will eat it. Oh yes. They gobble it down, down, down to nourish the mother, the nest. The newest born is always sick. Always small. We shall devour the sick little mouse, and she shall nourish us.

She shall nourish us.

We shall prey on her friends, her *friends*—a snarl tears from my throat at the word, at the empty promise—and we shall feed them until they are fat with grief and guilt, with frustration and fear. Where we go, they will follow. Then we shall devour them too. And when we deliver the sick little mouse to her mother at Chateau le Blanc—when her body withers, when it *bleeds*—her soul shall stay with us forever.

She shall nourish us.

We will never be alone.

L'ENCHANTERESSE

Reid

Mist crept over the cemetery. The headstones—ancient, crumbling, their names long lost to the elements—pierced the sky from where we stood atop the cliff's edge. Even the sea below fell silent. In this eerie light before dawn, I finally understood the expression *silent as the grave.*

Coco brushed a hand across tired eyes before gesturing to the church beyond the mist. Small. Wooden. Part of the roof had caved in. No light flickered through the rectory windows. "It looks abandoned."

"What if it isn't?" Beau snorted, shaking his head, but stopped short with a yawn. He spoke around it. "It's a *church*, and our faces are plastered all over Belterra. Even a country priest will recognize us."

"Fine." Her tired voice held less bite than she probably intended. "Sleep outside with the dog."

As one, we turned to look at the spectral white dog that followed us. He'd shown up outside Cesarine, just before we'd agreed to travel the coast instead of the road. We'd all seen enough of La Fôret des Yeux to last a lifetime. For days, he'd trailed behind us, never coming near enough to touch. Wary, confused, the matagots had vanished shortly after his appearance. They hadn't returned. Perhaps the dog was a restless spirit himself—a new type of matagot. Perhaps he was merely an ill omen. Perhaps that was why Lou hadn't yet named him.

The creature watched us now, his eyes a phantom touch on my face. I gripped Lou's hand tighter. "We've been walking all night. No one will look for us inside a church. It's as good a place as any to hide. If it *isn't* abandoned"—I spoke over Beau, who started to interrupt—"we'll leave before anyone sees us. Agreed?"

Lou grinned at Beau, her mouth wide. So wide I could nearly count all her teeth. "Are you *afraid*?"

He shot her a dubious look. "After the tunnels, you should be too."

Her grin vanished, and Coco visibly stiffened, looking away. Tension straightened my own spine. Lou said nothing more, however, instead dropping my hand to stalk toward the door. She twisted the handle. "Unlocked."

Without a word, Coco and I followed her over the threshold. Beau joined us in the vestibule a moment later, eyeing the darkened room with unconcealed suspicion. A thick layer of dust coated the candelabra. Wax had dripped to the wooden floor, hardening among the dead leaves and debris. A draft swept through from the sanctuary beyond. It tasted of brine. Of decay.

"This place is haunted as shit," Beau whispered.

"Language." Scowling at him, I stepped into the sanctuary. My chest tightened at the dilapidated pews. At the loose hymnal pages collecting in the corner to rot. "This was once a holy place."

"It isn't haunted." Lou's voice echoed in the silence. She stilled behind me to stare up at a stained-glass window. The smooth face of Saint Magdaleine gazed back at her. The youngest saint in Belterra, Magdaleine had been venerated by the Church for gifting a man a blessed ring. With it, his negligent wife had fallen back in love with him, refusing to leave his side—even after he'd embarked on a perilous journey at sea. She'd followed him into the waves and drowned. Only Magdaleine's tears had revived her. "Spirits can't inhabit consecrated ground."

Beau's brows dipped. "How do you know that?"

"How do you *not*?" Lou countered.

"We should rest." I wrapped an arm around Lou's shoulders, leading her to a nearby pew. She looked paler than usual with dark shadows beneath her eyes, her hair wild and windswept from days of hard travel. More than once—when she didn't think I was looking—I'd seen her entire body convulse as if fighting sickness. It wouldn't surprise me. She'd been through a lot. We all had. "The villagers will wake soon. They'll investigate any noise."

Coco settled on a pew, closed her eyes, and pulled up the hood of her cloak. Shielding herself from us. "Someone should keep watch."

Though I opened my mouth to volunteer, Lou interrupted. "I'll do it."

"No." I shook my head, unable to recall the last time Lou had slept. Her skin felt cold, clammy, against mine. If she *was* fighting sickness, she needed the rest. "You sleep. I'll watch."

A sound reverberated from deep in her throat as she placed a hand on my cheek. Her thumb brushed my lips, lingering there. As did her eyes. "I'd much prefer to watch you. What will I see in your dreams, Chass? What will I hear in your—"

"I'll check the scullery for food," Beau muttered, shoving past us. He cast Lou a disgusted glance over his shoulder. My stomach rumbled as I watched him go. Swallowing hard, I ignored the ache of hunger. The sudden, unwelcome pressure in my chest. Gently, I removed her hand from my cheek and shrugged out of my coat. I handed it to her.

"Go to sleep, Lou. I'll wake you at sunset, and we can"—the words burned up my throat—"we can continue."

To the Chateau.

To Morgane.

To certain death.

I didn't voice my concerns again.

Lou had made it clear she'd journey to Chateau le Blanc whether or not we joined her. Despite my protests—despite reminding her *why* we'd sought allies in the first place, why we *needed* them—Lou maintained she could handle Morgane alone. *You heard Claud.* Maintained she wouldn't hesitate this time. *She can no longer touch me.* Maintained she would burn her ancestral home to the ground, along with all of her kin. *We'll build new.*

New what? I'd asked warily.

New everything.

I'd never seen her act with such single-minded intensity. No. Obsession. Most days, a ferocious glint lit her eyes—a feral sort of hunger—and others, no light touched them at all. Those days were infinitely worse. She'd watch the world with a deadened expression, refusing to acknowledge me or my weak attempts to comfort her.

Only one person could do that.

And he was gone.

She pulled me down beside her now, stroking my throat almost absently. At her cold touch, a shiver skittered down my spine and a sudden desire to shift away seized me. I ignored it. Silence blanketed the room, thick and heavy, except for the growls of my stomach. Hunger was a constant companion now. I couldn't remember the last time I'd eaten my fill. With Troupe de Fortune? In the Hollow? The Tower? Across the aisle, Coco's breathing gradually evened. I focused on the sound, on the beams of the ceiling, rather than Lou's frigid skin or the ache in my chest.

A moment later, however, shouts exploded from the scullery, and the sanctuary door burst open. Beau shot forward, hotfooting it past the pulpit. "Bumfuzzle!" He gestured wildly toward the exit as I vaulted to my feet. "Time to go! Right now, right *now*, let's *go*—"

"Stop!" A gnarled man in the vestments of a priest charged into the sanctuary, wielding a wooden spoon. Yellowish stew dripped from it. As if Beau had interrupted his morning meal. The flecks of vegetable in his beard—grizzled, unkempt, concealing most of his face—confirmed my suspicions. "I said get *back* here—"

He stopped abruptly, skidding to a halt when he saw the rest of us. Instinctively, I turned to hide my face in the shadows. Lou flung her hood over her white hair, and Coco stood, tensing to run. But it was too late. Recognition sparked in his dark eyes.

"Reid Diggory." His dark gaze swept from my head to my toes before shifting behind me. "Louise le Blanc." Unable to help himself, Beau cleared his throat from the foyer, and the priest considered him briefly before scoffing and shaking his head. "Yes, I know who you are too, boy. *And* you," he added to Coco, whose hood still cloaked her face in darkness. True to his word, Jean Luc had added her wanted poster beside ours. The priest's eyes narrowed on the blade she'd drawn. "Put that away before you hurt yourself."

"We're sorry for trespassing." I lifted my hands in supplication, glaring at Coco in warning. Slowly, I slid into the aisle, inched toward the exit. At my back, Lou matched my steps. "We didn't mean any harm."

The priest snorted but lowered his spoon. "You broke into my home."

"It's a church." Apathy dulled Coco's voice, and her hand dropped as if it suddenly couldn't bear the dagger's weight. "Not a private residence. And the door was unlocked."

"Perhaps to lure us in," Lou suggested with unexpected relish. Head tilted, she stared at the priest in fascination. "Like a spider to its web."

The priest's brows dipped at the abrupt shift in conversation, as did mine. Beau's voice reflected our confusion. "What?"

"In the darkest parts of the forest," she explained, arching a brow, "there lives a spider who hunts other spiders. L'Enchanteresse, we call her. The Enchantress. Isn't that right, Coco?" When Coco didn't respond, she continued undeterred. "L'Enchanteresse creeps into her enemies' webs, plucking their silk strands, tricking them into believing they've ensnared their prey. When the spiders arrive to feast, she attacks, poisoning them slowly with her unique venom. She savors them for days. Indeed, she's one of the few creatures in the animal kingdom who enjoy inflicting pain."

We all stared at her. Even Coco. "That's disturbing," Beau finally said.

"It's *clever.*"

"No." He grimaced, face twisting. "It's *cannibalism.*"

"We needed shelter," I interjected a touch too loudly. Too desperately. The priest, who'd been watching them bicker with a disconcerted frown, returned his attention to me. "We didn't realize the church was occupied. We'll leave now."

He continued to assess us in silence, his lip curling slightly. Gold swelled before me in response. Seeking. Probing. Protecting. I ignored its silent question. I wouldn't need magic here. The priest wielded only a spoon. Even if he'd brandished a sword, the lines on his face marked him elderly. Wizened. Despite his tall frame, time seemed to have withered his musculature, leaving a spindly old man in its wake. We could outrun him. I seized Lou's hand in preparation, cutting a glance to Coco and Beau. They both nodded once in understanding.

Scowling, the priest lifted his spoon as if to stop us, but at that moment, a fresh wave of hunger wracked my stomach. Its growl rumbled through the room like an earthquake. Impossible to ignore. Eyes tightening, the priest tore his gaze from me to glare at Saint Magdaleine in the silence that followed. After another beat, he grudgingly muttered, "When did you last eat?"

I didn't answer. Heat pricked my cheeks. "We'll leave now," I repeated.

His eyes met mine. "That's not what I asked."

"It's been . . . a few days."

"How many days?"

Beau answered for me. "Four."

Another rumble of my stomach rocked the silence. The priest shook his head. Looking as though he'd rather swallow the spoon whole, he asked, "And . . . when did you last sleep?"

Again, Beau couldn't seem to stop himself. "We dozed in some fishermen's boats two nights ago, but one of them caught us before sunrise. He tried to snare us in his net, the half-wit."

The priest's eyes flicked to the sanctuary doors. "Could he have followed you here?"

"I just said he was a half-wit. Reid snared him in the net instead."

Those eyes found mine again. "You didn't hurt him." It wasn't a question. I didn't answer it. Instead I tightened my grip on Lou's hand and prepared to run. This man—this *holy* man—would soon sound the alarm. We needed to put miles between us before Jean Luc arrived.

Lou didn't seem to share my concern.

"What's your name, cleric?" she asked curiously.

"Achille." His scowl returned. "Achille Altier."

Though the name sounded familiar, I couldn't place it. Perhaps he'd once journeyed to Cathédral Saint-Cécile d'Cesarine. Perhaps I'd met him while under oath as a Chasseur. I eyed him with suspicion. "Why haven't you summoned the huntsmen, Father Achille?"

He looked deeply uncomfortable. Shoulders radiating tension, he stared down at his spoon. "You should eat," he said gruffly. "There's stew in the back. Should be enough for everyone."

Beau didn't hesitate. "What kind?" When I shot a glare over my shoulder, he shrugged. "He could've woken the town the moment he recognized us—"

"He still could," I reminded him, voice hard.

"—and my stomach is about to eat itself," he finished. "Yours too, by the sound of it. We need food." He sniffed and asked Father Achille, "Are there potatoes in your stew? I'm not partial to them. It's a textural thing."

The priest's eyes narrowed, and he jabbed the spoon toward the scullery. "Get out of my sight, boy, before I change my mind."

Beau inclined his head in defeat before scooting past us. Lou, Coco, and I didn't move, however. We exchanged wary looks. After a long moment, Father Achille heaved a sigh. "You can sleep here too. Just for the day," he added irritably, "so long as you don't bother me."

"It's Sunday morning." At last, Coco lowered her hood. Her

lips were cracked, her face wan. "Shouldn't villagers be attending service soon?"

He scoffed. "I haven't held a service in years."

A reclusive priest. Of course. The disrepair of the chapel made sense now. Once, I would've scorned this man for his failure as a religious leader. For his failure as a man. I would've reprimanded him for turning his back on his vocation. On God.

How times had changed.

Beau reappeared with an earthen bowl and leaned casually against the doorway. Steam from the stew curled around his face. When my stomach rumbled again, he smirked. I spoke through gritted teeth. "Why would you help us, Father?"

Reluctantly, the priest's gaze trailed over my pale face, Lou's grisly scar, Coco's numb expression. The deep hollows beneath our eyes and the gaunt cut of our cheeks. Then he looked away, staring hard at the empty air above my shoulder. "What does it matter? You need food. I have food. You need a place to sleep. I have empty pews."

"Most in the Church wouldn't welcome us."

"Most in the Church wouldn't welcome their own mother if she was a sinner."

"No. But they'd burn her if she was a witch."

He arched a sardonic brow. "Is that what you're after, boy? The stake? You want me to mete out your divine punishment?"

"I believe," Beau drawled from the doorway, "he's simply pointing out that *you* are among the Church—unless you're actually the sinner of this story? Are you unwelcome amongst your peers, Father Achille?" He glanced pointedly at our dilapidated surroundings. "Though I abhor jumping to conclusions, our beloved patriarchs surely would've sent someone to repair this hovel otherwise."

Achille's eyes darkened. "Watch your tone."

I interrupted before Beau could provoke him further, spreading my arms wide. In disbelief. In frustration. In . . . everything. Pressure built in my throat at this man's unexpected kindness. It didn't make sense. It couldn't be real. As horrible a picture as Lou painted, a cannibal spider luring us into its web seemed likelier than a priest offering us sanctuary. "You know who we are. You know what we've done. You know what will happen if you're caught sheltering us."

He studied me for a long moment, expression inscrutable. "Let's not get caught, then." With a mighty *harrumph*, he stomped toward the scullery door. At the threshold, however, he paused, eyeing Beau's bowl. He seized it in the next second, ignoring Beau's protests and thrusting it at me. "You're just kids," he muttered, not meeting my eyes. When my fingers wrapped around the bowl—my stomach contracting painfully—he let go. Straightened his robes. Rubbed his neck. Nodded to the stew. "Won't be worth eating cold."

Then he turned and stormed from the room.

THE COMPLETE SIZZLING TRILOGY!

Bound as one to love, honor . . . or burn.